THE
PUMPKIN
EATER

THE
PUMPKIN
EATER

A Sam Dawson Mystery

STEVEN W. HORN

GPP GRANITE
PEAK PRESS Cheyenne

Cheyenne, Wyoming
www.granitepeakpress.com

GRANITE
PEAK PRESS
Granite Peak Press
www.granitepeakpress.com

Although the author and publisher have made every effort to en-sure the accuracy and completeness of information contained in this book, we assume no responsibility for errors, inaccuracies, omissions, or any inconsistency herein. Any slights of people, places, or organizations are unintentional.

This book is a work of fiction. All references to real people, actual events or places must be read as fiction. The characters in this book are creations of the author's imagination. The dialogue is invented.

First printed in 2013

ISBN: 978-0-9835894-0-2
LCCN: 2013945056

ATTENTION CORPORATIONS, UNIVERSITIES, COLLEGES AND PROFESSIONAL ORGANIZATIONS: Quantity discounts are available on bulk purchases of this book for educational purposes. Special books or book excerpts can also be created to fit specific needs. For information, please contact Granite Peak Press, P.O. Box 2597, Cheyenne, WY 82003, or email: info@granitepeak-press.com.

Printed in the United States of America
10   9   8   7   6   5   4   3   2

FOR CARRIE BUCK

ACKNOWLEDGMENTS

It is truly a pleasure to thank the people whose encouragement and assistance made this story a reality.

V.A. Stephens, Peter Decker, Tonya Talbert, and Kristi Cammack all gave their time, expertise, and positive reassurance. Kate Deubert provided me with her extraordinary editorial skills. Tina Lyles-Worthman's and Rachel Girt's advice was invaluable. I am indebted to them all.

Special thanks to my daughters, Tiffany, Melissa, and Amanda, for their helpful reviews and enduring support.

I owe the completion of this book and its story to my loving wife, Margaret: a critic, a fan, and a sympathetic ear.

CHAPTER ONE

*NO ONE SUPPOSES THAT ALL THE
INDIVIDUALS OF THE
SAME SPECIES ARE CAST IN THE
VERY SAME MOULD.*
—CHARLES DARWIN

HIS DEAD SISTER GAZED BACK AT HIM. She was smiling. Sam could not breathe. A cold veil descended over him and the night became silent.

The flashlight's beam that illuminated her face began to shake. Her long blonde hair spilled over her shoulders, her blue eyes appeared dark behind the thick glasses, and her toothy grin reflected the light's beam back at him. She was as he remembered her.

Julie had been dead for nearly twenty-five years. She had remained seventeen for a quarter century, and now in 1999 she stared back at him from the darkness, unchanged since 1975 when he was twelve and saw her last. Sam forced a breath and inched the flashlight's beam upward on the stone marker. The name Genève Defollett was chiseled sharply into the polished red granite. She had been born nine years before Julie, but had also died at the age of seventeen.

The lump in his throat hurt as he swallowed, its corners as sharp as those cut into the stone depicting the American sign language symbol for "I love you" next to Genève's name. She had also been deaf.

Sam's heart pounded painfully in his chest; his eardrums kept cadence. But the initial shock of seeing his sister's likeness on the tombstone began to subside with the realization that he had been mistaken. He was a thousand miles and a lifetime away from his sister's disappearance. He tried to shake off the coldness that enveloped him, but his eyes refused to be drawn away from the ceramic oval that contained the photograph of Genève Defollett. The resemblance to Julie was frightening.

A twig snapped from the darkness to his left. Instinctively, Sam swung the flashlight's beam to the black wall of forest that bordered the cemetery. He shone the light in rapid, sweeping arcs against the impenetrable night. He heard the creak of barbed wire being pulled through fence staples as something pushed between the wire strands that separated forest from cemetery. Eye shine, eerie yellow reflections, stared back at him then began to move slowly toward him, flickering on and off at the edge of the flashlight's beam. Sam's fear was on the verge of panic as the golden dots became larger and brighter. The dog appeared magically within the shaking funnel of light, trotting slowly toward Sam.

"Elle!" he shouted, the sound of his voice strange and out of place in the dark cemetery. "Jesus, girl, you almost gave me a heart attack."

The bloodhound, tail waving, greeted him as though he had been gone for days instead of minutes. Drool glistened in long strands from the corners of her mouth.

"How did you get out?" He had left her in the motor home, which he had parked in the small, town park adjacent to the cemetery. Bending over, he scratched her ears and hugged her to his knee. The unmistakable fetid smell of death flared his nostrils. She had rolled on something dead. "Cur bitch. You're not riding with me," Sam said, wiping his fingers on his pants.

Once more he shone the light on the ceramic photograph of the girl who could have been his sister's twin. As troubling as the coincidence was, that's all it was, he reasoned. Besides, that was not why he was there.

"One more time, Elle, let's go see it one more time," he said, stepping around Genève Defollett's headstone.

Even in darkness, the older section of the cemetery was distinguishable. The giant oaks loomed overhead and the ground heaved around their bases, tilting headstones without reverence. The stones themselves were larger and more varied in style than in the new section. Gray and white were the colors, and none displayed pictures of the dead.

The tombstone he had come to see stood coldly on the dark hillside that sloped sharply toward the tangle of undergrowth and forest at the cemetery's edge. Just one more time; he had to be sure. In the morning, I'll come back and take pictures as proof, he said to himself. He shone the light at the face of the massive monument. It too was as he remembered it: Eugene Eris had died on August 4, 1930, and again on January 25, 1932. The two graves were nearly a thousand miles apart. The same epitaph etched deeply into the ashen granite of both headstones, the letters softened by seventy years, lay close to the ground, dead grass partially obscuring the words: "Wellborn Are My Children."

••••

The telephone receiver was cold against Sam's ear. He whispered the words of the epitaph again, this time more slowly. They had no meaning. He had repeated the words dozens of times since reading them.

First ring...

The names, the dates, even the identical tombstones could be explained as coincidental, but not the epitaphs.

Second ring...

"Pat, it's Sam. Sorry to bother you at home." He turned from the pay phone to see if anyone was watching. The small, town park was dark and deserted. The swings on long chains twisted slowly in the cold breeze blowing from the blackness of the cemetery. Dry leaves fell from the darkness above, clattering against the rusted floor of the merry-go-round. He turned his collar up and huddled close to the phone that hung against the gray cement block wall of the park restroom. The only light shown from the window of his motor home parked in the gravel lot beneath the silver water tower.

"It's Sam, Sam Dawson...No, I'm okay. Uh," he held his watch close to his face, "a little after midnight, Iowa time. Sorry, I didn't realize it was so late...

"Oxford," he said, looking up, following one of the erector-set legs of the water tower into the blackness above where the town name would appear with the morning sun. "Sort of east central, not too far from Maquoketa, if you know where that is." He knew Pat did not know. A transplanted New Yorker, Pat had escaped from the publishing industry to start his own small press in Denver. Pat would have been hard pressed to locate Iowa on a map.

"No, I'm fine, really. Something has..." He twisted anxiously toward the teeter-totters, heavy planks over deep depressions in the sandy soil. Shards of green paint, cracked and jagged, heaved upward from the boards' surface, foreboding even in darkness.

"Well, I..., I had this," he paused not knowing how to describe what had happened or whether he should tell Pat.

"Uh, tomorrow, I'll probably head out tomorrow, mid-morning. I should be back in Golden sometime tomorrow night. Pat, I've found..." He shook his head and scuffed rocks with his foot toward the dented oil drum that served as the park litter barrel. The word "trash" had been crudely hand-lettered with red paint across the side.

"It's about fifteen hours. Look, Pat...No, I'm maybe half-finished with this season's shots...Yes, I know there's a deadline. But...No, the advance is fine. It's not about money. I just need to come home. I had this, this..." He paused again. Revelation was the word he was searching for but reluctant to use. "I met a man in the cemetery here today. A caretaker, I think. Look, I'd just be wasting film until I get this figured out. I need my Colorado files, the negative files...

"She's fine. She stinks. She found something dead tonight and rolled on it. Look, Pat, this guy in the cemetery, the caretaker, I've seen him before...Probably a dead squirrel or bird or something, I don't know. She's a hound. Who knows why? But I've seen him before. I've taken his picture... The caretaker...No, not here. It was in Colorado a thousand miles from here...Maybe, I don't think so. I'm pretty sure it's the same guy...

"A salamander. He looks like an old salamander, flat mouth and beady eyes. All day I tried to remember where I had seen him before. It drove me crazy. It was like a song, the melody playing over and over in my head but I couldn't remember the name. Then tonight I..., all of a sudden like I've been electrocuted or something, one of those eureka moments, a revelation." There, he said it. "It's the same guy I saw a couple of years ago when I was working on the Colorado book. I just can't remember which cemetery, the eastern plains or maybe the San Luis Valley. But I'm sure I have some shots of him in my negative files. I remember taking the pictures...

"Nothing, I don't think there's anything you can do. But thanks for asking. I just needed to tell somebody, I guess. Your number was first on the list." The wind gusted loudly through the invisible tops of the giant oaks that towered above the playground. Dry leaves rained against the coarse concrete wall. T. C. plus J. I., ringed by a heart, was scratched into the paint on the side of the pay phone where Sam took refuge from the swirling debris. "There's something else, Pat. I found this tombstone...

"No, I haven't talked to him. The guy's creepy, he gives me the willies." Sam gently rubbed his finger across the scratched initials within the heart. "Pat, listen, I found this tombstone that's even creepier than the salamander guy. I'm certain that I've seen the same tombstone before, in Colorado...

"Yeah, yeah, I know, there are only so many designs to choose from. But you'd remember this one. I thought it was unique the first time I saw it. This has, I'm pretty sure, the same name on it and same date of birth as the one in Colorado...I don't know about date of death...No, I'm sure. I remember the birth date because it was the same month and day as my mother's, just seventy-some years earlier. It stuck in my mind...Because, it's a weird name on a weird stone, I remember it from Colorado. But here's the clincher. It has the same epitaph. What are the chances?" Sam turned restlessly away from the phone.

"No, it's not like that. It's not one of the little-lambs-in-heaven or resting-with-God type of quotes. It says "Wellborn Are My Children." I thought it was odd when I saw it a couple of years ago...I don't know what it means.

"Coincidence? Pat, are you hearing me? We're talking same stone, same name, same date, and same epitaph. The only difference is the thousand miles between cemeteries...

"Look, I don't know why I called you." Why had he called Pat? Because there was no one else to call, he thought. Divorced, no close friends, obsessed with his career, and only a dog for companionship was the answer. "I guess to tell you that I'm winding up early here. I'll come back midwinter to get the snow shots. We'll have to make do with what I have for the dead leaves shots...I won't let you down.

Have I ever let you down? Don't try to put a guilt trip on me, Pat. We'll go to press next spring like we planned. And, Pat, one more thing, the advance was a joke. See, I told you I was feeling okay. I just needed to hear your fatherly voice." Maybe that was it: He needed a father. "I'll call you when I get back. Goodnight, Pat."

He stood staring at the silver oil drum, mentally tracing the letters of the word "trash." A red teardrop descended from the bottom of the S as if the serpentine letter were bleeding. He listened for any movement within. He could not look inside. He had not told Pat about the snake. He had not mentioned how Elle had refused to enter the Winnebago when they returned from the cemetery or of the deafening buzz the large timber rattler had made when Sam opened the motor home door.

CHAPTER TWO

THE IOWA ASSIGNMENT WAS PURPOSEful. Sam had grown up with stories of the picturesque, small town of Oxford. It was his mother's home. Her adoptive parents, the Marshalls, were buried in the Oxford cemetery. It had been a belated pilgrimage, a quest for his roots.

That is what he tried to tell himself, but he knew it was much deeper than that. He was unsure of his motivation because he refused to think about it. But it gnawed at him, a disease that had plagued him for the past ten years. She had been dead that long. He had been too busy to say goodbye. She knew she was dying and, in a way, so did he. Maybe that was the reason for his ignoring her invitation to visit her. It was denial that soon turned into guilt. After all, wasn't that the real reason he was there? Ten years of penitence and now he sought absolution. He was angered that the sanctity of his mission had been interrupted by his accidental discovery of something that was bound to have a logical explanation, an explanation that lingered just beyond his grasp.

"Damn it, Elle," the anger in his voice surprising both of them.

The dog's ears dropped and her soft, golden eyes flashed as she looked away from Sam's uneaten breakfast. Strands of drool hung from the corners of her mouth.

"Begging is bad enough, but you smell like something dead. Is that your strategy?" he said, flaring his nostrils. "Ruin my appetite with your stench with the hopes of getting my food?" Sam turned from the dog and looked out the window of the motor home. In the half light of dawn the cemetery began to take shape. He knew he was redirecting his anger at Elle. He placed his plate on the floor.

••••

The sunrise shots were usually his favorites. All he ever wanted out of photography was to capture the light in the same way as his eyes. But Eris's tombstone repeatedly commanded his attention. With enough light to accommodate a longer lens, he had twisted his 300 mm Nikkor into the camera body and focused on the stone, which was still half-shadowed by a giant oak.

The marker appeared to be cast rather than carved. It was a very detailed likeness of a log, perhaps five feet long, complete with knars, knobs, growth rings, and missing chunks of bark. It was laid horizontally atop a more conventional headstone for a total height of over six feet. A stone wedge was buried deep within a crack at one end of the log and a stone single-blade axe with a recurved handle was sunk in the other. The discolorations of time and weather had streaked the monument in ghostly patterns. Green moss clung to the clefts of the north face.

Sam had carefully brought the big lens into focus, adjusting the f-stop to blur the foreground and background. The neatly carved, block letters of the deceased's family name were sharp under the close scrutiny of the polished lenses. "Eris" it declared for all who passed to remember. In the darkened lower half of the monument, Sam focused the name Eugene centered neatly between the dates June 18, 1852, on the left and January 25, 1932, on the right. There were no other names listed.

The barely distinguishable flowery script of the epitaph near the bottom of the base caused him to tilt the camera downward on its tripod, the epitaph that had beckoned him to the cemetery the night before. Grass had grown up along the edge of the base, partially covering the cursive inscription that undulated gracefully across the stone. The three-inch-high letters spanned two-thirds the width of the base and were almost unreadable through the long lens. He followed them along as he focused, his lips moving while he said the words to himself. "Wellborn are my children," he said, straightening. "What the hell does that mean?" he said aloud.

"Means nothing," a voice from behind him said.

Spinning around, Sam came face-to-face with the old caretaker. "Jesus, you almost gave me a heart attack," Sam gasped, suddenly remembering that he had said the same thing to Elle a mere seven hours earlier.

The old man stared at Sam. His watery blue eyes were so pale that the irises seemed to fade gently into the white corners. His pupils were abnormally constricted for the low light of dawn, beady, almost amphibian.

"I've read 'em all. They don't mean nothing. It's just words," the old man said, his eyes narrowing. "Sure, they wanted to say something, but most never got the job done. Flaubert said that language is a cracked kettle on which we tap out crude rhythms for bears to dance to while we long to make music that will melt the stars."

Sam raised his eyebrows in surprise at the contradiction between an old man in soiled, custodial clothes who used poor English and yet delivered an accurate quote from *Madame Bovary*. He studied the old man's face carefully while he sought the appropriate response. "So, you don't think that these last statements were true expressions of their lives?"

"No more than they themselves were true expressions of their lives," he quickly shot back.

The old man almost smiled and his eyes gleamed. "Life," he said slowly as if sharing some hidden knowledge, "'tis a tale told by an idiot, like the poor actor who frets and struts his hour upon the stage, full of sound and fury, but signifies nothing."

"Go on," Sam said calmly while trying to think of which Shakespearean work the old man had just quoted.

"Most people act out their lives as if they were performing in some great play. The true nature of a person can be found under the layers of makeup and wardrobe. The problem is that most people never step out of character long enough for anyone to discover the real person behind the scenes."

Sam scratched the back of his head. "So, all these people," he said, waving his hand in a sweeping arc around him, "were impostors who led deceptive lives. Why?" he said, challenging the old man.

"Social harmony," he smiled as if Sam should have known the answer. "Man by nature is a selfish bastard who'll do anything to achieve immortality. We'll even fake our lives in order to get other folks to help us achieve our own self-interests."

Sam's eyes narrowed as he looked at him suspiciously. He was uncomfortable continuing the conversation, especially with a total stranger in a cemetery at dawn. They had strayed from the original question concerning epitaphs. "What will your epitaph read?" Sam asked, trying to bring the discussion back with some closure.

"Here lies Fred, you thought I was dead," he said immediately, having obviously thought about it before.

Sam stared at him, a slight smile on his face, humoring the old man.

His watery, blue eyes flashing, the old man added, "To understand the actual we must contemplate the possible."

There is definitely something wrong with this man, Sam concluded, not taking his eyes from the figure in front of him. "And my epitaph, any predictions what it might say?"

The old man stared unwaveringly into Sam's eyes and said, "Three generations of imbeciles are enough." With that he turned on his heel and walked away. He had gone only a few feet when he stopped, turned slowly toward Sam, and said, "You favor her," a flat smile across his salamander mouth. He bowed his head as he turned and walked away.

Sam stared after him, a hundred questions racing through his mind. He wanted to call out for the old man to wait, to demand that he return and explain himself. He stood there silently, feeling helpless, watching the figure slowly weave between the graves. The old man's head was bowed, his shoulders slumped, and his torso bent forward as he stumbled along. His shuffling gait reminded Sam of a child who has just learned to walk. But he made steady progress, finally disappearing around the base of a grave-studded hill. His dark figure seemed to meld into the background, distinguished only by his motion, a moving blotch of camouflage that grew shorter with each step beyond the hill's horizon.

When he had disappeared completely, Sam continued to watch the hillside, partially in anticipation of the old man's return and partially because he did not know what else to do. He had an unsettled, unfulfilled feeling of something important that had been cut short. Sam continued to stare; he was confused and tired. He had slept little after searching the motor home. Everything was coincidental, he reasoned. The explanations were logical; he just hadn't thought of them yet. Rising repeatedly from the fog of confusion, the porcelain picture of a seventeen-year-old girl surfaced. He was a long way from home and suddenly felt very alone.

CHAPTER THREE

WHAT WAS MORTAL OF THEM RESTS BELOW
UNTIL THIS MORTAL PUT ON IMMORTALITY.
EPITAPH
—ALEXANDER KENNEDY

MIDNIGHT HAD ALWAYS AFFECTED Sam in a peculiar way. Not morning, not evening, it was time teetering on a fulcrum that, he secretly hoped, could go either way. With a foot planted in both worlds, he was momentarily hesitant, superstitious. The green numerals of the dashboard clock caused him to hold his breath. At 12:01 he could breathe again and the fear of uncertainty became the past.

The yellow glow of the log house reflected warmly in the headlights of the motor home. He was home. His trip odometer read 878 miles. It had taken him a little over fourteen hours of nonstop driving from eastern Iowa to the foothills west of Denver. Massaging his stiff neck, he unlocked the side door while Elle made her rounds to urinate on what she considered hers.

The red blinking light of the answering machine in his studio pulsed impatiently. He had finally broken down and purchased it only to satisfy Marcie, his ex-wife. It was probably Pat or Marcie, both wanting something he did not have time to give, but he pushed the play button anyway.

Beep. "Dad, it's me, Sidney. Can you call me as soon as you get home, please? Mom is being unreasonable again. It's really important. Love you."

Beep. "Sam, it's Marcie. Sidney is under the mistaken belief that you can somehow grant her permission to go to homecoming. God himself doesn't have that authority. She's fifteen, for God's sake. Call me before you talk to her. I mean it, Sam."

Beep. There was silence except for a faint static sound in the background. After several seconds Sam heard the phone at the other end hang up. He continued to stare at the answering machine, unsure of what to do next as an uneasy feeling swept over him. He looked at his watch. He would call Marcie in the morning.

He began pulling folders from one of two filing cabinets. Most of the files contained only an eight-by-ten-inch contact sheet with most of a roll of 35 mm exposures and a second contact sheet with a few two-and-a-quarter-inch exposures. It was just after 1:00 a.m. when he saw the old man. Sam grabbed the magnifying glass as he moved toward the brighter desk lamp on his rolltop. Surrounded by the light-colored tombstones, the old man seemed to rise from the dark ground; the black-and-white film made no distinction between his clothes and the grass. The old man's anemic face and snowy crest of hair melded with the stones in a field of markers. His right hand clung to the well-worn shovel that stood upright at his left side. Sam remembered taking the picture because of the cryptic nature of the old man's presence. A human chameleon, he blended perfectly into his surroundings.

Sam located the corresponding negative from a separate file using the numbers written on the file tab after Cambridge, a small ranching community in southeastern Colorado. This can't be the same person, he thought as he headed for the darkroom. Old men were a little like babies: They all looked alike, Sam believed. Surely the white hair and custodial clothes were the only common features the two men had.

• • • •

Sam watched a Steller's jay hop mechanically along the rail of his deck in the soft light of the Colorado dawn. He needed sleep. Again he fumbled on the table for the magnifying glass. He was tired of thinking, tired of asking himself questions that he could not answer. He inspected the two photos, one from Iowa and the other from Colorado. The old men were identical. "Twins," he said with a note of finality. "They've got to be twins." It was not unheard of for twins to be engaged in the same profession.

He placed the two photos side by side, Iowa on the left and Colorado on the right. The old men nearly filled the frames of each print. Their white hair, pallid skin, washed-out eyes with dark beady centers set above flaring nostrils, and salamander-like mouths were the same. They were old, but identical. A logical explanation would come, he told himself. There had to be one. It could be the same person. People move. Once a gravedigger, always a gravedigger. "Twins," he said as if dismissing further debate.

Pushing the Colorado photo away, Sam did a classic double take. He had been so intent on studying the old man that he failed to notice the tombstone in the background. Again he grabbed the magnifying glass. He looked beyond the old man who was framed in the center of the picture to the tombstone with the cast log laid horizontally across the top of the gray rectangle. His jaw muscles tightened. Without taking his eyes from the Colorado photo for fear that it might disappear, he brought the magnifying glass into focus. The name Eris appeared on the face of the stone. He was suddenly wide-awake.

CHAPTER FOUR

WE SHALL SLEEP,
BUT NOT FOREVER.
EPITAPH
—SARAH DOVE

MARCIE, IT'S SAM." He paused, staring at the coil of air hose that hissed below the pay phone at the corner of the Texaco station. "Pick up if you're there." He paused again. "I got your message. I'm in Pueblo. I should be back tomorrow night. I'll give you a call then and we'll work this out. Not to worry, okay? I haven't talked to Sidney, but she's a big girl. She should take part in the discussion." He winced at his last statement and wished that he could take it back, somehow delete it from the answering machine. He could see Marcie's disappointment, her frown and slumped shoulders. He knew she would leave another message on his answering machine, a stored recording designed to instill guilt. "We'll talk soon," he added, his voice weak with frustration.

••••

He turned south at La Junta and quickly left the fertile farmlands of the Arkansas River for the rolling hills of the

Comanche Grasslands. Cambridge was not on the official
Colorado state map. Sam had discovered the tiny community while studying the more detailed Las Animas County
map. He often used this technique when searching for possible inclusions to his book on forgotten cemeteries. He had
thought it strange that a town would be called Cambridge in
an area with such a dominant Hispanic history and culture.
But he found that many of the towns were Anglo in name.
Kim and Branson lay to the south; Tyrone and Thatcher
to the west; and Springfield, Walsh, and Stonington to the
east. It was the physical features of the land, the creeks and
canyons, that carried the names given them by the original
Spanish explorers and Mexican settlers. Vachita Creek, Jesus
Canyon, Trinchera Creek, Pinon Canyon, and Tejana Ar-
royo could have been located in Mexico.

Red dust billowed from behind the motor home into
the fading light of southeastern Colorado. Sam could
smell the rotting leaves from the dense stands of cottonwoods, willow, and tamarack that lined the valley floor
and hung with foreboding over the road in the semidark-
ness. The red sandstone walls of the canyon were reduced
to gently eroding hills a half mile apart at this end of the
valley. At the mouth of the canyon where the wider valley funneled into the deep, red cleft cut by the Purgatoire River, a second, smaller canyon intersected from
the south. Chacucao Canyon meandered gracefully into
the Purgatoire. The oxbows of its tiny stream had cut a
fertile green swath from the sandstone mesas above it.
It was here, where two steep canyons had come together

forming a small, level valley, that the Cambridge settlement had been built.

The cemetery was located above the floodplain on a grassy knoll where Chacucao Creek gently slipped into the Purgatoire. By the time Sam pulled the motor home into the short, grass-lined wheel paths of the lane leading to the cemetery, darkness had settled over the valley floor, a blanket of uniform murkiness with changed perspectives.

Beanee Weenees and a can of Coors satisfied his hunger. Exhaustion had finally taken hold of him in the security of the well-lit motor home. Its thin, aluminum walls served as impenetrable barriers to the darkness beyond. Its yellow, battery-powered lights provided the mental security that Sam hated to admit he needed.

Elle began to snore, normally a source of irritation to Sam who would respond with a thrown tennis shoe or a gentle nudge.

"Stink Dog," he managed with half-closed eyes, too tired to throw something.

••••

Confusion swirled with the remnants of sleep as Sam sat bolt upright in the narrow bed. From the floor below him a deep, throaty growl poured from Elle's frozen face. The inside of the motor home was ablaze with a white light that shone through the rear window and bounced from chrome to glass with the intensity of a welder's arc. The tapping that had awakened him was repeated. It was the unmistakable sound of human flesh stretched over bony knuckles wrapping against the aluminum door of the camper. Sam squinted at his watch. It was 10:15, but 10:15 what? From the opaque blackness on the other side of the windshield, he determined it was still night.

"Easy, girl," he whispered reassuringly to Elle as he slid from the bed, being careful not to step on her.

Hazy with sleep he opened the door without caution. An even brighter light exploded in his face. Defensively, he threw up his left hand to shield his face.

"Sorry," said the feminine, yet assertive, voice from behind the flashlight. Turning off the light she said, "Just wondering if everything was all right. I thought you might have had mechanical trouble or something." She paused then added, "We don't get many visitors down here."

Sam had turned his head sideways and was squinting through the halo of retinal after-flashes from the flashlight. He could hear the engine of the vehicle parked behind the motor home. "Everything's fine," he managed through a mouth that seemed stuffed with cotton. "Just pulled in for the night," he added, still straining to make out the woman's features.

"I didn't mean to wake you. I was just checking. This is our land."

"Sorry. I didn't mean to trespass. I thought it belonged to the city."

The pale, white glow of a three-quarter moon reflected softly from the gray felt Stetson atop her head. Its wide, nearly flat brim shadowed her face mysteriously. Sam could see puffs of blonde hair swept upward and tucked under the hat's brim.

"Cambridge is not much of a city," she said as if admitting a long-kept secret. "Isn't even a town," she added suddenly with a smile, the moon reflecting from a row of perfect, white teeth. "My great-grandfather gave them the ground for the cemetery. We still run cattle all around it. We've lost a few head again this year to rustlers." Looking down nervously, she added "that's why when we see a strange vehicle..."

"You thought I was a cattle thief?" Sam asked with surprised amusement.

"You just may be one, mister. I don't know you from Adam," she said, losing her smile and staring directly up into his face from under the hat's shadow. "The one thing I do know is that you're trespassing and I'm missing six yearling heifers."

Sam suddenly felt defensive, a condition that usually led to anger. He hated being at the receiving end of an accusation. "You're welcome to search the premises," he said, stepping to one side of the narrow doorway and extending his arm in a mock gesture of welcome. "Don't forget the bedroom closet. That's where I usually keep the cattle I've stolen."

She stared at him, her eyes burning with the desire to meet his sarcasm with an equally caustic response. Instead, she smiled politely and said, "That won't be necessary. Enjoy your stay here in Cambridge. I'm sorry I bothered you."

"No bother at all. Come back anytime you're missing livestock," he called after her as she walked into the glow of headlights behind the camper, her slender frame outlined by the harsh light. She wore snug-fitting blue jeans. A pair of leather gloves hanging from her back pocket flopped rhythmically, accentuating the movement of her hips. Her torso was covered by a short jean jacket that gave her the appearance of having wide shoulders and a narrow midsection. He wished he could have seen her face more clearly.

"Oh, by the way, mister," she called as she disappeared behind the headlights, "nice boxers!"

Sam quickly looked down. He raised his head slowly, eyes closed, a grimace of embarrassment on his face. In his confusion he had answered the door in his underwear. He was now suddenly aware of the cool night air rushing through the gaping slot in the front of his shorts, which his mother had always referred to as the "worm hole." Marcie had given them to him as a Valentine gift. White with pink hearts and tiny cupids, the kind you hoped you never were wearing if involved in an accident. "Damn," he hissed as he shut the door in an attempt to end his humiliation.

••••

The pungent aroma of sage, intertwined with the sweet, wet smell of prairie grasses, added to the dawn's beauty. Sam held his coffee mug between his hands, savoring the warmth against the crisp morning air. He stared pensively at the orange horizon, studying the land's features as the jagged landscape slowly, almost magically appeared from the night's darkness. He felt alone. Elle's presence helped, but it was not enough. He loved the dawn, even though it made him feel small and insignificant. A tide of memories would wash over him, pushed explosively ahead of the sun. His dead mother was usually the first to arrive. Committed to his work, Sam had immersed himself in it in order to escape the realities of a life gone stale. But at dawn the realities arose with the sun, illuminated, the details bright.

He could trace his disappointment back to when he was still in junior high school. He had just rounded the corner of the block on his bicycle when he saw the police car at the curb in front of his house, the starched and stiff young officer standing on the front porch step, his arms stiffly holding up his mother. His mother's screams of grief and disbelief still echoed deep within him. She never fully recovered from losing her firstborn child. Four years later his father, who went through the motions of life but never overcame his grief, was eventually consumed by his misery. Officially a heart attack, his mother was convinced he died of a broken heart. After college, after marriage, a few hectic years into his career, his mother had begged him to come home. She was sick and lonely; Sam was the only family she had. Born late in his mother's life, there had been a special bond between them. She even played her orphan card in a desperate attempt to impart guilt, but Sam was too busy. She died a week later, having never complained about the cancer that consumed her from within. All she had wanted was to say goodbye. He had been too busy. Ten years of regret seemed to rise up in his throat on mornings like this. He sipped his coffee.

Marriage had been the crushing blow. Life is so full of regrets, he thought. Why did it take a lifetime to realize one's mistakes, to understand the things that should have been said and done? A failed marriage and deep financial debt seemed to be the icing on the cake. That was nine years ago. Now at age thirty-seven, Samuel Theodore Dawson had recovered. And, a miraculous recovery it was. He sipped his coffee and stared blankly through the rising steam.

The headstones stood erect in the dusky light. They appeared cold and stark, uniform in color. Sam silently read the names and dates as he slowly made his way toward the crest of the hill. The names were old: Myra, Emma, Clara, Zode, Brittie, Briann, Nellie, Augusta, Flora, Agnes. And they had been dead a long time: 1908, 1909, 1907. There seemed to be a preponderance of little white lambs lying docilely atop thin, rectangular stones.

"God will grant me eyes and ears," he read aloud, the flowery script barely legible on the sun-bleached stone of Lorna Wertz, born in 1950 and dead a short sixteen years later.

"I shall be satisfied when I can hear Thy voice and see Thy likeness," proclaimed Sarah Cawlfield, a seventeen-year-old who died in 1969. "What the hell...," he said, spilling the remains of his coffee. "Were they vision and hearing impaired too?" He thought of Genève Defollett and his sister who, like Lorna and Sarah, had died as handicapped teenagers.

A cool morning breeze with a hint of fall stole his breath, a giant blowing into the face of an infant. "What's going on here?" he said, turning around then back again. He felt a flush of fear sweep over him as the hairs on his arms bristled over bumpy gooseflesh at the sudden realization that there were no boys buried beneath him.

CHAPTER FIVE

*AFFLICTIONS SO LONG TIME I BORE
PHYSICIANS SKILL IN VAIN
UNTIL GOD WAS PLEASED TO GIVE ME EASE
AND RID ME OF MY PAIN.*
EPITAPH
—MARY JOHNSON

THERE WERE OLD MEN WHO HAD LIVED long lives. But there were no boys. Thad Dougherty was eighty-two in February of 1943 and Thomas Pough was just short of ninety when he died in June of 1958.

A light breeze blew cool air down the back of Sam's neck and he shuddered. I've got the heebie-jeebies in a cemetery in broad daylight, he thought. "That's a first," he said quietly.

"All is not here for our beloved and blest. Leave ye the sleeper with his God to rest," the tombstone of Clifford Major, dead in 1949, proclaimed.

"Let not your heart be troubled In my Father's House are many mansions." Edith Phillips' prose was block letters with no punctuation and a stretch for proper capitalization. She had died in 1967 at the age of seventy-eight.

John and Rebecca Anderson had a span of bad luck with their offspring:

Mary died May 3, 1908

Age 3 weeks

Louisa died September 28, 1911
Age 8 months, 2 weeks

Emily died June 15, 1917
Age 7 months, 6 days

All three stones lay flat against the earth, stretching
south from the larger, upright monument of their parents.
They served as cold reminders of the lives that could have
been and the pain of losing a child. Sam inhaled deeply and
exhaled with a prolonged sigh. He thought of Sidney and
how horrific it would be to lose her, and how his father must
have felt after Julie's death. Sam had wanted to be Joe Average with a house in the suburbs, a station wagon, an ador-
ing wife, and a couple of kids who would revere him. He
blamed Marcie, but knew he shared the responsibility for a
failed dream. He tossed the remainder of his coffee, which
had gone cold, between two graves.

The marker he had traveled so far to see lay at the
very top of the grassy knoll, now covered with angular
tombstones. The concrete log with axe and wedge lay
atop the granite headstone. It was more conspicuous here
in the treeless, shortgrass prairie than it was in the lush,
oak-covered cemetery of Iowa, he thought. Out of place
might be a more accurate assessment. Eastern Colorado
was noted for its treeless plains. Colorado in general had
never been a significant lumber-producing state. This
guy was obviously a lumberjack or a timber baron, he
reasoned.

The stone appeared to grow larger as Sam approached. The edges of the block letters that spelled the name Eris were dangerously sharp. Similar to the Iowa stone, the name Eugene was centered between the dates June 18, 1852, and August 4, 1930. The Eugene Eris buried in Iowa had died on January 25, 1932, almost eighteen months after the Colorado Eris.

The sun was fully up when Sam heard the sound of a vehicle approaching. Gravel ricocheting and crunching under rubber popped and cracked in contrast to the mechanical drone of the engine. Sam watched as the pickup slowly climbed the serpentine ribbon of gravel upward from the valley floor toward the cemetery. Its large, green, rounded fender cowls with bulbous headlamps, and tiny cab with a divided windshield dated the old Chevy as late forties.

Turning off the motor drive and light meter of his camera, Sam turned to stare at the inscription at the bottom of the stone one more time: "Wellborn Are My Children." His jaw muscles rippled as he clenched his teeth in frustration.

The pickup came to a noisy halt at the side of the road next to the cemetery driveway. The door opened slowly as the old man slid from behind the wheel. His white hair contrasted sharply with the brown and red surroundings of the countryside. Even at a distance, Sam could see the salamander-like appearance of the old man's face. His wide, flat mouth was expressionless as he walked in old-man fashion toward the top of the hill.

"Good morning," Sam called out as the old man approached him straight-on, still twenty yards away. The salamander did not respond but continued to make his way toward Sam. "Looks like it's going to be a beautiful day," Sam added cheerfully.

The old man stopped in front of Sam, uncomfortably close. The tiny, black beads in the center of his watery, blue eyes stared directly into Sam's face. The square chin, sharp nose, and flaring nostrils were the mirror image of, if not the same, features he had noted only two days earlier in eastern Iowa, right down to the janitorial green, heavy cotton trousers and shirt. Sam glanced quickly at the pockets of the old man's pants. They were clean and showed no soiling. But they were old, and the left pocket displayed the frayed effects of preferential use, just as it did in Iowa.

"Back again?" the old man said through cracked lips rimmed with white beard stubble that held a hint of brown tobacco juice at both corners of his mouth.

Sam did not know how to respond. Back again where? Was the old man referring to Iowa, to this cemetery in particular, or to all cemeteries in general?

"You were here about two years ago," the old man said, seeing Sam's confusion.

"Yeah, right," Sam said with obvious relief. "But I don't believe we met. I didn't think anyone noticed me."

The old man smiled. "We don't get many visitors to this part of the country, especially ones that take pictures of tombstones. I noticed you," he stated flatly. As if an afterthought, he added with a smile, "Say, you don't have any cattle hidden in that camper, do you?"

Sam stared at the old man for a long moment. "News travels fast in a small town," he said, scratching his head. "Did she mention my underwear too?"

"Hearts," the old man shot back with a larger smile.

Sam shook his head and looked down.

"Oh, don't worry about it. It'll take close till noon before everybody in town knows about it," the old man said wryly.

"I guess I offended the lady," Sam said.

"Good thing. That'll be the most exciting thing Blair has happen to her all summer."

"Blair?"

"She's my grandniece," the old man said, still smiling. "She's home for the summer and thinks she's a range detective."

"She's a student somewhere?" Sam asked with a curiosity that was all too obvious.

"Professor," the old man stated proudly. "She's up at the university in Boulder. The kid's got brains. Don't know why she comes back here every summer. Says she's doing field research, but my guess is she's just getting away from the city."

"This looks like a great place to kick back and escape the pressures of the world," Sam said.

"Those of us who don't know any better, think it's a pretty special place," the old man said, his salamander eyes still staring studiously at Sam as if waiting for a particular response.

Sam stared back, unable to rationalize the fact that he had just seen the old man in another cemetery a thousand miles away. "Do you work here?" he said suddenly.

"Yep, I'm the caretaker, among other things."

"My name's S—"

"Sam Dawson," the old man interrupted sharply.

The surprised look on Sam's face begged the obvious question.

The old salamander managed another half-smile. "Even we country folk get to town once in a while. Some of us even been known to go inside a bookstore." He paused and looked Sam up and down. "I'll have to admit that you are a mite larger than the photo on the dust jacket indicates."

"I'm sorry, but I didn't catch your name," Sam said, trying not to show his pride in being recognized.

"Tennyson," the old man said with an air of pride, "Al Tennyson."

Sam smiled. "As in Alfred," he said with a hint of sarcasm.

"Alfred L.," beamed the amphibian.

Sam chuckled and shook his head. "I should have guessed, coming from a town named Cambridge. Is your middle name really Lord?"

"Don't know. All I ever got was the initial."

"Don't tell me there are a Byron, a Shelley, and a Keats in town too," Sam said, smiling.

"No Keats," the old man shot back. "What brings you back?" he said, changing the subject abruptly.

Sam was caught off guard. He had not contemplated an answer to that question. "More pictures," he said vaguely. "This is one of my favorite cemeteries."

"That so," Tennyson said as if playing along. "How come we never saw any pictures of it in your book?"

"We?" Sam questioned.

"The whole darned town! We huddled around that book and examined every picture, looking to see a familiar one."

Sam scratched the back of his head, a nervous habit he was well aware of. "Guess they got lost on the cutting room floor," he said apologetically.

The old man stared at him with no sign of understanding. He clearly was waiting for another explanation.

"Editing," Sam said. "The publishers were unmerciful. They cut some of my favorite shots. We had some knock-down, drag-out battles and I lost most of them."

"Good," Tennyson shot back abruptly.

"Excuse me?"

"I said it was good," the old man growled, his eyes narrowing. "We don't want reminders of our loved ones appearing in your godforsaken book. It's commercial and it's blasphemous," his voice rising with anger. "The last thing we want is a bunch of souvenir-hunting tourists from the city crawling over our town cemetery."

Sam stared back in disbelief. "I'm sorry if I've offended anyone," he said softly, not taking his eyes from Tennyson.

The old man had expected an argument and now seemed confused, the wind taken from his sails. "We live way the hell out here because we want to be left alone," he said in a less threatening tone. "Our father would turn in his grave," he said, gesturing toward the grave with the log headstone, "if he knew strangers were trampling through his cemetery."

"Father?" Sam questioned with a puzzled look.

"Founder is more like it. But he was like a father to most of us," he said with an air of reverence as he gazed pensively toward Eris's grave.

"You knew him?"

"Hell yes, I knew him! He was the only father I ever knew. Doctor Eris took care of my mother and me and most of the rest of the kids in town."

"Doctor," Sam said, somewhat surprised.

"Yep, he doctored all of us. He got his training in England, an aristocrat. But that's no business of yours," he said as if catching himself. "He demanded privacy when he was alive and would surely want it now."

"What did he mean by the epitaph, 'Wellborn Are My Children'?" Sam asked quickly, ignoring the old man's attempt to end the conversation.

Tennyson stared through amphibian eyes, at first a cold, dispassionate glare then a curious scan, his eyes searching Sam's face, mellowing with a hint of recognition. There was an uncomfortable moment of silence. "You're trespassing," he said suddenly, turned, and walked away, weaving with a slight limp through the headstones toward the road.

The cool morning breeze again caused Sam to shiver. Dark clouds had gathered to the west, a sign of the long, harsh winter ahead. The granite monolith with the curious epitaph appeared darker and colder than it had earlier. Sam stared at the chiseled angles, the smooth flat surfaces, and the granular appearance of the mottled stone. The dark letters engraved in the lower half represented the name of a long-dead human being. A man, a doctor, a founder was all that he knew about this person who had existed for seventy-eight years. There was more, Sam thought. There had to be much more.

Sam watched the cloud of red dust rolling restlessly upward from behind the pickup as the old man wound his way back down the hill toward town. The morning breeze stirred the stalks of dead grass that had grown high around the base of Eris's gravestone, floating across the cold, sedentary inscription. Sam held his breath as he again read the epitaph.

CHAPTER SIX

*FRIENDS, AS YOU PASS BY,
AS YOU ARE NOW SO ONCE WAS I.
AS I AM NOW YOU SOON WILL BE.
SO PREPARE YOURSELF TO FOLLOW ME.*
EPITAPH
—RAYMOND E. HALL

THE DANK CELLAR SMELLED OF DUST and moldy paper as Sam descended the creaking open-backed stairs that plummeted downward at an acute angle into the limestone-walled cavern. A single low-wattage light bulb hung from two, frayed cloth-covered wires in the center of the room. Stacks of yellow-brown newspapers on crude, wooden shelves lined three of the walls.

The *Tribune Democrat* occupied one of the oldest buildings in La Junta. The upstairs had been remodeled to resemble a modern newspaper office, but it was only a facade. The back rooms were the repositories for a hundred years' worth of newspaper junk stacked helter-skelter, a bonfire waiting for a match.

Lupe Guerrero smacked her gum incessantly through lipstick-smeared lips. Her black eyes shone as she listened to Sam explain his need to search the stacks for August 1930. Unfortunately she did not know a microfiche from a silverfish. It was noon and most of the staff had gone to lunch. Lupe dismissed herself as an intern on loan from the high school, but led Sam to the cellar door with the small-town trust so common to most of rural Colorado.

The thought of microfilm had been a long shot. He knew how costly it could be for a small newspaper to shoot their stacks. But he had expected something a little more sophisticated than the fire hazard he now faced. Sophistication was represented by the fact that the tattered and crooked piles of old newsprint were arranged chronologically from left to right and top to bottom. Sam was amazed that it took him less than two minutes to find the August 1930 collection. He discovered there were two newspapers dating back to 1897, the *Daily Democrat* and the *La Junta Tribune*. The papers had merged sometime after the 1930s.

News traveled more slowly in those days. He reasoned that if Eris had died on August 4, the obituary would not have run until several days later. The obits were a good deal larger than the present-day two-column inches, but were still buried on the next-to-last page along with the funeral notices and ads for mortuaries.

Sam was skeptical. Perhaps it was his innate pessimism, but he did not expect to find a thing. His heart raced a little when the name Eris appeared in the dark, bold print of the August 9 edition of the *Daily Democrat*: "Eugene Eris, 78 of Pueblo, died August 4 at home. There were no services. Burial was in Cambridge Cemetery. Dr. Eris was the Director of Medical Care at the State Insane Asylum in Pueblo for 22 years before retiring in 1926."

The *Tribune* treated it even more casually by simply printing a death notice under the "Vital Statistics" column on August 10: "Eris—Eugene, Pueblo, Aug. 4. Harold McLavey."

"Pueblo?" Sam said. Eris, the founder of Cambridge, father of the town, lived and worked in Pueblo. He scratched the back of his head as he read the notice again. "Pueblo?" he repeated.

••••

The sign at the west edge of town read, "Pueblo 64 miles." With Cambridge another thirty-five road miles southwest of La Junta, it was more than an afternoon jaunt in a Model A for Eris to visit the town he had founded, Sam thought. Of course there was probably passenger service on the Atchison, Topeka and Santa Fe Railway between Pueblo and La Junta in those days. Sam knew those old steamers covered ground much faster than their modern diesel-electric counterparts. He was willing to bet that more than one train per day had headed east from Pueblo. He calculated that Eris could be in Cambridge in less than three hours after leaving Pueblo.

Elle sat awkwardly in the passenger seat, a long strand of drool hanging from the corner of her mouth, as he raced west on Highway 50, occasionally looking at his watch. "You sow," he said with mock anger.

Elle's amber-colored eyes glanced quickly toward Sam as she shrank in response to his criticism. Just looking at her provided the comic relief that Sam often needed when he was anxious.

He checked his watch again. It was just after 3:00 p.m. Four o'clock in Iowa, he thought. Elle nearly fell from the seat when he turned abruptly into the Sinclair station at Fowler.

••••

Liz Seymour had a disgusted look on her face as she plopped down behind her desk at the *Jackson County Herald* in Maquoketa, Iowa. She looked at the Seth Thomas clock on the wall above the newsroom. It was 5:05 p.m. and she had wanted to leave early.

"What's wrong, Liz?" asked Jenny Edwards from across the aisle.

Liz shook her head and sighed. "Just when I thought I could get out of this pit early for once in my life, I get this nutcase on the phone. Some jerk calling long distance from Colorado wants me to look up an obit from 1930, for Christ's sake."

"Did you?"

"This guy was persistent, wouldn't take drop dead for an answer."

"Probably one of those necrophiliacs," Jenny smiled. "This was his idea of an obscene phone call."

"I don't think so. Least I didn't hear any heavy breathing," Liz said, grabbing a stack of papers from her in-box.

"Who'd he want?"

"Anybody who'd talk with him," she said.

"No," Jenny whined. "Whose obit did he want?"

"A guy by the name of Eris who croaked on January 25, 1932," she said. "I had to read the whole thing to him twice."

"Must have been a relative, huh?"

"Don't think so," Liz said, looking up pensively. He didn't seem to know much about this guy. He was mostly interested in where he lived."

"Where'd he live?"

"Independence, I guess. At least I assume that's where he lived. He was a doctor at the state hospital. But his family must be local since he's buried just west of here at Oxford."

"Oxford?" Jenny asked quizzically.

"Yeah, it's about twenty-five miles west of here and off to the south. It's a dinky, little farm community next to the Wapsipinicon River, sort of isolated in a wooded valley. Very picturesque! I was there once. Quite by accident. It was one of the highlights of my relationship with Roger. He took me squirrel hunting and we got lost." Looking up thoughtfully, Liz said, "I guess that's when I realized that Roger was a squirrel, a squirrel with no nuts!"

Both women burst out laughing.

••••

Sam knew several people on the staff of the *Pueblo Chieftain* from his days as the governor's press secretary. It was a modern, professionally run newspaper that served southern Colorado from the San Luis Valley in the west to the Kansas border in the east. He was in no mood to visit old acquaintances and make small talk. He was on a mission of discovery. The old familiar pangs of obsession beyond curiosity were stirring and he wanted more information.

The desk clerk had been reluctant to let him use the microfiche library. It was close to 5:00 p.m., when they closed to the general public. She had tried to convince him to go to the public library since they had duplicate services. But when Sam asked to talk with Preston Dean, the editor, she suddenly became very cooperative.

The *Chieftain* titled them "Funeral Notices" and devoted an entire page to the dead. Sam found the notice in the August 7, 1930, edition. He had held only minor hope for a picture and was not overly disappointed by the lack of one. Pictures of any sort were a bit rare in the tabloids of the earlier part of the century. Even the advertisements were drawn by staff artists. It was a longer piece than published in the *Daily Democrat*, but the shortest on the page: "Eugene Eris, 78, passed away in Pueblo on Aug. 4, 1930. Dr. Eris, believed to have been born in England, has no known surviving relatives. He was Director of Medicine at the Insane Asylum for more than two decades before retiring in 1926. Dr. Eris was known as a quiet man who never turned someone less fortunate away. No services will be held at the deceased's request. Interment: Cambridge Cemetery, Las Animas County."

Sam read the notice one more time, hoping to see something he may have missed the first time. "This tells me nothing," he whispered to himself. He quickly scanned the page, looking at other obituaries. Each was a biographical narrative of the dearly departed. They were the beloved husband, wife, father, son, mother, daughter, or friend of someone else. They were each survived by specific people from specific places. They were born and educated someplace. They had hobbies and were members of professional and fraternal organizations. It was 1930 and they all had religious affiliations with funeral services, liturgies, Masses, graveside services, commendations, or military honors. They were all people with lives. Lives compressed into twelve-to-fifteen column inches, but lives nonetheless. Eris, on the other hand, was an enigma. How could a man live seventy-eight years with so little information published about him? he wondered.

On the way out Sam asked the obviously irritated desk clerk if he could borrow a phone book. He quickly, almost destructively flipped through the yellow pages, first to Mortuaries then to Funeral Directors.

Lawrence McLavey, Director, Piedmont Funeral Home & Historic Chapel, 901 Broadway; a family friend since 1885. "Do you know where Broadway is?" he said somewhat impatiently.

The desk clerk glared at him contemptuously. "Yes," she said flatly as she placed the closed sign on the desk, turned, and disappeared into the inner office.

"Just checking," Sam said quietly, knowing he deserved what he got. He was acting like an impatient jerk. Since leaving the more structured workforce, he had developed a mild intolerance for the eight-to-five mentality. He seemed to always be pressing the five o'clock limit of the rest of the population. He knew the mortuary would be no better. He dreaded the pompous, dark-suited, hands-folded, after-five type confrontation that awaited him there.

With one detour to ask directions from a convenience store clerk, Sam rolled to a noisy stop in the circular driveway of the Piedmont Funeral Home and Historic Chapel. Elle needed to go outside, her eyes desperate from a tortured bladder. Sam looked around at the manicured grounds and decided that dog urine was not the calling card he needed. "Stay, girl! I'll be back in a few minutes."

The heavy, wooden front doors were locked. A small brass plate just above the latch was neatly engraved to instruct that after hours one should ring the bell. Pushing the large black button to the left of the door, he heard nothing. He pushed it again, paused, then a third time. Sam had turned to walk back to the motor home when the door behind him suddenly opened.

"Can I help you?" the man called out before Sam could turn around.

"Yes, would it be possible to talk with the funeral director or owner?"

"You're talking to him. What can I help you with?"

Sam did not respond immediately. He was studying the young man before him. Late twenties or early thirties, Sam guessed. He was handsome with wavy brown hair worn well over the ears. He wore running shoes, faded blue jeans, and a bright orange Broncos sweatshirt. "My name is Sam Dawson," he said, offering his hand.

"Larry McLavey," the young man beamed.

Sam did not know how to begin the conversation. He was so eager to get there that he had not thought of what to say or ask when he arrived. "Uh, I'm working on a book and was wondering if…I'm doing some background stuff, you know, historical research, and was wondering if you kept records on the people that you, uh, um, your clients, you know."

"Sure," McLavey smiled. "We've got files that go clear back to the first corpse my great-grandfather embalmed in the mid-1880s. Are you looking for somebody in particular?"

"Yeah, a guy that died in 1930 by the name of Eris."

Holding the door open, McLavey said, "Come in. I'll show you what I've got. If he was laid out here, we'll have paper on it."

Larry McLavey had been busy embalming himself, Sam determined as he passed beside him into the chapel foyer. His breath reeked of vodka, which stood in sharp contrast to the spring floral scent of the chapel.

"Relative?" McLavey asked cheerfully.

"No," Sam said hesitantly. "Just a prominent figure in a period piece I'm working on east of here."

"Are you from Pueblo?"

"No, Golden. Hey, I really appreciate you taking the time tonight."

"No problem," McLavey said. "I'll be here half the night. Got a rush job in late this afternoon that I need to have ready by tomorrow."

He led Sam through two sets of doors and down a long hallway toward the rear of the building, which adjoined the chapel. "Not squeamish, are you?" he said, pausing, his hand on the knob of yet another door.

"Not usually," Sam said, bracing himself for whatever surprise McLavey had in store.

"All of our old files are in the storeroom and there's only one way to get there, and that's through the prep room. Please excuse the mess," he said, opening the door. "I didn't expect to have visitors back here today."

The smell was not unpleasant, Sam thought, a cross between disinfectant and dry cleaning solution. McLavey's rush job commanded Sam's total attention. The huge, blanched corpse of the woman seemed to fill the room. Her naked body was so obese that Sam could not help staring. He was momentarily captivated, in the same way he had been intrigued as a child by the sword swallower or the rubber man at a carnival sideshow. Her bulbous form appeared to be rising at the center. Her breasts hung to the sides of her rib cage. Mounds of white, corpulent flesh completely covered the exam table and gave the appearance of being rolled and pleated. Her feet were dirty and misshapen, ravaged from the weight above. Long, yellow nails covered her cyanotic toes. Her feet seemed small compared to the beefy quarters they were attached to. Rough, unwashed calluses darkened her elbows. He could not see her face. Her auburn hair hung over the edge of the table, radiating from a head that was obscured by its body.

Seeing Sam's fascination, McLavey looked as if he was about to say something. But he maintained a sense of professionalism and said nothing.

Sam too repressed his desire to comment.

"Here we go," McLavey said as they entered a small cement-block room with no windows. "Everything up to 1950 is in these three file cabinets. What'd you say his name was?"

"Eris."

Opening a drawer and finger-walking across the tops of the files, he said, "Eris, Eugene?"

"He's the one."

"We received him on August 4, 1930. My grandfather, who served as a deputy county coroner, signed the death certificate. Cause of death is listed as natural," he said, holding the file so Sam could read it also. "This shows his home address as the state asylum. Next of kin: none. Religion: Anglican. You don't see that one very often. He must have been English."

"That's what I understand," Sam said, still scanning the file.

"Let's see, the body was released to an Alfred L. Tennyson on August 7 for burial at Cambridge Cemetery, wherever that is."

"Las Animas County, southwest of La Junta," Sam said.

"He got a mahogany casket with pewter fixtures, satin lining and pillow. No services were held here," he said, raising his eyebrows. "It was probably conducted locally."

"Nothing else?" Sam asked, disappointment evident in his voice.

"I'm afraid that's all we have on your man Eris," McLavey said, returning the file to the drawer. "Did that help you any?"

"Yes," Sam responded enthusiastically. "You've helped me a great deal." Actually, he was disappointed. He had hoped for more, much more. At least he knew that salamander man was the one who had picked up Eris, indicating an obvious relationship.

One more time past the huge woman. Her clothes were folded neatly and stacked on a side table next to her shoes and a stainless steel bowl containing her personal effects, jewelry, barrettes, dark glasses, and a pair of hearing aids. Sam exchanged cordialities at the front door, promising that if he ever dropped dead in Pueblo, he would leave instructions to be brought to Piedmont.

Elle almost knocked him down as she rushed by him when he opened the motor home door. She squatted immediately, forgoing her usual routine of looking for just the right spot. In a few days there would be a small yellow circle of dead grass in Piedmont's front lawn for McLavey to remember them by.

••••

"Barb?"

"Yes."

"Sam Dawson. Sorry to bother you so late. Were you in bed?"

"Yes."

"Were you asleep?"

"Yes."

"Are you still asleep?"

"Yes."

"You want me to call you back in the morning?"

"For Christ's sake, Sam, you've called me up in the middle of the doggone night. What the hell do you want?"

"I'm sorry, Barb, it's important and I need a favor," he said. He had known Barbara Sinclair since the governor hired her as director of Institutions. She was one of the few cabinet members who had a sense of humor. For a Yale Law School graduate, she was unpretentious. Sam had saved her from the media when it was discovered that the state's institutions were feeding hamburger to its residents that contained tracheas, anuses, salivary glands, and other such unsavory innards.

"You bastard, this better be important," she said, sitting up and turning on the light. She fumbled for her glasses on the nightstand. Barbara Sinclair was a plain woman in her mid-thirties, not unattractive but slightly overweight. She had dedicated her life to her career, never finding time to get married. She liked Sam and he knew it.

"Listen, Babs, you don't need any more beauty sleep," Sam smiled through the phone. "It's important and I need a big favor."

"The last time you needed a big favor, I almost got fired." She was referring to the pro bono legal work she had done for Sam during his divorce. The governor found out about it and chewed her butt out for consulting, when she was supposed to be working for him eighty hours a week. If she needed work to do, he would be happy to give her additional responsibilities, he had told her.

"This one won't get you in trouble. I promise!"

"What is it?" she said, trying to act disgusted.

"I need everything you can find on a dead guy that used to be the medical director at the state hospital. Check with personnel to see what they have. Call archives to see if they have anything. The state hospital itself may have some records..."

"Whoa, whoa, whoa," she said, "a dead guy?"

"Yeah, name of Doctor Eugene Eris. He died August 4, 1930, in Pueblo. He had worked at the hospital for more than twenty years, retiring in 1926."

"Christ, Sam! I can't find the records of people we hired last week. I have almost three thousand employees. I don't even know what our policy is about record storage."

"Now's the time to learn, Babs," he said excitedly. "I wouldn't ask if I didn't really need it."

"What do I get out of this?" she said sarcastically.

"How about lunch and my undying gratitude?" he shot back quickly.

"Wonderful, the last time you bought me lunch it came in a bag with fries and a Coke. When do you need all this?"

"Tomorrow."

"Sam, tomorrow is twenty-eight minutes from now," she said calmly.

"I meant by noon or so."

"Oh, in that case, there shouldn't be any problem. You jerk!"

"Thanks, Barb. Get some sleep."

"You jerk."

"Bye."

••••

Wind rushing through aspens created a white noise that Sam always found soothing. The pine trees hissed and, with strong enough gusts, they hummed. But the aspen clattered softly, a constant rustling of leaves. Nights in the foothills had become very cool as the first hints of winter filled the air and touched the landscape.

The coolness of the bedsheets surrounded him. Sleep would come quickly. He was exhausted, confused, and slightly depressed. Again, he had returned too late to call Marcie. She would be angry. He sighed and closed his eyes.

All he had wanted to do was create the perfect pictorial essay of Iowa's dead, to show their stone tributes and to stir the reader's curiosity and imagination about the deceased, their life and times, their contributions and societal sins. He was fascinated by the mystery contained under every etched stone, captivated by the story that each grave had to tell. They seemed to call out to him, beckoning him to recognize them, to give them individual attention, to hear their story above the stories of all those around them. But he had wanted this book to be a secret book, produced just for him and nobody else. Perhaps in that way, he, the reader, could share in the revelation of the secrets exposed through his lens. He wanted this book to be simple, yet tell a story. At times he became depressed by his inability to capture his mind's eye on film. His photographs were awkward attempts to visualize things for which there were no words. Now the last thing on his mind was photography. His stride had been broken, his life interrupted by something he did not understand, something he felt compelled to investigate.

The house strained under the pressure of a now steady wind. A cold, light rain pelted against the bedroom windows. The floor creaked and then creaked again. When it creaked a third time, Sam raised his head and stared toward the doorway. His first thought was that Elle was cruising through the house.

It was not a faint odor that captured his attention. It was the strong, nostril-searing stench of disinfectant and dry cleaning solution that seized his heart. She stood to the left of the bedroom door, partially obscured in shadow. Her white flesh gathered the small amount of available light and radiated it back in ghostly fashion. The floor creaked in protest as she took a graceful, almost dainty step toward the bed, moving from the shadow of the door. She did not lumber as Sam had envisioned. She was still naked. Her huge breasts hung pendulously above her distended abdomen. A second, somewhat smaller abdominal section rolled gracefully outward from below her naval, intersecting the vertical chasm created by her two man-size thighs.

He tried to scream, to yell in horror, to frighten and threaten, but nothing more than an unintelligible squeak emerged. Her face was still hidden in shadow as she slowly but purposefully made her way to the foot of the bed. He wanted to leap up and run, but he could not. Only his head moved, thrashing from side to side, his mouth opening and closing.

The bed moved gently as she bumped against the foot. Sam was frozen in horror, unable to breathe. She leaned forward from the waist, her huge breasts suddenly swinging free, the burning odor now corroding the back of his mouth and throat. Her face slowly came into view, framed by ringlets of dark auburn hair. It was Tennyson. His broad, flat, salamander mouth was fixed in a perpetual smile and the beady ebony of his pupils filled his eyes. He slowly raised his swollen hands and signed, "You are trespassing."

Sam shrieked, a forced, garbled, extended "No!" pushing through the barrier that separates the conscious from the unconscious. His eyelids sprang open as he bolted upright. The faint odor lingered only in his memory. His body trembled in fear, his face was wet with perspiration, and his lungs heaved for air. He looked around the dark room.

Outside, the aspen leaves rustled restlessly, writhing against one another in wind-induced confusion. A cold sleet pattered with an irregular rhythm against the windowpanes.

CHAPTER SEVEN

I WILL TAKE MY HAT OFF WHEN
I MEET A MAN WHO CARVES IN STONE,
FOR HIS IS THE ONLY WORK THAT ENDURES.
EPITAPH
—GEORGE W. MATHIS

COLORADO DEPARTMENT OF HEALTH, Vital Records Section," the woman said flatly over the phone.

"Yes," Sam said with hesitation, not knowing where or how to begin the conversation. "I would like to get a copy of a death certificate."

"Name?"

"Mine?"

"No sir, the name of the deceased."

"Oh, I'm sorry. Eris. Eugene Eris. E-R-I-S," Sam spelled into the phone.

"Date of death?"

"August 4, 1930."

"Place of death?"

"Pueblo."

"County?"

"Pueblo."

"Reason for request?"

"Excuse me?" Sam said in an attempt to buy time. He had not thought of a legitimate reason.

"Reason for your request?" she repeated slowly as if talking to a child.

"Legal considerations," he said, biting his lip. "It has to do with the settlement of his estate," he added. He cringed at the stupidity of his last statement. Why would he be settling the estate of a man who died in 1930?

"Age at time of death?" she said mechanically, moving to the next question on the application, having met the minimum requirement for a response.

"Seventy-eight," Sam shot back with self-confident certainty.

"Your name?"

"Samuel T. Dawson."

"Relationship to deceased?"

"No relation," Sam said without thinking.

"Are you the legal representative of the deceased?" she said, emphasizing the word legal.

"No," he said cautiously with the realization that he may have hit a snag.

"Are you the legal representative of the parents, grandparents, stepparents, siblings, spouse, adult children, stepchildren, or grandchildren of the deceased?"

Sam hesitated. The bureaucrat had him. "No," he said almost apologetically.

"Are you a probate researcher?"

"No!" He was starting to get angry.

"Can you demonstrate a direct and tangible interest in the information about the deceased for determination or protection of a personal or property right?"

"Yes," he responded in desperation. What's to lose? he thought.

"Sir," she said, sounding more official every second. "Pursuant to Colorado Revised Statutes, 1982, 25-2-118, and as defined by Colorado Board of Health Rules and Regulations, the applicant must have a direct and tangible interest in the record requested. There *are* penalties by law for obtaining a record under false pretenses."

"I believe this man is my biological grandfather," Sam said.

"You believe?"

"Yes. My mother was an orphan." Now he was telling the truth.

A short period of dead air traversed the line between them before she began her perfunctory recital. "There is a $12 charge for the first copy or for a search of the files if no record is found, and a $6 charge for each additional copy of the same record ordered at the same time. How many copies do you wish to order?"

"Just one," he said, smiling.

"Your complete address?"

All right, he thought to himself. Now we're getting somewhere. He gave her his address and she repeated it with the efficiency of a machine.

"Sir, you *are* required to come to our offices at 4300 Cherry Creek Drive South in order to sign this application for a certified copy of a death certificate."

"Can you just send me an uncertified copy that I don't need to sign for?"

"VISA or Master Card number," she said, having lost patience.

Sam recited his VISA card number from memory, even giving her the expiration date before she asked.

"Sir, there is an additional convenience charge of $4.50 for use of a credit card. Your total comes to $16.50 unless you want the certificate sent to you by certified mail, Express Mail, or Federal Express, at which time I will have to add another $5.00."

He had forgotten the exasperation he had felt while working for government when encountering such bureaucracy. A frustrating career that culminated as press secretary to an egotistical governor had left him disappointed and disillusioned. Disappointed with his journalistic career and disillusioned with the politics he had once found captivating. "Can you send it Overnight Mail?"

"That will be an additional $9.00 for next-day service, bringing your total to $25.50," she said without hesitating. "Will there be anything else?"

"No. Thank you. You've been very considerate."

"Thank you, sir. Goodbye."

"Goodbye," he said and hung up the phone. He had lied, and that troubled him. Taking a deep breath, he said, "One more time," as he picked up the phone.

"Information. What city?"

"Des Moines," he said.

"What listing?"

"Under state government, Department of Health."

••••

Wharton Mortuary was perhaps the biggest in the state. They owned several cemeteries around the city, including one that took up nearly a square mile of a western suburb. Early in the last century, Mr. Wharton had assured his posterity by erecting mammoth edifices in the form of chapels and mausoleums and plastering them with his name. They had achieved landmark status with the natives and could be seen from any high spot in a five-county area.

Sam did not go to many funerals and only now did he realize how little he knew about mortuaries and the burial process.

Wharton's business office was sunny and attractive, remodeled from the Tudor-style home that most likely belonged to Wharton himself. It was attached to the funeral parlor, now an elaborate chapel.

Niva Gibbs greeted him with a cheerful smile and seemed eager to answer anything she could. Although she had worked at Wharton's for twenty years, she seemed dumbfounded by Sam's somewhat dark line of inquiry. In order to relax her and keep the conversation going, he skipped over the hard questions and asked her about the process in general. She knew little of the technical area of embalming that was done across town at their preparation facility. However, she was a fountain of information concerning funerals. She explained in great detail the process of casket selection, types of services offered, and all the paraphernalia and options that existed from flowers to flags, musicians to pallbearers. He did learn that death certificates could only be issued by an attending physician or the coroner. She talked briefly about the circumstances that would trigger a coroner's inquest. He discovered that the county administrator assumed custody of all unclaimed bodies and was required to issue a release permit prior to burial. Sam was interested in the fact that a transit permit was required if a body was shipped out-of-state and that bodies could only be sent to other funeral directors.

"Niva, let me go back to a couple of the questions I asked earlier," Sam said, feeling that he had gained her trust. "How do you know the deceased is who they are purported to be?"

She looked at him blankly as if the thought had never occurred to her.

"Let's say I bring a body in here and tell you it's my father, Joe Schmo."

"You'd have to have a death certificate," she interjected as if that were the answer.

"Got one," Sam said. "Joe died in the hospital and the attending physician, a first year resident from New Delhi, signed the certificate."

"It's never happened," she said defensively.

"But you wouldn't know if it had," Sam said, smiling and trying to be polite. "If I bring you Joe Blow and tell you it's Joe Schmo, how are you to know who the deceased is?" he said, smiling even more broadly. "Do you do any I.D. check on the deceased? What about fingerprints?"

"No. But I'll often ask for a picture so that we can match hair styles and facial expressions when we prepare the body."

"Sure, but all I have to do is give you a photo of Blow and tell you it's Schmo," he responded as if pleading for her acceptance.

"Well, I suppose anything is possible," she said, dismissing it with a "when pigs fly" attitude.

"Scenario number two," Sam said, pushing his luck. "Joe Schmo arrives here with a death certificate. I show up the next day with my pickup truck and tell you I'm Joe's next of kin and I want the body. How do you know I'm his next of kin?"

"You have to sign the release."

"No problem. I'll sign anything. I just want the body."

Niva tried to crack a smile of concession, but it appeared more like a nervous twitch.

"Scenario number three: I tell you to ship the body to Iowa for interment. How do you know that the person greeting the body at the train station or airport is who they say they are?"

"Look, Mr. Dawson," she said, her voice rising in pitch, "if bodies come up missing, which they don't, the authorities would be notified and criminal investigations would be launched."

"Only if they thought the body was missing. Are caskets sealed when they are shipped?"

"Of course, they're watertight."

"No. Are they sealed with a seal like the one that's on your electric meter to insure there has been no tampering?"

"Well, no," she admitted.

"So, the body could be removed either prior to shipment or upon receipt, prior to interment?"

"I suppose so," she said, her voice indicating that she was getting tired of the third-degree routine.

"One more," Sam said, standing as if to leave. "If a body is arriving at the airport this afternoon for burial at Wharton Gardens, who would you send to pick it up?"

"Since it will be interred at our own cemetery, we would send the sexton."

"Bingo," Sam proclaimed with a broad grin. But he could see by the confused look on Niva's face that he was now viewed as just another crazy from off the street. He thanked her profusely and retreated to the parking lot. He took a deep breath, staring across the road at the field of tombstones.

••••

The campus at the University of Colorado in Boulder was an exciting place in the fall. The freshness in the September air smelled of new beginnings, of hopes, and newfound independence. Sam felt out of place as he walked among the students who scurried between stone buildings. Each time he visited a college campus, the students appeared a little younger.

At the university bookstore Sam found a stack of freshly printed campus phone directories. Acting on a hunch, he looked up the name Tennyson in the blue pages, which listed faculty. There was only one listing: "Tennyson, Blair. Asst. Prof., E.P.O. Biology; C-204 Richardson Bldg." My lucky day, he thought.

After asking directions from a young man on Roller-blades, leading a dog with the classic red bandanna around its neck, Sam found the Richardson Building. The directory outside the administration office read: "Department of Environmental, Population, and Organismic Biology."

"Sounds dirty," he mumbled to himself as he mounted the stairs for the second floor.

The placard next to the door read: Dr. B. Tennyson, Genetics. She's a geneticist, he said to himself with a note of surprise. For some reason he had envisioned her as something else. What, he did not know, but something more feminine perhaps. When he thought of geneticists, he thought of Mendel, Watson, Crick, and the like. But he had only seen her briefly in the dark through sleep-filled eyes. How could he possibly form an opinion? If anything, he should have thought of her as an animal scientist, a beef cattle specialist, a range scientist, or something else associated with cattle.

Sam knocked but there was no answer. Her schedule was taped to the door, indicating class and office hours. Glancing at his watch and then back to the schedule, he determined she was halfway through a lecture in General Genetics in room C-101 of the same building.

The lecture hall was huge. Two sets of double doors leading into a terraced amphitheater with a capacity of at least 300 student desks, each filled by an undergraduate, their polished, young faces still attentive. The staggered rows of desks funneled downward to the small lecture floor. An oak podium stood off-center, surrounded by sliding whiteboards covered with rather elaborate drawings of the inheritance pattern of the X and Y chromosomes of the always useful fruit fly, *Drosophila melanogaster*. Colored chalk neatly displayed matrices of mono- and dihybrid cross ratios.

The acoustics of the room were surprisingly good. Professor Tennyson had stepped from behind the podium and walked to the center of the stage. "So, what generalizations can be drawn from the experimental findings of Mr. Mendel and his peas?" she asked in a voice that was as confident as it was clear. Raising her hand and enumerating the first point with a long slender finger she said, "One: In F1 only one of a pair of alternative characters that typify the different parental lines appears. Two:...," a second finger raised, "In F2 both of the alternatives that define the parental lines appear. And, three:...," she now appeared to be giving the Girl Scout pledge, "In F2 the character that appeared in F1, to the exclusion of its alternative, is found about three times as frequently as its alternative."

As with the first time he had seen her, Sam was captivated by her appearance. Not so much by what he could see, rather it was what he could not see that intrigued him. It was as though she purposefully disguised her beauty. Her straw-colored hair was pulled back into a loose French twist. She wore large, round, thin-rimmed glasses that accentuated her professorial look, the wise owl impression. A gray wool suit covered her slender frame. The long-sleeved jacket with wide lapels and thick shoulder pads was matronly at best, masculine at worst. A simple white blouse, open at the neck, exposed her slender, tanned throat. She wore no jewelry. Her skirt, a bit tighter than expected, hinted at a shapely figure.

It ended at her knees. Pale white nylons, more sheer than those of a nurse, disappeared into short but thick-heeled pumps that could have belonged to anyone's grandmother.

Looking at the clock high above the whiteboards, she said, "In our society, knowledge comes in fifty-minute blocks and your installment is up. See you on Friday. Don't forget your reading assignments," she yelled above the din of books slamming, papers shuffling, and desktops banging downward.

Suddenly Sam found himself in the traffic lane of a fast-moving highway of bodies. Students poured around him as though he were a construction pylon. He decided the best thing he could do would be to stand still and allow the writhing mass of noisy people to flow by him. Taller than most of them, he looked over their heads toward the podium. Blair Tennyson, surrounded by several students, looked past them and was staring directly at him. As suddenly as the chaos had begun, it ended as the last student filed past him. Sam had made his way to the lecture platform, and he now found himself alone in the giant room with the woman who had held him captive with a flashlight. She had her back to him as she erased the whiteboards. Stretching upward, her coat lifted above her narrow waist. The gray wool skirt was pulled taut across the same buttocks that Sam had watched depart into the darkness at the Cambridge cemetery. Meticulously placing the eraser in the tray, she hesitated before turning around, perhaps wishing to avoid the confrontation she knew was behind her.

"Doctor Tennyson," Sam said in a voice that was disappointingly weak.

"Mr. Dawson," she said with a pleasant smile and unwavering eye contact.

It was Sam's turn, but he said nothing. The silence became awkward. "You remember me!"

"How could I forget? I'm not often insulted in the middle of the night by a strange man wearing funny underwear."

Sam blushed involuntarily. He could feel the rush of warm blood to his ears that betrayed his confidence. "Insulted?" he said with disbelief, a tinge of anger in his voice. "If anyone should have been insulted it was me. Roused from peaceful slumber and accused of rustling by a pugnacious cowgirl is not my idea of western hospitality."

She continued to smile pleasantly, her eyes sparkling, unyielding. Again there was silence.

Sam was intrigued that this woman had once again pushed his hot button in less than ten seconds of conversation. "How did you know my name?" he said, trying to change the subject.

"The same way you knew mine. Good old Uncle Al."

"So you admit genetic relatedness to that old—" he caught himself still attempting to insult her. "I'm sorry. Perhaps we should start this conversation over again. Doctor Tennyson, it's great to see you again."

"Why?" she said flatly, her smile dissipating.

Now he was completely unarmed. Sam matched her unnerving stare, but could not think of a response. He was too captivated by her beauty. Her blonde hair had been pulled loosely, almost carelessly behind her, a casualness of spirit that intrigued him. He felt the urge to reach behind her and remove the bobby pins that restrained that spirit. Her large, wide-set blue eyes, soft and alluring, belied her verbal armor. Her mouth seemed a bit small for the wide-spaced eyes, yet the lips were well defined, full and almost pouty in their expression. But when she smiled, her entire body radiated a spunky enthusiasm. Her flawless skin contained more than a hint of honey-colored tan, suggesting her outdoor orientation. There was a small brown freckle off-center on the left side of her willowy neck. It reminded him of the lure of a predacious fish, an attractant that demanded to be kissed despite the threat of being enveloped and consumed by its owner.

"That's not a fair question," he said, finally. "Look, is there any chance that you and I can communicate civilly?"

Her smile returned slowly and with it, an inner warmth that was disarming. "Sure," she said, her eyes radiating a determined confidence.

"Could I buy you lunch?" Sam said nervously.

"Mr. Dawson, I'd love to, but—"

"Please call me Sam," he interrupted with a smile.

"Very well, Sam, I'm sorry but I've scheduled student appointments over the lunch hour and I have another class, a lab, to prepare for this afternoon."

"How about dinner?" he blurted out, suddenly feeling like a pimply-faced teenager asking for his first date.

"Was there something in particular that you wanted to discuss with me or is this purely a social request?" she said, sensing his desperation.

"Both," Sam said, unsure of how to answer the question.

"I see," she said, nodding her head and pursing her lips. "Mixing a little business with pleasure, or is it a little pleasure with business?"

This woman is tough, Sam thought. She's playing with me. But he had no choice other than to continue the game. "I'm a little unsure of what my motivation is," he said, looking down. "All I can tell you is that it is changing rapidly."

The perfect answer, he thought. Totally without a hint of what his intentions were.

"When?" she asked matter-of-factly.

"Tonight?"

"Can't."

"Tomorrow?"

"That will work," she said, nodding.

"Great," Sam smiled, a sense of relief washing over him. "I'll pick you up at seven."

"Fine."

"Not to hint at my motivation," Sam said slowly, "would it be all right if I called you Blair?"

"Doctor Blair," she said, smiling broadly.

"I can accept that compromise," he said, knowing that she was joking, but the hint of social dominance was apparent. "Great," he said after of moment of silence. "It's a date then, I mean it's an appointment," he corrected himself.

"See you tomorrow night," he sang out over his shoulder as he took the wide stairs two at a time.

"Sam," she called.

Stopping and turning, he said, "Yes?"

"Don't you want my address?"

Feeling as sheepish as he looked, Sam slowly returned to the podium where Blair scribbled her address onto a blank note card.

"A first order of business," she said, sarcastically emphasizing the word business, "is to get your client's address."

"Right," Sam said, trying not to show his embarrassment, whereupon he turned, tripped over the first step, and fell awkwardly to his hands and knees.

••••

Sam pounded the steering wheel and shook his head on the way home. He cursed and called himself names. Why was it that he felt compelled to embarrass himself whenever he was around Blair Tennyson? he wondered. In spite of his anger, by the time he reached the turnoff to Golden Gate Canyon, he noticed that the sky seemed a little more blue than usual, the fall colors a little brighter, and the afternoon clouds unusually white. "Easy, big fella," he said aloud. "You've been through this before. It's not that great," he cautioned himself.

Elle greeted him with the usual "I can't believe you're alive, I thought you were dead" routine. The answering machine greeted him with the familiar routine as well. Pat, threatening and mad as hell, demanded that he call him immediately. Beep. Marcie, in tears, called to notify him that her mother had been diagnosed with diverticulitis. Beep. What about senile dementia? he thought, smiling. Then Marcie again, this time angry that he had not called about Sidney.

The next message, however, got his attention. "Sam, this is Barb Sinclair. Sorry it has taken me so long to get back to you. Had to go to archives, but found some stuff you'll be interested in. It seems your boy Eris created quite a stir in the early twenties. He took a real media bath. He should have had you doing his press, not that you were that good, of course. Anyway, he was the local grand wizard, so to speak, of the eugenics movement. He got himself accused of baby killing at the asylum. I made copies. Give me a call. You owe me big-time, buster." Beep.

The next call was from Sidney. "Dad, homecoming is next week. I need a decision. Either I'm going or I'm running away, each of which requires a totally different wardrobe. I need to plan. Please call me." Beep.

The last call at first confused him and then caused him to freeze in terror. It started the same as it had before, dead air with a hint of static in the background. Then weakly: "Dad, homecoming is next week. I need a decision. Either I'm going or I'm running away, each of which requires a totally different wardrobe. I need to plan. Please call me." Beep. This was followed by a second louder beep. Someone standing where he was now had recorded Sidney's message, called Sam, and played back the recorded call to the same answering machine from which it had been taken.

CHAPTER EIGHT

*A MOTHER IS A MOTHER STILL
THE HOLIEST THING ALIVE
EPITAPH
—HAZEL J. CANFIELD*

MARCIE? PICK UP IF YOU'RE THERE." Sam waited. He looked at the clock; it was nearly 8:00 in the morning. He had waited to call, knowing Sidney would have already left for school. "Look, we need to talk." He hesitated, not wanting to say any more. He was not sure what he wanted to say, but he had an uneasy feeling that somehow Sidney was at risk. The phone message on his recorder had him spooked. The homecoming dance was the least of his concerns, but he realized that it was the most important issue in his daughter's life at the moment. Sidney had a habit of playing back phone messages before her mother had a chance to delete them. He decided not to tip his hand about the dance. Also, Marcie was an alarmist who tended to act like Chicken Little each time a cloud appeared. That was the last thing he needed, he thought. "Call me."

• • • •

"Good morning, Babs," Sam said cheerfully as he entered Barbara Sinclair's office.

"Spare me the pleasantries, Sam. The day is off to a miserable start. I've got a nine o'clock cabinet meeting and the governor's on the warpath this morning about funding for Youth Services."

Her office was similar to her appearance, disheveled but functional. Sam always thought she looked like somebody's mother or sister. She had gained at least twenty pounds since assuming her cabinet post. She wore too much makeup, especially rouge and lipstick, which gave her the appearance of being overheated. Thick glasses made her eyes look large and watery, on the verge of tears. She was his friend.

Sam had been impatient, barely able to sleep in anticipation of seeing what Barbara had discovered. The morsel of information provided by his dictionary had only whetted his appetite. The discovery that "eugenic" was from a Greek word meaning wellborn had caused the hair to rise on his arms. The dictionary's single sentence definition stated: "Eugenics, the science that deals with the improvement of races and breeds, especially the human race, through the control of hereditary factors."

"How is our fearless governor?" Sam beamed at her.

"You're disgusting! Speaking of disgusting, how's Marcie?"

Sam smiled. Barbara Sinclair, one of the strongest, most self-reliant women that Sam had ever known, disliked his ex-wife intensely. Marcie was weak and clinging, the very things that Barbara pretended not to be. "What have you got for me, Babs?"

"Mostly news clippings, and some correspondence and findings of a legislative committee that investigated the charges of official misconduct. There was never any court action that I could find, just allegations of misconduct."

"You mentioned baby killing in your phone message."

"Yeah, but it seems it was a bit inflated by the local press. He was accused of performing an abortion on a young inmate of the asylum. His claim was that she had miscarried. The entire thing would probably have been dismissed if he hadn't created such a ruckus a couple years earlier by pushing for the introduction of eugenics legislation."

"Legislation?"

Barbara handed him a manila file folder, and he thumbed through the photocopies as she talked. "Can you believe it? Right here in River City! There was a pretty sensational Supreme Court case in the late twenties in Virginia, *Buck vs. Bell*, if I remember correctly. We studied it in law school. That's the one where Oliver Wendell Holmes delivered his famous line, 'Three generations of imbeciles are enough,' in defense of Virginia's sterilization bill."

Sam stopped suddenly. The look of surprise on his face caught Barbara's attention.

"You've heard of the case?"

"Ah, no," he stammered weakly. "But I've heard that line by Holmes before." He could see the stained, white stubble on the old salamander's face and the icy blue light that shot from his eyes as he spat the vile statement at him in the wet Iowa cemetery. "Go on," he encouraged.

Barbara looked at her watch. "Well, I'll tell you what I remember, but it's not much. The movement for compulsory sterilization, I think, began during the 1890s. Early in the century some states passed laws that mandated eugenic sterilization of anyone in the state's care that was viewed as feeble-minded or a threat to society. By about 1930, two-thirds of the states had passed similar laws. Not only did they sterilize sex offenders and retarded people, they went after drug addicts, alcoholics, and people with convulsiveness and hereditary defects. It seems that Eris led the crusade here in Colorado for legislation. You'll find copies of letters to and from Harry Laughlin, superintendent of the Eugenics Record Office in Washington."

"You're kidding! There was a federal agency?"

"Yep, and Harry-baby used it as center stage for his crusade for eugenic sterilization. He proposed a model sterilization law in 1922. There's a copy of it in the file. Eris used it as his prototype when he championed the introduction of a bill in 1924."

"Did it go anywhere?"

"Yes, but not without a lot of tail twisting. It seems the president of the senate was an elder in some fundamental Christian group that, believe it or not, got their backs up about man doing God's work. Anyway, it made it out of committee, but almost died in a media-induced flame of oratory sensationalism on the senate floor. It became law on July 1, 1925."

"What about the abortion? Were there any sanctions against Eris?" Sam asked as if desperate for some resolution.

"Not that I could find. There was an endless parade of character witnesses who came forward in his defense. Appears the old boy was well liked and highly regarded. His retirement a few years later was probably coincidental rather than forced." She looked at her watch and, feigning impatience, said, "Look, buster, it's been great seeing you again, but I'm late for my meeting. Give me a call next time you want to use me for something. Christ, Dawson, you're the only person I know who takes the term public servant literally."

Sam smiled broadly. "Thanks, Babs. You're too good to me."

"Like I said, you owe me big-time, buster." She paused and turned toward the wall beside her desk. "You know, one of your black-and-whites would look great on that wall."

"You got it. Framed and matted. I'll let you go. Tell the gang hi for me. Ask the governor if he's seen the latest polls."

"What polls?"

"Got me, but I'm sure it will get his attention."

"Get," she said, pointing sternly toward the door.

"Thanks, pal. See ya."

••••

Sam spent most of the afternoon in the Denver Public Library studying the information Barbara Sinclair had given him and looking up articles on eugenics. The library had provided the *Reader's Digest* version that he needed. Many of the popular pieces were sponsored by conservative religious groups or antiabortion advocates. Most of them attacked social Darwinism, eugenics, and designer babies.

He found that many notable Americans had been active in the eugenics movement. Margaret Sanger, founder of Planned Parenthood, was a staunch advocate of eugenic sterilization and, along with Lothrop Stoddard, campaigned for passage of the Immigration Restriction Act of 1924. She had ties to Ernst Rudin, director of the leading German eugenics institute, who influenced the political views of Adolf Hitler regarding racial purity.

He found that everyone from Teddy Roosevelt to Winston Churchill to Henry Ford had been tied either justly or unjustly to the eugenics movement. But it was Francis Galton, born in 1822 and died in 1911, an Englishman, whose name was mentioned in every article. Galton, a cousin to Charles Darwin, was a credible scientist who had created the world's first weather maps, invented the questionnaire and word association test, developed the fingerprint classification system, and discovered the regression line, a useful analytical tool that plagued Sam in high school and college calculus. Galton believed that intelligence was hereditary and that society should encourage superior individuals to procreate while discouraging those with lesser mental abilities. He coined the term eugenics to denote the improvement of the human species through selective breeding. As far as Sam could tell, Galton was only interested in positive eugenics, the practice of encouraging the "best specimens" to breed.

Sam quickly discovered that the American approach, which Nazi Germany adopted nearly three decades later, was negative eugenics, where the "worst specimens" were prevented from breeding. Sam straightened in his chair when he read that Galton was the first investigator to study twins who had been separated from each other, pursuing the merits of the nature versus nurture controversy. Sir Francis Galton was knighted in 1909 for his lifetime achievements in science.

He found nothing on Eugene Eris. The name Eugene was from the Greek word meaning "wellborn." He doubted it was coincidence that "wellborn" appeared on Eris's tombstone. Eris was a goddess in Greek mythology, the one responsible for strife, discord, and war. She rejoiced in bloodshed. Eris appeared to be the model for the evil witch in the fairy tale "Sleeping Beauty." When she was not invited to the wedding of Peleus and Thetis, the eventual parents of Achilles, Eris showed up anyway. Denied entrance, she tossed a golden apple inscribed "To the Fairest One" amongst the goddesses in attendance. The three bridesmaids all laid claim to the title and a fight broke out, which resulted in the Trojan War.

Sam yawned, his eyes glassy from reading. He looked at his watch. "Crap," he said a little too loudly. A cowboy reading a newspaper looked at him over the top edge of the *Rocky Mountain News*, the headline declaring the latest Washington sex scandal.

•••••

If you don't like the weather, just wait a minute, Sam thought as he strained to make out the turnoff to his driveway. It was a familiar saying often repeated to nonnatives who were dumbfounded by how quickly the Colorado weather could change. It had been a beautiful fall day, sunny and crisp. Seemingly without warning the sky turned gray and the temperature dropped to freezing. First rain then freezing drizzle, followed by snow and wind as the sun disappeared behind the foothills.

He hurriedly changed clothes, fed Elle, and punched the ever-blinking red light on the answering machine. Marcie had returned his call. She was near tears, something about her mother's latest medical emergency. Call her.

It would have to wait, he decided. He would be late.

On the way out he noticed vehicle tracks in the fresh snow that showed someone had come most of the way down his driveway before turning around and heading back to the canyon road. Somebody's lost, Sam thought. "Tourists," he said, a term the locals used for anyone they didn't recognize, and he pulled onto the highway. He saw only one vehicle on his way back to Golden: a white pickup truck parked at one of the turnouts on the canyon road. It continued to snow.

CHAPTER NINE

OUR DARLING ONE HAS GONE BEFORE,
TO GREET US ON THE BLISSFUL SHORE.
EPITAPH
—MABEL KING

HIGHWAY 93 BETWEEN GOLDEN AND Boulder was bad when it was dry in broad daylight. In the dark during a snowstorm, it was a game of Russian roulette with three thousand pounds of glass and steel serving as the weapon. Sam was glad he had chosen to drive his pickup; the four-wheel drive gave him some comfort.

He was nervous about how, or if, he should present what he had found to Blair Tennyson. The two times in his life he had been around her, he had made a complete fool of himself. The thought of doing so again unnerved him. While the mystery of Eris intrigued him, Blair intrigued him more. He was not sure if it was her alone, or the fact that she could help him solve the bewildering puzzle that had taken over his life. Based on his behavior the day before, he guessed it was Blair alone, and that increased his anxiety about telling her about Eris. The man was the patriarch of Cambridge. If she was the grandniece of Alfred L., and the old salamander viewed Eris as the only father he ever knew, then Blair probably considered Eris her great-grandfather.

That, of course, meant that Alfred L. had another brother who would be Blair's grandfather. He took a deep breath in an attempt to quell his confusion.

By the time he reached Boulder, his neck was stiff and his fingers ached from the tension of driving in the worst fall blizzard he had seen in years. Street signs were almost impossible to read through the blinding snow. Traffic was nonexistent, a rare sight in Boulder on a Friday night. He made his way slowly, following the directions that Blair had given him. He had expected her to live up Four Mile Canyon or on Sugarloaf, trendy mountain subdivisions with small acreages. But this small-town-country-girl-turned-geneticist lived in old Boulder.

A warm, yellow glow through lace curtains shone from the windows of the tidy, brick Victorian home. Gingerbread trim above the front porch and along the roofline, a large bay window, and a turret protruding from the corner of the second floor all contributed to the warmth radiating from this safe haven in the snow. A shadow behind the curtained window passed quickly toward the door as he ascended the steps of the porch.

"You made it," she said, opening the door wide before he had a chance to ring the bell.

"Doctor Tennyson, I presume," he said, shaking the snow from his hair.

"Please come in. I tried to call you to tell you not to come in this, that we could reschedule. But you've got an unlisted number."

"After I get to know you better, I may give it to you," he grinned.

Blair took his coat and hung it on a mirrored hall tree just inside the door. Sam stole a quick look at her as he stamped the snow from his shoes. She still wore her hair pulled loosely into a French twist above her slender neck. A bulky, white, knit pull-over sweater and black slacks contrasted with the more businesslike attire he had observed in the classroom.

He could smell the distinct aroma of Italian food.

"When I didn't hear from you, I assumed you were on your way," she said. "I took the liberty of starting dinner, figuring it was too awful to go out. I hope you don't mind?"

"Not at all, but I hope you haven't gone to too much trouble." He had made reservations at the Hotel Boulderado, but decided to say nothing.

"Do you like Italian food?"

"Love it! What are we having?"

"One can of SpaghettiOs mixed with a can of ABC's & 123's," she said, trying to contain a smile.

"With or without meatballs?" he asked.

"With, of course," she said as if nothing else would do. "Make yourself comfortable," she motioned toward the living room, "while I check on dinner. May I get you anything, a drink?"

"No thanks. Go ahead, I'll be fine."

The entire house appeared to be furnished with antiques. Honey oak, mostly Victorian with gaudy lions' heads and feet, Thors with puffed blowing cheeks, and hideous gargoyles appeared to be the standard appointments. An open doorway off the living room captured his attention. It was Blair's study. Boldly, yet realizing the potential impropriety, he entered the room and turned on the lights. Hundreds of books lined the oak bookshelves. Oak wainscoting suggested that originally the house had been done in the more opulent manner of turn-of-the-century wealth. Beautifully refinished antique oak file cabinets, an ornate rolltop desk with snarling lions at each corner, and a huge library table cast an intimate, golden glow throughout the room.

All three of his books about Colorado were stacked neatly on an end table next to a morris chair, a baroque floor lamp looming above them. He noted all were first editions. Since his first book, *Historic Ranches of Colorado*, had sold out quickly, there was little chance she had purchased it since meeting him. That had to mean that she, at least, liked his work.

The books lining the shelves were mostly textbooks, genetics being the dominant theme. A section of literature hinted at her tastes in the arts. There were many female authors represented. Charlotte and Emily Bronte, Jane Austen, Willa Cather, Edna Ferber, and Edith Wharton provided much of the fiction, although Dickens, Hawthorne, and Thackeray were present as well. Her more modern tastes ran toward Anne Tyler and Larry McMurtry. Several books of English and American poetry were shelved together next to the fiction. *The Complete Poetical Works of James Whitcomb Riley*, in five volumes, caught his eye. The stub of a bookmark protruded from the center of the third volume. Pulling

the book from the shelf, he opened it to the marked page. The
poem was titled *Little Orphant Annie*. Sam began to read:

> *Little Orphant Annie's come to our*
> *house to stay,*
> *An' wash the cups an' saucers up, an'*
> *brush the crumbs away,*
> *An' shoo the chickens off the porch, an'*
> *dust the hearth, an' sweep,*
> *An' make the fire, an' bake the bread,*
> *an' earn her board-an'-keep.*

"It was my mother's favorite," Blair said from behind
him.

Startled at the sound of her voice, he nearly dropped the
book as he whirled around to face her. "I'm sorry, I didn't
mean to pry," he offered apologetically.

"Yes you did! But that's okay. Her name was Ann, and
everyone called her Annie. When she was sixteen my grandparents told her she had been adopted, thus, her affinity for
the poem."

"Is she still living?"

"No. She died quite suddenly from a stroke last March."

"I'm sorry."

"That's her with my grandparents when she graduated
from high school," she said, pointing toward a faded color
portrait in an ornate wood frame on the library table.

He walked to the table and, bending over the picture,
studied it carefully. The young woman standing behind her
seated parents bore a striking resemblance to her daughter.
Her blonde hair was swept upward in a gentle roll that en-

circled her head in the typical hairstyle of the late 1940s or early 1950s. Her features seemed more delicate than Blair's, but he reminded himself that the photo was taken when the woman was about eighteen years old. He guessed that Blair was in her early thirties. Her mother had the same flawless skin and perky look that seemed to radiate self-confidence. Her eyes sparkled with the determination and naïveté of a young person about to take on the world. He wanted to say something flattering, such as she's beautiful just like her daughter, but decided that was somewhat presumptuous this early in their relationship.

"I certainly see a strong resemblance between mother and daughter. She was a very pretty woman," he added casually, as if an afterthought.

He was about to turn away when he noticed the tiny mole on her neck. Attempting to avoid looking surprised, he bent lower to examine the photo. The small, dark speck lay just off-center on the left side of her neck. The photo was old but the mole was unmistakable. Most photographers of that period retouched their portraits and removed blemishes that they considered unsightly or less than flattering. But this tiny fleck on such a long and flawless neck only seemed to enhance her attractiveness, as with Blair. A true beauty mark, he thought.

"I lost my mom almost ten years ago," he said.

"That's a long time to be without a mother," Blair said.

"She was an orphan too. What are the odds?" he added rhetorically.

"Are you hungry?" Blair said.

"Ravenous."

"Great. Let's eat," she said, an uncertain smile passing over her lips.

She had not been joking about dinner. A steaming bowl of artificially orange SpaghettiOs and ABC's & 123's sat like a centerpiece on the claw-foot oak table in the dining room.

"Would you care for a glass of vin rosé? I have a whole gallon," she said, lighting a long, white candle on the table.

"What year?"

"Last week."

"You know, I think beer goes better with SpaghettiOs," he said, scrutinizing the main dish.

"With or without a glass?" she asked, smiling.

"Without, of course."

Sam was hungrier than he had realized, having skipped lunch to read the materials Barbara Sinclair had given him. He ate two large helpings of the orange gruel after offering a bottle-clinking toast to Gregor Mendel and his peas. After dinner he helped her with the dishes over minor protests from Blair that he was the guest and not required to assist.

The conversation had been light: life in Boulder, academia, government. He did not know how to broach the topic of Eris, or if he should. He watched her build a fire in the living room fireplace. The flickering, yellow glow provided a soft backlight that danced warmly through her golden hair. He was intensely attracted to her and was aware that it was more than a mere physical attraction. She was beautiful, intelligent, athletic looking, and all the other things that Marcie had not been. The last thing he wanted to do was to alienate her by asking about Eris. She would surely think his motivation for seeing her was only to gain additional information.

"So, how did you become interested in genetics?" he said, hating himself immediately for asking the question.

"I've often wondered that myself. It's hard to point to any single event that set me on a career path in the life sciences. I sometimes think that I was predestined to do what I do, but I'm not much of a believer in destiny. I do believe in genetic predisposition for certain traits, but career choice isn't one of them. Why did you become a photographer?"

"Because I was sick of being a propagandist," he said. "And," he paused, "I wanted to be creative. Like many people, I wanted to make a contribution."

Blair smiled and her eyes indicated that she understood. "You wanted to leave something for posterity, something to be remembered by."

"Exactly," he said, returning the smile. He looked down, "I guess it sounds a little selfish, doesn't it?"

"Not at all. Remember, I'm a geneticist, and that's one of the underlying principles of the science. Each of us strives, either consciously or unconsciously, to achieve partial immortality by contributing a part of ourselves to future generations." It was her turn to look down as if embarrassed. "Most organisms achieve this through sexual reproduction."

There was a long, slightly uncomfortable lull in the conversation. Sam turned toward the window when a sudden gust of wind pushed hard against the panes. "From a biological perspective," he said, "I've been there and done that. I was married for a while, but it failed on all fronts. With the exception that we produced a beautiful daughter, Sidney, fifteen going on twenty-five. What about you?" he said, trying to direct the conversation away from himself. "What's your contribution?"

"Biologically, it's one to nothing, your favor. Not that I haven't tried, understand. My last serious relationship burned itself out about a year ago. It seems that I'm a little too independent for most men, who want to protect me, to dominate me, to turn me into a wife."

Sam detected a sharp tone in her voice, the resentment of an equal having been treated unequally.

Detecting her own anger, she chuckled and smiled broadly. "No, my contributions have been through my work. I sometimes think my true passion is for research. Then I see the light go on in the eyes of my students and I realize the contribution I've made through teaching. Mine is science, yours is art and a daughter. We're both trying to establish a legacy."

The wind buffeted the house and the flames of the fire flickered wildly from a downdraft in the chimney. The atmosphere was so warm and comfortable that Sam felt like burrowing into it, pulling it over his head, and wallowing in his own contentment. He tried to suppress the thought of Eris and the drive home. He suddenly became aware that Blair was staring at him.

"A penny for your thoughts," she said.

His silence had been obvious. He smiled apologetically and repressed the urge to tell her his thoughts. Thoughts of how beautiful she was, of how he wanted to touch her face and stroke her hair; thoughts of his desire for her, for the taste of her lips upon his own, of holding her warm body next to his.

"Sorry. I was just thinking of Eugene Eris. What do you suppose his legacy was?" He cringed, the words barely out of his mouth, he regretted saying them. He waited in fear of her response, unable to meet her eyes.

"You are a strange one, aren't you? Whatever possessed you to think of him?"

"I don't know. When I get philosophical, I have visions of tombstones dancing before my eyes. One of the hazards of the trade, I guess."

"But why would you remember his?" she asked somewhat skeptically, her back straightening.

"We were discussing biological legacies and I remembered his epitaph: 'Wellborn Are My Children.' What do you think he meant by that? Did he have any children?"

"Uncle Al said that you were asking questions about Doctor Eris. What's your fascination with a man who has been dead since 1930?" her voice becoming defensive.

"The mere fact that you know the year he died I find fascinating."

"That cemetery is on our ranch," she said sharply. "I played there as a child. I remember lots of things about the people buried there."

"Then surely you remember that there were no boys buried there between 1905 and 1925." He disliked the way his last statement had rushed out, accusingly.

Blair stared at him, obviously insulted. "So, is this the business part or the pleasure part that motivated you to ask me out?"

He ignored the question. "Did you know that Eris lived and worked in Iowa during the same time he worked in Colorado?"

"Jesus, what's going on here?" her voice raised. "I wish you'd give me some warning when you're about to become a total ass. If you wanted to pump me for information, you could have sent me a questionnaire. If you wanted to pump me in any other fashion, you just lost all hope." She stood up suddenly, coffee cup in hand, a look of hurt rather than anger on her face. "It's late! I think you better go before the weather gets any worse."

He was a desperate man now as he watched her turn and walk toward the kitchen. Panic grabbed at his stomach. He had nothing to lose. "Did you know your Uncle Al has an identical twin in Iowa?"

Blair stopped and turned slowly toward him with a look of total disbelief. She said nothing.

I've got her attention, he thought to himself. Now give her the coup de grâce. "Did you know that Eris has a grave in a small cemetery in eastern Iowa with an identical headstone as the one in Cambridge, right down to the epitaph, but with a different date of death? If, in fact, it's Eris. Unless he had a twin, somebody else is buried in that grave," he added as the clincher.

"Why are you doing this?" she said with a mixture of skepticism and appeal for mercy. "What do you want?"

"Blair, I'm sorry," he said, coming to his feet. "My purpose wasn't to offend you." He paused, "I'm not sure what my purpose is. I needed to talk with someone about this. I had hoped you could help me by giving me logical answers to the questions that have been burning inside me since I discovered all this." He could feel his ears burning with emotion, fear that he had lost her.

She turned and met his desperate look.

"When I came to Boulder yesterday, it was business," he said. "But I swear to you that when I saw you, my questions became secondary. Do you think I would have driven through the snowstorm from hell just to get information? Blair, please don't be angry with me."

"Doctor Eris was not married. He had no children of his own," she said without expression.

"Of his own, what do you mean?"

"I mean figuratively. He was viewed by many as the town father. They were all his children." She stared at Sam without speaking. "Look, this man is still held in high esteem by the folks in Cambridge. I grew up believing in his benevolence as if he were some saint. People would thank him in their prayers and acknowledge him when they said grace. There are a lot of people who owe their lives to Doctor Eris and, in a way, I'm one of them."

"You?" he said, shaking his head. "I don't understand. He died in 1930. How could he have helped you?"

"Not me directly, but my mother owed her life to him. Do you want that glass of wine now?"

"Sure." He felt the fear he had experienced only moments earlier drain from him at the realization that she was willing to continue the conversation.

After returning with the wine and adding a log to the fire, Blair sat next to him on the couch. She sipped her wine and stared pensively at the fire before speaking. "When my mother discovered that she was adopted, she tried to research her ancestry. Who was she? Where had she come from? How had she ended up in Cambridge? Seeking one's biological heritage in those days was not viewed sympathetically and she quickly ran into a dead end. The only information she came up with was that Doctor Eris had obtained her shortly after birth and given her to my grandparents to raise. But it was more than a simple case of adoption. Years later Mom discovered that there had been a financial arrangement between Doctor Eris and her adoptive parents. Sort of like foster parents, they had been paid to care for her."

"Was all this legal? Are there records?"

"Yes and no. You have to remember that things were much less formal from a legal perspective in those days. But my mother was never able to find any records relating to who she was or where she had come from. What she did discover was that she was not alone."

"What do you mean?" This piqued his interest even more.

"There were others. Other children in Cambridge had been adopted over the years. Apparently secured and paid for by Doctor Eris."

Sam shook his head. "No questions asked? Here's a kid. Here's some money. Have a wonderful life."

"I can't answer that, but the people of Cambridge practically worshiped Doctor Eris. He was viewed as the most kind and gentle person to walk the earth, next to Jesus Christ. He apparently loved children and wanted them to grow up in a healthy environment. He had access to unwanted children through his position with the state. He was a physician and people trusted him. And there was probably a financial incentive for people to cooperate. The 1920s weren't that prosperous in rural areas."

"You mean it was a business venture," he laughed sarcastically. "Like a feedlot, he engaged an entire community in finishing out somebody else's kids."

"You're being much too cynical," she said, her voice tightening. "People then were more altruistic than they are now. It was a society where people cared about other people. There were no gangs, no drive-by shootings, and no carjackings. People helped each other. There was no welfare system, no Social Security, no Medicare or unemployment insurance. It was people helping people. They took care of their own and they took care of others too. No questions asked. It was expected. These people loved the children they raised and they thanked Doctor Eris every day of their lives for the opportunity."

The faraway gleam in her eyes told him that she was romanticizing a time and a place that represented, in her mind, Utopia. To shatter that vision was a dangerous proposition. He felt as if he were in a dark room groping for the light switch. He needed the light. He wanted to see. But he was fearful of tripping, of breaking something valuable. He had to be cautious. "Your Uncle Alfred was adopted, wasn't he?"

"Yes," she said meekly as if admitting a shameful family secret, "probably one of the first."

Reaching into the breast pocket of his corduroy sports coat, Sam pulled out the black-and-white photograph of the caretaker from Iowa. He handed it to Blair carefully. "I took this photo two weeks ago in eastern Iowa, a cemetery in a small town named Oxford. It's almost nine hundred miles from here."

She examined it carefully without speaking. Sam watched her eyes dart back and forth, up and down across the photo. She even turned it over as if the solution lay on the back. When she finally looked up at him, he could see her eyes were filled with tears, almost to the point of spilling over.

"I don't understand," her voice was weak as if pleading for the answer. "He's never been farther away from home than Denver in his life."

"I don't understand either. This damn thing has taken over my life. I can't work, I can't think of anything but this," he hesitated then added softly, "and you."

Wiping the corners of her eyes with her fingers, embarrassed by her emotion, she looked openly at her watch. "I need to think about this," she said as she rose from the couch. "There has to be a logical explanation." Her tone was now professional and businesslike. "In the meantime, we better figure out how to get you home." She walked across the living room and turned on the television. "Let's get a weather report first."

The ten o'clock news had just started. The anchorman for Channel 4 opened with the headline that a major fall

storm was sweeping across the Front Range of the Rock-
ies and that there were many road closures. For details they
switched to their meteorologist. Sam watched the weath-
erman's mouth move, his arms flailing about at the various
maps and radar images projected behind him, but he did
not hear him. His mind was racing through the events of the
evening. He thought of what he should have done or said
differently. He tried to outline his approach for continuing
his relationship with Blair.

"Highway 93 between Golden and Boulder has been
closed due to strong winds and drifting snow," the weather-
man said with a hint of melodrama. "The Denver-Boulder
Turnpike is reporting zero visibility, numerous accidents,
and abandoned vehicles. The state patrol is advising they are
turning back all but emergency vehicles."

Sam picked out all the usual warnings, "winter storm
alert, travel advisory, stockman's advisory." He suddenly
wished he had never mentioned Eris. It was a disaster inside
as well as outside, he thought.

"Well it looks like you're stuck here," she said, attempting a hesitant smile.

He did not know how to respond. He wanted to clap
his hands and shout that it was his lucky day, a fantasy come
true. Instead he took the martyr approach. "Oh, I couldn't
impose on you like that. I'll be fine! I've got four-wheel
drive."

"Don't give me the Joe Macho crap, Mr. Dawson," she said,
her smile becoming more assured. "You're staying here tonight
and that's an order. We're both adults, civilized people," she

added awkwardly in an attempt to warn him that he should not read into the situation anything that was not there.

Sam understood. "Are you sure?"

"Positive! I'll get some blankets and a pillow. You can sack out here on the couch next to the fire. There's a half bath down the hall past the kitchen. I'll even throw in a new toothbrush. What more could you want?"

He could think of several things, but decided not to press his luck. He let it pass as the rhetorical question that it was intended to be. "Thanks, Blair. Someday maybe I can return the favor."

"Perhaps," she said with a slight flair and then disappeared up the stairs.

Sleep came slowly, if at all. He was unsure. The gentle fire was soothing and tempered the competing images that flashed across his mind. Outside the storm raged. Inside the fire crackled and the mantle clock resonated its monotonous cadence.

It was difficult to sleep in a room filled with the material possessions of someone else's life. Objects seemed to radiate a karma of their own, especially antiques. Immobile, silent, and with cold objectivity they presided over a room, each with its own history and muted story.

The unfamiliar surroundings, the storm, the fire's flickering reflection from oaken gargoyles all combined to give him an uneasy feeling. He suddenly had the impression that he was not alone, that he was being watched. It was this feeling that caused him to open his eyes from what may have been sound sleep.

Blair stood next to the couch. The orange embers of the fire glowed behind her bare legs. She wore a short, flannel nightgown that appeared pink in the subdued light. Her golden hair spilled over her shoulders, much longer than he had envisioned. He was not startled. He did not speak.

The fire's embers reflected from the metal flashlight she held at her side. Dream-like, she bent over him and carefully pulled back the blanket. He winced at the explosion of light from the flashlight as she shone it squarely at his midsection, illuminating his white boxer shorts.

"Just checking," she said softly. "I couldn't sleep from curiosity."

Sam reached out and gently took hold of the hem of her nightgown. She stood motionless as he slowly, deliberately raised the gown above her thighs, exposing her satin white panties. He stared up at her and with a raspy nighttime voice said, "Curiosity killed the rabbit."

"Don't you mean cat?"

"No," he said, not taking his eyes from hers and releasing her nightgown.

She stared back then nodded with a smile. "Yes," she whispered, backing away from the couch. She turned and disappeared into the darkness.

CHAPTER TEN

O Brother, first to leave our band,
Life's song as yet unsung
While gray hairs gather on our brows
Thou are forever young.

EPITAPH
—ANDREW PEARSON

THE LANDSCAPE WAS UNIFORMLY covered with a heavy blanket of snow. The blemishes and ravages of time lay beneath its cleanliness. The world was silent. By midmorning there would be movement as the wet snow slid from the bowed branches of resistant trees and life emerged to assess its possibilities.

Highway 93 had been plowed and sanded before daybreak, Golden Gate Canyon sometime later. Sam had ample traction in four-wheel drive to negotiate the long, winding driveway to his house. Most of the snow would be melted by the end of the day.

Elle emerged from the dog door in the garage. Her thick, yellow tail waved rhythmically, which belied her stoic bloodhound face.

It felt good to be home. He needed time to think, to sort through the swirling mix of emotions he felt for Blair. He was more than attracted to her. When around her, he could not take his eyes off her. There was a possession over him that was frightening. The way she moved, the way she talked, the way she looked at him, and even the way she smelled, all made him feel as though his head were filled with cotton and his stomach with helium. It had been a very long time since he had experienced that type of infatuation. He supposed he had felt that way at one time regarding Marcie, but he could not envision it now.

The morning had been awkward. No one spoke of Uncle Alfred or Eris, nor had there been any reference to her nocturnal mission of curiosity. When he stood in the doorway, coat on, with a blank look on his face, she simply said that she needed some time. Time for thought, he was sure, but thoughts about what? Did she need time to think about him and their future relationship, or time to think about his discoveries concerning Eris? He said he understood, but now regretted lying. The ball was in Blair's court. She had asked for time. He would not pressure her.

••••

Marcie cried on the phone. Every frustration, no matter how insignificant, caused her to cry. She had been trained to cry by overly indulgent parents who raised her as though she were royalty. Tears had been rewarded.

"All right," Sam interrupted, "I agree. Sidney's too young to go to the homecoming dance. But what if we offered her the consolation of a chaperoned date where you or I drove them someplace—a movie, a burger, the mall, something less intimate than a dance? She's only a freshman, for crying out loud." Sam twirled the spiral phone cord around his finger.

Marcie explained that the boy who had asked her to the dance was a junior who had his own car and it was unlikely he would accept the consolation.

"Look, this isn't about him. I could care less about what he will accept. If he wants to date Sidney, these are our terms."

She continued to cry.

"What's going on, Marcie? Is there something more serious than teen dating going on here?"

Between sobs Sam was able to determine that the school counselor had called Marcie to alert her to the fact that Sidney's grades were slipping, that she seemed distracted and isolated. Two of her teachers had sent up red flags in response to her lack of attention in class and her often confusing answers to questions. The counselor wanted to know if there was something going on at home that might be facilitating Sidney's downward spiral. Sam wanted to blame it on Marcie's neurotic helicopter approach to child rearing, but decided against muddying the water.

"Sounds like typical adolescent behavior to me. She'll probably snap out it. Our intervening might make matters worse."

Marcie was not convinced and agreed with her mother that she should take Sidney to a doctor.

Sound advice coming from a hypochondriac, Sam believed, but he bit his tongue and agreed. "I promise to spend some quality time with her. Maybe she'll open up and tell me what's bugging her." He knew the promise was idle, in that a fifteen-year-old always had something to do other than hang out with a parent. Marcie continued to sob.

••••

Eris was running a close second behind Blair in terms of occupying his thoughts, but now Sidney had entered the equation and forced him to reevaluate his priorities. He took Elle on the long walk to the mailbox, hoping to clear his mind. The Colorado and Iowa death certificates for Eris had both arrived. Elle grew impatient and followed her nose into the timber as Sam scanned each document. The forms were different but the information they contained was nearly identical. Eris had been born on June 18, 1852, in London, England. Manner of death was listed as natural causes on both forms. The Iowa date of death was January 25, 1932, and Colorado's certificate showed August 4, 1930. Father's and mother's names were left blank. Each form listed an informant's name; both showed Alfred L. Tennyson. "What the hell is going on here?" he said, looking up but seeing nothing.

"Elle," he shouted in frustration. He waited, but she did not come. Sam followed her tracks from the driveway into the timber. Elle snuffled about frantically at the base of a huge ponderosa pine. Something shiny about five feet up on the trunk caught Sam's attention. It was a picture of him, cut crookedly from the dust jacket of his book on Colorado cemeteries, stapled to the tree. A bullet hole was centered between his eyes.

CHAPTER ELEVEN

NOT LOST BUT GONE BEFORE.
EPITAPH
—GRACE REID

THERE HAD BEEN A BRIEF MENTION OF Mount View in Eris's file from Barbara Sinclair. Sam recognized it as one of the state's institutional properties, the one for girls, located in Lakewood. It fell under the general and somewhat misleading heading of Youth Services in the institutional hierarchy. The services Mount View provided were locking up the state's female juvenile offenders. There was a rehabilitation and educational component to their detention. But mostly it was a wasteyard where the state dumped huge sums of money in an attempt to protect society from the infections of poverty, hate, and parental disinvestment. Sam knew what it was now, a repository for mostly minority gang members, child prostitutes, and truants. Too young for lockup at the state penitentiary, too violent and disruptive for public schools, they lingered in and out of this institutional purgatory. But what had it been in the 1920s and what was Eris's connection?

Barbara Sinclair had reluctantly returned his phone call. "Christ, Dawson, I've got real work to do! Do all you people in the private sector spend your time playing fantasy games?" she had asked somewhat angrily. The bullet hole in his picture was no fantasy. He was now convinced that someone had been sending him clear warnings to back off. The snake, strange phone messages, and threatening photo were somehow related. He was undeterred; if anything, he was even more committed to solving the puzzle. Sam knew Barbara's agitation was a front, and easily pulled from her the name and phone number of a contact person for Mount View.

●●●●

Norbert Crowell had been retired from Youth Services for nearly a year. Barbara had dubbed him the unofficial historian for the division. Crowell had received Sam's telephone call skeptically, waiting for the sales pitch. With some coaxing, he agreed to meet Sam for lunch. "You pick the day. I'm retired! I can go anytime," he boasted, proud of his retirement. Eagerly, Sam suggested they meet at a local diner on West Colfax.

Sam had told Norbert Crowell he would be wearing a leather jacket and baseball cap. Fortunately, at the diner, the construction crowd was into Carhartt, Dickies, and Levi's as the preferred outerwear. The man in the corner booth waved uncertainly at Sam.

Norbert Crowell was younger than Sam had envisioned him. He was a big man with dark hair, thin on top and graying at the temples. A dark complexion gave him the appearance of being suntanned. After the usual exchange of pleasantries and ordering the least greasy thing on the menu, a bowl of soup, Sam got down to business, asking the questions he had mentally rehearsed on his way to town.

"When was Mount View established?"

Crowell acted a little shocked that Sam had gotten to the point so quickly. Sam recognized his discomfort and decided he better let the man talk rather than interview him.

"The home itself has a long history," Crowell began slowly. He raised his eyes to stare at Sam through the top half of his glasses. The lenses were smoked a dark gray and surrounded by thick, black frames.

"I'm sure it does, but—"

"The property was originally homesteaded by the Hampton family in the early 1860s." Crowell was slow and deliberate in his delivery. "Through a succession of land acquisitions, John Hampton, the family patriarch, acquired much of the Bear Creek Valley, from Morrison to the town of Sheridan. The Victorian home that still serves as the central administration building was constructed in 1876, the year Colorado was granted statehood."

"What about the—"

"Mr. Hampton's first wife died shortly after moving here from Pennsylvania with their four daughters. He remarried a short time later to a widowed woman from Denver, who herself had three daughters."

"When did—"

"As one of the more prosperous cattlemen of the day, Mr. Hampton was determined to build a home where each child could have their own room. With servants' quarters, library, parlor, and all the other amenities of the day, the home was considered a mansion by its overwhelming size. With seven daughters the locals began referring to the house as Hampton's Home for Girls."

"Is everything all right here?" said the waitress in a dirty pink uniform, her cigarettes clearly visible through the breast pocket.

Crowell seemed to assign the same weight to the question as if asked his views on capital punishment. Before he could answer, Sam said, "Everything is fine, thank you."

The waitress stared at him blankly. "If you want pie, we've got apple, cherry, banana, coconut cream, and pecan," she said flatly without smiling.

"Nothing just yet," Sam smiled. He looked at his untouched bowl of soup, the grease congealing on the surface.

The waitress rolled her eyes and muttered something about him being a big spender as she walked away.

"Let's see, where were we?" Sam said. "I think you were at the point when Mount View became a state institution?"

Clearing his throat, Crowell began his dissertation again. "Mr. Hampton died in January, no, excuse me, it was February of 1892. By then, of course, the children were all grown and moved away. He and his wife had taken a smaller residence in a fashionable neighborhood in downtown Denver. He bequeathed the original home to the state with the express purpose that it be used to help young girls."

Sam was voluntarily giving himself leg cramps in order to stifle a monstrous yawn that was forming deep within him. He watched Crowell's lips move, thinking of how a cobra watches a charmer's flute. He picked out the salient points and let the rest slide by. Crowell continued in a slow monotone.

The lunch crowd had disappeared and the waitress had stopped offering coffee. Crowell was at 1912 when Sam interrupted. "Why were girls institutionalized at Mount View?"

Crowell pondered the question. "For any number of reasons," he said deliberately. "But mostly for being incorrigible. They were runaways and truants for the most part. Sometimes parents would drop them off claiming that they were unmanageable, often evidenced by the fact that they were pregnant."

"You mean that unmarried girls were institutionalized, locked up because they were pregnant?"

"It was a noncriminal offense, of course. They were considered status offenders. Pregnancy was considered an indicator of more serious antisocial behaviors. But in most cases judges removed the girls from society as a charitable act, sparing them the embarrassment and ridicule of their peers."

"What happened to the babies?"

"Adoption, but mostly they were placed in orphanages. And the cycle repeated itself."

Sam stared at him for a moment. "Repeated itself? I don't follow you."

"Many of the girls at Mount View were orphans themselves, the results of teenage pregnancies."

"It's hard to believe that a town the size of Denver at that time could have had an orphan problem, or that many runaways," Sam said.

"The residents of Mount View came from all over the state and the country. Often more than 250 girls at a time were housed there." Crowell droned without inflection. "Many even came from the larger East Coast cities. Have you ever heard of orphan trains?"

"Orphan trains?" Sam asked, finally taking interest.

"Yes, the large East Coast orphanages were periodically purged of those inmates old enough to work, sending them west. Entire trains of orphans! They would stop at every farming community in the Midwest and West and herd the children onto the loading docks where local farmers bid on them like slaves at auction."

"What?" Sam said with disbelief. "You mean they became indentured servants?"

"Yes, I suppose that is one way to look at it," his eyes never changing expression. "For many of these children, though, it was their first and only opportunity to become part of a family. The farmers sometimes legally adopted the children and they were integrated into the family and community. In some cases, the children were overworked or abused and they simply ran away, usually running toward the biggest city around so they could meld into the transient community of the streets."

"How long were the girls locked up at Mount View?"

"Locked up," Crowell said slowly, "is perhaps too harsh of a term. The girls were detained at Mount View usually until they were eighteen."

"How young could they have been?"

"In the early days they were ten, now twelve."

"What happened when they reached eighteen?"

"They were released."

"Even for serious crimes, felonies, murder?"

"Until relatively recently, children and teenagers were adjudicated as juvenile delinquents, regardless of the crime. They could not be tried as adults no matter what the offense. At eighteen they were released. Of course those laws have now changed to allow for a court to decide whether a juvenile will be tried as an adult or not."

"And, what if an inmate was insane?"

"Of course, the mentally infirm were often transferred to the state asylum in Pueblo, in later years to the State Home and Training Academy in Wheat Ridge."

Pueblo got Sam's attention. "Ever hear of a guy named Eris?"

"Eris?" Crowell pondered again. "Eris," he said, only his mouth moving and nothing else. "No. That name is unfamiliar to me."

"Who would have provided medical care for the inmates at Mount View?"

"When?"

"Say in the late teens and twenties."

"They had a resident nurse. For more serious medical needs they relied on the staff physicians from other institutions."

"Who made the decision to send girls to Pueblo?"

"In those days, it was probably the director of medicine at the state asylum."

"Would there be records for these girls?" Sam asked with some excitement. "Records of admission, medical records, transfer documents, anything?"

"Certainly there were records, but how far back they go, I can't be sure. All records, boxes and boxes of them, were stacked in the basement of the central administration building at Mount View when I retired a year ago."

Sam looked at his watch in an exaggerated fashion. "Oh boy, I'm late for another appointment. I'm afraid I have to run."

With no change of expression, Crowell, who remembered precisely where he was when Sam had interrupted with his questions, said, "Do you care to hear about 1913 and beyond? You know the girls were quite industrious, raising their own food and making their own clothes."

"You know, I'd love to hear more, but I'm truly late for another appointment."

Even after Sam had paid the bill and left the diner, he could see Norbert Crowell still sitting in the corner booth. He undoubtedly was pondering what to do next. Sam waved awkwardly to him from the parking lot.

••••

His other appointment was Pat Bateson. He had promised Pat on the phone that he would stop by his office in the afternoon to give him a progress report on the Iowa project. He resented having to report to anyone, but was sympathetic to the fact that Pat had a substantial investment at risk. As successful as he was, Sam still depended on the advances from Silvercliffe Publishing to get him through a project.

Pat Bateson had seen through Sam's unimpressive attempt to cover up the fact that he had done little on the

Iowa project. Sam had received one of those father-and-son talks that left him with mixed feelings of depression and triumphant determination. Depressed because he had let Pat down, determined because he possessed the talent to get the job done.

Pat was the first to discover Sam's talent as a photographer. Taking pictures had always been Sam's hobby and when he decided to combine it with his true passion, writing, he knew he had finally found himself. His first work, titled *Historic Ranches of Colorado*, had sold out in six months. The second printing had done well but tapered off sharply at the end of the first year. His second book, *Colorado Dawn*, pulled him from debt and made it possible for him to relax for the first time in years. So successful was this pictorial essay of alpine imagery, that he had earned more than his previous year's salary from the sale of calendar rights alone.

Pat had slowly convinced him that his strengths were in photography and that the public, who possessed a ninth-grade intellect, wanted pictures, not prose. Sam accepted this reluctantly, but only temporarily. To him the measure of true success was the ability to indulge in frivolous pursuits. If nobody wanted to read what he wrote, that was fine with him. He was going to write it anyway.

It had been his third book that set him and his publisher on their present course. For Sam it was an experiment in the medium to which he was most partial, black-and-white still photography. He had taken the concept into the field, to the one place where things did not move—a cemetery. He found the big city cemeteries too clean, too uniform.

They reminded him of national burial grounds with their row upon row of uniform white crosses. His boredom led to *Colorado Graveyards: A Pictorial Essay of Forgotten Cemeteries*. He had received a surprisingly good review in the *Denver Post*. There were book signings at the historical society and the Tattered Cover, and radio talk show interviews along the Front Range and in Grand Junction on the western slope. Pat had read the market well. They were currently holding off on a second printing in order to better assess the demand. Out-of-state sales were almost nonexistent, thus the attempt to mine another state. Inspired by his mother's stories of Iowa, he had convinced Pat that its rural cemeteries were fertile ground for repeating his Colorado successes.

He had wanted to tell Pat of his amazing discoveries, but decided it was too bizarre for a logical thinker like Pat. It would sound like a weak excuse. After all, what did he have to show for the time he had spent thus far: a mysterious, yet kindly old doctor who paid people to raise babies, some of whom must have been twins? The twins argument would explain the salamander brothers, one of whom knew Sam's mother. Eris's duplicate graves, however, were more than a little strange. And where did Eris get the babies? he asked himself. There had to be a connection with Mount View.

Less than twenty minutes had passed since Sam had received Pat's lecture about focusing his attention on finishing the Iowa job. Yet he found himself parked outside the administration building at Mount View. He had convinced himself that all he wanted to do was see the place, to experience for a moment what thousands of young girls had experienced as they arrived through the front gates on the way to their imprisonment.

It was a sprawling campus with a disrespectful mixture of old and new architecture. The original Hampton home was a stately Victorian structure that seemed to preside over the other buildings. Its red bricks had faded to pinkish-orange during the last century, but its angles were as sharp and ominous as the day it was built. He was nervous as he climbed the steps and opened the white wooden door labeled "Director's Office" at the rear of the building.

Inside were narrow hallways, high ceilings, and numerous tiny rooms that had been converted to offices. The wooden floor creaked loudly as Sam made his way down the hallway looking for life. A portly, middle-aged woman was as surprised to see him as he was her when she popped from a doorway in front of him.

"May I help you?"

"Hi, I'm Mark Ambrose," he lied with impressive confidence. "I'm with the Department of Administration, Division of Archives. You should have received a letter from Barbara Sinclair some time back. I'm here to inventory Mount View's historical records."

Her eyes narrowed and she cocked her head as if trying to hear the nonexistent letter. She studied him for a moment and then without question led him down narrow, wooden stairs to the basement.

"You know the reason these records are here and not down at Archives," she admonished, "is because they are not public documents. You can look and inventory all you want, but you'll need a court order to take anything out of here."

"Right, I understand," he said, sidestepping a broken chair amid the clutter. He watched her ascend the stairs and heard the door close behind her. His heart pounded and there was lightness in his chest.

Cardboard file boxes were stacked haphazardly upon one another along one wall of the basement. The lids of some were crushed downward from the weight of others piled on top. A gray blanket of dust and cobwebs covered every surface. Two boxes marked "Annual Reports" caught his attention. Here he found flowery testaments of the social good that had been accomplished, complete with black-and-white photos depicting college-like life. Obviously staged, the girls wore white dresses and happily posed in front of buildings as if sending snapshots from summer camp. The reports from the turn of the century, teens, and twenties, although incomplete, bragged mostly of agricultural production and accomplishments in various domestic skills, such as sewing and quilting. Submitted to the legislature and governor, they were signed in the flowing script of the day by long-dead directors and head mistresses.

The other boxes were labeled "Personal Records" and were stored alphabetically in five-year increments. The 1930s far and away outnumbered the other years, probably depicting the effects of the Depression, he reasoned. Sweeping the sticky cobwebs from the box labeled "A–H 1920–1925," he opened it with a sense of reverence. Brown folders were neatly arranged in alphabetical order starting with Adams and ending with Huffnagle.

Sarah Veronica Adams was admitted on April 23, 1921. Her date of birth was January 7, 1905. Her mother was named Mary with deceased written in parentheses after it, and the blank for her father listed "Unknown" in cold cursive. Next of kin was left blank. Her home address was "605 Grove St., Denver, Colo." There was a confusing one-page court order dated April 20, 1921, the bottom line stating, "Therefore, it appearing that all proper parties have been duly served with proper notice of these proceedings, and have been heard or given opportunity to be heard, it is ordered that Sarah Veronica Adams be committed to Mount View Home for Girls until the day of her eighteenth birthday or until this order is challenged by a responsible party who can demonstrate the ability to provide her with proper care." District Court Judge Clifton A. Harper commanded her to Mount View for the heinous crime of having a dead mother coupled with being indigent. Sarah Adams had been orphaned.

The admittance form contained the usual descriptive information of height, weight, hair and eye color, and health assessment. Curiously, the form contained a column of potential checks under the heading of "Race": "Negro, White, Mulatto, Indian, Mexican, Italian, German, Irish, Jewish, Other." Sarah was categorized as "White." Sam wondered what special treatment she would have received had she been "Irish."

There was a report card with no indication of grade level, but listing the month and year the grades were recorded. In June of 1921 she had received A grades in reading, spelling, and writing, and a B in mathematics and English. An A in deportment indicated that she was a good kid.

Sam was about to pick another file randomly from the box when the name Eris jumped out at him from Sarah Adams's folder. It was a simple form; Hospital Form No. 107 was printed in tiny letters in the upper left corner. In bold typeface across the top it read, "Before the State Insane Asylum Board." A blank space with "(Institution)" written under it was filled in with the blossomy script of someone writing "Mount View." The same pen strokes recorded "Sarah Veronica Adams" in the line reserved for "Inmate." "Upon the petition of...," then the signature of "Eugene Eris, Director of Medicine for the State Insane Asylum Board." White space then: "Upon consideration of the evidence introduced at the hearing of this matter, the Board finds that said inmate is," then a blunt list of conditions to check: "insane, idiotic imbecile, feeble-minded, epileptic, other"; a small inky check mark next to feeble-minded had sealed Sarah's fate. The same girl who had received As and Bs on her report card..."and by the laws of the State of Colorado established to protect the health, safety, and welfare of both society and the inmate and that such welfare will be promoted by the institutionalization of said inmate, it is hereby ordered said inmate shall be transferred to the State Insane Asylum at Pueblo, Colorado for detention and/or treatment." More white space then a signature line with Eris's inscription again and dated July 15, 1921. Another signature line with "(released by)" typed under it was signed "Darryl G. Moody, Director of Mount View."

Laying Sarah's file aside, he quickly scanned the next folder for a similar transfer form. By the time he reached Marianne Hufftnagle, his hands were shaking, his lips were moving, and he heard himself talking aloud. "Christ Almighty," he said as he glanced at the stack of purged file folders on the floor, each containing a transfer form signed by Eris. He looked at his watch—it was almost 3:05 p.m.— and he stared at the mountain of boxes in front of him. The woman upstairs would shut him down promptly at either 4:30 or 5:00. He had to hurry.

He scanned the remaining folders like a machine. He had formed a searching image for the transfer form and mechanically picked his way through each box from beginning to end. The form changed over the years as did the director of Mount View. But the name Eugene Eris remained the same. He remembered Eris had retired in 1926 and that his obit had stated he worked at the state asylum for more than two decades. He went back as far as 1905, finding nothing earlier than 1907. The number of transfers tapered off sharply after 1925 with none occurring after 1926.

The door above the stairway opened suddenly causing Sam to jump. "You'll have to finish up down there," the woman yelled down the stairs.

He looked down at the stack of file folders he had purged from the boxes. They would fill a box themselves, and he had not had time to study them. His mind raced.

"Do you hear me?" she shouted again, her voice impatient.

Sam grabbed a file box and emptied its contents on the floor. Hurriedly, he stuffed the segregated files into the box while looking around him. The stone-lined basement was windowless. Even the coal chute had been bricked in. The only way those files were leaving Mount View was up the stairs and out the back door, he determined.

"Are you down there?" she questioned, uncertainty in her voice as she descended to the first step.

"Whoa!" Sam yelled with mock astonishment.

"Excuse me?"

"Did you see it?

"See what?" she said from the top step.

"The rat! Big as a wiener dog. They're all over down here. Whoa! He's headed up the stairs."

The top step groaned as the woman, without so much as a shriek, mounted her escape. Sam listened to the heavy footfalls down the hall. He wasted no time in ascending the stairs. Poking his head into the hallway, he saw the back door swinging listlessly in the late afternoon breeze. "Yes!" he said to himself as he scurried, rat-like, down the hall, the file box tucked securely under his arm. As he approached the door, he could see her pounding the pavement headed toward the next building labeled "Maintenance," her stumpy high heels clacking on the asphalt.

He never stopped looking in his rearview mirror until he turned off Crawford Gulch onto his own property.

"I can't believe I did that," he repeated to himself over and over, glancing at the box on the seat next to him.

He overfed Elle, who acted starved. Grabbing a beer from the refrigerator, he sat on the couch and opened the box.

He had not noticed the darkness that had enveloped the world around him. Nor had he noticed that another day had begun at the stroke of midnight. Only the empty beer bottles and Pepsi cans marked the passage of time.

Sam loved a good book. He especially liked the way he always felt when he finished reading the last page. Regardless of the ending, happy or sad, he would feel as if he had just said goodbye to his best friend for the last time. But most of all, it was the sense of accomplishment, of knowing and understanding something new that perhaps no one else had seen in the story, that made him feel enlightened. Enlightened, awed, and depressed were the same emotions that he felt as he closed the last file folder. He placed his hands over his eyes and rubbed his forehead then massaged his scalp, leaving his hair standing comically on end. Fatigue was tightening its grip.

A third of the way through the folders, he had started over. This time, with shaking hands, filling in a crude table he had drawn on a yellow legal pad. The headings were basic: date, age, various physical characteristics, ancestry, kin, medical condition all on one axis, the girls' names on the other. Massaging his temples, he whispered, "What the hell was going on there?" He knew that a statistical analysis was not necessary to show the positive correlations that leaped from the pages of the taped-together tablet paper. He had noted the associations from the beginning, but to see them charted before him with such graphic conclusions was unsettling. Eris had selected these girls, pure and simple. There was no randomness. A large population to draw from over a twenty-two-year period should have yielded diverse characteristics. Sam stared at the data showing just the opposite. The girls were so similar that the hair on his arms stood up and a cold shiver raced down his spine. He inhaled slowly and exhaled noisily. "What the hell was going on there?" he said again, this time much louder.

Eris had transferred 120 girls to the state asylum between 1907 and 1926. The only things they should have had in common were their sex and some form of diagnosed mental illness. Instead, Sam found they all fell between sixteen and eighteen years of age. Nearly all of them were seventeen when Eris transferred them. A few were sixteen but within a few months of seventeen. None were eighteen since that was the age of mandatory release from Mount View, but there had been many within weeks of being set free. Without exception they were orphans with no next of kin listed. They were all white, blonde, blue-eyed, of medium build, between 5 feet 4 inches and 5 feet 9 inches, tall for the day. There were no names that ended with "o" or "ski." Names such as Johnson, Peterson, and Wilson seemed to be the rule. If report cards were contained in the file, they all showed good marks. The Mount View intake forms indicated that all of them were in excellent health upon arrival. Eris's transfer forms, however, depicted each as being epileptic, syphilitic, schizophrenic, or having "unspecified" mental illness. Most had been at Mount View for less than a year before being transferred.

Beyond the limited illumination of the floor lamp next to the couch, the house had grown dark. Only Elle's deep, rhythmic breathing from her dormant body at his feet and the faint ticking of the schoolhouse clock interrupted the stillness of the night. He stared at the mound of file folders on the coffee table. Tattered and brown with age, they were all that remained of the young lives stolen so many years earlier.

One hundred twenty young women, a lifetime ago, had their lives changed because they looked like each other and had similar backgrounds. "Why?" he said aloud, startling Elle. "It's okay, girl." But it's not okay, he thought. There was something terribly wrong here. Something dormant that was now awakened.

Outside a sudden breeze swept through the aspen. Their dead leaves rained against the windowpanes in noisy protest of their final journey toward the dark earth below. Each looking like the other, each from similar spore as they helplessly descended toward their unrevealed providence.

He stared out the living room window into the night sky with full moon and clouds. The sky appeared smoky, a huge circle of illuminated white haze on the western horizon. Sam watched as the moon inched its way behind a large ponderosa pine. The needle clusters were black along graceful limbs, nature's shadow box. Fear spread across his shoulders and down his arms as he suddenly realized why he could not turn away from these young women.

He ran his fingers through his hair and shook his head. He remembered. He never talked about her, not even to his mother. No one knew of her, not even Marcie. Not even Elle, and he told her everything. She was his secret and he did not know why. The moon, lower, appeared on the other side of the tree, a celestial game of peekaboo. The sun would rise soon and force the moon even lower. He recalled her voice, wise beyond her years. When he closed his eyes he caught faint wafts of her fragrance, a mixture of soap, skin, and hair. Twenty-five years, where had they gone? Twenty-five years and she had not changed. She was as he remembered. Sam was twelve years old when his sister, Julie, was kidnapped, raped, and murdered.

CHAPTER TWELVE

HER FEARLESS BUOYANT YOUTH
WILL ALWAYS LIVE,
REVEALING LOVE AND TRUTH
AND RADIANT JOY.
SHE IS ASLEEP, NOT DEAD.
EPITAPH
—PAMELA ROSE WHALEN

W HEN SHE SPOKE, THE DARKNESS of her mouth appeared from between thin lips, the antithesis of a blinking light.

"I am sorry, sir. Without a court order, I cannot give you that information," she said precisely.

Sam always became suspicious of someone who refused to use a contraction when speaking. "Can't you at least tell me if you have records for them?" he said, almost pleading.

"The mere identification of an individual who resides here or once resided here casts certain aspersions upon their character," the records clerk offered with a note of apology.

"They're probably all dead," he said.

"They have families that could be embarrassed by such disclosure."

"They were all orphans! They didn't have any families."

"I have no way of knowing that," she smiled apologetically.

"What am I going to tell my boss? She sent me all the way to Pueblo to get this information and you won't give it to me."

"Who is your boss?" the dark hole flashed amid the whiteness.

"Barbara Sinclair. I'm her executive assistant."

"Barbara Sinclair, director of Institutions?" she said, the black hole remained open this time.

"Yeah, didn't I mention that earlier?"

"No. You should have said so. I am very sorry. We get requests for patient information all the time and we have to take a pretty hard stand. Ms. Sinclair, of course, has access to anything she wants at the state hospital."

"Sorry if I didn't make myself clear. I guess I assumed you knew who I was. I'm used to working with her division heads who all know me." Sam looked at his watch, but he did not notice the time. Forced into another lie, he was anxious to search the files and leave. "Barbara is expecting me to call my findings in before noon."

"It's the first door on your left. When you hear the buzzer, open it and come in," she said, stepping back from the glassed-in counter labeled "Records Clerk" in neat blue-and-white letters.

An entire wall moved up and down, rotating trays of color-coded files in an enlarged version of a dime-store jewelry case. "Could I see your list?" she asked, peering upward at Sam.

"Sure," he said, handing her a handwritten, alphabetized list of the 120 names. He had a feeling that what he really needed was archives.

"Adams, Sarah V.," she said slowly as she typed the name on a computer keyboard beside the moving wall. Almost as quickly as she entered the request the monitor flashed in all-caps: "NO RECORD FOUND." "No Sarah V. Adams here," she smiled. "When was she a patient?"

"All of them were between 1907 and 1926."

"That explains it. What you need is archives. This system only goes back to 1945."

Sam looked nervously at his watch again. "Where would that be?" he asked, remembering the half hour of wandering it took to find the records office.

"Oh, it's right here, just a different program." Her fingers tapped across the keyboard, pausing occasionally to make menu selections. "We got a big fat grant in the late seventies to put all our archives on microfiche. Two years ago we got another grant to put the microfiche on a CD-ROM. I worked on that one. Believe me, if they were a patient here, everything in their file will show up on the ROM."

"That's impressive," he said, but he was thinking of the mashed file boxes piled in the basement of Mount View.

"Adams, Sarah V.," she half-whispered as her fingers typed. "NO RECORD FOUND" flashed boldly on the screen. "That certainly is strange. Are you sure she was a patient here?"

"Yes. Try another one."

She scanned the list and typed in Katherine E. Douglas. Again, "NO RECORD FOUND." Rebecca Sharp, Allison Farnsworth, Eleanor Drummond, and Rosemary Talbot all yielded the same white letters against the blue screen: "NO RECORD FOUND." "Could these people be listed under different names?"

"I don't think so," Sam heard himself say, his voice sounding distant. His mind raced. "Please keep trying," he said.

The dark eyes set deeply within the creamy white face looked nervous, almost frightened, as she turned to him twenty minutes later. "I'm sorry sir, but none of these people were patients here. Are you sure they—"

"Yes," he said, cutting her off. He turned away, inhaled deeply, and told himself to remain calm. "Is it possible that the records were lost in a fire or maybe archived in Denver or something?"

"No, sir. All the records for that time period are on this CD. They go clear back to the eighteen hundreds."

"Look, I'm sorry I put you to all this work. I really appreciate your help."

"No problem," her eyes appeared frightened. "Tell Ms. Sinclair that if records for these people existed, they would show up on the system. I am very confident of that," she said, pride displacing the fear.

••••

Sam remembered little of the drive between Pueblo and Denver. Just before Colorado Springs, he pounded the steering wheel in frustration. Embarrassed, he looked into the side mirror to see if anyone had seen his display of anger. A white pickup truck followed in the lane behind him, too far back to see Sam's minor tantrum. He had asked himself the same questions repeatedly, but he had no answers. Eris had taken 120 young women to the state asylum where they had disappeared. They were celestial matter sucked into a giant black hole; nothing remained. As hard as he tried to resist it, a kinship was developing, not unlike that of his sister, Julie. It was an obsession with discovering their fate, with acknowledging their existence. They had become his mental poltergeists, restless souls wandering aimlessly through his mind in search of resolution, of recognition and remembrance.

Why am I assuming they are dead he thought to himself suddenly. What if some of them are still alive? "Excuse me," he said aloud in response to his silent question. Sure, a teenage girl in 1925 could easily be living today. She would be in her nineties, but alive. "Yes," he proclaimed with resolve. But how do I find someone who has had over three-quarters of a century to disappear? he asked himself. The odds of their staying in Colorado for that long were surely low. Women get married and change their names. These girls were orphans with no family to help him track them down.

At Colorado Boulevard he pulled off and headed for the department of health. A place to begin was at the end, he reasoned. Perhaps he could narrow the field by determining who was dead. Remembering the difficulty he had encountered at the Vital Records Section concerning direct and tangible interest in dead people, not to mention the twelve bucks per name it would cost just to search the files, he headed straight to the director's office.

Dr. Nolan Patrick had come to the post of director of the Colorado Department of Health under a cloud of controversy. A coalition of environmental groups asserted that he had been too soft on water quality issues in his previous capacity as county health director in an industrialized area outside of Seattle. His specialty was environmental and occupational medicine, but public health and epidemiology were his passions. When things got rough and it appeared that he might lose his bid for senate confirmation, the governor, trying to save political face, directed Sam to put the appropriate spin on some press releases and get support for Patrick. With the journalistic flare and ethical standards established by Joseph Goebbels, Sam was able to develop enough public support to get him through the senate and into the highest-paying cabinet post of the administration.

Dr. Nolan Patrick owed Sam and he knew it. He left a meeting to see him, had his secretary photocopy the list of names, agreed to search the death records as soon as possible, and never asked Sam what it was for. Sam did not offer an explanation, figuring the whole thing was too weird for a logical person like Patrick.

His next stop was the Department of Revenue on Capitol Hill. As its name implied, the department was responsible for everything that earned a penny for the state. Sam was specifically interested in driver's licenses and income taxes. Unlike Barbara Sinclair and Nolan Patrick, Ronald Fay owed Sam nothing. An attorney who came out of the legislature, Fay was an easy confirmation who never warmed to his new peers in the executive branch. Sam bypassed him and went directly to his old friend Dale Lashly, the public information officer for the department. Dale loved a little adventure, especially if it was illicit. Dale, who had been there long enough to warrant a cubicle with an outside window, was staring across the street.

"This is exactly why taxpayers have such a low opinion of government workers," Sam said.

Startled, Dale spun around. "Screw the taxpayers. And up yours, Dawson," he added.

"Where are your shoes?"

"Where are your manners?"

"Nice shirt," Sam said while nodding approvingly. He had known Dale since his first days with the state. Dale never wore shoes while indoors and always wore a short-sleeved Hawaiian shirt, even on the coldest of winter days. Today's offering displayed a surfboard laden woody with palm trees towering above.

"Glad you like it. If I had known you were coming, I would have worn a tie. To what do I owe this pleasure, my friend?"

"I need your help, Dale. I'm tying up some loose ends on my latest book."

Dale listened intently then studied the list of names Sam had given him.

"I'll run these ladies through the system and give you a shout tomorrow."

"Thanks, pal, I owe you."

Crossing Sherman Street, filled with hope and smiling at Dale's weirdness, a horn blared with the intensity of a passenger liner as he nearly stepped in front of a passing fire engine. "Use the crosswalk, butt wipe," a fireman clinging to the back yelled at Sam. Looking both ways, he jogged across the street, heart pounding. Fortunately, the man in the white pickup truck parked on the other side of the street was more interested in his newspaper than seeing Sam's near-death experience.

••••

Sam was tired and glad to be home. It had been a long day. He built a fire and plopped on the couch with a beer in one hand and the list of names in the other. He was tired of his obsession, but there was no escape. He needed resolution. It was the same drive that he had once experienced for his work. But there was a competing compulsion that lurked even closer to the surface. It was always there, sometimes bubbling into his consciousness with little provocation. It was Blair.

He closed his eyes and forced himself to concentrate on recalling her image in detail. It was a feat he had mastered in college when taking exams. He had discovered he possessed the ability to visualize an entire page from a book or class notes in such detail that he could simply read the answer from the image projected within his mind. It often gave him a headache if he had to recall very obscure material. He could even do lengthy arithmetic calculations by simply projecting a blackboard and chalk.

At first he had difficulty visualizing her; his emotions swirled recklessly around him. It was more than her physical appearance that he wished to recall. He wanted to capture her total essence, her fragrance, to imagine the taste and feel of her lips tenderly pressed against his. He generally used his recall ability to conjure up stationary images, but now he sought living detail.

With the grace of a great poet, he flashed her living image before him. More than an image, all dimensions were represented. There was depth and atmosphere and color. He could synthesize the sound of her voice, the warmth of her skin, even the sweet smell of wine on her breath. He could speed up or slow down her movements, add shading for atmosphere, and include vivid audio, complete with background noises. He enjoyed freezing a particular scene, rewinding the mental film, and playing it again, sometimes over and over while adding details that were overlooked in the earlier versions.

Her flawless skin glowed with a warm bronze radiance in the Victorian light. The downward cast of her eyes followed by slow-motion bats of long, dark lashes presented a childlike innocence. Her nose, straight and slender, was slightly animated as she spoke, wrinkling playfully to accentuate her dialogue. From her cheekbones to her chin there was symmetry; not too long or too wide, nothing out of proportion. Her hair pulled neatly back presented her face openly, unashamed. Soft and tiny ears appeared translucent at their edges, pinkish with emotion. Flat, gold earrings adorned each ear. Her left ear sported a small diamond post above the gold clasp. The one-sided luster, along with the additional mutilation it implied, suggested a breach with conformity and a hint of rebelliousness. The thought that it represented an uninhibited or even licentious penchant was exciting to him.

But what he found most stimulating was the slender pinnacle on which her head was set. Her neck was long, descending with arrow straightness from beneath both sides of her jaw, flaring sensuously as it approached her shoulders. It was difficult to pinpoint the location of her larynx due to its unobtrusive, feminine qualities. There was an unspoiled chasteness in the vast whiteness of her throat that caused his heart to race with the thought of kissing her there. The tiny brown freckle, the bait of the damsel fish, the genetic link to her past, had a hypnotic effect on him. It held his attention, distracted him. He focused his mental lens back and forth on her long, silky neck. He especially liked the image when her head was turned to the side. Her profile, like the rest of her, was perfect. He wondered if he could capture his perceived image of her on film. After all, he was a photographer, he thought, challenging himself. He rolled his imaginary film of her in a thin, white cotton dress, dancing innocently in a field of golden wheat. The next clip was of her naked body, distorted beneath the shimmering waters of a remote, forest pool. Her head and sumptuous neck above the surface, beads of spring water on her face reflecting brightly in the sun's rays. He could hear the foil shutter of his Nikon rhythmically opening and closing in slow-motion sound.

"Blair?"

"Yes."

"It's Sam Dawson. Did I wake you?"

"What time is it?"

"Eleven thirty, I guess."

"Is something wrong?"

"No, I just...," he paused trying to think of a good excuse for waking her, "just wanted to hear your voice, I guess."

"You guess it's eleven thirty and you guess you just wanted to hear my voice? Can you guess what I'm going to do next?"

"No, what?"

The click of the receiver was unmistakable.

He wanted to dream of Blair and the images of her he had created. Instead, he dreamed of young girls, blonde girls in white dresses. They danced and twirled in foggy slow motion amid gray tombstones on a grassy knoll. Heads back, their long hair flowed in golden swirls. They held each other's hands, a circle of living uniformity sprouting from the dark granite markers of the dead. They sang an uncertain children's nursery rhyme, their voices muted by distance. If only he could capture the scene on film, it would be the perfect photograph for the dust jacket of his new book. But each time he raised the camera to his eye, they disappeared.

••••

"Sam, it's Barbara Sinclair."

"Good morning, Babs."

"Sam, the next time you impersonate an employee of mine or misrepresent me, I will personally see to it that you are committed to one of my institutions. I am furious with you. I have given you everything you have asked for and yet you go to Pueblo and pull a stunt like you did yesterday."

"But—"

"No buts, Sam. Those records were confidential. The records clerk who assisted you is in serious trouble with her supervisor. At best she will receive a corrective action for not verifying your identity. I hope you're happy."

"But there were no records."

"You lied and you violated my trust, Sam."

"But, Babs—" Again there was the unmistakable click of a telephone receiver being placed in its cradle. "Ouch," he said as he hung up the phone.

"Elle," he said, looking at the lazy bloodhound, her forehead oozing over her eyes, "did you ever notice what a talent I have for making women angry? At least you still love me, don't you, girl?"

Elle raised her head, unsure if she was being addressed. A long, thunderous fart rolled from beneath her tail. With a surprised look on her face, she jumped up, as best a bloodhound jumps, spun around to face the fart-eating predator that had attacked her then trotted from the room, head and tail lowered in submission to the unseen force of flatulence.

"That's a class act, Elle."

For a day that had started well with much anticipation of things to come, events were certainly taking a turn for the worse, he thought. He wanted to call Blair to apologize for the late call the evening before, but thought better of it. He was scared that she was truly angry with him. Blair was important to him, very important. He stared at the phone.

Splitting wood was the therapy he needed. It cleared his mind, focused him mentally and physically, and passed the time that tortured him when he was impatient. Even though the day was cool, sweat rolled downward from his temples as he entered the house for a cold drink. The blinking red light gave him promise.

Beep. "Sam, Nolan Patrick here. My people in statistics just called. They didn't find a single death certificate for any of the names on the list you gave me. Either they're all still alive or they died in some other state. Just for fun, I had them do a search for birth certificates. Again, there were no results. But, considering the time period you told me these were from, I'm not surprised. Many births were delivered by a midwife at home and no reports filed. Does seem a bit strange though that we didn't find any in a sample that large. Like the deaths, they could have been born out-of-state. The only thing they did find was both a birth and death certificate for a baby girl dated the same day in May of 1922, probably a stillborn. The baby was unnamed, but the computer kicked it out because the mother's name was Sarah Veronica Adams, one of the names from your list. The father was unknown. The baby was born at Glenwood Springs and the mother's address was listed as New Castle. Let me know if you need anything else." Beep.

The files he had appropriated, a word he liked better than stolen, had been placed neatly in the file box in alphabetical order. Adams, Sarah V., was in first place. She was sixteen when admitted to Mount View in April of 1921. Eris had committed her to the state asylum on July 15, 1921. The time frame was in the ballpark, he thought. She was a bright kid. Her only crime was that she was an orphan. Perhaps Eris had discovered his misdiagnosis and released her. But why not back to Mount View? She was still underage, only seventeen, when she had the baby in Glenwood. Counting backward on his fingers, assuming the baby was full-term, he calculated that she had become pregnant in August of 1921. "Christ," he said aloud at the realization that she had become pregnant within a month of being sent to Pueblo.

"Information, what city?" the male operator intoned quickly.

"New Castle."

"Go ahead."

"For a Sarah Veronica Adams."

There was a short pause then, "I'm sorry, we are not showing a listing for anyone by that name."

"Thank you," he said with little disappointment. It had been a long shot at best.

"Thank you for using AT&T."

The chances of her still being in New Castle were slim as well, he thought. The tiny western-slope community had probably turned over several times in the past seventy-eight years. She could be anywhere.

"Dale Lashly, please," he said into the phone. "This is Sam Dawson." There was a pause and click but no ring as his call was transferred.

"Hey, Sam. I was just about to call you."

"What'd you come up with?" Sam said, trying to sound casual.

"Not a thing. Sorry! I even checked our tax records, which would cost me my job if anyone found out. God himself and a court order couldn't get those records. Only the IRS has access to them. Anyway, I found nothing."

"What about driver's licenses?"

"I went to DOT, it's public information, anybody can pull it up. Again, nothing, but they only go back as far as 1963. Everything before that has been purged. The other problem is that until recently, we had no way of cross-checking maiden names. When a woman was married, her previous identity vanished. From a record-keeping standpoint, most women have no history prior to marriage. It's up to us men to give them true identity," he added in a deep voice.

"Or take it away," Sam added soberly, the image of a seventeen-year-old girl before him.

"Sorry I couldn't be of more help."

"No, that's great, Dale. Now I know where not to look. You saved me a lot of time. Thanks!

"Elle," Sam shouted after hanging up the phone and placing Sarah Adams's file back in the box. "Oil your dog door. I'm going to New Castle."

••••

At Vail he noticed the ache in his set jaw and the stiffness in his tight knuckles. His determination engulfed all other thoughts and feelings. He stared only at the target, envisioning the path of the arrow and projecting its impact at the center of the bull's-eye. Sarah Adams was his target. She had left Pueblo and had given birth to a dead child, three quarters of a century ago. He would find her. Dead or alive she would provide resolution. He knew it would be difficult. A person can cover a lot of ground in seventy-eight years, but there would be traces, indelible footprints left behind, he reasoned. He would catch up with her, find what was left, be it a cold, stone marker or a woman in her nineties. He would find her.

CHAPTER THIRTEEN

*DEATH IS ONLY A SHADOW
ACROSS THE PATH TO HEAVEN*
EPITAPH
—JOHN PREISENDORF

THE TINY GARAGE STOOD DEFIANTLY on the side of the hill, poking up from the rocky ground, listing slightly toward the stream below. Asphalt shingle siding that imitated brick, covered the wooden structure in an attempt to hide the imperfections of add-on construction and the gravitational effects of age. A broken window, a crooked door, and a sagging beam seemed to mirror the western character of its owner.

Chuck Wiley stood one foot atop the other, leaning against the whitewashed garage door. A single Standard Oil gas pump and an orange sun-faded Allis-Chalmers tractor sat in the driveway. In his late sixties, he still had the physique of a much younger man. He wore blue jeans and a short-waisted down jacket with corduroy collar that was soiled with dried mud. The bill of his camouflage baseball hat was black from being taken on and off with greasy fingers a few thousand times. Chuck had shaved earlier in the day, but had missed several spots on his chin and neck. He talked without opening his mouth more than a slit.

Chuck Wiley had been easy to find, although it had been quite by accident. The plan Sam had developed in the three hours on the road had yielded nothing. There was a record of the baby's burial at the cemetery district office. She was given a pauper's grave with no marker, on the hill above Glenwood. It was the same cemetery that held the remains of one of Glenwood Springs' most notable characters, Doc Holliday. County health, social services, telephone company, county assessor, sheriff's office, town marshal, mayor's office all drew blanks. Frustrated and defeated, he had stopped for gas at a tiny Conoco station at the end of Main Street, the only street, in New Castle. An old man in bibbed overalls with a Walter Brennan limp emerged from the rubble that served as his office. He did not speak.

"Fill it up," Sam stated just in case the old guy wanted to know how much he needed. There was no response, only a long uncomfortable silence as the old man clung to the gas nozzle, seemingly for support. "I'm looking for a woman, she'd be in her nineties, named Sarah. Know anybody 'round these parts like that?"

"Yep."

Sam waited, his heart suddenly pounding faster. "Is she still alive?"

"Yep."

"Where's she live?"

"Up the canyon."

"What's her last name?"

"Wiley."

"Know her maiden name?"

"Yep."

Sam was starting to lose patience but controlled himself. "What was it?" he asked calmly.

"Adams."

"You sure?"

"She was married to my dad's cousin, Bob Wiley. He's been dead for years. But Sarah's fine. She lives up the canyon with one of her boys, Chuck. Hope you got cash; there's another customer waiting for the pump."

Looking up, Sam saw a man in a white pickup truck double-parked with his turn signal on. The motor home took up the entire driveway of the tiny station.

After prying directions from the attendant, Sam found himself face-to-face with the boy, Chuck. Chuck Wiley was polite, even friendly, but displayed the typical western restraint when talking with a stranger. He was a retired government trapper. The last of his lion dogs, a scared and arthritic Plott hound, urinated on Sam's tires. Even though Sam had asked for Chuck by name, the trapper seemed little interested in what business Sam might have with him.

"Chuck, is your mom's middle name Veronica?" Sam finally asked when the small talk became obvious.

"Yes, yes it sure is," he smiled, unconcerned as to how Sam knew that fact.

"Would it be possible for me to talk with her?"

"Sure. She's down to the house," he motioned toward the small frame home downhill from the garage. "Go on down. She likes company."

Sam realized it was the true western ethic that Chuck was displaying: Never pry. If someone wants to tell you something, they will. Judge a man by looking into his eyes and believe what comes out of his mouth.

The sidewalk was little more than a path of cracked and broken concrete, heaved upward in several spots, making it difficult to walk casually, confidently, knowing that someone was watching you from behind.

The aspen in the yard were bare; their white bark with black scars complimented the small, white, frame house set among them. It was in need of paint. Several huge blue spruce towered over it, lending a storybook atmosphere.

Sam was slightly out of breath as he walked toward the house. What will I say to her? Where should I begin he asked himself. It was quite possible that she had kept her past, including the baby, a secret. He looked quickly over his shoulder in time to see Chuck and his dog disappear into the crooked garage. He was on his own.

The curtains on the door stirred as he approached. When he reached to knock, the door opened slowly and he found himself face-to-face with Sarah Veronica Adams.

She was taller than he expected. He assumed she would be a little old lady. Bent in the usual fashion of a person her age, she still gave a stately impression. She was thin, perhaps abnormally. She wore a long cotton dress. The small blue-and-white check reminded Sam of a tablecloth in a country restaurant. A white hand-knitted sweater covered her shoulders. Her short snow-white hair was sparse and tightly curled above her mottled forehead. Her eyes, although pale, were still blue and distinctively wide-set, giving her the appearance of an aged Lauren Bacall.

"Mrs. Wiley?"

"Yes."

Her voice was much stronger than he expected. "My name is Sam Dawson and I was wondering if I could speak with you?"

"Do I know you, Mr. Dawson?"

"No, ma'am. I'm from Denver and I've driven all the way over here to see you," he looked down, a little embarrassed by his attempt to bribe her with his investment of time and energy.

"Come in, Mr. Dawson," she said, backing away from the door. "Please sit down," she gestured toward the couch. "I was just about to have my afternoon tea. Would you care for some, Mr. Dawson?"

"Yes, ma'am. That would be nice. Thank you."

She disappeared into the kitchen, moving smartly on spindly, lumpy legs covered with brown cotton hose. Sam looked curiously around the room. It was over-decorated with a lifetime of memories. There were pictures everywhere, old people, young people, groups of people. Knick-knacks of every sort filled each available space throughout the room, generations of gifts from friends and family. The house smelled of things that were old: the familiar odor of a brown-with-age book, musty with a hint of mildew.

She returned with a tray containing a porcelain teapot, a matching cup and saucer, creamer and sugar bowl, and a plain white coffee mug. "The mug is mine," she explained, her voice wavering slightly. "I've a bit of the palsy and I can't make a teacup work for me anymore."

When the tea had been served, she sat across the coffee table from him, smiling pleasantly in anticipation of his business. Sam sipped at his tea and looked uncomfortably at her. He did not know how to begin.

"Mrs. Wiley, I'm a photographer." He paused suddenly, realizing that being a photographer had very little if nothing to do with the reason for his visit. She continued to stare at him patiently. "I've discovered some things while doing research on an individual who died in 1930," sipping more tea to buy time. "You sure have a beautiful home, Mrs. Wiley."

"Thank you."

"Have you lived here all your life?" He immediately regretted asking the question. He knew she had not and it might appear that he was trying to trap her.

"Almost my entire life. Is that your trailer out there?"

"Motor home. Yes, ma'am."

"Where do you live, Mr. Dawson?"

"Denver. Actually I live in the mountains west of Golden."

"I have a niece who lives in Golden. She works at Coors. Maybe you know her?"

"I..."

"Where do you work, Mr. Dawson?"

"I'm self-employed, a photographer. I used to work for the state."

"Chuck, my son, worked for the state, a trapper for the Department of Agriculture. He lives with me now. His wife and daughter were killed in a car accident in 1964. When he retired a few years back, he came to live with me. He's a good boy."

"Yes, ma'am. He seems like a fine man," he said, smiling at her. It seemed strange to hear of a man that old referred to as a good boy. "How many children do you have?"

"Three sons. Chuck is the youngest. I lost Virgil, the oldest, in World War II. He was killed in France. Raymond died of cancer in 1973."

"Mrs. Wiley, the only way I was able to find you was through a death certificate that was filed for your daughter in 1922." There, it was out. He braced himself in anticipation of her reaction.

Sarah Adams stared at him without emotion. Slowly, with shaking hands, she placed the mug of tea on the coffee table. Her eyes began to fill with tears, although the expression on her face remained the same, an alert, pleasant smile on her lips. "Who are you, Mr. Dawson?" she finally said, her voice breaking.

Swallowing the lump in his throat, he said, "Just an interested photographer trying to piece together the past."

"All my life I feared this day, when they would come for me." She smiled broadly as a tear rolled down her wrinkled right cheek. "But I'm a very old woman now. I had hoped to die here where I have lived my life, not in Pueblo. It probably doesn't matter. Chuck is all I have left. The rest, family and friends, are mostly gone. I've outlived them all."

At first he did not understand what she was saying. Suddenly, he realized that she feared being sent back to the state hospital. "Mrs. Wiley, I'm not here to take you back to Pueblo."

"My husband, Robert, was the only one who knew," she said, ignoring his admission. "He knew I was a fugitive from the loony bin." She laughed as she dabbed at the tears in her eyes with her handkerchief. "He knew about the baby too. But he still married me and gave me a lot of good years and three healthy sons."

"Mrs. Wiley, from the records that I've looked at, you didn't belong at Mount View or Pueblo. I assure you, no one even knows you were there. You're the only one I have been able to find."

"I'm probably the only one who ever escaped," she interjected quickly.

"Escaped?"

"Mr. Dawson," she studied him intently, her eyes still filled with tears, "nobody was ever released from Oxford Hall."

"Oxford Hall?"

"We called it the Pumpkin Shell behind his back."

"Pumpkin Shell? Behind whose back? Doctor Eris's?"

The old woman's head rose slowly up. Through her tired, tear-filled eyes there was a look of determination, perhaps hatred, perhaps fear. Sam could not be sure.

"I've not heard his name spoken in over seventy-five years. It seems strange to hear it now." She paused, gazing past Sam. "We called him Peter-Peter." Again she was silent; tears welled up and flowed from her eyes. "The Pumpkin Eater," she added in a high, almost inaudible whisper.

Sam could feel the hairs on his arms stiffen. He watched her face, which seemed to alternate in expression between anger and relief.

"He was a monster, you know."

There was no doubt about the anger he now saw in her eyes. He suddenly thought of Blair and wished she were there to hear this. The compassionate, benevolent town father of Cambridge was regarded as a monster just sixty miles to the west at Pueblo. The atmosphere was tense and the moment awkward. He sipped his tea.

"I'm an old woman. I've probably forgotten more than some people know. But I'll never forget that place. Do you know, Mr. Dawson, that I can still smell it! It was a strange combination of odors—alcohol and horses. The alcohol was used to sterilize his instruments in the infirmary. The building itself was a converted stable. When it rained, the smell of horses rose up through the floor and damp earth outside. I used to close my eyes and imagine the great dark horse that would carry me away from that place, hooves flashing in the night. Nothing could catch it." She again stared blankly past him, savoring the pleasant memory of an imaginary horse.

He did not interrupt. "Infirmary?" he finally said.

She stared directly at him this time. "It was the first time I had ever been on a train. I had ridden street cars in Denver with my mother before she died, but never a train. Many of the other girls had come west on orphan trains, but it was my first time. He seemed like a nice man at first. He sat next to me and talked softly about the countryside. I was very frightened. We had heard such terrible tales about the insane asylum. But he was reassuring and told me that I would live with other girls my own age—I was only sixteen, and that we had our own dormitory separate from the rest of the asylum and wouldn't have to work as hard as we did at Mount View. The infirmary was the first stop after arriving at Oxford Hall." She swallowed the lump in her throat, looked down then smiled. "Would you like some more tea, Mr. Dawson?"

"Yes, ma'am, thank you."

With unsteady hands she poured him another cup. "I had never seen such fancy equipment, so bright and shiny. Glass cabinets filled with medicines and medical instruments. Having never been to a doctor or hospital in my life, I had no fear. Not like today, where the mere thought of going to the doctor causes you to shy a bit." Using both hands, she sipped from her mug. "It was the first time I had seen a doctor's examination table. Back then they were made of quartersawn oak and all the gadgets were nickeled. It had more adjustments on it than a steam engine. Do you know, Mr. Dawson, I still have nightmares about that table?"

He said nothing, but nodded reassuringly.

"It must seem hard to believe by looking at me now, but I was a pretty girl at one time, and well-developed for my age," she added. "Women were much more modest in those days, Mr. Dawson." She paused again as if debating how to proceed. "The humiliation I felt that first day at the asylum has stayed with me my entire life. He made me strip naked and climb onto that table, my feet strapped into those stirrups, not even a sheet to cover myself with. When I cried he pinched my breasts so hard that my nipples bled. We all learned very quickly to keep still. He poked and probed all over and within me. He put things inside me, made measurements, and wrote things down. He asked me dozens of questions, private questions about my cycle. Always writing things down, he was, at that fancy desk of his. I can still see those lions staring at my nakedness."

Embarrassed by the discussion, Sam nervously scratched behind his ear.

"I'll not forget him either. Not the sight, the smell, or the sound of him. Like the monster that lives under every child's bed, The Pumpkin Eater is burned into my memory. I still see him sometimes late at night, standing at the foot of my bed. I even hear his voice whispering my name in the dark. He was an evil man, Mr. Dawson." Looking directly into Sam's eyes, she added: "Maybe the most evil man to ever live on this earth."

He nodded slightly, demonstrating that he understood.

"He wasn't a very big man, almost womanish in some ways. He had tiny hands for a man and he carried himself different from most men. His hair was white as snow, the same as his whiskers. He wore long, white muttonchops, but no moustache or chin whiskers. Thick spectacles were always slid way down his nose. I suspect he was of fair complexion in his younger years, just like I was, Mr. Dawson. It's hard to tell by looking at me now, but I was as blonde and blue-eyed as they come when I was young."

"So were all the other girls, weren't they, Mrs. Wiley?"

"Yes," she smiled with the faraway look of a fond memory. "To look at us, we could've all been sisters. And, you know, Mr. Dawson, there wasn't a crazy one in the bunch. We were as normal as apple pie," she said defiantly.

"How many girls were there?"

"There were six in our ward. The Pumpkin Shell was divided into several wards with locked doors between them. We seldom ever saw any of the other girls. The Pumpkin Eater and the matron had the only keys."

"Matron?"

"She was a deaf-mute from the asylum who supervised and attended to us. She lived in the hall somewhere. She watched us like a hawk. Brought us fresh bed linens and gowns once a week and kept us in food. There was a kitchen in the center of the hall and we took turns doing kitchen duty and cleaning. That's how we knew there were other girls in the hall somewhere. We fixed their meals on a rotation schedule."

"How many?" he asked again.

"I remember fixing meals for as many as twenty girls. But the number went up and down quite a bit. Once we stopped cycling we were moved and never seen again." She could see by the puzzled look on his face that he did not understand. "When we missed our period, Mr. Dawson, we were taken to another ward."

"How long were you there?"

"I don't know, just for a few months, I suppose." She paused then sighed deeply. "It was such a short time for me to carry this big of a burden all these years. But he never stopped messing with us. I spent a lot of time on that oak table. He never said much, just kept sticking stuff inside me. There were injections too. Sometimes he had me in there twice a day then nothing for a week. Then one day he found whatever it was he was looking for. That afternoon, I was moved to another part of the building. There were two other girls there, both of them pregnant."

"Did you ever see any babies?"

"No, but we could hear them crying in the ward next to us." She smiled slightly, a distant look in her eyes. "We weren't the smartest bunch of kids, but we were smart enough to know that none of us was the Virgin Mary. Yet we were pregnant. At least I was pretty sure I was, since I hadn't gotten my period. It was a mystery to all of us. None of us had been with a man, if you know what I mean, Mr. Dawson."

Sam nodded. "Do you know how it happened?"

"For most of my life, it remained a puzzle. But what I've read about in the papers in recent years about women getting fertilized in a test tube, I suppose that's what happened to us."

"In 1921?"

She smiled. "I know what you're thinking, Mr. Dawson. How could something like that happen prior to the industrialized age? Let me tell you, young man, that when I was growing up in the Roaring Twenties, we were as awestruck by our scientific advancements as you were in the sixties when man was walking around on the moon."

The light had shifted as the sun prepared to set behind the western foothills. It now streamed in the window behind Sarah Adams, silhouetting her, filtered through thin, white, linen curtains. The backlighting was distracting him, teasing him with its visual theatrics. He wanted to take her picture. He visualized the black-and-white image. Old people have so much character, he thought. There was a story, perhaps a book of stories wedged within each wrinkle of her face, amid the brown blotches of age. She had lived so long. There was so much life, so much experience in that face that he wanted to record. He forced himself to pay attention. "Who do you think was the father?"

She sipped her tea then stared down at the table. "The Pumpkin Eater was an old man at the time. Until I became an old woman, I didn't think it possible for him to be the father. At the time I believed that he had somehow made us pregnant without the male spore. But later on I learned that couldn't be. So I assumed that he had gotten it from himself or the men at the asylum. Maybe somewhere there was a ward of men that he performed his experiments on, just like us women."

"How did you escape?"

Sarah Adams smiled broadly. "It was one of those times when he was gone. Sometimes we wouldn't see him for a week or more. I had found a painted-over trapdoor to the attic in a broom closet. I waited for just the right night. The matron had made her rounds and left, thinking we were all asleep. It was raining cats and dogs outside, thunder and lightning too. The other two girls helped me. We stacked a chair on top of a trunk and I used a table knife to pry up that trapdoor."

"What about them, the other two girls?"

"Becky was too far along. She wouldn't have fit through the trapdoor, even if she had wanted to go. Matty could have gone with me but was too scared, afraid of being caught. At the time, Mr. Dawson, we all thought we were supposed to be there. Becoming a fugitive was a big decision for a young girl. We tended to be more like sheep than people. Twenty years later when I learned what had happened to the Jews in Germany, I understood how they had been led to the gas chambers and ovens. They did what they were told, simple as that. They were frightened. I thought about the other girls many times over the years, wondering if they were ever released, if they're still alive."

Again, Sam nodded his understanding.

"I laid in the attic for a long time myself, debating whether I should go or stay. Finally, during the peak of the storm, I pushed out a vent at the end of the building and lowered myself to the ground. I had no idea which direction to go. I just ran. It was raining so hard that it hurt. And so dark that I couldn't see more than a few feet in front of me. I hadn't gone far, crossing a grassy field, when I fell into a hole. Half-filled with mud and water, it was deep." She pulled at the sweater and held her arms to her chest. "It was as cold as ice, Mr. Dawson. The mud sucked off one of my shoes and I had to feel around underwater for it. It smelled too, that dank wet-earth smell, like a fresh-turned grave. And when the lightning flashed, I discovered that was just what it was, a grave. I must've stumbled into the asylum's cemetery. But there were no markers, just a grassy field. I had a devil of a time pulling myself out of that hole. But somehow I managed and I just kept on running. I found a river, not far either, and I followed it upstream. I walked and ran all night long. I couldn't stop until the sun was well up, else I'd of frozen to death. I was cold and wet and covered with mud from head to toe."

"Still following the river?"

"Yes, the R-Kansas," she pronounced it the way Sam had heard a few old-timers do. I was well into the mountains when I finally stopped to rest. I was exhausted. I stripped down naked and washed myself and my clothes in that river. I laid facedown on a big warm boulder and fell fast asleep while my clothes dried on some willows."

Sam watched as she smiled and looked down at the floor as if embarrassed. Whether she was embarrassed now or only showing empathy for the young girl lying naked on a rock seventy-five years ago, he could not determine. She raised a bony, mottled hand to her head, running her fingers through her hair, perhaps remembering the long, blonde strands that once covered her cheeks.

"That's how Robert found me," she said, still smiling and looking down. "He'd sold a bull for his father at the La Junta sale barn and was on his way back here to New Castle. Robert was a fisherman, Mr. Dawson," she said, as if admitting some dark perversion. "Until the day he died, he was never without a fly rod in his truck. Wherever we went, no matter for what purpose, if he saw some interesting-looking water, he had to wet a line. We'd be late to church because of it. Anyway, that river, the R-Kansas was too much for him and he'd pulled off the road and started working his way upstream. Imagine his surprise when he came around a bend and spied me laying on a rock in my birthday suit," she shook her head again and gently slapped her knees. "We secretly laughed about that all our lives. Don't know how long I had been asleep, but it was long enough to turn my backside pink as a lobster. Robert thought I was dead. We scared each other near to death when he reached down to push the hair from my face." She said nothing for several seconds, but continued to gaze at the floor, her eyes glassed over with the tears forming there. "We were married less than a month later, Mr. Dawson. And we stayed married for the next forty-nine years," she added proudly.

He wanted to ask about the baby, but did not want to steal her pleasant memory.

"The baby, Mr. Dawson, was stillborn, the cord wrapped around her neck. I gave her my maiden name and let the county bury them both. I never considered the child mine."

That was the last thing said about the life of Sarah Veronica Adams. Noting the hour, Sarah Wiley invited him to stay for dinner and he accepted. Chuck Wiley said little during the meal. Sam determined that Chuck was the kind of man who would never ask and, if told, would only listen. Sarah talked about the changes in the Colorado River Valley over the past seven decades, especially the evils of population growth and urban expansion.

After dinner, at the door, Sarah looked him straight in the eyes and he saw a hardness there he had not noticed earlier. She simply said, "Goodbye, Mr. Dawson." By the finality in her voice, he knew she meant it as a request. He smiled an unspoken thank-you. Like her son, she had not asked him to divulge his intentions. And without speaking she had asked that he not involve her further. Moments earlier he would have honored her request unconditionally. But the picture hanging near the doorway caused him to reconsider. It was a sober young Sarah seated next to an equally stoic young man. The finery of their clothes suggested it was a wedding picture. She was truly beautiful. Her blonde hair was pulled upward into a bun. Her porcelain skin was flawless except for the tiny mole on her neck.

CHAPTER FOURTEEN

PEACEFUL BE THY SILENT SLUMBER,
PEACEFUL IN THY GRAVE SO LOW;
THOU NO MORE WILL JOIN OUR NUMBERS,
THOU NO MORE OUR SORROWS KNOW.
YET AGAIN WE HOPE TO MEET THEE,
WHEN THE DAY OF LIFE IS FLED
AND IN HEAVEN WITH JOY TO GREET THEE,
WHERE NO FAREWELL TEARS ARE SHED.
EPITAPH
—CYPRUS LUGY

"HELLO?"

"Blair, it's me, Sam. Please don't hang up. I know it's late. I'm sorry to wake you, but I've got to talk with you."

"Who is it?"

"Sam Dawson."

"What time is it?"

"It's eleven thirty."

"Let me get this straight. You're the same guy who got me out of bed at eleven thirty the night before last?"

He paused before responding, knowing that she was about to hang up. "Blair, it's important. I really need to talk with you," he said with all the sincerity he could muster.

Now she paused, debating whether or not to hear him out. "What's so important that it couldn't wait until tomorrow?"

"I need your help. I've discovered something and it's complex, too complex to discuss over the phone. Can I see you?

"Right now?"

"Right now!"

"Where are you?

"At the 7-Eleven down the street."

"Here in Boulder?"

"Yes."

"Sam," she whined.

"Please, Blair, it's important."

"All right, but—," she heard the click of the phone at the other end. He was on his way.

In the four hours it had taken him to drive from New Castle, Sam had attempted, unsuccessfully, to formulate the questions he wanted to ask Blair. He knew that he needed her technical assistance, but more importantly he needed to share what he had discovered with someone. But it could not be just anyone; it had to be with Blair. He struggled with what his true priorities were and then cursed himself for lacking focus, allowing his life to spin out of control. First he had an obsession with a dead man, then with a beautiful geneticist. Sometimes he felt as if he were just along for the ride.

Blair greeted him with a friendly hug, a light brushing of cheek to cheek, the type of mock kiss that women of society use when greeting friends, male or female. It was a gesture that always made him feel awkward. It was too intimate for casual acquaintances, too artificial for friends, and too fraudulent for lovers. He wondered which category Blair had placed him in.

Blair sat cross-legged on the couch across from him, gently sipping the wine she had poured for them. She had pulled on a pair of faded blue jeans and a bulky sweatshirt before he arrived. She looked comfortable yet seductive with her hair pulled loosely behind her. She listened without interrupting him.

Sam, still unable to frame the questions, simply recounted his discoveries at Mount View and Pueblo and the lack of information in state records for the 120 girls that Eris had sequestered at Oxford Hall. Blair listened attentively as he described how he had found Sarah Veronica Adams-Wiley and as he gave a detailed account of the interview with her. He offered no speculation of his own as to what had occurred at Oxford Hall more than seventy years ago. He did not want to bias her response in any way.

It was just before 1:00 a.m. when he finished. He sipped his wine and was silent for several seconds as he attempted to think of details he may have forgotten, other than the mole that he thought was too personal to mention. "Well, there you have it. What do you think?"

Blair was silent, staring down at the floor between them. A hint of a smile tugged at the corners of her mouth. "I think you're a man obsessed, Sam Dawson."

"Only by your unequaled beauty, Blair Tennyson," he shot back quickly. He thought he noticed her blushing slightly. He liked that. "My obsession aside, what do you think was happening with your kindly old country doctor seventy-five years ago?"

"Based on your story, what I want to think and what I know as reality are two entirely different things."

Now it was Sam's turn to be patient and listen. He chose not to respond to her initial challenge.

"What you've done, Sam, is built a case for artificial insemination. When you couple that with your earlier proposition of independently produced twins, what you've done is suggest embryo transfer and embryo splitting, and even the possibility of sexing semen." She twisted on the sofa and smiled at him. "These procedures are all currently being used in livestock production and to a very limited extent with human infertility. But I'm here to tell you that most of this technology simply did not exist in the teens or 1920s."

"Embryo splitting," he muttered slowly, a distant look on his face. "The wedge and maul on Eris's grave."

"What?"

"Oh, nothing. I'm guessing that Eris was not a lumberjack."

"I don't follow you," Blair said, her eyes narrowed.

"Never mind. How can you be sure the technology didn't exist?"

"Sam," she said defensively, "eighty years ago nobody had ever seen a human ovum or embryo. There was virtually no understanding of the mammalian reproductive process from a physiological, genetic, or biochemical standpoint. In livestock the first transfer of a bovine embryo wasn't reported until the late forties, and it took several more years before anyone produced a live calf. It was a complex surgical process. The techniques for today's nonsurgical embryo recovery, transfer, and cryopreservation didn't come about until the late seventies and early eighties."

"I love it when you use big words," he smiled.

"How do you know your Sarah Adams is telling the truth? Pregnancy has a way of justifying itself in the mind of a young girl. Could be that Doctor Eris was simply administering prenatal care to pregnant inmates."

"What if Eris was ahead of his time? What if he understood artificial insemination and whatever else you said? Blair, we're only talking a difference of twenty or thirty years before the concepts were tested."

"Twenty or thirty years in science represent a very long, long time. I'm not saying that the vision wasn't there. Man had long dreamed of going to the moon, but had to wait patiently until the technology in a number of scientific disciplines became available. With artificial insemination and embryo transfer, it wasn't so much technology that was needed as it was knowledge of the human reproductive system." She was silent for a moment as if questioning her position. "I know a guy at CSU who routinely splits cow embryos with his naked eye using a razor blade. It's not that technical," she added, doubt creeping into her voice.

"What if Eris had it all figured out, ahead of his time? Let's assume he was some sort of genius."

"But what was his motivation?" she said, smiling. "Most researchers develop a hypothesis then test it using a model, or in this field, laboratory animals. Why didn't he use rats, dogs, monkeys, or cows?"

Sam rubbed the back of his neck; fatigue was beginning to take its effect. "I don't know. Why use lab animals when you have access to a steady supply of humans? All orphans, all incarcerated, no future, no past." He looked up suddenly, eyes flashing. "You're assuming that he was a researcher doing research. We're forgetting the old boy was into eugenics. He wanted to improve the race—"

"Eugenics," Blair interrupted, "during his time was primarily confined to institutionalization or sterilization. It was negative eugenics, discouraging reproduction among people believed to have undesirable genetic traits. Hitler perverted the concept to the extreme, but basically his goal was to prevent the production of children on the part of people he thought of as having inferior genetic traits."

"But," Sam said, positioning himself on the edge of the couch, "if there was a negative eugenics there must have been a positive eugenics. Eris was selecting these girls for positive traits: They were healthy, intelligent, blonde, and beautiful." He paused and looked squarely at her. "Just like you," he said. "Aryan in the way the Nazis used the term. Maybe he believed himself superior. Maybe he was impregnating them."

"I'll ignore your insinuation that I am a product of some oversexed, deranged scientist," she said with a serious edge to her voice. "Yes, there was and still is, to some extent, positive eugenics, but it has always been a bit vague. Who should be encouraged to reproduce? What are the qualities that should be selected for? Physical? Intellectual? Who decides?"

"Eris, that's who," he said forcefully. "The old boy was working both sides of the issue. Publicly he was promoting negative eugenics, encouraging sterilization of the asylum's regular inmates, even aborting those who somehow became pregnant. He got his ass in trouble over that!"

"What do you mean?"

"He was accused of abortion in 1926, I believe. The local press did a number on him. They linked him to Harry Laughlin, who was the superintendent of the National Eugenics Record Office in Washington. There was a legislative investigation and a fair amount of public outcry. Eris had even lobbied for a state sterilization law a couple of years earlier. He was this state's resident eugenicist," he said conclusively. "But nobody dug deep enough. They didn't discover his little baby factory in the stables where he practiced positive eugenics." He paused. "The pumpkin shell," he added solemnly. "There he kept them very well."

Blair was silent. "Inclusive fitness," she finally muttered.

"What?"

"Inclusive fitness," she repeated. "It's a term that the sociobiologists came up with a few years back that refers to reproductive success. Actually, it was a rather bold genetic theory advanced in the mid-1960s by Hamilton that had to do with the origin of sociality, assigning a wholly different role to haplodiploidy. Basically, what it says is that for an altruistic trait to evolve, the sacrifice of fitness by an individual must be compensated for by an increase in fitness in some group of relatives by a factor greater than the reciprocal of the coefficient of relationship to that group. According to Wilson, the full effects of the individual on its own fitness and on the fitness of all its relatives, weighted by the degree of relationship to the relatives, are referred to as the 'inclusive fitness.'"

Sam stared at her with a look that was comprised of equal amounts of astonishment, bewilderment, and irritation. "Christ, Blair! What the hell did you just say?"

"If you leave out the selfish mutant gene theory, it's simply a measure of one's genetic representation in future generations. It usually involves some genetic expression that confers an advantage to the individual. In many respects it's the opposite of altruism. Eugenics in general is a selfish process whereby one raises their own fitness by lowering that of others."

"Now I understand," he said facetiously.

Blair smiled her acceptance of his confusion. "Think of it like the ram or the bull elk that gathers a harem and prevents all other males from breeding with his females. What he effectively has done is increase his genetic contribution to the next generation while limiting or eliminating that of other males. In monogamous species, the individual competes through parental investment in the offspring's success. Polygamous species generally take the strength in numbers approach. There are even some species, like the cuckoo, that demonstrate social parasitism. By laying their eggs in the nests of other birds, they exploit their hosts by having their own young raised, often to the exclusion of the host bird's young. The beauty of the scheme is that the more altruistic host spends its time and energy incubating and looking after the young, while the social parasite simply breeds and lays eggs. Guess who gets greater genetic representation in future generations with the least amount of investment?"

"Eris!"

"You're making too many assumptions. I'm telling you that the technology didn't exist."

"And I'm telling you that you're the most beautiful woman I've ever met," he blurted out, his tone serious.

"Sam," she paused, looking at him then down at the couch then at her watch. "It's really late. I have classes in the morning. I'm going to feel like crap if I don't get some sleep. Can we talk about this later?"

"When?"

"I don't know, during daylight perhaps."

"Do you *want* me to go?" he said, emphasizing the word want. He was suddenly very nervous as he waited for her response. He feared that he had pushed her too far.

"Unfair question, Dawson."

"It's an honest question that deserves an honest answer."

"What do you want from me?" It was now her turn to ask the serious question.

"A monogamous relationship, I guess, using your vernacular, a chance to perpetuate the species, to go from haploid to diploid."

"Take a cold shower, Sam. You had your chance and you started talking about dead rabbits. By the way, they haven't used rabbits for that test in decades. Besides, I'm not sure that I want a relationship with a crazy person just now."

"You know I'm as rational as you are. I'm on to something here. You're just taking your role as devil's advocate too seriously."

"You're taking your role as Sherlock Holmes too seriously. Sam, there are hundreds of unanswered questions here, dozens of assumptions, and little substantive data to make your case. And you have gorgeous eyes," she added as if admitting some long-kept personal secret.

"All the better to see you with," he smiled, reaching out and taking her hand tenderly. It was soft and warm and responsive as their fingers clasped.

Neither spoke, nor did they look at each other. Instead they sat silently staring at their groping hands, fingers intertwined. There was a passion that flowed from her, hot and electric. It washed over him. His heart raced, and for an instant he was transported back to high school and the remembrance of his first love, with his first kiss amid pounding heart and shortness of breath. To feel young again, even for a second, was euphoric. He pulled her toward him.

"Sam," she protested softly. "We—"

He ignored her mild resistance. Her lips were as tender as he had imagined them, but not passive. She kissed him back. At first delicately then passionately, her mouth opened and closed, her tongue probed teasingly. His hands found the softness of her face and neck and he gently explored her beauty, his fingers nested seductively in her hair. He found the large hair clip that held the loose bundle behind her and pulled it slowly downward. Her hair spilled forward around her neck and over her face, and drifted over his face as he pulled her toward him. There was no resistance as her body settled with all her weight upon his. The infatuation that he had felt moments earlier was suddenly transformed into something more carnal. The intellectual discussion in which they had engaged was irrelevant. He was quickly consumed by a physical appetite that craved for fleshy gratification. He was no longer a man.

The unencumbered firmness of her breasts pressed against his chest. The acknowledgment of their naked presence under the loose sweatshirt blinded him with passion. As the intensity of his desire escalated, she responded equally, pressing her body almost painfully against him, writhing with sexual anticipation.

So singular was his focus, so consumed by his animal-like drive, that he remembered little of the experience, the details did not exist. The lions, Thors, and gargoyles with menacing faces were mute as they watched the torrid spectacle below their lofty perches. The mantle clock marked cadence but was not heard.

••••

At dawn they showered together in the narrow, claw-foot tub on the second floor; Sam's head loomed comically above the shower curtain. It was there, after yet another round of consummatory passion, that Blair suggested he meet her after class. She wanted to introduce him to Ivan

Manfred, the resident reproductive endocrinologist who specialized in embryo transplant research. Perhaps then he would give up the notion of eugenic conspiracy.

••••

Sam intentionally arrived early so that he might hear the end of Blair's lecture.

In spite of her lack of sleep, she looked fresh and vibrant, more so than the first time he had seen her in front of a class. Perhaps a little frayed around the edges; her hair appeared as if it might spill loose at any moment. The silly black ribbon bow tie at her neck was off-center, giving the impression she had dressed in a hurry. His infatuation with her seemed no less than the first time he had seen her in front of a class.

"In general, we can speak of the total of all genes contained in the sperm and ova produced by the parents in a particular population as constituting the gene pool of that population," she lectured as she hurriedly printed "Gene Pool" on the whiteboard, her black marker squeaking frantically. "This is a very useful concept, which we will use frequently. In our present example, half of the genes in the gene pool are big B and half are little b. So, we can generalize by saying that in a population whose gene pool is composed of 1/2 B genes and 1/2 b genes, the offspring will be expected to occur in the proportions of 1/4 BB, 2/4 Bb, 1/4 bb," the blue marker squeaking in unison with her lecture. Next she grabbed the green marker.

"Let p = the relative frequency of gene B..."

Sam's eyes became glassy as Blair energetically scribbled on the board.

"In our present example," she continued as the students slumped over their desks writing furiously, many with a fistful of colored pens, "then...," she tapped out a series of equations, the room filling with the chemical odor of the markers.

"Note," she said with emphasis as she wrote more letters and numbers on the board while announcing some revelation. "So," she said with equal emphasis as she repeated the findings she had presented moments ago. "Remember the little checkerboard we drew a few minutes ago," she said, pointing to a matrix drawn in red on the whiteboard that was slid above the one on which she now worked. "This formula is simply an algebraic way of expressing what is shown in that little checkerboard." She was now using the red marker again. "In terms of our formula...," she continued, talking louder when she faced the board. The students hunkered lower, their pens scribbling. "In filling in the checkerboard, we did diagrammatically the equivalent of multiplying...," her blouse pulled free of her skirt, exposing the tanned flesh near the small of her back as she stretched to pull the upper whiteboard down. "Or, in other words...," she continued, but Sam had tuned her out, captivated by her beauty. "Which equals, of course,..." she scribbled another equation. "The application of this squared binomial to panmictic populations was stated independently and almost simultaneously by two men, Hardy and Weinberg in 1908. Hence," she stated slowly, but with obvious emphasis as she printed in large, black, block letters, "it has come to be referred to as the Hardy-Weinberg law."

The students wrote silently without looking up. Sam glanced at his watch and noted that she had less than five minutes of the period remaining. He was thankful that he was no longer in college, he thought as he stifled a yawn. He did not care about Hardy-Weinberg. He cared about the professor. Quietly he slipped inside the projection room at the rear of the hall. The tiny room was a full story above the lecture floor and was littered with slide projectors, VCRs, and spare parts of audio-visual equipment. The room was nearly soundproof and he watched with fascination as Blair paced in front of the class, pointing to the whiteboard. She was beautiful. The tight wool skirt only hinted at the curvaceous body beneath. Her long, sensuous neck disappeared into the plain collar of her white blouse, giving little indication that it graded into muscular shoulders. He liked her shoulders and arms. The muscle groups had definition. Not like a body builder, they were more subtle, indicative of an active outdoor lifestyle. He thought it fascinating that the tight stomach he had repeatedly kissed that morning was now parading in front of nearly three hundred people, covered only by a thin layer of cloth.

Sam leaned his elbows and hands against the glass of the projection booth; he peered down at her and smiled. He had the sudden urge to pound against the glass and yell, "Elaine!" as he had seen Dustin Hoffman do in the movie *The Graduate*. He thought he saw Blair acknowledge his presence with a quick smile as she pushed her owl glasses up on her nose, but he was not sure. Looking around the booth, he found both poster board and Magic Markers. He grinned as he printed in large, squeaky letters the words "You Look Great Naked!"

"To summarize," Blair said, stepping close to the first row of students, "the Hardy-Weinberg law states in algebraic form the fact that a panmictic population tends to attain genetic equilibrium, with regard to a pair of alleles, in one generation, and to maintain that equilibrium thereafter. Of course," she paused looking at the projection booth at the rear of the room, "this is somewhat ideal," she said slowly, having difficulty finding the words, never taking her eyes off the sign that Sam held at chest height against the window, "in that it assumes that mating is truly random and that the alleles do not differ in their, uh effects on viability and, uh fertility. Excuse me," she smiled to the class, "but there's a guy in the projection booth that thinks I look great naked," she held out her hand as if to introduce him to the class.

Taking the cue, the entire class swiveled in their chairs, craning their necks upward to stare at Sam with his obscene placard.

Caught completely off guard, Sam froze. Slowly lowering the poster board, he managed a sick smile as a form of greeting to the six hundred eyeballs fixed upon him. The silence caused his ears to ring.

A clean-cut young man in the front row began to slowly applaud. He was quickly joined by those around him, and within seconds the entire lecture auditorium resonated with the full-bodied sound of their ovation. There were no whistles or catcalls, only the polite thunder of their approval. At first, Sam thought they were mocking him, but then realized they were vicariously agreeing with him. They too saw the beauty beneath her professorial costume.

The bell sounded and the students responded with the usual conditioned response of gathering their materials and moving hurriedly toward the exits. They filed past him, eager to get to the next fifty-minute installment of their education. Some reached out and shook his hand and said, "Yes!" or "Right on!" as he stood in the projection booth doorway.

Blair leaned casually against the podium, still smiling as he approached the lecture floor. The room seemed cavernous with the students gone. "Here," he said, handing her the placard, "a souvenir to remember the time you totally humiliated me."

"You deserved it," she said, looking past him to make sure the room was empty. Placing her hand on the back of his neck, she pulled him toward her and kissed him passionately. The kiss was broken off prematurely as she recoiled in laughter. "If you could have seen your face," she giggled.

Sam smiled, slightly embarrassed. "The score is zero to one. When you least expect it, Tennyson..."

••••

Ivan Manfred was nothing like Sam had expected. He had pictured an elderly scientist of Volga-Deutsch ancestry with a plaid bow tie. Instead he found a gum-chewing paunchy remnant of the sixties from British Columbia wear-

ing a Beatles t-shirt in a tiny unkept office. His pronuncia-
tions of "out" and "about" were classic. Graying hair pulled
into a short ponytail and a minimally kept beard marked
his eccentricity. A full professor in the Biology Department,
Manfred shared his appointment with the CU School of
Medicine in Denver.

After the usual pleasantries, Blair got right to the point.
"My friend wants to know if embryo transplant, bisection,
and artificial insemination were possible eighty years ago."

Manfred looked at Sam, his eyebrows raised. He did not
answer immediately, but stroked his beard then plunked
down in his office chair and reclined, his hands folded across
his paunch. "It's an interesting question, Mr. Dawson," he
grinned. "It seems so easy now, given our technology and
knowledge of the reproductive process. I'd love to dismiss
your question with a simple 'Hell no.' But I learned a long
time ago to never say never." He paused. "Yes, the concept
was there. It had been around since at least the mid-nine-
teenth century and probably long before that. Egyptians
AI'd horses in the thirteen hundreds. Italians did it in dogs
and Russians were the first to do it with cattle and sheep in
the 1930s."

"AI'd?" Sam said.

"Artificially inseminated," Blair offered.

"Artificial insemination was being used worldwide by
the 1950s," Manfred continued. "The first official record
of artificial insemination in humans was in 1884 in Phila-
delphia. Embryo transfer was demonstrated in lab animals
more than eighty years ago in England. But, and this is a big

but, there was only a rudimentary understanding, by today's standards, of reproductive physiology, especially of the biochemical and hormonal aspects. All the gadgets we use today didn't exist. If you're talking about delays in transfer or insemination, I don't think cryopreservation was being used yet. Sure, they knew about liquid nitrogen and how cold it was. But I'm not sure anyone had thought about using it for tissue preservation. As far as artificial insemination is concerned, hell, scientists have been fooling around with that for nearly two hundred years."

"What's the primary purpose or advantage of embryo transfer?" Sam asked.

"The main use today is in cattle for amplifying reproductive rates of valuable females. Of course, embryo transfer procedures are nearly always at the expense of reduced reproductive rates of the recipients, from a genetic standpoint.

"As far as my work is concerned," Manfred explained, "I use it to circumvent infertility in humans. The aggies up at CSU actually perfected the procedures because of cows with cystic ovaries or uterine infections. At the fertility clinic in the med center, we get women who chronically abort or have adhesions of the ovaries or blocked oviducts. Basically, we superovulate them with prostaglandin F2 alpha, AI them, flush 'em, and implant the embryo where it's supposed to be. Like falling off a log, eh," he grinned.

"Does it require surgery?" Sam said.

"Used to," Manfred said. "Both recovery and transfer were surgical procedures in both animals and people. Again, the aggies perfected the nonsurgical techniques. Of course they could stick their entire arm up the vagina of a cow and palp for corpora lutea to determine when and from which side to flush. We had to wait for the development of fiber optics and microsurgical techniques in order to do the same thing in humans. We've also been able to exploit other technologies, including in vitro fertilization, sexing, production of transgenic animals, bisection of embryos, and cloning by nuclear transplantation. Hell, there's an old boy at Fort Collins who's doing in vitro work from slaughterhouse oocytes in a twinning program in order to increase calf crops without increasing the number of cows. Mama may have croaked last year, but she's produced fifty sets of twins last month alone. When it comes to humans, you can get into some pretty heavy ethical debates about the potential of all this wonderful science."

"You mean religious?" Sam asked.

"Yes, in part, but more from the standpoint of genetic superiority or the preservation of germplasm. The potential for misuse, as with all areas of science, is certainly there."

"Is there such a thing as genetic superiority?" Sam asked as if baiting him.

"Damn right there is. Anybody who tells you different is a lying fool."

"Who determines what is superior? Who sets the standard?"

Manfred smiled broadly and looked squarely at Sam. "You do," he said softly.

There was a long pause in the conversation as Sam debated to himself whether to pursue the issue further. It was Blair who decided for him.

"We can argue that one over lunch sometime," she laughed. "We wanted to know if it was possible in 1920."

"Possible? Yes! It would have been crude as hell and based on trial and error with low success, but possible," Manfred admitted.

"What if...," Sam started to say and paused. "Let's say that you were...," he stopped again, unwilling to divulge his real interests. "Tell me how you'd go about it. You said it was like falling off a log. How easy is it?"

"It just seems easy given today's technology. It's actually somewhat involved. I could give you a six-hour lecture and you'd probably not understand a thing I said."

Sam hated academic snobbery. He especially disliked being dismissed as being intellectually inferior. "Try me," he said in a challenging tone that caused Blair to raise her eyebrows.

"Sorry," Manfred said. "I didn't mean you personally. Christ, it took me twelve years of college to get the basics and I'm still only a damned mechanic. I haven't the foggiest about how or why the system works like it does. What part are you most interested in, Sam?"

"Tell me how you get embryos."

"Well, to increase our efficiency, we begin with super-ovulation in order to obtain enough embryos to screw with. Pardon the pun. There are a couple of different methods based on two different gonadotrophins. The simplest is to give an intramuscular injection of gonadotrophin called equine chorionic gonadotrophin, followed by a luteolytic dose of prostaglandin F2 alpha or an analogue intramuscularly two to three days later. A second prostaglandin injection is often given twelve-to-twenty-four hours after the first."

Sam was already regretting he had asked the question.

"The second method of superovulation is to give eight-to-ten injections of FSH, follicle stimulating hormone, subcutaneously or intramuscularly at half-day intervals. Intramuscular injection is more reliable under outpatient conditions."

Sam had already tuned him out. He studied Manfred's mouth opening and closing.

"As with the equine chorionic gonadotrophin, prostaglandin F2 alpha is...The most common FSH regimen is...," he paused to observe Sam's reaction.

"Where do you get the FSH?" Sam asked as if he had understood everything Manfred had said.

"We used to get it from swine pituitaries! Now most is synthesized in a lab. Equine anterior pituitary extract and human menopausal gonadotrophin are being used. But each has their problems, expense being one of them."

"What's next?"

"Well, we then wait for ovulation to occur, oestrus in the animal world. If you're using hubby's frozen semen, one ampoule or straw is inseminated at twelve and twenty-four hours after the onset of oestrus. There are lots of variations on this theme, including in vitro insemination or, as we like to call it, sex in a petri dish. Personally, I like the one that starts with dinner and a movie, eh."

"Okay," Sam said as if he were getting somewhere. "You got egg and sperm together and the embryo has formed. How do you get the little rascal out of there?"

"Prior to the mid-seventies, we used a surgical technique called a midline laparotomy about six-to-eight days after the beginning of oestrus. Next we palpated the ovaries to esti- mate the formation of corpora lutea. Ultrasound nowadays makes this easier. We scrub her, give her an epidural of pro- caine, which makes her peepee numb, retract the labia, and let them dry. Disinfectants will kill an embryo slicker than snot. Next we insert the cervical dilator. We then run a spe- cial catheter up there. Did I mention the cervical expander, eh?"

"Yes," Blair said with painful identification.

"Anyway, as with everything else, there are forty ways from Sunday to do uterine flushes. I generally use the contin- uous-flow system with about a liter of medium in an Erlen- meyer flask held about yea high," he said, holding his hand above his head. "Nothing works better than simple gravity for filling up a uterus at the optimum rate. Whatever system you use, the principle is to fill and empty the uterus four- to-six times. You ought to see how some of those old girls swell up; it looks like they're a couple of months pregnant. I like to massage the horns a bit to get those sticky little suck- ers from the endometrial folds. The whole time, I'm collect- ing fluid from the uterus through a 75 micron mesh filter. I pour the contents into a searching dish and, like panning for gold, I swirl those little babies to the outside, rinse 'em, swirl 'em, and rinse 'em again. We take a peek at the flush fluid at about twelve power magnification to locate the embryos, transfer them to fresh medium, and wash them through at least three more changes of medium. Once that's done, we either prepare them for immediate transfer or cryopreservation. Now, think you can do it? Blair, hop up on this desk."

Blair rolled her eyes in mock disgust.

Ignoring Manfred's attempt at humor, Sam said, "Without cryopreservation, how long could you keep an embryo?"

"About twenty-four hours. The little suckers get their nutrients from the fluid in which they're bathed. By the way, light will really screw 'em up, even from a microscope. You got to keep 'em in the dark or in subdued light."

"So, you have about twenty-four hours to get it to wherever you're going with it?"

"Yeah, roughly. Did I mention serum? You can feed 'em blood serum. They like big fat protein molecules. Sterile macromolecules derived from serum keeps 'em soft, supple, and nubile. And they won't make a chocolate mess in your hands!"

"How would you transport them?"

"A small test tube, a petri dish, or multiwell plates work fine too. A thin layer of nontoxic paraffin oil over the top will regulate the rate of gas exchange. Keep 'em in the dark and at room temperature and you'll be fine."

"Okay, I've got them out. Now I've got twenty-four hours to do something with them. What next?"

"Well," he said, rubbing his chin. "Unless you've got crackers and vodka, you better transplant them, eh."

Blair stifled a laugh.

"I transplant them with a standard Cassou inseminating gun for French straws, which we call ticklers 'cause they're not as smooth at the tip as other straws," he smiled, but decided not to elaborate. "The whole thing is similar to the artificial insemination process; a shot in the twat, up the cervix, past the uterus ipsilateral to the corpus luteum, right to the bifurcation of the uterine horns. Slam-bam-thank-you-ma'am! The key is to get up there without damaging the endometrium. You gotta be fast, but not too fast. You gotta be gentle, but not too gentle. It's like makin' love, eh. It's an art!"

Sam could not help smiling. There was a crude side to this academician that was amusing. He could tell by the gleam in Manfred's eyes that he was one of those rare individuals who was married to and made love to his work. Sam could identify with that, although his marriage was in trouble if he did not return to it soon. "That's it? Doesn't the recipient have to be chemically receptive or something?"

"Absolutely! Good question, Sam. Probably the most venerable principle of embryo transfer is that the stage of the reproductive cycle of the recipient must correspond to that of the donor or physiological stage of development of the embryo. Synchrony doesn't have to be perfect."

"Can you induce synchrony?"

"You bet. Lots of different methods. Lock those rascals up with one another for long enough and they'll synchronize themselves. Ever hear of the Radcliffe studies? Never mind. Trust me, women are animals." He glanced sideways at Blair to see if he had achieved a reaction. She simply smiled and nodded approvingly. "The best way to synchronize them is to give the recipient a luteolytic dose of prostaglandin F2 alpha or some suitable analogue during the luteal phase."

"Are there adverse side effects?"

"Oh, once in a while they'll dry hump your leg, which is really embarrassing in front of company, eh."

Blair snickered and held her hand to her mouth.

"Seriously," Manfred continued, "I've never observed any side effects, but I've not looked at it from a behavioral standpoint."

Sam looked at his watch. "I didn't mean to take up your morning. I know you're busy, but one last question, if you don't mind?"

"Shoot."

"How do you split embryos?" Sam said. The vision of Eris's grave appeared, the maul and wedge atop the stone.

"To my knowledge, Sam, it has never been taken to term in humans. I've split a few for fun, but never had the occasion to implant the pieces. But it's done every day in this state in the livestock industry. It's not brain surgery. My friend at Moo U in Fort Collins can do it with a razor blade using his naked eye. But it's usually done with a broken fragment of razor blade held in a special handle using a dissecting microscope. Embryos can be bisected from the two-cell stage through the hatched blastocyst stage. Actually, you can split them more than once, but it will lower your success rate."

"But what's the purpose?"

"Basically, there are two main reasons for splitting embryos. The first is to obtain identical twins. That's real use-

ful if you're filming Doublemint commercials or doing research. The second is to increase productivity. In cattle you
can get fifty percent more calves by implanting two demi-
embryos than if you just do whole embryo transplants."

Sam ran his fingers through his hair. He was remembering again why he majored in journalism and not biology. He
was at that point of intellectual overload where he needed
time to digest and sort through his newfound knowledge.
He suddenly felt very confined. He needed to be outside. In
his mind he could see the tall brown grass waving between
the headstones at the Cambridge Cemetery. He began to
read the names. He jerked his head upright and looked at
Manfred. "Can you sex the embryos?"

"Absolutely, it's on the verge now of being used com-
mercially by the livestock industry. The procedures are a bit
clumsy and the embryo can be damaged, but they're getting
there."

"Could it have been done seventy years ago?"

"I'd like to say 'Hell no.' They hadn't heard of karyotyp-
ing, male-specific antigens, or DNA probes. But a couple
months ago I ran into a young lab tech at a private lab in
Platteville who said she could visually tell male from female
embryos in cattle. The vet who runs the lab said she was hitting at about eighty percent. I guess if your job was to stare
at the little buggers all day, you'd eventually pick up subtle
differences. Sort of cracks me up that researchers have spent
years and millions developing techniques for sexing embryos, and some gum-smacking little thing in tight jeans and
running shoes can simply look at 'em and tell the difference."

Manfred smiled and shook his head in disbelief. "Maybe there is something called woman's intuition, eh."

"You're a real sexist, you know that, Van," Blair said, smiling.

"Sorry, Blair," he beamed. "I just can't help myself. But I wouldn't expect a woman to understand, eh," he added with mock sarcasm.

"I'll ignore that this time," Blair smiled. She looked at her watch. "Thanks, Van. We'll let you get back to whatever it is that you do."

Manfred frowned. "You know what I do, Blair! I add meaning to whatever it is that you do."

Sam thanked him profusely and accepted Manfred's business card.

Blair walked Sam to the visitor parking lot. The sun shone brightly and a gentle breeze played through her hair. She squinted up at him as she spoke. "Well! Did you get the answer you needed?"

"I don't know. After all that, I'm not sure of the question I asked. I think I have a case of information overload. I need some time to digest all this."

"Sam, you heard him. This is complex stuff. The chances of Eris being able to—"

"But the chances were there," Sam interrupted. "That's what I heard Manfred say. He never discounted a thing. He left the door wide open. I wish he hadn't. I wish he had told me 'No way, Jose.' But he didn't. No," he said, looking down and shaking his head, "there are way too many possibilities here."

Seeing his conviction, Blair said nothing.

"Why girls?" Sam asked. "If Eris had the ability to distinguish female from male embryos, why did he choose females? It seems to me that males would have a bigger genetic payoff. They could breed with many more females producing more offspring. A female can only get pregnant every nine months or so. But a male can get someone pregnant every thirty minutes or so."

"Whoa, big fellah," Blair smiled. "Every thirty minutes? You're having delusions of grandeur."

"You know what I mean," he said, slightly embarrassed.

"You're off into sociobiological theory again. I can sum up the very long and very complex answer in one word: Cuckoldry!"

"Excuse me?"

"Cuckoldry," Blair repeated. "From a parental standpoint, you want your offspring to reach sexual maturity, breed, and pass on your genes to the next generation. With male children, you're never really sure that their kids are theirs. Their wives could've been having sex with anybody. But with female offspring, it doesn't matter who they've been sleeping with. Since they're the one that's pregnant, you're assured that the resultant offspring shares twenty-five percent of your genes with you. In other words, there is no doubt that the kid is related to you. With a son, you're never sure, unless you do DNA testing."

"So, if my goal was to ensure my genetic contribution to future populations, I would try to have girls rather than boys?"

"Exactly!"

"Do you know that my life was much simpler before I met you?" he said, sighing deeply.

"But not nearly as interesting," she cooed then kissed him dryly on the lips. "I've got a lab to teach. Call me?"

"Count on it!" He watched as she hurried across the parking lot. "Blair," he suddenly called out to her, unsure of why. It was as if he was afraid he would never see her again. She stopped and turned to face him. She shielded her eyes from the midmorning sun. He wanted to tell her he loved her, but knew it was too early in the relationship to disclose something so profound. "Thanks," he said, the uncertainty apparent in his voice. "I appreciate all your help."

"I'd do the same for a sane person," she smiled. She turned and danced across the street, where she joined a throng of students and bicycles.

"Blair," he called again even louder. She stopped, hesitated, then turned around slowly. "I'll call you."

She nodded several times then called back "I know." And then she was gone.

He stood for what seemed like several minutes trying to pick her out of the crowd. He had been there before. He was reliving some familiar experience. When he realized what the association from the past was, he felt a wave of panic sweep over him. He had called out to his sister on the day she disappeared. He challenged her to a game of one-on-one after school, an inhibited substitute for the "I love you" that he was unable to say. He never saw her again. He had looked for her for the past twenty-five years. He always looked for her. Occasionally he would rush awkwardly through a crowd to see the face of a girl who, from behind, looked like Julie. She never aged. Sometimes, especially early in the morning, he heard her voice whispering his name. She had been his best friend. The four-and-a-half years that separated them was enough to almost eliminate the usual competitions that led to anger. She was a beautiful young woman, tall, blonde, and athletic. She had tried out and made the varsity cheerleading squad shortly before her disappearance. She was in uniform the day she was abducted. The gold-colored shorts she wore under the short, pleated skirt were found three days and twenty miles after she stopped to buy a soda at a local convenience store. Tossed into a ditch along a country road, the blood- and semen-stained panties were all that was found.

CHAPTER FIFTEEN

WHETHER WE CLIMB, WHETHER WE PLOD,
SPACE FOR ONE TASK THE SCANT YEARS LEND,
TO CHOOSE SOME PATH THAT LEADS TO GOD,
AND KEEP IT TO THE END.
EPITAPH
—RACHEL DOROTHY FOUNTAIN

THERE WERE NO RED LIGHTS OR SIRENS as Sam felt there should have been. Instead, the sheriff's deputy had arrived unceremoniously in a white Chevy Caprice that someone on a low budget had made look like a police car. The deputy, an overweight young man with bad skin who had attempted to grow a mustache that involved fewer than two dozen whiskers, acted like Joe Friday, a seasoned veteran of big-city crime. He referred to Sam as "sir" and used the term incessantly. He instilled little confidence with Sam and made Elle nervous, as evidenced by the long, glistening strands of saliva that descended from the corners of her mouth.

"Are you sure nothing else is missing, sir?"

"No!"

"Sir?"

"I'm not sure. I haven't had time to inventory everything. There were thousands of negatives and proofs in those cabinets," he said, waving his arm in the direction of the file cabinets with their drawers ajar and their contents strewn over half the room.

"Sir, then how can you be sure there's anything missing at all?"

"Because everything that was in the darkroom is gone and there are entire files that are missing."

"Which files, sir?"

"I told you, the ones marked 'Oxford, Iowa' and 'Cambridge, Colorado.'" He thought how lucky he was that he had taken the box of files appropriated from Mount View with him to New Castle.

"Do you know why those particular files have been stolen, sir?"

Sam hesitated before he answered. He wanted to shout "Hell, yes, I know!" But did he really know why? And if he thought he knew, did he want to share it with Joe Friday, Jr.? He was on to something and this confirmed it. The robbery was deliberate and specific. Nothing else appeared to be missing. There was no attempt to cover up their singular mission. They could have stolen the other files, cameras, and darkroom equipment. It was the Eris material they were after.

"Sir?"

"Oh, not really," he said indifferently as he ran his fingers through his hair. "Those files contained photos of a project I've been working on."

"Project, sir?"

"A book. A book on rural cemeteries."

"Do you know who would want those photos, sir?"

"Hey, this is a cutthroat business I'm in," Sam smiled. "It was probably one of my competitors wanting to slow me down. You know the public can only afford so many coffee table books. If they buy my book on cemeteries, they won't buy somebody else's book on wild horses or the amazing world of mushrooms. This happens more than you realize. It's just that it has never happened to me before."

"Sir, do you know the names of these competitors?"

"No, it's anybody with a camera and an idea. Look, are you going to dust for fingerprints or something?"

"I don't think that would be of much use, sir. This was a professional job. They wouldn't have left any prints."

Sam stared at him in disbelief. A professional job? he thought. The guy crawled through Elle's dog door then went through the house with the finesse of a freight train. He may have been focused, but certainly lacked the precision and grace of a professional.

"I see this sort of thing every day in my job, sir."

Here comes the seasoned veteran speech, Sam thought.

"From Evergreen to Conifer to Pine Junction, it's an everyday occurrence, sir. You people move up here and think you're immune from crime."

The term "you people" caused Sam to raise his eyebrows. He had heard it before, usually from the blue-collar crowd and government services. It was class distinction, a form of discrimination that the haves and the have-nots often displayed to show their contempt for each other. "Not me," he said sarcastically, "I've always known that your ilk would eventually stumble upon me in one of their criminal forays from the city. I only wish I had been here to administer a sound thrashing with my polo mallet."

Joe Jr. looked at Sam quizzically. He was unsure if he had been insulted. Giving Sam the benefit of the doubt, he ignored the statement. "I'll need a detailed list of the missing items, sir. You can mail it to me or bring it by the sheriff's office."

"I'll bring it by first thing in the morning." Sam had no intention of supplying the sheriff's office with anything. He knew it was a paper exercise. At this point, he only wanted the offensive deputy, who resembled a sadist's Christmas tree, to jingle-jangle back to Golden. Sam had witnessed the ineptitude of small-town cops before. When Julie disappeared, they hadn't a clue of what to do. They were too embarrassed to ask for help. Short on specifics, they spoke in vague generalities about their investigation. More comfortable with routine police work, they quietly gave up. When challenged by Sam's father, they cited lack of manpower, time, and money. They seemed immune from the little media attention that a small Front Range town could muster. Had the crime occurred a few miles to the south, the Denver media would have forced the issue. Had the people of Colorado known his sister, they would have forced the issue. Perhaps it was then that the seeds of a career in journalism were planted in his head. Truth and justice needed Sam Dawson. He had been righteous early in his career, but politics had stolen his sense of right and wrong, replacing it with the nebulous adulterations of spin. When he realized that he could no longer distinguish between fact and fiction, he dropped out. The camera, he believed, did not lie.

"Sir, I'll leave you a copy of our pamphlet on ten easy things you as a homeowner can do to prevent burglaries. One of those things, sir, that you might consider," he said as he rattled noisily toward the door and stepped around Elle, "is to get a dog."

Touché, Sam thought, the deputy has a sense of humor. "That's a wonderful idea. I can't believe I didn't think of that before."

He watched as the white cruiser disappeared down the long, winding driveway. A slight chill caused him to embrace himself, arms held tightly against his chest. He suddenly felt very alone. He was frightened and he was not ashamed to admit it to himself. Someone had violated him and in the process destroyed the confidence he had in his well-being. He was vulnerable.

Sleep did not come easily for him that night. Every creak and groan of a log home drying and settling caused his eyes to spring open. He held his breath in anticipation of something human. His thoughts were random, scattered images of a confused life. Images of suspects flashed before him. Who knew what he had stumbled upon? Why would they care? It was more than seventy-five years ago! What was the link to the present? Who could he trust in the future? When Blair's image appeared, he immediately went to the next image, mentally suppressing the possibility that she could be involved. At first he thought she had the perfect alibi. She had been with him the entire night. There had been unbridled passion. He had held her in his arms. He loved her. But why had he not called her to tell her of the robbery? He knew that the time of the robbery had not been established. He had gone straight from New Castle to Boulder the day before without stopping home. The robbery could have taken place before he went to Blair's. No, he almost shouted to himself. He would not entertain the possibility of her involvement.

His sleep was fitful, but at least it had been sleep until the phone rang.

"Hello," he said weakly.

"Sam? It's me, Blair. Were you asleep?"

"What time is it?"

"Eleven thirty. I've been waiting all evening so I could call you at eleven thirty."

"Why?"

"Payback, big fellah. What's fair is fair!"

"But I never did it maliciously. I always had a good reason," he said.

"Me too," she said seriously. "I've been thinking about what happened last night." There was a long pause and he did not know if he was to respond. "And I just wanted you to know that I've never done anything like that before. I mean, that spontaneous. Do you understand what I'm trying to say?"

"I think so," he said, rubbing his eyes.

"There's more," she said. Again she paused as if searching for the words. "Sam, I've never felt this way about someone before. What happened, happened. I couldn't control it." Again, silence. "I just wanted you to know that I care about you. I care about you a lot."

There was silence as Sam debated what to say. She had made a bid and he wanted to see it and raise her with an "I love you," but the emotional stakes were too high. He would call her. "I care about you too," he said weakly.

Again there was an uncomfortable silence. "Goodnight, Sam," she whispered then hung up.

••••

The flight to Cedar Rapids was crowded and noisy with squalling children strategically placed throughout the cabin, a reminder of why he preferred to drive.

Somehow amid the noise of humankind he fell asleep. He dreamed of Blair. They were making love in the berth of a Pullman, the train swaying gently from side to side, Blair on top of him, her hair tickling his face. People passed by in the corridor inches away; sometimes they brushed against the heavy curtain that concealed his and Blair's nakedness.

"Something to drink?" Blair asked.

Confused, his head leaning into the center aisle, he looked up at the flight attendant.

••••

For a small town, Cedar Rapids was sprawled over a large area. It was early afternoon when he passed the city limits and pressed northward toward Independence. The Ford from Budget held tightly to the road as he negotiated the sharp turns and steep hills of the eastern Iowa landscape.

Fall colors were in full bloom. The endless sea of golden corn undulated into the horizon.

True Iowan flowed from the pores of the office staff at the state hospital at Independence, friendly people who treated Sam without suspicion. They gave him the use of a small conference room and provided him with the records he requested. German chocolate cake, homemade summer sausage, and fresh Wisconsin cheese were brought to him in courses on paper plates. A clerk's birthday had prompted the staff to bring food, but Sam gathered that nearly any event would trigger a potluck.

Eugene Eris's signature appeared on hundreds of documents dated from the teens through the late twenties. Like Colorado, everything had been scanned on to CD-ROMS. He was unsure of exactly what he was looking for, but hoped that something would present itself. At 4:20 p.m. he found it. He did a keyword search from 1920 to 1930 and was stunned that he had not seen it before. A similar search from 1930 to 1940 and again from 1940 to 1950 yielded data in sharp contrast to his baseline search. During the ten years prior to Eris's death, seventy-eight female patients were diagnosed as pregnant.

Unlike his stolen files from Mount View, these records showed no uniformity or commonality among the women. They were all over the map, ranging in age from nineteen to thirty-five. Last names indicated a hodgepodge of ethnicities. Likewise, physical characteristics showed no pattern. Feeblemindedness seemed to be the catch-all diagnosis. Some indicated a condition of dementia praecox, and many were classed as idiots, imbeciles, or morons. He quickly counted sixty-two who had been taken to term with live births recorded. The same sweeping script was used in the narratives to mention pregnancy, almost incidentally, that described mental and physical conditions. Without exception, all babies born were female.

It was 5:30 p.m. when Sam emerged from the conference room. Doris, a middle-aged woman who had appeared to be in charge, was waiting patiently for him; the rest of the business office staff had left for the day. She furrowed her brow when Sam asked about the disposition of babies born to inmates.

"Our residents are not inmates," she said, staring hard into Sam's eyes. "In most cases they are segregated by sex, and extreme caution is taken to insure that no sexual behavior occurs between them."

"But what if it does," Sam said, "and a resident becomes pregnant?"

"It doesn't happen," Doris said without blinking.

"It happened seventy-eight times between 1920 and 1930 with sixty-two live births," he said, not backing down.

"Look, I just run the accounting functions here. But I've been here long enough to know that great care is taken to keep that sort of thing from happening."

"You've never heard of a resident becoming pregnant?"

"Mr. Dawson, I've been here twenty-three years. I've heard everything. From male orderlies having sex with eighty-year-old women in diapers, to virgins claiming divine insemination and going through false pregnancies. Believe me, I've seen it, heard it, or smelled it at one time or another. The place is a madhouse."

"If someone becomes pregnant—," Sam started, but Doris quickly answered before he could finish.

"The babies would become wards of the state. They're turned over to Human Services and placed for adoption. It's rare, Mr. Dawson, very rare."

"It wasn't so rare eighty years ago."

Doris looked at her watch. "You should come back tomorrow and talk with somebody in administration. You know, back then they sometimes institutionalized unwed women who became pregnant." She looked at her watch again. "Hardly seems fair, does it?" she added.

Sam wanted to argue the point that these women had been diagnosed mentally ill and committed long before becoming pregnant. But he could see that Doris was impatient to leave and defensively supportive of the institution.

"No, it wasn't fair," Sam said.

••••

"Blair? It's Sam."

"Sam," she said in a sleepy voice. "What time is it?"

"It's eleven thirty. Did I wake you?"

"Yes."

"Blair, are you awake yet?"

"I don't know. I'm hoping this is a dream and that I'm really sound asleep getting the rest I need before the killer day I have planned for tomorrow."

"Sorry, I didn't realize what time it was."

"I don't believe that for a second," she said. "Where are you?"

"I'm in Iowa, Independence, Iowa."

There was a moment of silence before she responded. "It's twelve thirty in Iowa, Sam."

"Yeah, I guess it is, but I needed to talk to you."

"Obviously," she said.

"Your kindly town father was a busy boy here in the Corn State. Frankly, I don't know where he found the time. I'm beginning to think there were two of them."

"This couldn't wait until tomorrow?"

"During the 1920s Eris presided over seventy-eight pregnancies resulting in sixty-two live births at the state hospital."

"Uh-huh. He was a doctor. That was his job," she said.

"I scanned the records clear up to 1960. He was off the charts in the twenties. I'll check with Human Services in the morning, but I doubt if there will be any record of adoptions. I have this sinking feeling that Oxford is Iowa's counterpart to Colorado's Cambridge."

"Jesus, Sam, you can jump to a conclusion faster than anyone I know."

"They were all girls, Blair," he quickly added.

"Who were all girls?"

"The babies. There wasn't a boy in the lot. And I think my mother may have been one of them. She was an orphan. She grew up in Oxford. That's why I went there in the first place."

"Where are you?"

He knew he had her attention now. As a geneticist, she knew the probability of sixty-two girls and no boys was a statistical impossibility. "I'm in the Overland Motel in Independence. What are you wearing?"

"Excuse me?"

"Just wondering what you had on."

"I'm in bed, Sam. I don't have anything on. Why?"

"I miss you. I wish you were here."

"You wish I was there naked?"

"I just wish you were here," he said in a serious tone.

"There may be a logical explanation for what you've found. Perhaps you've discovered only a single data set that was purposely skewed. The total lack of randomness is not a statistical anomaly. You're looking at one component of an experimental design. Don't jump to conclusions, Sam. And by the way, what are you wearing?"

"Standard issue boxers. Come to Iowa, Blair. I'll pick you up in Cedar Rapids. I really need to see you."

"Take a cold shower, Sam. I've got classes the rest of the week. I can't just pack up and fly to Iowa to chase after some warped notion that—"

"Would you come to Iowa to see me?" he interrupted.

"Yes," she said softly.

"But?"

"But you're a crazy person who scares me with your fantasy games. Furthermore, you better stop calling me in the middle of the night. Goodnight, Sam. Call when you get back to Colorado, preferably during waking hours."

Sam heard the gentle click of the receiver as Blair hung up the phone.

He stared at the ceiling of the darkened room. A blinking neon light from Bob's Always Open Cafe across the street produced a flashing wedge of light through a gap at the top of the curtains. His odyssey played out in a collage of visual fragments: Sarah Adams, a teenager escaping from a converted stable; his mother as a young girl twirling and dancing with other orphan girls in Oxford. He quickly interrupted the realization that Eris might be his grandfather with the image of Blair. He had wanted to tell her of the break-in and burglary at his house. The fact that he did not troubled him.

CHAPTER SIXTEEN

IT CAME UPON US BY DEGREES.
WE SAW ITS SHADOW WHEN IT KISSED HER.
THE KNOWLEDGE THAT OUR GOD HAD SENT
HIS MESSENGER FOR OUR SISTER.
EPITAPH
—SYLVIA P. MCKENDRICK

THE SUN HAD BEEN A THIN, PINK LINE between earth and sky when Sam left Independence. The morning was chilly and smelled of silage and feedlots. Tidy white farmsteads surrounded by trees dotted the rolling hills on both sides of the highway. In the small town of Jones, the pickup trucks were lined up neatly in the gravel lot of the Tenderloin Grill, suggesting the local farmer hangout. He decided to stop, remembering there were no services in Oxford a few miles away.

It could have been 1955. Classic Americana was more than an ambiance in the grease-smoked air of the cafe. Men in bibbed overalls and seed caps, men with potbellies that tugged their trousers down below the cracks of their butts as they leaned over the breakfast counter. The smell of bacon, eggs, and coffee was so strong that Sam's stomach gurgled loudly as he slid into the only available booth. A round, little farmer not more than five feet tall in Key overalls and in bad need of a haircut turned toward Sam and said, "Say, you know why fire departments have Dalmatians?" Long gray hairs grew from both the insides and outsides of the little man's ears. His face was reddened and elfish. Before Sam could respond, the farmer blurted out, "So they can find the fire hydrants."

Sam grinned and nodded. The man then turned toward the waitress behind the counter, a strikingly attractive woman who Sam thought looked a little like Blair, only a few years younger and with brown hair. The elf was reciting a story about a farmer who tells his wife that her butt's as wide as a nine-row corn picker. His voice was too high and he spoke much too fast, lacking any sense of joke-telling rhythm. But he was obviously amused by his own performance, turning toward other patrons for reinforcement. The punch line was the wife saying, "You don't expect me to start up this expensive piece of machinery to shuck one little ear of corn, do you?" The furry-eared farmer squealed with delight at his own joke and repeated the punch line twice more.

No one paid any attention to the man, including the waitress, who walked away without expression. She brought Sam coffee without asking and took his order without benefit of a menu. Four middle-aged men in the booth behind him were engaged in an intellectual debate about Saturday morning cartoons.

"Whatever happened to the good old days when the Road Runner beat the stuffing out of Wile E. Coyote? Or, when Tweetie Pie electrocuted Sylvester? Now, Saturday morning kids shows are filled with a bunch of milk-toast characters teaching nonviolence. Whatever happened to animal characters that could talk or light a fuse?"

Sam smiled with amusement as their conversation drifted toward the liberal media, Hollywood's fascination with
homosexuals, and the always nebulous Trilateral Commission, which was run by old-money New Yorkers.

He was mopping up the yellow remains of his eggs with
a piece of wheat toast when the waitress brought him more
coffee and the morning paper. It was a countywide paper in
small-size format, eight pages of local information that turned
his fingers black. The headline on page three caught his attention: "Oxford Harvest Day Parade Selects Queen." A picture
of Annie Dillon, an elderly woman supporting herself with a
cane, appeared below the headline. She was smiling broadly
beneath the sparkling tiara perched in her pure-white hair. A
short article about Annie Dillon gave the usual biographical
information. She had been a resident of Oxford since 1922,
the daughter of, the wife of, the mother of, now living at
Riverview Acres in Dubuque. What was unique about Annie Dillon was the fact that this was the second time she had
been selected Queen of the Oxford Harvest Day Parade. She
had reigned as Queen in 1941 at the age of nineteen, less than
three months before Pearl Harbor. Bold print indicated the
article was continued on page four.

"Can I get you anything else?" the waitress said, returning with more coffee. She was smiling, a smile with an uncanny resemblance to the one on Annie Dillon's face.

Sam could not take his eyes from the pretty young woman. "No, just the check."

"She's my grandmother," she said, nodding toward the
newspaper.

"You both have the same smile," he said, slightly embarrassed, glancing back at the photo of Annie Dillon. "I didn't mean to stare. If I were any older, you might accuse me of leering."

"Oh, that's okay, I'm flattered. Turn the page if you want a real shock."

Sam flipped to the center section. Centered at the top of the page was a grainy black-and-white photo taken in 1941 of Annie Dillon, who was wearing the same tiara. He suddenly felt weak, his heart raced, he steadied his trembling hands against the table.

"That's Nana when she was eight years younger than I am now. What do you think? See any resemblance?"

"She's beautiful," Sam said without thinking, his voice breaking. He looked nervously at the waitress, "Yes, the resemblance is amazing."

The waitress blushed and appeared at a loss for words. Indirectly, he had just told her she was beautiful, an unexpected compliment from a total stranger.

"You must be very proud of her," Sam said, attempting to relieve the awkwardness of the moment.

"Yes, Nana is a dear. We've always been very close."

"Hey, sweet pea, what's a guy gotta do to get some more coffee around here?" a smiling farmer called from the counter.

"I'll be right there, Milt," she replied over her shoulder. Turning back to Sam, "I've got her with me for the weekend. The parade's at noon today in Oxford if you want to see her in person." She started to walk away then stopped and turned to face Sam, an Annie Dillon smile on her face. "I'm Annie too. And thanks for the compliment. A girl needs one every now and then." She then made her way back to the counter, apologizing to Milt for making him wait.

Sam started to lift the coffee cup, but quickly placed it back in the saucer. His hands were too unsteady; the black liquid sloshed over the edges of the cup. He stared at the nineteen-year-old Annie Dillon, admiring her the way he had the first time he had seen her: her long, slender neck with the mole low and to the left, her eyes shining, a young woman with her entire life ahead of her. It was the same woman who stood behind her parents in the framed photograph on Blair's library table. "Little Orphant Annie's come to our house to stay," he said softly, gazing out the window, but seeing nothing.

••••

He did not remember the drive to Oxford. It had magically occurred while his mind raced in other directions. A frustrating call to the Iowa Department of Human Services yielded what he had expected. There were no records of adoptions from the 1920s that could be traced to the state home.

The picture of Annie Dillon haunted him. Logical explanations seemed illogical. The most plausible interpretation was one that he had been thinking about for some time. He reasoned that the human gene pool was actually somewhat limited. There were only so many phenotypic combinations. Everyone he encountered looked, at least partially, like someone else he knew. He called them morphs. It was primarily facial characteristics that reminded him of a past or even present acquaintance. Body size and shape had little effect. He was unsure of the influence hair had, but knew color was unimportant. Even facial hair seemed to play a minor role. He assumed that the older he became and the more people he met, the greater the likelihood of recognizing a morph. He engaged in games, while sitting in boring meetings or while in a restaurant or airport, of pairing as many people in the room as he could with their morph. He tried to determine what characteristics the person possessed that were similar with those of someone else he knew. He quickly discovered that it was not only physical similarities, but behavioral likenesses that triggered the association. Often there were subtle mannerisms that he had observed in other people. Behaviors that, perhaps, in combination with shared physical traits, triggered the recognition. Small eyes, beak-like noses, no chins, thin lips, tight faces, horse faces, dog faces, crooked Quasimodo-like faces. Everybody looked like somebody else. But Annie Dillon looked exactly like Annie Tennyson. If they were not the same person, they were twins.

••••

The Oxford cemetery was as he remembered it, small, but eloquent and well-maintained. The midmorning sun was too harsh for shooting the high contrast photos he pre-

ferred, but felt good on his face and shoulders. The camera
body and single zoom lens that he brought were an excuse
to be there. He had seldom visited the same cemetery more
than once, especially one so far away. His first stop was at
the grave of Genève Defollett. Her picture sent a chill down
his spine and across the tops of his shoulders. "I love you,"
the carved hands signed. He had purposefully pushed to the
back of his mind thoughts about Genève, Julie, and all the
teenage girls' graves in the Cambridge cemetery. He knew it
was more than coincidental, but was still unclear as to what
the connection might be.

Unsure of exactly what he was searching for, he walked
among the graves noting names and dates. Women and girls
born in the 1920s were a red flag, but he saw nothing un-
usual. Most were buried next to their husbands. There were
far more dead husbands than wives, representing the ineq-
uity in longevity, he speculated. He knew that over a lifetime, people dispersed from the places where they were born
or raised. Some came back to be buried in family plots, but
most created their own families and identities. They wanted
their remains to be associated with the people and geogra-
phy of their new lives.

The Marshalls' graves were as he had remembered them,
low to the ground and simple, carved granite atop the remains of his maternal grandparents, dead before he was
born. So much death in his mother's life, he thought. She
was the strong one, at least on the surface. After losing Julie,
Sam noticed the little things that had changed. Dust where
it had never been allowed before, weeds that were tolerat-

ed, and a distance in her words told of her anguish. They never again talked of Julie. Sam accepted that when he was young. When he was older, it was too late, too remote. No one wanted or could articulate the pain. At his father's funeral, when the procession had moved to the cemetery, Sam discovered his sister's tombstone. The polished red granite rectangle, angled over her unfilled grave, presented Julia M. Dawson's date of death as the day she disappeared, two weeks short of her seventeenth birthday. There had been no mention of his parents' feeble attempt at closure. A single lot remained next to his sister's vacant grave.

Eris's grave was also as he remembered it. Standing in front of it, he felt his jaw muscles tighten with anger. If there was such a thing as a perfect crime, he thought, here lay the perpetrator. Sam looked at his watch and discovered it was nearly time for the parade to begin. He wanted to meet Annie Dillon, to talk with her, to determine what she knew, if anything, about where she came from.

Turning, he came face-to-face with the caretaker. "Christ, you shouldn't sneak up on people like that, especially in a cemetery," Sam said angrily. "Where's your shovel?"

"I ought to charge you admission," the old caretaker said with neither smile nor smirk from his flat salamander mouth. His beady eyes flashed from beneath his dirty green cap.

The old man's sudden presence made Sam flush with irritation. He was in no mood to play cryptic word games with a crazy person. "You can charge the media admission when they visit you in prison."

The old man stared menacingly at Sam but said nothing.

"I've a mind to get a backhoe and dig that dirty bastard up," Sam said, gesturing toward Eris's grave. "I'll need a DNA sample before this is over."

Still, the old man only stared at Sam.

"Complicity," Sam spat accusingly. "You and your littermate from Cambridge, the guardians at the gate, the keepers of the secret, you can both spend the few years left of your miserable lives stamping out license plates and showering with other men. But rest assured, you won't be forgotten. When I'm done with you, you'll be immortalized as an accomplice to one of the greatest mass murderers of the last century."

They stared at each other fully for five seconds, the old man seemingly passive, Sam rippled with anger.

"We'll be late for the parade," the salamander finally said then turned and walked stiffly toward the gate.

Sam watched him disappear over the hill. He brushed his fingers through his hair and exhaled loudly. "Who's the crazy person here?" he mumbled, shocked by his own explosive outburst.

● ● ● ●

Downtown Oxford was less than a block long, consisting of Olive's Fashions, Natalie's Nails, NAPA Auto Parts, and Nutrena Feeds. The rest was abandoned, boarded up in stark, weathered gray lumber. The feedstore served as the True Value hardware store, UPS shipping station, and

Oxford Real Estate Agency. From rubber mice and remote-controlled fart machines to truck tires and woodstoves, everything was crammed together in the most eclectic collection of merchandise Sam had ever seen. He bought a roll of film and a pack of Black Jack licorice gum that he had not seen in many years. He wondered if his mother had bought candy in the same store. He momentarily envisioned her there as a little girl, standing on tiptoe, pushing pennies across the wooden counter.

The parade was assembling at the far end of the block and would evidently move to Optimists Park at the edge of the treelined cemetery.

"You made it," the waitress said, squeezing beside him on the curb in front of the feedstore.

At first he did not recognize her. She had changed from her uniform into blue jeans and a white blouse, a blue sweater draped over her arm. She had released her long, brown hair from the ponytail she had worn earlier in the day. She was very pretty—no, beautiful, Sam concluded, and he was flattered that she had sought him out. She had Blair's eyes, flashing with intensity. Even her facial expressions were similar to Blair's, especially how the corners of her mouth turned upward into a warm and slightly sexy smile. "Wouldn't miss it for the world," he said, staring intently at her. "Forgive me for staring, Annie, but you remind me of someone I know in Colorado. Do you have any cousins?"

"That's the second time today you've stared at me, and yes, I have loads of cousins. Nana had six children who made her a grandmother twenty-two times and a great-grandmother many times over. I lost count years ago. Reunions are great fun, we have enough cousins for eleven-man football," she said, smiling broadly.

"Any in Colorado?"

"Why do you ask?" she said, smiling but tilting her head and wrinkling her brow.

"Your resemblance to my friend in Boulder is uncanny," he caught himself staring again. Looking down, he said, "Besides, my mother grew up right here in Oxford. You and I might be cousins."

"Really?" she said, raising her eyebrows.

He wished he had not brought it up. "Well, probably not genetically related cousins," he said, attempting to cover up his disclosure. "She was an orphan. She never mentioned adopted siblings, but it's possible."

"What was her maiden name?"

"Marshall," Sam said.

"Boy, that doesn't ring a bell with me. You might ask Nana. I'm sure she would know the family. But the answer to your question is no. Most of the family is within a couple-hundred-mile radius of good old Oxford. It's funny, we're a highly educated lot, doctors and lawyers and such, but pretty much all came home to roost."

"And you, why are you here?" Sam said.

"I honestly don't know. Trying to determine what's next, I suppose."

"Have you ever lived anywhere else?"

"Sure, I was gone for nine years. I went to school at Drake and picked up a bachelor's degree in molecular bi-

ology then a master's in environmental microbiology from
Southern Illinois University at Carbondale. I ended up in
Washington, D.C., developing policy for the President's
Council on Environmental Quality for a couple of years. I
hated it back there. I came home four months ago. I'm wait-
ressing at the Tenderloin to make ends meet while I figure
out what I want to do with the rest of my life. I'm much
older than I look."

Sam smiled. "You're not that old. As a matter of fact, I
can guess your age."

Annie's eyes widened a little. "You're on."

"And if I win?" he said.

"You get the prize."

Sam thought she was flirting with him, but was not sure.
"And what would that be?"

Her eyes sparkled and she smiled broadly at him. "Pie
and coffee, my treat."

"I'll have to look in your mouth."

"Excuse me?"

"To guess your age, I'll need to see your teeth," he said,
trying not to smile.

She whinnied softly, exposing a row of perfect teeth,
then covered her mouth and looked down, embarrassed by
her behavior.

"Twenty-seven," he said.

"You cheated."

"How's that?"

"You obviously counted the annual rings of cementum
on my central incisors."

"This morning you told me you were eight years older than your grandmother was in 1941. Annie Dillon was born in 1922. I'll be by the restaurant to collect my pie and coffee. And my name is Sam, Sam Dawson from Colorado."

"I'll still expect a tip, Sam Dawson from Colorado."

He stared at her for a moment. He wanted to tell her the best tip he could offer was to get out of Oxford. Suddenly the music blared with a teeth-grinding shrillness that caused him to wince and turn toward the parade that was starting down the street.

The Jones Junior High School Marching Band was playing something, but Sam could not tell what. Members of the Oxford Volunteer Fire Department clung to the sides of their shiny, lime-green fire truck, occasionally hitting the siren followed by the air horn. Old men with fake, white Springfield rifles and VFW campaign caps marched out of step behind the band. Kids with dogs, dogs with kids. A John Deere tractor pulled a hay wagon float stacked with agriculture's bounty and waving farmers who tossed candy at the children in the crowd. The mayor rode atop the backseat of a Mustang convertible, followed by several palominos that left a scattered line of horse droppings in their wake.

Annie Dillon rode in the backseat of a red 1959 Cadillac convertible, the huge tail fins with double rocket taillights rose from behind the car. The rhinestone tiara was nestled brightly within her snowy hair. She smiled and waved a bony hand at the crowd. She blew a kiss to her granddaughter, who caught it with both hands against her heart. The band's noise seemed distant and the cheering crowd was suddenly muted as Sam watched Annie Dillon pass by in slow motion. She wore her seventy-eight years and six children well. She appeared thin, not frail, slightly bowed at the shoulders. But her smile and strong blue eyes belied her age. He wondered, if Blair's mother had lived, how closely she would have resembled her twin.

At the park, Annie helped her grandmother from the car and gave her a hug. Sam stood back and took several pictures of the two of them, posing and hugging.

"Nana, this is Sam Dawson. He came all the way from Colorado to see the parade."

Annie Dillon extended her age-spotted hand to Sam and smiled. "It's a pleasure to meet you, Mr. Dawson, but I find it hard to believe you came this far just to see the Oxford Harvest Day Parade."

"No, Mrs. Dillon, I was here on other business, but when I saw your picture in the paper, I couldn't resist attempting to meet you in person. Your granddaughter was kind enough to make it happen."

The elderly woman looked at each of them, and Sam could tell she was trying to connect them somehow.

"We met at the restaurant in Jones this morning," Sam added before she developed any false conclusions.

"What is your business, Mr. Dawson, if I might ask?"

"I'm a photographer, Mrs. Dillon. I publish books of photographs. I'm currently working on a book about Iowa's cemeteries."

"Are you here to take pictures of the Oxford Cemetery?"

"Yes and no. I already shot the cemetery a couple of weeks ago. I was curious about a particular grave and I came back to get more information."

"And which grave would that be? Since I know a good share of the folks buried there."

"Doctor Eris," Sam said, not taking his eyes from hers.

"I know that headstone," the younger Annie said. "It's the one with the axe and log on top."

Sam did not respond but continued to stare at Annie Dillon, waiting for her response, waiting for any clue that she knew what may have happened in Oxford so long ago.

Annie Dillon only smiled politely then turned toward her granddaughter. "My dear, I'm supposed to go to the gazebo so the mayor can introduce me. You know, I could tell a few tales about him when he was younger."

Annie took her grandmother's arm and led her toward the center of the park, where the band had gathered and the mayor waited.

The Mayor talked about the importance of agriculture and lauded the community's farm families. He then introduced Annie Dillon, gave a biographical overview, and listed her civic contributions. Annie was relaxed and addressed the crowd in a familiar tone, calling many individuals by name. She was brief and appreciative. The crowd loved her. Her granddaughter, standing next to Sam, beamed with pride.

Watermelon, fried chicken, horseshoes, and softball presented a scene straight from a Faulkner novel, Sam thought, as he sat at a picnic table beneath a giant oak tree, its leaves golden brown. The younger Annie had insisted that Sam join them at their picnic lunch that both Annies had prepared. The conversation was light with no discussion of physical ailments or the shortcomings of friends and relatives. After lunch, granddaughter Annie circulated among the families as she greeted people, laughed, and smiled. Annie Dillon looked across the table at Sam and studied him.

"I can remember Doctor Eris," she said suddenly. "I was just a young girl when he passed away, but I remember him. He always had a piece of candy and a gentle pat on the head for me when he visited."

Sam returned her stare but said nothing. She was old, but not frail, he determined. He sensed a leathery toughness beneath her aged exterior.

"I have a strong suspicion that you want more than a photograph of Doctor Eris's headstone, Mr. Dawson."

"I want to know what happened here in the 1920s," he said quickly. "My mother, Agnes Marshall, grew up here. She was an orphan adopted by the Marshalls. That's all I know of her life in Iowa. She never talked about it and I was always too busy to ask. She's been dead almost ten years and now I'm finding out she was not the only orphan in Oxford."

"I've often wondered what happened to Aggie," Annie said, a faraway look in her eyes and a slight smile on her lips. "She was one of the older girls, you know, a sweet girl, always so quiet." There was a long pause, her eyes turned glassy.

"When we were young," she continued, "before most left the nest and moved away, we lived in constant fear that someone like you would come along and expose us. We were ashamed. Our secret hung over this black bottomland thick as morning fog, but stayed in this valley. People in these parts respected our privacy. Sure there was talk, but only to each other, never to outsiders." She paused and looked toward the river where the fall colors fluttered to the ground. She tugged at the neck of her sweater and her eyes became glassy with tears. "There was a whole bunch of us, you know," she said, looking down.

"Are you cold, Mrs. Dillon? Would you like my jacket?"

She smiled slightly and shook her head.

"Yes, I know," he said, an acknowledgment to her last statement. "There were sixty-two by my count."

"My folks took in five themselves. With two of their own, they had their hands full. The state built us a new school to handle the crowd of children that flooded our one-room schoolhouse."

"You must have had one heckuva girls' basketball team."

"We didn't have organized sports for girls back then, Mr. Dawson. But yes, we had all-girl basketball and baseball teams. We were quite athletic. The handfuls of boys in each class were in hog heaven. We wondered why there were only girls. We figured the boys were probably in another town somewhere, kept separate so as to not pass on any mental illness."

"There were no boys, only girls," he said.

She raised her eyebrows in surprise.

"Even if there had been, none of you were related to the inmates of the state home."

"I don't understand, Mr. Dawson. We assumed our real mothers, and perhaps fathers, were locked up at the insane asylum."

Sam hesitated, looked away, but saw nothing. Turning back he looked directly into Annie Dillon's eyes. "Do you really want to have this conversation, Mrs. Dillon?"

"I've lived a long time, Mr. Dawson. It's been a wonderful life. I doubt there is anything you can tell me that can change that. I am who I am." She smiled and reached across the table and took his hand in hers. "You can't change that," she repeated.

Sam cleared his throat and swallowed. "I'm not sure yet about your fathers, but your mothers were as normal as you and me and lived in Colorado. The women who gave birth to you were surrogates."

"Surrogates?"

"They were mentally ill, perhaps, but physically able to provide the warmth and nourishment necessary to carry a baby to term. They were incubators, not your mothers."

"Why?" she said, her jaw quivering slightly.

"I don't know for sure, a grand plan to improve the race perhaps. Eris was some kind of a genius with a forty-year jump on reproductive science." Sam turned away toward the crowd. Granddaughter Annie was standing, talking with a group of people. She looked beyond them, stared at Sam and her grandmother, a mild look of concern on her face. He needed to hurry. "Do you want more, Mrs. Dillon?"

"Yes, of course. Please go on."

"You had an identical twin in Colorado. I've seen her picture. I suspect you all had twins. They were reared in a little town, much like this one, in southeastern Colorado."

"I had a twin, Mr. Dawson?"

"She passed away last spring. Her name was Annie too."

"We looked alike?"

"Identical, at least when you were younger."

Tears formed in her eyes, spilled over and ran down her wrinkled cheeks. Sam handed her his handkerchief and she dabbed at her eyes.

"I'm sorry, Mr. Dawson. I guess I'm not as tough as I let on."

"I understand," he said, looking down at the table. Someone had carved their initials and date through the layers of green paint. "My mother may have had a twin too. It's all very confusing."

"A lifetime of missed opportunities is upsetting," she said. "I used to dream that I was somebody else who lived far from here. It wasn't me, you understand, it was somebody else. It frightened me when I was a girl. I thought it was the mental illness that only showed itself when I was asleep."

The younger Annie was making her way toward them, but was waylaid by a young woman who squealed with delight and began introducing her to several people.

"Annie, can you tell me anything about the caretaker at the cemetery?"

"Fred? Fred Tennyson? Actually his name is Alfred. He's got at least ten years on me. He's a bit loony now, but he's always been a little different."

"Alfred? Alfred Tennyson? Does he have a middle initial?" Sam said, shocked.

"Yes. It's L of course, but it doesn't stand for anything, just an initial. We used to call him Lord Tennyson behind his back when we were girls."

Sam had to look away for a second. The names were beyond coincidence. "Who pays him to care for the cemetery?"

"I don't know. He's had that job for as long as anybody can remember. I suppose the town pays him, or the cemetery district. He was Doctor Eris's protégé, you know. After the Doctor died, it was Fred who came to visit my parents every month. He was a young man then and we girls all had a crush on him. But he was always so serious. He never married. He could have had the pick of the litter with so many girls and hardly any boys around."

"Your parents were paid for caring for you?"

"We were just girls. We didn't pay attention to things like that. In later years, we realized that someone had been paying our father. We always had the things we needed, even during the Great Depression; we had plenty to eat and new clothes. All the girls did. When we graduated from high school, which you understand was rare, especially for girls in those days, we all had the opportunity to attend college. Our families had established a trust for each of us for tuition, room, board, and a fairly generous allowance. I met my husband at the university in Ames. We were married for half a century," she said, a faraway look in her eyes. She paused and then began again with a tired voice. "My father farmed three hundred acres of corn and oats and raised a few hogs. He didn't send us all to college on farm earnings."

"Where do you suppose the money came from?" Sam said.

"We assumed it came from the state. No one ever talked about it. The rumor was that Doctor Eris came from old English aristocracy."

"I've heard that before," Sam said, remembering his conversation with the caretaker of the Cambridge cemetery in Colorado. "Were there any records? When your parents died, did they leave anything, any record of transactions?"

"No, there was nothing out of the ordinary. They were simple and loving people who led uncomplicated lives. Their estate was divided evenly between us children. They were good parents, Mr. Dawson. They cared for us and loved us as their own. It wasn't just a business proposition, you understand." The old woman paused. She looked directly into Sam's eyes, her head shaking with the minute quivers of palsy. "Are you looking for your mother, Mr. Dawson?"

Sam stared back, searching her eyes, surprised by her question. Was it that obvious? Of course he was looking for his mother. Why else would he be here? As much as he tried to suppress what he knew to be his true motivation, it was always there, just one layer down. Sure he was curious, but curiosity was no justification for this obsession. He had screwed up, made the wrong decision, and had paid the price for ten years. Consciously or not, he was attempting to absolve his guilt of not seeing his mother before she died. He still had no idea of who she was, where she had come from, and how she had arrived in this world. Adding to his depression was the realization that he was somehow linked to all he had discovered. Each time the thought presented itself, he quickly changed the subject. But there was little doubt that Dr. Eugene Eris was his maternal grandfather. Blair was his cousin.

"Mrs. Dillon, there's a girl in that cemetery," Sam said, nodding toward the line of oaks on the other side of the park. "Her name was Genève Defollett. Can you tell me anything about her?"

"Oh my, Mr. Dawson, that was such a long time ago, more than thirty years, I believe."

"But you remember her?"

"Yes, of course. Everyone who was around here at the time remembers Genève. The poor girl was deaf and was losing her sight too. Such a shame! She was a very pretty girl. The Defolletts were good people, an old family that homesteaded here. They were French Canadian."

"What happened to her?" Sam asked.

"Genève was in high school. One day she got off the school bus, walked across the highway to get the mail, and a few moments later was struck and killed by a hit-and-run driver. The family and the entire community were devastated. She was such a sweet girl, everyone loved her," she said, pausing, remembering, her eyes filled with new tears. "They never found the driver or the car. Why are you interested in Genève, Mr. Dawson?"

"Nana, are you all right?" her granddaughter said, looking at Sam accusingly.

"Yes, dear, I'm fine," she said, dabbing her eyes one more time before returning Sam's handkerchief. "I was just taking Mr. Dawson with me on a walk down memory lane. I'm afraid I became a little emotional at some of the remembrances."

"We're here to have fun, Nana, not cry. Remember, you're the queen. You must uphold the dignity of your position." She straightened her grandmother's tiara then turned toward Sam. "And you, Mr. Sam Dawson from Colorado, you better quit upsetting my grandmother or there'll be no pie for you."

Sam smiled apologetically. "Yes, ma'am," he said, extracting his long legs from beneath the picnic table. "I think I'll circulate a little. I'd like to find Fred and have a meaningful conversation before I die."

"Fred?" the younger Annie said.

"Fred Tennyson," her grandmother said, slightly rankled.

"Good luck. The guy's goofy," granddaughter Annie said, smiling.

••••

"Hi, Sam," Blair said matter-of-factly.

"How'd you know it was me?"

"Who else calls me at eleven thirty at night?"

"Sorry, I lost track of the time. I didn't realize it was so late. Did I wake you?"

"Yes. What do you want?"

"I don't know. I guess I just wanted to hear your voice."

The line was silent.

"I met some people today," he began, but did not know how to proceed.

"And?"

"You would enjoy meeting them."

"Sam, I'm not coming to Iowa."

"I know. I'll be back soon. I'll show you the pictures."

"What pictures?"

"Oh, nothing of importance, just some scenic and human interest shots that you might like."

"Sam?"

"Yes."

"Are you all right?"

"I'm fine, why?"

"You sound a little down."

"Just tired, I guess. It was a long day. I needed to hear a friendly voice, that's all. Sorry I bothered you."

"That's okay. When are you coming home?"

"Soon as I get things cleaned up here," he said, looking around the motel room. The neon sign from across the street rhythmically illuminated the room's disaster. Overturned furniture, foam rubber from sliced-open pillows, the contents of his luggage strewn about the room. He doubted if anything was missing. They intended to send him a message, to intimidate him with a violent display of their seriousness. He swallowed hard. The disappointment he felt made breathing a conscious effort. Tears formed in his eyes.

"Where are you again?" she said.

"Independence, Iowa. Remember? I told you the other night. You're the only person who knows where I'm staying."

CHAPTER SEVENTEEN

WE CANNOT TELL WHO NEXT MAY FALL
BENEATH THE CHASTENING ROD.
ONE MUST BE FIRST, BUT LET US ALL
PREPARE TO MEET OUR GOD.
EPITAPH
—WILLIAM F. CAMPBELL

HUGGING MARCIE WAS STRANGELY different. There was nothing sexual, even though he could feel the softness of her breasts pressed against his chest. She could have been a cousin or a family friend. He heard a hollow sound when he patted her between the shoulder blades. The same hollowness he felt in his heart for the memory of their past together. They had been married for six years, but now she seemed only familiar, someone with whom he had shared his youth. She had dedicated her life to transforming him into someone her parents would accept, or at least forgive, for marrying their daughter. A Methodist, Sam had never heard the term Jewish American Princess before he married her. He always smiled politely at the JAP jokes, but they were a little too close to home to laugh at. Her obsession with living the princess dream put him in serious debt. In an attempt to placate Marcie and her mother, he sporadically attended synagogue and even began the process of conversion. But it was more than religious ideology that stood between them. It was his inability to reconstruct his personality. He would not yield to their persistent attempts to shape him into someone he was not. Marcie and her mother had a copyright on *Guidelines for Guilt*. For six years they led him to believe that he was a shameless underachiever who did not deserve a woman like Marcie. He finally agreed and left.

Marcie had left a message on his answering machine that there had been an emergency and she was at University Hospital. With little sleep, Sam was in no mood for her usual theatrics. While he was sure it had something to do with her mother, he was unable to reach her on her cell phone. She had only given him the name of Dr. Chapman. He slowed his pace when he learned that Dr. Robert Chapman was a resident in the Speech and Hearing Clinic.

Marcie sobbed deeply. Mascara ran in black streaks from her eyelids down both cheeks. Just when he thought she had calmed down enough to explain what the emergency was, a nurse came into the reception area and told them Dr. Chapman would see them.

Sidney was losing her hearing. Sam was stunned. Sucker punched, he sat holding Marcie's hand, thinking that this could not be happening. A concerned teacher had referred Sidney to an audiologist who, in turn, referred her to the Speech and Hearing Clinic at University Hospital where several tests had been conducted. All this had happened the week before, and no one had bothered to tell Sam. Now he had been summoned.

"At first I thought it was noise-induced hearing loss," Dr. Chapman said. "Not uncommon in this generation.

But when Sidney told me she was having trouble seeing, especially at night, my red flags went up. I sent her over to ophthalmology and they confirmed she's losing peripheral vision and has small clumps of pigment consistent with retinitis pigmentosa."

"Wait, wait," Sam said, holding up his hand to signal a time-out. "I thought she was losing her hearing. You're telling us she's going blind too?"

Chapman looked at Sam for a long moment. "Yes, I'm sorry. But understand that her particular condition is one that is progressively degenerative over a long period of time."

"How long?" Sam asked.

"It's hard to say. The hearing loss may stabilize for a number of years and then degenerate sometime in her late twenties or early thirties. Likewise, the degeneration of her retina is starting at the outer edge and working toward the center. Her macula may not be affected until she's in her sixties. We just don't know. The good news is that she has normal vestibular function. About half of the people with this condition have difficulties with maintaining their balance."

Marcie buried her face in Sam's shoulder and continued to cry. Sam felt weak, his ears burned, and his throat was scorched by the acid squeezed upward from a stomach that had been tied in a knot.

"Usher syndrome is a genetic mutation," Chapman continued. We recognize three subtypes. Sidney has the least common and the least severe."

"It's inherited," Sam said, straightening in his chair.

"Yes, it's an autosomal recessive. We did a swab on Sidney last week and the chromosomal mutation is there. Since it's a recessive, both of you are carriers, unaffected obviously, but carriers."

"I had a sister who was losing her hearing and sight when she was Sidney's age," Sam said, fear in his voice. "She died twenty-five years ago."

Marcie pushed away from him, a surprised look on her face.

"You had a sister?"

Sam nodded without looking at her.

"Again," Dr. Chapman interrupted, "the mutation is a recessive. Both of you are carriers. Assuming that you two are not related genetically, Usher syndrome is most prevalent in people of Jewish ancestry from central and eastern Europe, certain populations of French Canadians, people from Finland and from central England, Birmingham to be specific."

"My grandparents were Ashkenazi Jews from Hungary," Marcie said.

"It appears my maternal grandfather was from England," Sam offered. "But why did you say assuming that we were not related? What did you mean?"

"Consanguinity or having a common ancestor really increases the risk factor for transmitting the condition. Of course, that's the situation with many heritable diseases. That's why most societies frown on inbreeding."

Everyone was silent as Sam and Marcie tried to grasp the enormity of the issue. Finally, Sam said, "What do we do?" his voice catching.

"Be thankful that your daughter will enjoy a long and relatively normal life. She'll eventually need glasses in order to read and we can fit her with hearing aids to partially restore auditory function. Aside from not being able to drive at night, she'll continue to have a normal adolescence and young adulthood. However, she's homozygous for the syndrome. I strongly recommend genetic counseling if she plans on having children." Chapman leaned back in his chair, his hands on his thighs. "I think it is important that you continue interacting with Sidney as normally as possible. Don't treat her like an invalid. Encourage her rather than discourage her when she wants to do things that you might consider beyond her abilities. You'll be surprised at how she makes adjustments to deal with her deficiencies. Sidney and all those close to her should learn American Sign Language as soon as possible."

Dr. Chapman continued his pep talk, but Sam had tuned out the medical straight talk with all its optimism for Sidney's future. Sam was hurting. He suddenly felt trapped, confined by his physical space and behavioral norms. He wanted to run, cuss, and scream, throw things, break things. How could he interact with her normally? He wanted to hold her in his arms and stroke her hair, kiss the top of her head and tell her it would all go away. They should have allowed her to go to the homecoming dance. He felt sick to his stomach with guilt. Mental images shot at him like jagged bolts of lightning. Julie, Genèvc Defollett, dead teenage girls buried in the Cambridge cemetery, and Eris, who somehow was responsible.

"Above all, treat her normally. You'll be inclined to feel sorry for her and yourselves. Don't," Chapman warned. "If you want your daughter to be handicapped, treat her like she's handicapped."

Marcie's mother rushed into the waiting room as Sam and Marcie were leaving. Mother and daughter became totally consumed with self-pity, their grief inconsolable. Sam left the light-green antiseptic clinic alone.

The elevator doors opened on the third floor and Ivan Manfred stepped in. He wore a white lab coat over a colorful Hawaiian shirt, blue jeans, and running shoes.

"Well hello, Blair's friend," he said, extending his hand.

"Sam Dawson. It's good to see you again, Doctor Manfred," Sam said, taking his hand. It wasn't good to see him again. The last thing Sam wanted was to see anyone he knew.

"Call me Van. What brings you here, Sam?"

"An old acquaintance, nothing serious," he lied. "How about you?"

"Vicarious and completely artificial sex, eh," he said, smiling. "I spend a couple of half-days a week at the fertility clinic here," Manfred said, reaching into his coat pocket and pulling out a tin of Copenhagen snuff. "Pinch?" he said, extending the can to Sam.

"No thanks, I'm trying to quit."

"How," he said, placing the tobacco inside his lower lip, "goes your quest? Did you ever find whatever it was you were looking for?"

"Oh that. I'm afraid it was a bit of a wild-goose chase. You were right, the technology just wasn't there in the

1920s. But I learned a lot. Thanks for taking the time." The elevator doors opened on the first floor and they stepped into the bright openness of the lobby. "I did have one more question that I thought of later. Let's see, what was it?" Sam said, stopping and lowering his head in thought. "Oh yeah, I remember. You know when you talked about inducing ovulation with gonadotrophin or something like that? You mentioned that you got it from horse or pig pituitaries."

"Equine chorionic gonadotrophin or follicle stimulating hormone from swine," Manfred said.

"Right," Sam said. "Why couldn't you get it from humans?"

"Theoretically, you could. But you'd screw up a live person and there just aren't enough organ donors out there to provide a reliable source. Plus, there's no need. Hardly anybody relies on swine or horse pituitaries anymore. The hormones, which are basically pretty simple carbon molecules, can be synthesized in the lab. And, you can make big batches of it, which beats the hell out of munching up pig brains in a blender all day."

"But how would you get it out of a human?"

"Well, you'd want the adenohypophysis or anterior pituitary. Embryonically, it develops from the roof of the mouth. It's right there at the posterior base of the forebrain. I'm no neurosurgeon, but if I wanted to extract it from a live patient, I'd go through the nose. It's a frigging bloody mess, eh. You have to separate the upper lip and nose from the skull, basically pulling their lip up over their eyebrows then going in through the sinus cavity. On a cadaver you'd do a frontal craniotomy where the whole front quadrant of the skull is removed. Looks a little nasty, but you can jerk the brain out virtually intact."

They stepped away from each other to allow an elderly woman in a wheelchair, pushed by a teenage boy who looked like a Latino gang member, pass toward the elevators. "It sounds like a lot of work just to get some eggs," Sam said, stepping back toward Manfred.

"There's an alternative, you know."

"What's that?"

"Wait for them to come skidding down the oviducts on their own. It's a little hit-and-miss and you have to screen for them, but they'll show up once every twenty-eight days or so. Personally, I prefer to send out a search party."

"A search party?" Sam asked.

"Yeah, a few million of those tail-wagging, gung-ho little gangbangers. If there's an egg in that jungle, they'll find her."

"Jesus, Van, you ought to write children's books with your ability to reduce complex subject matter to something so simple," Sam said.

"I could be a regular Doctor Seuss, eh. How about *Green Eggs and Slam Bam Thank You Ma'am* for a title?"

Sam shook his head and forced a smile. "You take care, Van."

"You do the same, Sam."

Sam's eyes burned with tears. He walked absently through the visitor parking lot remembering the look on Sidney's face when he held her in his lap and read Dr. Seuss books to her. He had no idea where he had parked his truck.

CHAPTER EIGHTEEN

*NOTHING NEITHER GREAT NOR SMALL
REMAINS FOR ME TO DO
JESUS DIED AND PAID IT ALL
ALL THE DEBT, I OWE*
EPITAPH
—AGNES MACGREGOR

HELLO?"

"Annie?" Her name was Annie George. With a mouthful of blueberry pie, he had asked for her name and telephone number before leaving Iowa.

"Yes."

"This is Sam Dawson from Colorado."

"Hi, Sam Dawson from Colorado. It's good to hear from you."

"I know it's only been a couple of days, but I was wondering if you could do me a big favor?"

"Sure, Sam. What is it?"

He liked Annie George. She was easy to be around. There was some tension, he believed. After all, she was extremely attractive. But the ten years that separated them seemed to allow for a comfortable relationship. Sex and all the emotional baggage that came with it were not in the equation. She was refreshingly honest.

"Do you remember me asking if you had any cousins in Colorado?" Sam said.

"Yes, and I said they all lived in this part of the country."

"I believe you said most of them," he said, trying not to sound accusing. "Annie Dillon has six children, twenty-two grandchildren, and an unspecified number of great-grand-children."

"I'm impressed, Sam. You have an amazing memory."

"Those great-grandchildren are your second cousins, Annie. Is it possible that one of them ended up out here?"

"Sure, I suppose so. But, where's all this going, Sam?"

He was lying to her. The lie was getting bigger and harder to swallow. He wanted to trust her, to confide in her what he suspected, but he had to be cautious. Blair would be her aunt, and Annie would not accept that; neither would Blair. He needed hard evidence. "Annie, could you send me some of your grandmother's hair?" There, he asked her. He closed his eyes and waited for her response.

"What for, DNA analysis?"

"Yes."

"Wouldn't it be easier to ask someone if they're related?" she said.

"Been there and done that. I need tangible proof to convince this person."

"What person? To convince them of what?"

"A friend of mine. She's a geneticist and needs solid, scientific evidence that she has relatives in Iowa."

"Don't you think this is a little intrusive, Sam? Have you thought through the consequences?"

"Yes, I think so. You'll have to trust me."

There was a long pause.

"Is this geneticist my second cousin?"

"No." He closed his eyes.

"Then who is?"

"I don't know."

The line was again silent. "Sam, why are you making me play twenty questions?"

"Please trust me, Annie."

"I just met you. This could be some sort of con game."

"What? I'm going to extort pie from you?"

Sam heard her exhale loudly.

"Nana is still here. I'm taking her back to Dubuque tomorrow. I suppose I could borrow a few strands from her hairbrush."

"I'd be forever indebted. Try to get some with the follicles still attached."

"Sam?"

"Yes."

"I'm trusting you."

"I know, Annie. I won't do anything to hurt you or your grandmother. I promise."

"Sam, did you know it's eleven thirty at night?"

"I'm sorry. Did I wake you?"

"Yes."

"Will you remember this conversation tomorrow?"

"Tomorrow is only thirty minutes away," she said. "I'll be awake and I'm pretty sure I'll always remember this conversation."

••••

The cloudless fall day was crisp. Sam was glad he was wearing a wool jacket. The students were, as usual, under-dressed. Guys wore t-shirts without coats, girls with pierced navels preferred midriff blouses. Elle watched with droopy eyes and saliva hanging from the corners of her mouth. Blair saw them as soon as she stepped from the Richardson Building, briefcase in hand.

"Well, this is a surprise," she said, walking toward them. "And who is this?"

"Blair, Elle. Elle, Blair."

Blair petted Elle then tousled the bloodhound's ears.

"Elle?" she said, looking puzzled.

When people asked that, he usually responded by asking if they too thought the dog presented an uncanny re-semblance to Eleanor Roosevelt. But he had named her after Australian supermodel Elle Macpherson. He had found the dog walking down the side of a desolate eastern Colorado dirt road. At a market in Springfield he stopped to buy dog food and was drawn to the cover of a magazine at the check-out counter. It was one of the glossy periodicals that invari-ably had a beautiful girl on the cover exposing the bulk of her silicon-enhanced breasts. Filled with ads for beauty and feminine hygiene products and photo-filled articles about fashions that nobody wore, Sam determined they were de-signed to make the average American woman feel ugly, in-adequate, and self-conscious. This particular issue featured Elle Macpherson on the cover wearing a string bikini that looked as if it was irritating. Returning to the motor home, he smiled and shook his head at the wonderful comparison of his new travel-mate with the vision of Elle Macpherson still fresh in his mind. He named the bloodhound Elle. "It's a long story," he said.

"I was wondering when I would hear from you again," she said. "When did you get back from Iowa?"

"A couple of nights ago, but I've learned my lesson about calling you, so I thought I'd try to catch you during the day. Is this a good time?"

"Catch me? Sounds more like business than pleasure."

"With you, Blair, it's always pleasure," he said, smiling. "Can I buy you lunch?"

"This is Boulder, but I doubt any restaurant would allow that mass of wrinkles in the door," she said, gesturing with her thumb toward Elle.

"Ouch. I was hoping you could get past her exterior and see the beauty within."

"Sorry, but that's one ugly dog, mister."

"C'mon, Elle, we needn't stand here and be insulted."

"Tell you what, I've got a couple of hours before my next class. Why don't you and Elle come over to my house and I'll fix you a sandwich? She can play, or do whatever bloodhounds do, in the backyard."

"I'll meet you there in ten minutes," he said. They received curious stares from passersby as they hustled toward the parking lot. "We're in, old girl. Good job," he said from the corner of his mouth.

Blair greeted them at the front door. She had already kicked off her matronly shoes and removed her professorial jacket. She led Elle by the collar through the kitchen and out the back door. "She kind of smells like a giant beagle," she said, wrinkling her nose.

"She can't help it; she's a hound," Sam said defensively.

"Take your coat off. I'll fix us something to eat."

"I'm not really that hungry," he said, taking her hand and pulling her to him.

"Saaaam. Is this why you came to see me? You don't call, you don't write. I have no idea where you are until you suddenly show up looking like a love-crazed—"

He put his arms around her and covered her lips with his. Her resistance faded quickly and she returned the kiss with passion, her thighs pressed tightly around his right leg.

"Mongoose," she said, breaking off the kiss suddenly and finishing her sentence.

"And just where do you keep your cobra, lady?" he said, unzipping the zipper at the back of her tweed skirt.

"You just can't show up here in the middle of the day and—"

He again kissed her deeply. Her skirt slid silently to the floor as he pulled the ribbon tie from around her neck.

••••

Sam gritted his teeth with frustrated confusion, his knuckles white with tension as he drove the winding Highway 93 toward Golden.

Elle sat in the seat next to him, surprised by every vehicle that whooshed past them.

He thought he loved Blair. He wanted to love her without suspicion. The smell of her hair, the sound of her voice, the taste and texture of her ear made his heart race. He wanted to call her as soon as he had left her, to be with her constantly, to feel her next to him, the warmth of her body pressed against his. How could he love her and deceive her at the same time? he thought, glancing at the tissue protruding from his jacket pocket. If he went through with this, he would lose her forever. There had to be a better way. All he had wanted was a few strands of her hair, but they had never made it upstairs where her brush may have been. Blair had suddenly interrupted their passion with a quick trip to the guest bathroom. He suspected she was having her period. He found the tampon wrapped in tissue in the bathroom wastebasket. He fought back the lump that had formed in his throat.

CHAPTER NINETEEN

THE COLORADO BUREAU OF INVESTI-gation's Forensic Science Research Unit was sterile and bright. Young men and women in white laboratory coats, wearing safety glasses and latex gloves, moved quietly around the room. The week before, Bill Westbrook, the Director of CBI, was happy to receive a signed copy of Sam's book *Colorado Dawn* and introduced him to Michael Donovan, an anemic-looking young man with red hair wearing Buddy Holly glasses. Donovan was their DNA fingerprinting expert. Sam had received Donovan's call mid-morning asking him to stop by the lab to discuss the results of the analyses.

"I was able to isolate DNA from both the samples you provided me, Mr. Dawson," Donovan said as he closed the door to the small conference room that he had led Sam to.

"And?"

"And I performed a Southern blot, made a radioactive probe, and created a hybridization reaction."

"And?"

"And I came up with a number of very specific VNTRs."

"VNTRs?" Sam said, fearing that he was about to hear the watchmaking lecture again.

"Variable Number Tandem Repeats. Every strand of DNA has genetic codes that reveal how a particular gene developed. Do you know anything about exons and introns?"

Sam stared at him blankly.

"Each person has a particular pattern of VNTRs. It's this pattern that we call the DNA fingerprint. The pattern is inherited, Mr. Dawson. You get it from your mother or your father or a combination. It's unique. We can even reconstruct a parental VNTR from information found only with the children. VNTR pattern analysis generally has a very high probability of match, say one in twenty billion."

"Michael," Sam said sternly. "You're killing me, here. Are they related or not?"

"Absolutely, the DNA extracted from the hair follicle belongs to the parent of the individual from whom the vaginal epithelial cells were taken."

"Parent?"

"Yes, with a little more work, I can give you the sex if you want."

"No, it's a woman," Sam said, running his fingers through his hair, the image of Annie Dillon appearing in his mind, her tiara sparkling in her white hair.

Donovan glanced at the clock on the wall. His eyelids were ringed in pinkish red.

"I guess I'm just a little surprised," Sam said. "I thought you might tell me that she was an aunt or something."

"An aunt?"

"Yeah. What if the mother had an identical twin? Could you distinguish between the mother and the aunt?"

"I'm not following you. Are you asking if we can distinguish between identical twins when assigning parentage?"

"Exactly."

"Interesting question, Mr. Dawson. The answer is yes and no. They would, of course, have the same DNA chemical structure. Theoretically, there should be some differences, whether endogenous or environmental in the order of the base pairs. There are millions and millions of base pairs, you understand."

"Uh-huh," Sam said, pretending to understand.

"Every person should have a different sequence, and it's that sequence that is unique to the individual. It would take a very long time to identify those sequences. That's why we developed a shortcut method to look at the repeating patterns in DNA. We try to look at a few sequences that we know differ a great deal between people. It's that analysis that gives us the probability of a match. Those repeated sequences of base pairs are the Variable Number Tandem Repeats, in other words, the DNA fingerprint."

"Back to my original question, Michael."

"Well," he said, glancing at the clock again and pushing the dark frames of his glasses up the bridge of his nose. "Going in, if I knew the suspected parent was an identical twin, I'd ask for a DNA sample from the twin."

"The twin is dead," Sam shot back.

"Then I'd do a lot more VNTR probes. The larger the pattern I can expose, the higher the probability of showing the genetic match."

"But you've already said there was an absolute match using the standard number of probes. What if you didn't know of the twin's existence? What if the twin didn't know they had a twin? You just testified establishing parenthood."

"You're making too many assumptions, Mr. Dawson. The incidence of identical twins is very low. Even lower would be the question of paternity or maternity."

"I understand," Sam said, not wishing to challenge him further, but he was suddenly angry. "The point I'm trying to make is that I just blew a hole the size of a basketball through your once-in-twenty-billion probability against a wrong match. There's doubt here, Michael, and lots of it. I'd hate to be sitting on death row, convicted on evidence like this."

"I guess that's why we have a jury system of jurisprudence, Mr. Dawson. They get to hear the evil twin argument and then make an informed decision."

"They would only hear the evil twin argument if the suspect knew he had a twin," Sam said, looking at the clock too as a way to break off the conversation. "I'm late for another appointment," he lied. He thanked Michael profusely and pumped his arm until the kid's glasses slid down his nose as he attempted to smooth over his impatient behavior.

••••

Sam hated Capitol Hill in Denver: the traffic, the dichotomy of its people—rich, poor, and government workers thrown in the middle. He was reminded of the children's book, *Little Black Sambo*, where the tigers chased each other 'round and 'round, faster and faster until they turned into butter. He was on his third trip around the block searching for a parking place, getting angrier by the minute. His lack of patience bothered him. Since learning of Sidney's condition, he had become driven, a man obsessed with assigning blame. But he concluded it was his deception of Blair that made him most irritable. He had what he wanted. There had been no debate. Now there was remorse, but he had expected that. He tried to put it out of his mind with the logic that he should feel guilty only if he shared the information with Blair. What she doesn't know won't hurt her, he tried to convince himself. Besides, if it shed any light on what had happened to Sidney, it was worth the guilt he felt.

Barbara Sinclair was in a meeting. Cabinet officers spent most of their lives in meetings. When they were not attending meetings, they were traveling to meetings. The whole business seemed repulsive to Sam, now that he was on the outside looking in. Her secretary, Oliver, was new. His mannerisms and voice dripped with femininity.

"Ms. Sinclair's schedule is booked solid the rest of the afternoon," Oliver said. "Is there anyone else that could help you?"

"Could you slip her a note telling her that Sam Dawson is here to see her?" Sam said.

The young man dutifully obeyed, and seconds later Barbara emerged from her office, closing the door behind her.

"This better be damned important, Dawson," she said. "You've got a lot of nerve barging in here and interrupting my meeting."

He could tell she was bluffing. When she was really angry, her throat covered over with red blotches. "I was in the neighborhood, Babs, and was wondering if I could take you to lunch?"

The presumptuousness of his offer caught her off guard. The lawyer with a master's in psychology didn't know what to say. "Up yours, Dawson," she finally blurted out.

Oliver's eyes widened.

Sam smiled but said nothing.

She stared at him, her eyes flashing, nostrils flaring. Turning toward Oliver, she said, "Cancel my lunch with Senator Rossen." She looked at the door to her office then back at Oliver. "And tell that pack of bureaucratic anal sphincters in there that I've been called over to the governor's office. If they ask to reschedule, tell them not in my lifetime."

Sam offered his arm and she took it without hesitation. They walked silently from the office without looking back.

••••

Barbara Sinclair stared straight ahead without speaking. She appeared overdressed to be riding shotgun in Sam's pickup. He reached over and squeezed her hand but said nothing. He took her to the El Condor, a low-rent, family-owned restaurant on South Broadway that served authentic Mexican food, not catering to the yuppie-gringo perception offered by the chain restaurants. The Capitol Hill gang never made it that far on their lunch hour.

Barbara chugged her Dos Equis straight from the bottle and wiped her mouth with the back of her hand. "I wish I had the balls to do what you did, Sam. To just walk away, tell the state to stick it, and enjoy life."

"The fact that you even think about it tells me that you'll probably do it," he said, not taking his eyes from hers. "You'll know when the time is right."

"How the hell will I know when the time is right?"

Sam was caught off guard. He searched for a witty comeback. "I guess when you have enough money, or meet someone who does."

"Meet someone?" she said, shaking her head. "Christ, Dawson, I don't have time to shave my legs. When am I going to meet someone? That's a laugh," she said, lifting the bottle to her lips again. "What about you? Are you seeing someone?"

"Yes."

"Who? Anybody I know?"

"No, she's a professor at CU."

"My, my," she said with a tinge of mockery. "How do you communicate?"

Sam smiled but did not respond.

"I'm sorry, Sam," she said, reaching across the table and taking his hand. "I didn't mean to redirect at you. But thanks for being my punching bag."

"What's wrong, Babs?"

"The usual frustrations. The tight-assed conservatives in both houses are after my budget and the governor doesn't give a rip. The chief of staff and the budget director are playing politics for him. We're talking major cuts. These people haven't a clue as to what it takes to keep the doors open at institutions. On top of that I've got personnel issues that are about to turn ugly, nothing that a decent pay raise couldn't solve. At last count I had nineteen lawsuits pending, all naming me as the devil incarnate. My mother's ill, my tires are bald, and I'm about to start my period for the second time in less than a month. How was your day, dear?"

Sam chuckled. "That's why I like you, Babs. You make me feel good about my life."

She smiled and took another pull from the beer bottle. "Whew, I feel better knowing that I'm of service to someone. But you didn't come by to get a dose of feel-good, Sam. What do you want?"

He knew she was in no mood for him to play games. "I need your help. Again," he added with apology.

"Can I get fired?"

"Maybe."

"Great, I'm your gal. Shoot."

It was nearly three o'clock when Sam ran out of story to tell. He had told her everything except his suspicions about the genetic defect causing Usher syndrome. Barbara's eyes appeared glassy behind her too-thick glasses from the four beers she had drunk. Her face was red and shiny. Green chili sauce stained her blouse. She had listened intently with few

interruptions, eating two baskets of nachos and a beef bur-
rito, washing them down with beer.

"So, there you have it. What do you think? Can you get
it for me? Are you going to be sick?" he said.

"Jesus, Sam. This is all pretty incredible. It's fascinating
stuff that probably has a dozen other explanations. You're
suggesting some sort of conspiracy exists. I have to admit
that the salamander twins are a little beyond coincidence.
But the rest of it sounds pretty far-fetched. Eris was some
sort of zealot, I'll give you that, who may have adopted out
a set of twins or two. But to engage in the sophisticated, un-
derground activities you're suggesting sounds like a stretch."

"Can you get it for me?"

"Where's all this going? What is it that you want to
accomplish? Even if you found what you're looking for, it
would be a media circus. I need that like a hole in the head."

"Can you get it for me?"

"What's in it for me, you big jerk?"

"I'll make a few phone calls to some friends in the press
and we'll turn this run on your budget into political suicide
for anyone stupid enough to go there," he smiled slyly. "I'm
talking major pain and suffering here," he added.

"Now you're talking, buster. Give me a couple of days
and I'll see what I can dig up." Barbara Sinclair looked at
him with blurry eyes, smiled, and shook her head in disbelief that she had again been talked into helping him.

••••

There were agencies within agencies, boards upon boards, and commissions set up to study other commissions. There were subdivisions of state government that Sam had never even heard of after years in the governor's office, each with a board, commission, or agency that provided oversight, channeled state funds, collected mill levies, conducted elections, appointed representatives, certified or licensed people. He found state agencies that inspected carnival rides and ski lifts; a board of deans for the distribution of unclaimed human bodies; boards that licensed barbers, beauticians, veterinarians, electricians, and morticians. From pesticide applicators to butchers, there were state statutes established to govern their profession. He discovered it was against the law to give away ice cream, to let dust blow, and to sell cars on Sunday. Government had always been somewhat of an enigma to Sam, but he had never realized how encompassing it was, how pervasive it was in the lives of people who had no idea how regulated their goods and services were. He was reminded of the protection rackets of organized crime. For a fee, the state would protect your profession and regulate your competition. It was a cancerous mass of bureaucracy that thrived just below the surface of stately marble buildings. It espoused free trade and a market-driven economy while controlling both.

Sam yawned and stretched his arms above his head. The clock on the wall indicated a new day was about to begin. Volumes of Colorado Revised Statutes were scattered across the couch on either side of him. Elle lay in a melted heap next to the coffee table. He concluded that in spite of government's controlling complexities, it was an incredibly successful example of how to maintain social order. It worked. Perhaps better than any other society, America's form of governance worked and worked well.

He found the original eugenic sterilization laws. He found laws prohibiting miscegenation and laughed out loud with the discovery that not only was it illegal to marry someone of a different race, it was also illegal to cohabitate with a man or woman of a different race. He wondered if Marcie, being Jewish, would have been considered a different race. His question was quickly answered when he found a series of legislative acts adopted in the mid-to-late 1920s that followed the U.S. government's Immigration Restriction acts. Jews were listed as one of the "undesirable" groups that Colorado wished to restrict, along with most eastern European ethnic and racial groups. Italians brought to Colorado to burrow in the coal mines, and Chinese to build the railroads, were given specific mention in terms of restricting their admittance to the Centennial State. The narratives were sprinkled liberally with the words feeblemindedness, genetic defectives, social dependents, shiftlessness, pauperism, criminality, and inebriate. By the mid-1940s, with the social horror of Nazi Germany as the tragic backdrop, the eugenic and immigration laws were repealed.

He had not found what he was looking for and was about to give up when he decided to thumb through the statutes dealing with agriculture. He had saved them for last, giving higher priority to those involved with social services, institutions, health, and regulatory affairs. Agriculture, by far, was represented in statute more than any other entity or organization. Highly regulated and promoted, it was served disproportionately by government. Marketing, animal health and welfare, predator and rodent control, invasive plant species, pesticide laws, biological pest control, consumer protection, market orders, weights and measures—more than a thousand pages of duties and responsibilities of the Colorado Department of Agriculture and its commissioner. Sam was close to giving up when he stumbled upon the State Board of Stock Inspection, referred to as the Brand Board, one of the divisions of the ag department.

Sam had known the Brand Board was the oldest agency of state government, having been organized a dozen years before Colorado became a state in 1876. The agency was governed by a gubernatorially appointed board whose primary purpose was the enforcement of the state's livestock brand laws. What caught his attention was a reference to the establishment of a Eugenics Section of the State Board of Stock Inspection, created to represent Colorado with the American Breeder's Association in 1907. Amended in 1923, the section was given the added responsibility of preparing a report to the legislature titled *Eugenics: The Science of Human Improvement by Better Breeding*. The statute boldly proclaimed that human populations, like breeds of livestock, needed to be managed to insure genetic purity and fitness by encouraging only the healthiest individuals to breed while culling less-fit members from the population. Apparently the American Breeders Association, with experience in the selective breeding of cattle, had devoted itself to exposing the hereditary differences between races of human beings. The statute repeated the themes of positive breeding and controlling heredity in human populations. It warned of the biological threat of "inferior types" of people being allowed to propagate. The section was to manage and account for funds provided by the Race Betterment Foundation in Battle Creek Michigan, founded and funded by J. H. Kellogg.

"Jesus, Elle. This is where they hid it," he said, standing. "Leave it to the cowboys to hide it in the Brand Board." He ran his fingers through his hair triumphantly and began to pace around the room. Elle raised her head and opened one eye before going back to sleep. From his earlier research, he knew that thirty-three states had enacted statutes and either created agencies or assigned responsibility to existing units of government to oversee the involuntary sterilization of tens of thousands of Americans. There was a federal agency called the Eugenics Record Office, an International Eugenics Congress, the American Eugenics Society, and even high school and college curricula developed around eugenics as a legitimate science. But in 1923, Colorado was still run by the Colorado Cattlemen's Association. You didn't become a political figure unless the cattlemen endorsed you. He had heard repeatedly how the cattlemen had selected every governor of the state up until the 1960s. "They put it in the Brand Board," he repeated, smiling and shaking his head.

He guessed that the American Breeder's Association was the forerunner of the National Cattlemen's Association. His experiences dealing with the cattlemen and the Brand Board when he was in the governor's office were mostly positive. He found some to be occupational zealots interested in preserving their culture at everyone else's expense. They cast an aura of righteousness over themselves and professed God to be on their side. With a combative history first with the Indians, then with sheepmen, and finally with sodbusters, they fought anyone who threatened their use of the land, land that sometimes belonged to the public. Sam imagined that when it came to genetic fitness, the cattlemen volunteered the answers. Cigar-chomping, mustachioed, white males with cow crap on their boots had decided the fates of immigrants and orphans. He thought it ironic that the cereal magnate, Kellogg, a sodbuster of gigantic proportion, was the financier of a cowboy-run death squad.

The statute was cross-referenced with the Genetic Integrity Act and it referred to the Bureau of Vital Statistics in the Colorado Department of Health's statutes. There, he found what appeared to be Colorado's cross-references to the original eugenics and immigration acts. The Genetic Integrity Act directed the health department to provide pamphlets to those planning to marry and to ensure sexual segregation of the genetically unfit at the state's institutions. That statute was repealed in 1945 along with the original eugenics and immigration laws. But he found no amendments or repeals to the directive creating a Eugenics Section of the State Board of Stock Inspection. It was a vestige of an earlier time that had never been scoured from state law. The statutes were filled with the remnants of history. There were bounties on wolves, horse and buggy traffic laws, and capital punishment for someone cutting a barbed wire fence. By law, the Brand Board was to have a Eugenics Section.

Elle growled a deep, throaty gargling sound that Sam seldom heard. "What's the matter, girl?" he said, placing the heavy book of statutes on the coffee table. Glancing at the clock, Sam noted it was 12:37 a.m. Elle's head was up and her nose twitched. She was oriented toward the picture window in the living room, ears perked as best a bloodhound could perk them. There were no curtains in the entire house. He had no need for them. His reflection peered back at him, the darkness beyond the window a shiny, ebony mirror. "It's just the wind, girl." But there was no wind. "It's just a deer." Not likely at this hour, he thought. Elle growled again, this time rising to her feet. "Okay, it's Charles Manson. Let's check it out, girl," he said, rising and walking to the front door. Elle rushed out the door, her tail held high. This is the same dog that lets burglars crawl through her dog door, he thought. Sam turned off the lights and quietly slipped out the kitchen door. The night was cold and the stars bright in the moonless sky. Somewhere between the house and the county road, Elle gave voice, a melodious bay, the one she used when running a hot scent. Through the trees he saw the flash of headlights, a vehicle turning around in the driveway, the engine noise fading in the distance. When Elle returned she ignored Sam's words of praise and scented the ground at a run toward the front of the house. Sam followed. Elle worked the ground in frenzied circles, snuffling like a pig. She seemed oblivious to the one-gallon gas can sitting next to the front porch.

••••

It was a little past 1:00 a.m. when the phone rang, startling both Sam and Elle.

"Hello," he said, the weakness of his voice sounding strange to him.

"Sam?"

"Yes."

"It's Blair. Did I wake you?"

"No, I was just sitting here reading," he said, attempting to sound wide-awake.

"Rats. I was hoping to wake you up so I could claim some payback for all the times you got me out of bed."

"What about the times I got you into bed?"

"What about them?" she said.

"Don't they count? Are they on the positive side of your tally?"

"My accounting practices are none of your business. What are you reading?" she said in an obvious attempt to change the subject.

"A cowboy story," he said.

"I didn't know you liked westerns. What's it about?"

"It's about a cowgirl that falls madly in love with a handsome photographer."

"Yeah? How's it end?"

"Don't know yet. I'm only half-finished."

"How do you want it to end?" she said, a note of seriousness in her voice.

"Happily ever after, I hope."

There was a long pause. "I hope so too, Sam. Keep reading. Goodnight."

"Blair."

"Yes."

"Are you a member of the Colorado or National Cattlemen's Association?"

"Both. Why?"

"Just wondering. Goodnight."

CHAPTER TWENTY

TIS A LITTLE GRAVE, BUT OH!
HAVE CARE,
FOR WORLD-WIDE HOPES ARE
BURIED THERE.
EPITAPH
—ANNIE MAUD MCFALL

MARTA EISENOCH, A PLEASANT woman in her mid-sixties, volunteered on Wednesday mornings at the Colorado Historical Society. She quietly brought Sam everything he asked for without question. For that, he liked her. He had met Marta the week before when looking for a map of the grounds for the Colorado Mental Health Institute at Pueblo. The historical society was an important retail outlet for his books. The gift shop pulled in the Capitol Hill tourists and sold them Native American jewelry, wildlife and landscape artwork, historical nonfiction, and Sam's books of photography. Marta, who sometimes worked in the gift shop, was a lay historian with an encyclopedic mind. Her fountain of knowledge had already saved him considerable time and energy.

"Marta, I've found a cross-reference to another historical society record. Apparently, the burial ground for the Board of Charities and Corrections was recorded in the Pueblo public library as State Hospital Cemetery No. 2. The site number is 5PE527.6. Think we can find it?"

"Oh my, yes. I remember the controversy from a few years back," she said.

"Controversy?"

"Yes. The Department of Corrections was preparing to build a new building on the campus of the Mental Health Institute when they discovered an unmarked cemetery. The historical society's state archaeologist was called in."

"What was the controversy?"

"Oh, the controversy actually occurred in about 1899, if I remember correctly. It was called the Colorado Insane Asylum then. Their superintendent came under state investigation from allegations of mismanagement. One of those allegations had to do with the proper burial of inmates. During the legislative hearings there had been testimony from asylum staff that the dead had been buried on the grounds for many years. The superintendent emphatically denied the allegations and the joint legislative committee found nothing that substantiated the charges of mismanagement. Ninety-some years later, the archaeologist found between 120 and 140 people had been interred in an unmarked cemetery. The society cross-checked asylum ledgers with city death certificate records for the period and found nothing."

"Do you remember anything about who was buried there?"

"The skeletal remains and artifacts indicated they were inmates of the asylum. I remember they found a lot of striped wool fragments from their asylum-issued clothes."

"What were their sexes?"

"Both male and female, even a baby. It was the baby that helped trigger the scandal in the first place. There were accusations that the superintendent attempted to cover up the birth of a child between two inmates. The baby died within a short while and, according to witnesses, the child was buried on the grounds on orders of the superintendent. The superintendent, of course, denied all of this and was exonerated after the legislative inquiry."

"Any idea of when these people were buried?"

"They were all buried in the last twenty years of the nineteenth century."

Sam ran his fingers through his hair. "If this was Cemetery No. 2, there must be a Cemetery No. 1 someplace," he said, looking up.

"It was never found. They think it's somewhere near the powerhouse. The records are scanty and it doesn't show up on any of the maps."

"When was No. 1 used?"

"I would imagine from the late 1890s up until the late teens. They stopped burying inmates on the asylum grounds just after the great flu epidemic of 1918. I guess they ran out of space."

"What happened to all the bodies they dug up?"

"Oh, some are still in temporary storage, downstairs, here in the museum. Some went to a professor at Colorado College and I believe the county coroner had one or two. They were interested in finding out things like diseases, nutrition, injuries, and the like. They wanted to know the physical health of insane people in the nineteenth century, I suppose."

Sam located the powerhouse on the map. It was near the center of the campus. Cemetery No. 2, in the floodplain of the Arkansas River, was on the south end of the facility. Thumbing through the stack of maps and drawings on the table, he pulled one to the surface dated 1921. "Marta, I believe there may be another cemetery, a No. 3, somewhere near this building," he said, pounding his finger loudly against the map.

Marta lifted her half-glasses that dangled on a chain around her neck, to her nose. She peered down at the map, bending low to read the fine handwritten print. "The stable?"

Sam pulled out another map, an older one. "The stable shows up on this drawing, dated 1894," again, pointing with his finger. "Here it is again in 1921," he said, pulling the original map back to the surface. Then grabbing an aerial photograph of the campus taken in 1938, he said, "And, here we see nothing but an open field. The stable is gone, razed. I believe there is another cemetery somewhere between this stable and the river."

Marta studied the maps and again looked at the photograph. She slowly removed her glasses, peered at Sam, and smiled pleasantly. "Mr. Dawson, you've managed to find cemeteries in this state that few people knew existed. But there were always markers or headstones for you to photograph. What makes you believe there is a cemetery in that field?" she said, nodding toward the photograph.

"I didn't think you recognized me," Sam said.

"I've spent many hours upstairs behind the counter in the gift shop. I've admired your work for some time, Mr. Dawson. You have an amazing talent for capturing a mood along with the image. But, if I may, I'd like to suggest that you consider black-and-white as your medium sometime."

"Marta, I think I love you. Would you be my editor?"

Marta blushed and smiled.

"Has anyone else been here recently to look at these maps?" he said.

"Not on Wednesdays."

"Can I get a copy of this one?" he asked, pointing to the 1921 rendering.

"The best I can do without having it sent out for copying is to make you a letter-size copy of the portion you want."

"Shoot me the stable at one-to-one and a copy of the legend so I can get distances."

Marta disappeared to make the copy. He knew she was much too polite to press for an answer to her question about a third cemetery.

In his mind he could hear the frail voice of Sarah Adams: "The building itself was a converted stable. When it rained the smell of horses rose up from the floor...I hadn't gone far, crossing a grassy field, when I fell into a hole...I found a river, not far either..." There was a burial ground somewhere between that stable and the river. A burial ground that contained the genetic information needed to link the past with the present.

●●●●

"Damn it, Sam, why'd you up and leave me? I miss the hell out of you. We were a team," the governor said.

Der Fuhrer and Joseph Goebbels, Sam thought. "You've got an even better team now, governor. From what I read, your voter approval has never been higher." Sam had stopped by the governor's office to see Karen Steinkraus, the governor's appointments director. Sam wanted a list of the members of the livestock inspection board. But the governor saw him in the outer office and invited him in for a cup of coffee. Sam had had many partial cups of coffee in that office. Between the constant interruptions of staff trying to keep the governor on schedule, and the governor's extremely short attention span, a conversation and a cup of coffee almost never happened.

"What brings you to my neck of the woods, Sam?"

"I've discovered a sinister plot by state government involving rape, murder, and genetic engineering. I'm hot on the trail of the guilty bureaucrats. I think the Brand Board is somehow involved."

"Those bastards. They still think they run this state. Last election, I didn't get enough money out of the entire livestock industry to justify any representation on my part. I heard they're putting together a war chest to run Preston Holt next year. Can you believe that? I tried to reach out to the Republicans and the ag industry by appointing Preston commissioner of agriculture. How many Democratic governors do you know who would put a Republican on their cabinet? Dirty rotten pups. They're damn lucky I'm term-limited."

"I'll say."

Alice, the Governor's administrative assistant, opened the large wooden door just wide enough to stick her head in and look at the governor. She did not speak.

"Hey, Sam, it was good to see you," the governor said, standing and extending his hand.

Sam stood, his nearly full cup of coffee sloshing over the rim. "Good to see you too, governor."

"Sam," the governor called after him. "See Alice on your way out. She's putting together a book about my twelve years in office."

On his way out, Sam stopped by Alice's desk. He smiled broadly at her and said, "A book?"

She rolled her eyes, bit her lower lip, and exhaled through her nose. "Do you have anything you'd like to contribute? Stories, pictures, anecdotes, wonderful remembrances," she said in a flat monotone.

"Yeah, save space for the black-and-white I have of him at the cabinet retreat, the one where he's groping the policy analyst. What was her name?"

"Linda, Marcia, Natalie, Buffie, Teri, or Janet?" she asked with machine-gun precision.

"She was the one who had a lisp and groped him back."

"That would be Regina," she said, making it rhyme with vagina.

"Nothing could be finer," he sang.

"Great. Thanks, Sam. Will you write a narrative to go with it?"

"It would be my pleasure," he smiled and winked.

••••

Karen Steinkraus, a woman in her fifties with huge glasses and too much lipstick, gave Sam a current list of appointees to the Brand Board. Karen explained there was no geographic consideration, but they tried to get regional representation on the five-member board. There was a statutory requirement with two members from the minority party and one member from the cattle-feeding industry. It all seemed unremarkable.

"Karen, can I take a look at the historical list of appointees to the board?"

"Knock yourself out. They're all in that file cabinet. They're supposed to be in archives, but who has time to be that organized?"

"Thanks," he said, pulling open the file drawer marked "Stock Inspection Board." The files were unmarked. "How are they organized?" he called after Karen who was walking out the door.

"We use the cram-it method," she said seriously and disappeared into the hall.

It was nearly five thirty when Karen returned. "You want a job or what, Sam?"

"What's the process in making these appointments, Karen? Who makes the recommendations?"

"We get nominations directly into this office. Most often they're self-nominations. The brand commissioner makes recommendations to the ag commissioner who then advises me and the governor."

"Does anyone check for continuity or geographic distribution?"

"Are you kidding?" she said, placing a hand on her hip, her brow wrinkled. "Those appointments," she said, nodding toward the file cabinet that Sam was working on, "are for staggered four-year terms. They lop over from one administration to another. My job is a political patronage appointment. I raised money for him and campaigned hard to get him elected. He forgets my name all the time, but I've stuck with him for longer than most, nearly two years now. The turnover in this job is huge. Combine that with the fact that the commissioner of agriculture, who advises the governor on these issues, has an average tenure of about a year and a half, it's a wonder we even get these appointments made."

"What about the brand commissioner? Is there turnover there too?"

"Those guys are dinosaurs. There have been maybe four of them since the turn of the century. It must be the Copenhagen they chew. They live forever."

"By the way, you've got an open seat on the board. I only found four names on the current appointment list."

"Not on your life, Mr. Smarty Pants. I'm current on all board appointments. I just haven't had the time to update the list."

"You're amazing," he said, patronizing her. "I don't know how you remember who goes where and when."

"It's called a computer, Sam. But this one I remember. The governor jumped on it like a chicken on a June bug. This board had been all white male since Moby Dick was a minnow. Our most recent appointment is a woman. I liked to have had a heart attack." She pulled a manila folder from a file organizer on her desk and handed it to Sam.

He opened the file, scanned the application and handed it back to her. "Thanks, Karen. I appreciate your help," he said, closing the file drawer and gathering his notes. She said something in response, but he did not understand. He heard her voice and saw her lips move, but his mind raced and his ears rang; her words were unintelligible. He noticed his hands shaking as he fumbled for his keys when he reached his truck more than a block away. He had no recollection of walking there. Names and addresses flashed in his mind. The word Cambridge appeared over and over in his mind's eye, burned there indelibly from file after file where the board members listed their address as Cambridge. There had been continuous representation on the Brand Board by someone from Cambridge since 1920. The latest was Blair Tennyson.

CHAPTER TWENTY ONE

*A PRECIOUS ONE FROM US IS GONE
A VOICE WE LOVED IS STILL,
A PLACE IS VACANT IN OUR HOME
WHICH NEVER CAN BE FILLED.*
EPITAPH
—CECILIA K. PINTER

THE OLDER I GET, THE MORE I PISS ON myself," the old man said, stepping away from the urinal while zipping up his fly. "Christ, would you look at that?" he said, looking down at the front of his trousers.

Sam tried not to look; instead he sidestepped around the man to take his position in front of the huge urinal. Never in his life had he seen a urinal so huge. It was like peeing into your refrigerator, he thought. The porcelain fixture was a mosaic of web-shaped cracks and stains. Water spilled continuously down the back and sides of the cavernous receptacle. It was as old as any in the city. The Livestock Exchange Building was one of the few landmark buildings left in Denver. A broad, creaky, wooden staircase led him to the second floor where the State Board of Stock Inspection was located, just across the hall from the world's largest urinal. "George L. Byron, Commissioner" was printed in block letters on the frosted glass door.

Alice, the woman behind the desk, had an infectious smile and a beehive hairdo. A woman in her early-to-mid fifties, she was tall, perhaps five-eleven, slim, and attractive. "Hi," she smiled. "How can I help you?"

Sam had been unable to formulate an elaborate lie while driving across town to the Brand Board. "I'm Stan Lawson from archives."

Alice stared back at Sam blankly. Then her eyes narrowed and her brow wrinkled. "Yes?"

"I'm here to inventory your historical records. It's Thursday, isn't it?" he said, looking at his watch. "I'm sorry I'm a few minutes late, traffic was horrible this morning."

"You had an appointment?"

"Yes. You should have received a letter last month. We tried to give all the agencies at least a three-week notice of our scheduled visits."

Alice gave him a crooked smile then called over her shoulder. "Stella, do you remember getting a letter from state archives about an inventory?"

Sam heard the clicking of heels on the ancient hardwood floor as Stella emerged from an adjoining office. Even with her shoulder-length, bleached blonde hair, there was no mistaking Stella for Alice's twin. They were identical.

"Hello," he said weakly, his eyes darting back and forth between the sisters.

"Hi," Stella said, with the same irresistible smile that Alice had displayed earlier. "Nope, I don't recall seeing anything from archives," she said, looking at her sister.

To Sam she appeared as if she were looking into a mirror after trying on a wig. He stared shamelessly at them. They wore formfitting knee-length skirts, Alice in blue and Stella in black. Both wore plain white blouses that were pulled taut across their chests.

"I'm sorry, Mr. Lawson," Alice said. "We haven't a clue what you're talking about."

"Inventory," he said. "We're trying to determine if the various agencies of state government are complying with the governor's policy regarding disposition of historical documents."

"The Brand Board maintains its own archives, Mr. Lawson," Stella said.

"That explains why I couldn't find a thing for you guys," he said. "The governor's policy is law. I'm afraid I'm going to have to call the police."

Both women stared at him soberly.

"Was there something in particular that you were interested in seeing?" Alice said, suspiciously.

"Not really. But I'm doing the health department too, and I found some cross-references to the livestock board. That might be a good place to start. It had to do with the Eugenics Section of the board. Could I see those minutes perhaps?"

Both women looked at each other. "The what section?" Stella said, turning toward him, cocking her head and narrowing her eyes.

He was momentarily captivated by her animated cuteness. He wondered what these women looked like twenty or thirty years ago. Drop-dead gorgeous, he thought, a sailor's dream. "Eugenics Section," he said.

"Never heard of it," Stella said, turning toward her sister.

"Me either," Alice said. "And we've been here a long time. There's only the Brand Board. No sections."

He did not want to use his trump card this early in the game, but knew he was dead in the water without it. "Hmmm," he said, scratching his head. "I'll ask my girlfriend if she's heard of it. She's on the board," he added matter-of-factly.

"Blair Tennyson is your girlfriend?" Alice said, staring at him, her mouth open slightly.

"Yes." Somehow it seemed a lie and he regretted saying it almost immediately. If it was not a lie, it was sure to become one now.

The sisters looked at each other wide-eyed then back at Sam. "So you're the one," Stella said.

"We knew there was something different about Blair lately, but she wouldn't tell us who she had met."

There was something too familiar in their reference to Blair. "You know Doctor Tennyson, personally?" he said.

"Know her?" Alice said. "We used to change her diapers."

"I taught her to ride a horse," Stella said proudly. "A little paint pony."

"You're from Cambridge?" he said, a sinking feeling descending over him.

"Born and raised. Most people have never heard of it. Have you ever been there, Mr. Lawson?"

"That's where Blair and I first met. She accused me of rustling."

"That's our girl," Stella said proudly. "We're related, you know."

"I would imagine everyone in Cambridge is related," Sam said. "Don't tell me, Uncle Alfred is your uncle too?"

"Uncle Al is everyone's uncle, in a manner of speaking," Stella said. "No, Blair is our cousin, sort of."

"Sort of?" he said.

"Blair's mother was adopted," Alice interrupted. "And so was our mother. They were adoptive sisters, but ten years apart in age."

Sam stared at her blankly.

"We share the same maternal grandparents," Alice added in an attempt to clear up his confusion.

"Got any relation in Iowa?" he said flatly.

"No, not that we are aware of," Stella answered.

Sam's lie was now a giant piece of gristle in his mouth. He would be exposed as soon as the twins had a chance to talk with Blair. Any remnant of a relationship that he had with Blair would be lost forever.

"And it was Blair that told you we had a Eugenics Section, Mr. Lawson?"

"Dawson, with a D," Sam said.

"I'm sorry. I thought you said Lawson."

"That's okay. I hear that a lot. I need to learn to enunciate. No, Blair didn't tell me about the Eugenics Section. I discovered it while doing some research on state statutes involving the Department of Health."

Both women had regained their infectious smiles; their eyes shone with anticipation. They suddenly reminded Sam of schoolgirls admiring a puppy in a pet store window. No one spoke.

"And you work in archives, Stan?" Alice finally asked.

"Sam," he corrected. "I hear Stan a lot too. I mumble. I used to work for the state," he said, trying to minimize the lie.

It was apparent to Sam that they could care less who he worked for. Their little Blair had a boyfriend and they were inspecting him.

"Ladies," a man's voice boomed. "Try to stuff your eyeballs back in their sockets and show Mr. Dawson back."

Turning, Sam saw a man standing in the doorway of the office from which Stella had come. He was tall, made taller by the cowboy boots he wore and the slim blue jeans with a sharp laundered crease down the front. A large silver belt buckle with a bucking horse and rider inlaid in gold, the kind won at a rodeo, was centered at his waist. His western-cut shirt sported imitation mother-of-pearl snaps down the front and on the flap pockets. A gold watch chain disappeared into the left breast pocket and a fancy gold fob hung between placket and pocket. The right pocket bulged with the unmistakable outline of a snuff can. His short hair with a hint of gray at the temples was grooved just above his ears from the tight-fitting cowboy hat he obviously had been wearing. Bronco George, Sam thought, as Alice held open the old-fashioned swinging gate in the short railing that stretched across the room.

"This is Blair's gentleman friend," Stella said softly, her eyes cast downward.

Bronco George raised one eyebrow at her. "Bring Mr. Dawson a cup of coffee and then the both of you go to lunch. Lock the door on your way out."

A complete set of Brand Books from the 1860s to the present lined the shelves behind the large walnut desk. Crossed branding irons, a worn set of chaps, and cowboy art covered the walls. A dried bull scrotum served as a pencil holder.

Stella quietly handed Sam a steaming ceramic coffee mug covered with cattle brands. She closed the door carefully behind her as she left the room.

"Sit down, Dawson," Bronco George said, his back to Sam as he looked out the window toward the stockyards.

Sam hesitated. He felt the muscles in his jaw tighten in angry response to being told what to do. He placed the mug on a small table that had a lamp made of welded horseshoes at its center and stood his ground. "Don't tell me," Sam said sarcastically, "you're from Cambridge too."

"You're damned right I am," he said, turning to face Sam.

Sam smiled and shook his head. George L. Byron, the Brand Commissioner. Remembering his conversation with the old salamander from Cambridge, who admitted there was no Keats in town while implying the existence of a Byron and Shelley. "And the L?" Sam asked with a smirk.

"Just an L," he said without blinking. The two stared at each other for a long uncomfortable moment.

"You been nosein' around in business that ain't yours," Bronco George accused.

Still standing, Sam could feel his anger beginning to build. "Are you referring to my nosein' with Blair or my noscin' with your little secret genetic experiment?"

"Blair's a big girl. If she wants to diddle some jerk like you, that's her business."

Sam took a step closer to the walnut desk. The tendons in his neck began to bulge. "How much does she know about all this?"

Bronco George stared at him with narrowed eyes. "How much do you know is the question, Dawson."

"I know enough to blow this thing wide-open. We're talking national coverage, headlines for weeks, news shows, talk shows, congressional investigations.

"You're a crazy bastard. With balls," he added. "I'll give you that. More balls than sense. But what you think you know and what's the truth are two different things."

"Is this the part of the conversation where you try to convince me of the righteousness of your cause? Where you try to justify murder in the name of genetic purity?"

"Murder? I don't know what you're talking about. Nobody's murdered anybody, yet," he added with emphasis, his nostrils flaring.

"Is that a threat?" Sam said, staring back at the cowboy boldly.

"Take it any way you want it, Dawson. You're screwin' with the wrong folks here, powerful folks who aren't about to let some Hymie-loving bastard like you come along and destroy things."

Sam's ears burned with the flush of blood sent there in anger. He felt his fists tighten, clenched involuntarily. So this was what it was about. They were racists. The Klan gone bad. What had he been thinking? Eugenicists were racists from the start. "Do you suppose Eris was an Aryan supremacist like you? Or did he just like young blonde girls?"

"Doctor Eris was a visionary, a genius so far ahead of his time that he created a mechanism to insure his work survived."

"Is Blair a part of this?"

"A part of what?" he smiled.

"A part of this—this Nazi, racist baloney or whatever it is you think you're doing?"

"Hitler was an impatient man," he said, turning and gazing out the window. "Doctor Eris had the patience of Job. He was a scientist. Hitler was a gangster."

"But they were both after the same end result, weren't they? They wanted genetic purity, to build the super race."

Bronco George continued to gaze silently out the window. Without turning, he began to speak. "In the livestock industry we incorporate the strategies of both. Inferior animals are culled, separated from the herd and sent to slaughter. The best bulls are collected and the best cows AI'd. Embryos are flushed, split, and implanted in surrogates. The breed is improved. The breed is perpetuated."

"Your analogy, like Eris's experiment, is filled with holes," Sam said. "It's all artificial. It's all prejudicial. The criteria used to cull as well as to propagate are based on somebody's value judgment. Who makes those decisions and what are they based upon? Eris was a racist, pure and simple. What mirror on the wall told him he was the fairest of all? He inseminated at least a hundred girls that I know of. He eventually murdered the donors and the surrogates, at least here in Colorado. I don't know what he, or who I suspect was his twin, did in Iowa. But I'm sure I'll find an unmarked cemetery there too. Who gave them permission to overwhelm the gene pool?"

Bronco George grunted, smiled, and shook his head. "It was the process he was interested in, the science, not dominating the gene pool. Hell, one coon basketball player with more dick than brains will knock up about as many women. How do you compete with that? How do you compete with some greasy beaner on welfare who has twelve kids at home and is screwing the woman down the street too? How do you compete in a world where religion promotes it and government rewards it? And liberal, yuppie scum like you sanction the contamination by developing and supporting more programs to help them. All under the mistaken belief that all they need is equal opportunity and education. Jobs and books won't increase their intelligence, Dawson. People like you and the liberal media who promote hybridization of the races are only diluting our genetic capacity. Hybrid vigor is a phenotypic phenomenon that will eventually doom civilization to a regressive form of intellectual evolution. The browning of America is the dumbing of America."

It frightened Sam to hear this kind of talk. He knew people like this existed, but it was unnerving to actually hear someone articulate their racial hatred. Even more troubling was the fact that this stranger was openly acknowledging Eris's crimes. He looked at the door, reassuring himself that a way out still existed. "You can't honestly believe that," he said, his voice breaking.

"Don't get me wrong, Dawson. There's plenty of white trash out there too, dumb as posts and breeding like flies.

As a society, we're doomed. There's no turning back. It's just a matter of time before the most advanced civilizations on earth crumble and fall, destroyed by the exponential population growth of the least fit. Inferior people gobbling up resources at a rate that technology won't begin to keep up with. There'll be civil wars and world wars fought for control of food, water, and space. Hell, it's happening now in the Middle East and Africa, ethnic and religious factions killing each other. Our response, of course, is to deplore the violence and to intervene, just the opposite of what we should do. This country spends billions every year to provide food aid to a bunch of jungle bunnies whose response is to breed like flies."

Sam ran his fingers through his hair. "What's Blair's role in all this?"

"In what? You think you're on to something, Dawson, but you don't know jack squat. You're a gnat in the ointment, not even a fly. Who you gonna tell? Who's gonna believe you?" He smiled at Sam.

"I guess this means you're not going to show me the board minutes," Sam said.

"You need to back away from all this, Dawson."

"And if I don't?"

He continued to smile, not taking his eyes from Sam. "Goodbye, Mr. Dawson," he said finally then turned to stare out the window again.

"That's it? You threaten me then dismiss me like a schoolboy?"

"There is one more thing," Bronco George said without turning around. "Get little Sidney's tubes tied. You wouldn't want her to go missing like Julie, would you?"

It took Sam a moment to process what Bronco George had just said. "What did you say?"

"You heard me, Dawson. Just like cattle, the inferior are culled and sent to slaughter."

"You killed my sister?"

"It was bad enough that your mother married that fish-eating Finn. But you come along and knock-up that Jew bitch when you're still in college. The dice were loaded against you. We should have castrated you years ago."

Sam threw the chair aside and took two long strides toward Bronco George.

The brand commissioner turned quickly from the window to face Sam. He was pointing a pistol, a large-bore automatic, at Sam's midsection.

"Goodbye, Mr. Dawson."

•••

Driving home from the Brand Board, Sam at first was blind with rage. Then his thoughts became scattered. He had felt both anger and fear as he left the Stock Exchange Building and somehow found his truck. He thought of his sister, dead for so many years. But the hollowness in his chest and the warm cloak of tears that threatened to fill his eyes were for Sidney.

The right front tire of Sam's truck jumped the curb as he screeched to a halt in front of a pay phone outside the Travelodge motel on Pecos Street. It was a miracle that he found Bill Westbrook in. Bill was the director of the Colorado Bureau of Investigation. Bill listened patiently as Sam gave him Sidney and Marcie's address and phone number and the school that Sidney attended. He explained only that a credible threat had been made against Sidney's life. As a personal favor, he asked Bill to place Sidney under 'round-the-clock protective surveillance, put her in protective custody, to do whatever he had to do to protect his daughter. He told Bill to trust him, that he would explain everything as soon as he had a chance.

On the drive home he thought of Sidney, his mother, his own life, and the mistakes he had made. Unfulfilled expectations, a failed marriage, a career on indefinite hold, an endangered daughter, and how the woman he loved had betrayed him. His chest convulsed when he took a deep breath, the way it had when he was a child and had been punished for some wrongdoing.

Gray clouds laden with snow hung low over the foothills. He could feel the moisture in the air and taste the metallic bite of air pollution as he stepped from the truck and approached his house. He wanted to sleep. Sleep until it all went away. His ears rang from the collisions of competing thoughts. None of them completed. None of them solved.

The warm air of the house embraced him at the same time it repulsed him. The smell of dog poop was overpowering. "For crying out loud, Elle," he said loudly while scanning the room for the source of the odor. "Elle, get in here," he shouted. The odor was stifling. He felt the crow's-feet at the corners of his eyes tighten with the involuntary face of disgust as he walked toward the kitchen.

Elle's body had been laid carefully on the kitchen table. Her once-expressive brown eyes were fixed without emotion. She had been opened up and disemboweled. Her intestines were draped over the back of a chair, spilling down to the floor. Blood still dripped from the table to a large, red pool below.

CHAPTER TWENTY TWO

REMEMBER ME WITH LAUGHTER,
FOR THAT IS THE WAY
I WOULD REMEMBER YOU.
BUT IF YOU REMEMBER ME WITH SORROW,
DON'T REMEMBER ME AT ALL.
WE WILL HAVE TOMORROW,
AS WE HAD YESTERDAY.
DEAR ONE

EPITAPH
—MICHELLE EVANS

THE PINK FROSTING OF SUNRISE spread across the foothills. Night's blackness turned gray. The world was still without color as shapes slowly appeared. Two inches of wet snow pressed against the earth as a reminder of nature's dominance. Sam's muddy boots sat lifelessly inside the kitchen door. Their laces spilled out in long loops, descending into the brown water puddled on the floor. Sam stared at them. He sat slouched at the kitchen table, his head held up rudely by the fist of his right hand. A half-dozen beer bottles littered the tabletop. An Orvis catalog lay open among the clutter. "Pet memorials offer lasting remembrance," he read under item B on page thirty-four. He had his choice of Vermont slate or marble. The larger memorial allowed up to ten letters and spaces on the first line, twelve on the second, and eighteen on the third line. Punctuation marks were not available. He would order Elle a tombstone and take its picture in black-and-white on a gray, winter morning. A day like today, he thought. Then he would take his .300 Winchester Magnum to the stockyards and wait for Bronco George.

●●●●

At quarter to eleven the phone awakened him; his face was stuck to the glass of the tabletop.

"Hello," he said weakly.

"Sam, Barbara Sinclair. Did I wake you? It's ten forty-five in the morning, for crying out loud."

"No, I'm up."

"You sound a little strange."

"That's because my lower lip had dried and stuck to the tabletop."

"That's good, Sam. For a minute there, I thought you might have been normal."

"What's up?"

"You owe me big-time, buster. I'm expecting major media support for my budget."

"What'd you find?" he said, sitting up and rubbing his eyes.

"The good stuff, the stuff never sent to archives. I found some early maps of the asylum. They show the precise location of the stable, metes and bounds from the section corner."

"That's good, Babs. That's real good. Is there a date on the plans?"

"Uh-huh, 1894."

Sam said nothing. Marta Eisenoch at the historical society had already shown him that map. His silence conveyed his disappointment.

"But that's not the good stuff," she added cheerfully.

"What? What else did you find?" he said, sitting up a little straighter.

"I found an old photograph of the hospital staff. On the back someone had written the date and the names of the people from left to right. The third guy from the right was one Doctor Eugene Eris, dated September 9, 1923."

Now he was wide-awake. Without thinking about it, he scrawled the name Eris on the tabletop with a grease pencil he used for marking photos. "A picture of Eris? I can't believe it. What's he look like?"

"He looks like my grandfather. He looks like everybody's grandfather, kindly old gentleman in a baggy suit with white hair and wire-rimmed glasses. Nondescript really, not a very big man, slight features."

"Babs, it's important that you don't tell anyone about this, any of it."

"Not to worry. It's embarrassing enough just to be seen with you, let alone being caught helping you with your harebrained conspiracy theory."

"I'm serious, Babs. These people are alive and well and they're dangerous. Trust me on this."

"It's such a shame. You're so good-looking, smart, and successful. But you're mentally ill, Sam. Get help. And while you're convalescing, I'll expect some positive press about Institutions and our budget issues."

"Promise me," Sam said seriously.

"I promise," she said reluctantly. "The plans and the picture will be in an unmarked package in my office. The code word is 'Rosebud.' Oliver will know what to do. I'll be in C Springs the rest of the day."

"Thanks, Babs. I owe you."

"Damn straight. See ya, Sam."

The grease pencil fell from the tabletop, bounced, and rolled slowly under the table. His head pounding, Sam bent down to retrieve it, but could not reach it. On hands and knees he crawled under the glass-topped kitchen table and grabbed the pencil. Backing out, the black markings on the clear surface caught his eye. Looking upward from beneath the table, he stared at the name Eris written above. He froze, reading each letter, flipping them one by one, his lips moving as he silently spelled out the word "sirE." Sire, the anagram of Eris. Sire, the father of Cambridge, the patriarch of Oxford, the begetter of legions.

••••

Tears stung his eyes and blurred his vision as he drove into town. He had cried while showering, sobbing and shuddering over a dog. He remembered his mother's screams and uncontrolled sorrow over his sister's death. While there had been emptiness in his heart and weakness in his limbs, he had not cried for his sister or his mother. Now he cried for a dog. He loved Elle. But he had loved his sister and mother too. Before leaving the house, he had washed the blood from her collar and tags. The worn tags tinkled softly, the way they did when she entered the room. He hung the collar over a corner of the picture frame that sat on the mantle, the frame that surrounded the last-known photo of his mother, her sallow cheeks already showing the effects of the cancer that she had kept to herself.

••••

Oliver demanded the password in his most flirtatious voice. Sam was in no mood for games. "Give me the package, you little—," he said, the muscles rippling above his set jaw, his eyes flashing. Oliver complied, placed a hand on his hip, and attempted to look hurt.

His next stop was the Livestock Exchange Building. He had no plan, only anger. Waiting in the parking lot, he stared at the photograph of Eris. The unsmiling face with piercing eyes stared back at him. There was a bond here. A bond separated by eighty years, but as intense as if the two men had threatened each other the day before. Eris was not as unremarkable as Barbara Sinclair had stated. That was because she had never met Blair Tennyson or Annie Dillon or eaten blueberry pie with Annie George. Sam could see a little of Eugene Eris in each of them. But if he stared hard enough, to the point where his eyes began to narrow, he could see his own mother, her mouth and chin. He could see anybody he wanted if he stared hard enough.

It was just after one o'clock when Bronco George stepped from his white pickup in the reserved space at the south side of the building. Sam skidded to a halt behind the parked vehicle. He jumped from the cab of his truck, leaving the door open, and walked briskly toward the lanky cowboy who looked like a tall version of Eris.

"Well, well, look who's here," Bronco George said, his lunchtime toothpick dangling from the corner of his mouth. "Did you get my message, Dawson?"

Sam's first punch was straight-on and lightning quick. He felt the cowboy's nose crush against his knuckles. Bronco George staggered backward, his Stetson flying to the slushy ground. A left hook caught the man behind his ear and he spun around, falling against the door panel of his truck, his legs spread wide to keep him from buckling. Sam kicked him squarely in the groin, a sharp upward blow that nearly lifted the man from the ground. The cowboy groaned and collapsed to the wet, broken pavement, writhing into a fetal position, his hands tucked between his legs.

"I got your message, asshole. Here's my reply." Sam grabbed a fistful of the man's hair and yanked his head upward. He then delivered a smashing blow with a powerful right hand to the already bloody face of the cowboy. "You bastard," he yelled as he prepared to hit him again then hesitated. "If anybody comes near my daughter, I'll kill you. Slowly!" He lowered his cocked arm and flexed his painful knuckles. He hovered over the semiconscious man for several seconds. He wanted to threaten him, to spit in his face and tell him that next time it would be *his* bowels draped over *his* kitchen table. Sam walked away, shaking his bruised hand.

••••

Boulder had received more snow than Denver, but it was melting quickly. He approached Blair's house on foot from the alley. His ball cap was pulled down low on his forehead, and he carried a clipboard he found under the seat of his truck. He entered her backyard through a wire gate and approached the electric meter on the wall next to the back door. Pretending to write something down, he slowly turned to scan the yards and houses behind and to the side of Blair's. He saw no one. Holding his breath, he was about to place his elbow through the windowpane nearest the door handle, when he decided to try the knob. The door was unlocked. Rather than feeling pleased about his good fortune, Sam bristled with the thought that Blair was so careless. A beautiful, single woman living alone in Boulder needed to be more cautious.

The kitchen was warm and smelled of ripe bananas, a bunch of which sat in a mixing bowl on the counter. He wiped his feet on the rug next to the door. Flexing his stiff knuckles, he realized his shortness of breath and the fear in his throat. He had just assaulted a man who undoubtedly had called the police. Now he was breaking and entering, although he had not broken anything. Even more troubling was the fact that he was spying on the woman he had thought he loved. He took a deep breath and headed for the study.

He would have to work quickly. The fall afternoon was short and the sun was already low, casting an eerie glow on the Thors and lion heads that watched him carefully. He started with the oak file cabinets, opening each drawer and picking through the file tabs. Two drawers were dedicated to personal business. There were files with bank statements, insurance premium notices, credit card and utility bills. The remainder contained reprints of scientific literature alphabetized by author. The titles were long and made little sense to a nongeneticist. He poked around in the pigeonholes and drawers of the rolltop desk but found nothing. He was not sure what it was he was looking for, but would know it when he found it. He scanned the bookshelves and noted his books still stacked neatly on the end table next to the Morris chair. The study was comfortable, warmly appointed with Blair's books and treasures. He stopped, suddenly aware that he was being watched. He turned and saw the frozen snarls of the lions on the corners of Blair's desk, their immobile eyes dispassionately overseeing his every move. He felt exposed, naked. There was something familiar, déjà vu-like that momentarily captured his attention. Stay focused, he told himself.

The stairs creaked as he tiptoed up to her bedroom. Halfway up, he realized that he need not tiptoe. The room smelled of Blair's perfume, not in the least overpowering, just a hint of the fragrance he associated with her neck and ear. Like the rest of the house, the room was clean and orderly. The bed was made crisply, with oversize pillows in ruffled cases piled against the antique headboard. He had made love to her on that bed, in that room, but remembered nothing of his surroundings. The second drawer of the bureau held Blair's undergarments, dainty sheer panties in a rainbow of colors. Sam held up a white satin thong not much larger than an eye patch. He thought of her smooth, muscular body, how he had made love to her in the very house he now had broken into. And love it had been, not just sex, he thought, as if trying to justify his carnal pleasure. But if he had truly loved her, why was he ransacking her house? He suddenly felt very guilty and wanted to leave, scurry down the alley, hat pulled low and collar up, a criminal on the run.

A row of photo albums lined the lower shelf of her dressing table. They appeared to be in chronological order from left to right. There were old family photos, black-and-whites of lean people, cow dogs, and shaggy horses. Brandings and holiday meals were overrepresented. He recognized Blair as a little girl, her long, blonde hair varying between ponytail and braids. Her tiny legs were tanned and often sported Band-Aids on her knees. There was a period of years, lasting into high school, when it was difficult to find a photo of her where she was dressed in anything but blue jeans. Blair had been a tomboy. He watched her grow, inches at a time. He saw her mature, her body developing under western attire. Blair's mother, Annie Dillon's identical twin, appeared in many of the photos. Uncle Alfred showed up when haying crews were being fed at long tables in the front yard. From baptism to confirmation to homecoming queen, Blair's life passed before him with each flip of a page. Alice and Stella, Blair's cousins, had the same hairdos twenty-five years ago. They were as cute as he had imagined them to be, always smiling and bordering on being sexy. On a family trip to the

Royal Gorge, Blair waved bravely from the wooden-floored suspension bridge. A teenage Larry McLavey, the Pueblo mortician who had no idea where Cambridge was, stood next to her. Toward the back of the third album was a five-by-seven color photo of Blair and her prom date, Bronco George. Stunned, Sam stared at the photo, analyzing every detail from the straight pleats at the sides of her breasts to his large fingers at her waist. He wore blue jeans and a tuxedo jacket with tails, cummerbund, and a string bow tie. In cowboy fashion, he left his hat on for the photograph. Blair was wide-eyed with innocence and a hint of mischief. Her sleeveless, purple, satin dress was formfitting. She wore her corsage on her wrist.

Sam quickly leafed through the remainder of the photo albums. The image of Blair and Bronco George occluded all others. But it did not mean anything other than she was his prom date. The school was small. He was probably an upperclassman. Just because she went to a dance with the guy more than a dozen years ago does not make her his accomplice in organized bigotry and murder, he reasoned. He was seeing things that may or may not be there.

The girl in the third row of the church choir, the one wearing thick dark-rimmed glasses looked like a young Barbara Sinclair without heavy lipstick. He held the photo toward the window to gather the last of the afternoon's light. The girl was heavy and the hair was long and straight, but the sad eyes and fleshy lips were very familiar. It couldn't be, he told himself. It looked like Barbara, but it wasn't. It was someone else. It had to be. Stay on task, he told himself, purposefully diverting his attention away from Barbara Sinclair. He had not found a thing to indict Blair. Everything was purely coincidental.

The books neatly aligned on the nightstand were a mixture of topics. George Bernard Shaw, Henry Goddard, Aldous Huxley, E. L. Thorndike, Lothrop Stoddard, several by Margaret Sanger, even Henry Ford was represented. Eclectic nighttime reading to most, but Sam recognized them from his library research. They were all active in the eugenics movement. Ernst Rudin, author of *Rassenhygiene*, peaked his curiosity. *Aufgaben und Ziele der Deutschen Gesellschaft für Rassenhygiene* was published in 1934. The entire book was in German. He wondered if Blair could speak or read German. There was so much that he did not know about her, so much he wanted to learn. Wasn't that the reason he had broken into her house? he asked himself. What did he expect to find, a framed picture of Adolf Hitler in the bedroom and a Nazi uniform hanging in the closet? There was nothing here, no smoking gun, only a few books of interest to any geneticist. He was relieved. Blair's innocence was why he was there. If there was anything linking the present with the past, it would be locked in the giant walk-in vault he had seen at the Brand Board. They had been careful. They had survived for decades without detection. What made him think he would find incriminating evidence in Blair Tennyson's bedroom? She was an innocent bystander, Bronco George's prom date, a successful woman from Cambridge. An excellent choice for the Brand Board.

He poked his head into the bathroom then into the closet. He was about to walk out of the room when he stopped suddenly. He again looked into the closet, two neat rows of hanging clothes and shoe racks on the floor. He glanced into the bathroom. Something was wrong, spatially out of balance. The bathroom was deeper than the closet. The length of the closet was perhaps two-or-three feet less than the bathroom. Yet, both rooms were against the same outside wall of the house. It must be an optical illusion brought on by the presence of the window in the bathroom, he reasoned.

The closet smelled of cedar and of Blair. The walls were paneled with vertical, tongue-and-groove cedar boards. Maroon boards with creamy stripes and swirling dark knots broke the monotony of the flat wall at the back of the room. A horizontal shelf at eye level held shoeboxes and an assortment of caps, hats, ski goggles, and mittens and covered the top edge of the hidden door. The vertical edges were at the wall corners and covered by molding. He pushed against the door and it swung back easily, hinged on its left side. With racing heart he fumbled for the small light on his keychain. A lightbulb hung from a twisted fabric-covered cord in the center of the tiny room. Sam pulled the chain and the room exploded in a bright, yellowish light. It smelled of dust and dampness. The open studs on the bathroom side of the small room were filled with the pipes leading to the tub and shower. The gooseneck of the drainpipe bowed upward from floor level between the studs. The other two walls contained shelves, floor to ceiling. There were books, covered magazine boxes, ledgers, albums, small metal file boxes, large ringed binders, and a stack of dusty framed photos. An oblong ledger titled "Iowa" caught his eye. There were others: Colorado, Oklahoma, Montana, Texas, Indiana, Arkansas, and Oregon. Colorado was at the top of the stack. All were labeled F1.

He pulled down the ledger marked "Master" followed by "P1." Each page contained a name printed neatly in capital letters at the top left margin. The first entry was Sarah Veronica Adams. Katherine Elizabeth Douglas, Allison Matilda Farnsworth, Eleanor Margaret Drummond, Rosemary Francis Talbot all followed. The last entry, Jennifer Marie Wilson, was numbered 120 in the upper right corner. Sam recognized many of the names from the Mount View files. They were all here, 120 teenage girls, Eris's brood stock. One had escaped. He assumed the others were all long dead. He had told Blair everything about Sarah Wiley. He had exposed her. His hands trembled with fear as he returned to the first entry. Next to her name was an alphanumeric code, SVA00F1. Everything appeared to be in code, cryptic notes of scientific manipulations. He recognized dates written as six-digit numbers. The underlined subheadings were a mystery at first. Each girl had eight subheadings with indented numbers and letters listed under each. SVAF1ARK091822, SVAF1COLO090722, SVAF1IND091322, SVAF1IOWA091122, SVAF1OKLA091222, SVAF1OREG091022, SVAF1MONT090922, and SVAF1TEX091022 were the subheadings for Sarah Veronica Adams. All but the second had additional subheadings, indented progressively to the right and descending toward the bottom of the page. All entries were followed by a small square or a circle. The eight subheadings were all circles.

Sam squinted, the corner of his mouth pulled to the left. He turned the book sideways then back again. He flipped through the pages. Each girl had similar headings, the letters and numbers differing slightly. He realized that the first three letters represented the girl's initials. All were followed by F1. He had heard Blair talk about F1 in her lectures. First filial was the first generation product of the first parental cross, the P1. The letters that followed were the old abbreviations for states. The next six numbers were dates.

"There were eight of them," he said aloud. "Jesus Christ, there were eight of them." Arkansas, Colorado, Indiana, Iowa, Oklahoma, Oregon, Montana, and Texas: each with a different date, but all within days of each other. Eris had either both flushed and fertilized more than one egg from each girl, or he had split each embryo four times, producing eight identical embryos that he froze, shipped, and transplanted into surrogates in eight states. He was looking at a human pedigree. The coded descendants of Dr. Eugene Eris were all recorded. From the early 1920s to, in some cases, the F4 in the 1980s. He quickly calculated that one hundred-twenty girls, each producing eight identical embryos, yielded nine hundred-sixty offspring in the F1 generation alone. If each of them reached sexual maturity and conservatively produced two children each, the F3 would be nearly two thousand and the F4 close to four thousand. He turned back to the first page. There were no entries under the subheading SVAF1COLO090722. Sarah Adams had escaped. She carried with her one of eight embryos, a child born dead. No data available, he thought. The pedigree ended there. Somewhere in the ledger he would find Blair Tennyson, Annie George, and himself, all F3s.

He could not swallow and breathing was a conscious effort. Blair was part of it, part of what and to what degree, he was not sure. But the proof was in her closet. He wanted to cry.

A door slammed downstairs. Sam held his breath. He heard the click of Blair's heels on the hardwood floor then the dull rhythmic thuds as she ascended the padded stairs to the second floor. Quietly, he unscrewed the lightbulb in its socket and the room went dark. He closed the hidden door slowly and without noise as Blair entered the room.

The clicking heels stopped when she removed her shoes and softly walked into the closet to place them in a rack. Sam heard hangers being scraped across the wooden rod that ran the length of the closet. Light streamed into the secret room through a small knothole in the cedar paneling. He leaned forward and placed his eye at the source of the light. Blair was in the closet, so close that he pulled back suddenly. Again, he heard hangers being scraped against the rod. Looking through the knothole, he saw Blair walk out of the closet. She was wearing only her bra and panties. He heard the unmistakable sound of the toilet lid hitting the back of the tank then the soft tinkling of Blair urinating. The toilet flushed. Water pipes yelped and then screamed shrilly as the faucet above the bathtub was opened. Sam kneeled, unlaced, and removed his shoes. He hoped she would take a shower rather than a tub bath; the noise would mask his retreat.

The phone rang with an annoying electrical chirping. He heard the faucet crank shut and the singing pipes were suddenly silent. Looking through the knothole, he saw Blair pass in front of the closet door, turn, and approach the telephone on the nightstand next to the bed. She was naked.

"Hello?" She said nothing further, listening, turning impatiently, and exposing every angle of herself to him.

"Oh my god, are you all right?...Are you sure?...Did you go to the hospital?...How many stitches?" she asked into the receiver as she ran her hand across her flat lower abdomen. "No, no. Just sit tight. I'll call him...No. I mean it. I'll handle it. Let me find out...Yes, I'll call you...Okay."

She lowered the phone from her ear, her blonde hair hanging in her face as she dialed. Placing the phone to her ear again, she paced, taking the phone cradle with her. She stopped suddenly, facing the closet doorway. Her nipples had darkened and become erect in the coolness of the room.

"Sam, its Blair." She paused. "Pick up, Sam. I really need to talk with you." She paused again. "Please call me as soon as you get in, no matter what time, okay?" She hung up the phone and placed it back on the nightstand. She pushed her hair back with her left hand and stood staring at the phone for a moment, her slender back curving sensuously into rounded buttocks. She turned and walked quickly to the bathroom, her breasts bouncing roughly as she passed in front of the closet.

He heard the water faucets being cranked open, the curtain rings singing metallically on the curtain rod. There was a click, a pause, and then the spray of the shower against the tub. Sam opened the door slowly, his shoes tucked under his arm with the ledger and his clipboard.

Pausing at the door to the study, the sound of the shower above, he slipped on his shoes and quickly laced them. Once again, he sensed being watched. Looking up, he came face-to-face with the carved lions whose same unblinking eyes had beheld the naked innocence of Sarah Veronica Adams so long ago.

It was almost dark when he saw his truck. The slush in the alley was starting to freeze and crunched loudly as he hurried. He tried not to run. He tried not to scream.

CHAPTER TWENTY THREE

GOD'S FINGER TOUCHED HER
AND SHE SLEPT.
EPITAPH
—OLIVE SNYDER

S AM WAS AFRAID TO GO HOME, FRIGHT-
ened as much by the reality that Elle would not be
there to comfort him as by the threat to his own safety.
He grew weary of asking himself questions. The same questions over and over again, reworded, but the same questions.
He slept in the cab of the truck. Shivering and cramped, he
awoke several times to survey the parking lot of the Taco
Bell in Golden. It began to snow just after midnight.

The slamming of the dumpster lid woke him at sunrise.
A lanky teenager in an oversize uniform scampered across
the snow-covered parking lot, disappearing through the
back door of the restaurant. The sun was a flaming red slit
over the Denver skyline. Sam's toes were numb with cold as
he stepped from the truck and relieved himself in the fresh
snow beneath the open door.

At the diner on West Colfax he slurped coffee and studied the pedigree charts he had stolen from Blair's closet.
The letters and numbers blurred together, impersonal rep-
resentations of real people, people unaware of their role in
Eris's crime. People helplessly related to a demented killer,
his own mother one of them. Eris kidnapped young girls,

tortured and raped them. They incubated his young and then he killed them. And the woman Sam had loved was a product of the killer's depravity, an accomplice who carried on the family tradition of deceit.

"Are you ready to order, yet?" the waitress said, her arms folded across her chest, greasy stains on her pink uniform. She was the same woman who had waited on him and Norbert Crowell.

"I'm not hungry," Sam said, looking at her sorrowfully.

"I don't give a rat's behind," the waitress said, unflinching.

He stared at her for a moment and realized that she was making a statement about more than his nutritional need. She didn't want to hear his sad story. She had her own.

"Two eggs basted, bacon, hash browns, and wheat toast," he said.

She walked away without comment. He watched after her. There was no one to talk with. Barbara Sinclair, his friend for so many years, was now suspected of singing in the Cambridge church choir. Pat was ready to terminate his contract. Marcie was still feeling too sorry for herself to carry on a conversation. Sam talked with Sidney before she left for school. He and Marcie had agreed to not tell her about the severity of her condition until they themselves could understand the ramifications and cope with the predicted outcome. He simply told her to not talk with any strangers or accept a ride with anyone she didn't know well. When she asked what was going on, he lied badly about an investigation into health insurance fraud that he had been accused of and that they were questioning all the tests she had at University Hospital. She seemed to accept his lame excuse and agreed to avoid anyone she didn't know who might approach her.

"Thank you for using AT&T," the pleasant female voice said when he entered the last of his credit card numbers. The noise from the diner's kitchen forced him to cover his left ear with his hand. He heard the phone begin to ring on the other end.

"Hello?" she said, uncertainty in her voice.

"Annie?"

"Yes."

"It's Sam Dawson from Colorado."

"Hi, Sam Dawson from Colorado, this is a surprise, an early surprise."

"I'm sorry to bother you so early, but I—"

"Where are you calling from? There's a lot of background noise."

"A diner in Lakewood, one greasier than the Tenderloin Grill in Jones." He realized he was yelling into the receiver. Turning, he saw the waitress glaring at him.

"It's good to hear from you, Sam. I was thinking about you just the other day."

"Really? Good thoughts, I hope."

"Every time I serve a piece of pie, I remember how you tricked me to win the bet about my age."

"Annie, can you come to Colorado?"

"Excuse me?"

"I need to talk with someone."

"Get a dog, Sam."

"I had a dog and they killed her."

"Who?"

"Never mind. I'll buy the ticket. Can you come?"

"Why me?"

"You're implicated in something I've discovered."

"Implicated? In what? How?" her voice was now slightly defensive.

"Trust me, Annie. Please come. I'll explain everything when you get here."

"Sam, I barely know you. I—"

"No, no, it's not like that," he said, lowering his voice and placing his head between the phone and the wall. "It's just that I—," he paused. "It's just that I trust you, I guess. And right now I need somebody I can trust. Besides," he paused again, "it's not like that." He turned to see the waitress glaring at him again.

Annie was silent.

"Will you come?"

"When?"

"Today."

"Today! Gosh, Sam, I don't know."

"Please."

There was a long pause. The waitress brushed by him, his order in her hands.

"I need some adventure in my life," Annie said assertively. "It'll take some finagling, but I could do it."

"Great. That's really great. Thanks, Annie."

"I must be crazy," she said.

"I'm headed home," Sam said. "Leave a message on my machine with your flight number and arrival time. I'll pick you up at your gate." He gave her his telephone number. She asked about the weather, what to pack and for how many days. She never again asked why.

••••

"Directory assistance. What city?"

"New Castle."

"What listing?"

"Wiley, W-I-L-E-Y," he spelled, "Sarah Veronica."

As the phone rang, he watched the waitress stop at his table and slap the bill squarely into his plate.

"Hello?"

"Chuck? Is this Chuck Wiley?" Sam said.

"Yes. Yes it is," the retired trapper said sincerely.

"Chuck, this is Sam Dawson from Golden. Do you remember me from a couple weeks back?"

"Yes, yes I do."

"Chuck, I was wondering if I could speak to your mother?"

There was an uncomfortable silence on the other end, a pause even too long for Chuck Wiley. "Chuck?"

"I'm sorry, Mr. Dawson, but Mother passed away just yesterday."

Now the silence was at Sam's end. His mind raced. "I'm very sorry to hear that, Chuck. Please accept my deepest sympathies for your loss."

"Thank you, Mr. Dawson," Chuck said, his laconic western nature still intact.

"I guess I'm a little surprised, she seemed very healthy for a woman of her age," Sam said, doubtfulness resonating in his voice.

"Yes, yes she was very healthy. I figured she would probably outlive me. It was an accident that took her, Mr. Dawson."

Again there was silence. Sam knew that Chuck would offer no details unless asked. "An accident?"

"Carbon monoxide. The heat exchanger on the furnace had somehow worked loose from the flue. She fell asleep on the couch and never woke up."

He could not remember if he said goodbye to Chuck. He placed a ten-dollar bill on the table without turning over the grease-soaked check. He had led them to SVA00F1, the only eyewitness, the only survivor. Sarah Veronica Adams was dead because of him. How could he have been so stupid, so self-absorbed that he did not see what was happening? A person was dead. But she was old and it was a painless death, he justified to himself. The house was old, there was seismic activity in the area, the wind. It was probably just an accident. "It was an accident," he said out loud. Why make more out of this than there really is? It was just an accident, a tragic accident.

••••

There were no vehicle tracks in the fresh snow of the long driveway to his house. He drove past his turnoff and parked the truck on an old logging road out of view from the county road. Following a snow-covered dry creek bed, he made his way amid towering ponderosa pine and aspen trees back to the house, stopping frequently to look for tracks. There were no signs that anyone had been there, at least since the snow the night before.

The house reeked of the pine-scented disinfectant he had used to clean the kitchen. Without Elle, the house seemed cold and empty. The red light on the answering machine blinked furiously. Three calls were from Blair. In the second one there was a recognizable change in her voice when she said, "You have something that belongs to me and I want it back. You have no idea of what you're involved with, Sam. Bring it back and I'll explain everything to you. But you'll need to hurry. I can only hold them off for so long." The third call was desperate, her voice pleading. "You're part of this now, Sam. You're linked to the family by blood. You always have been. We're related for God's sake." There was a long pause. "I didn't want to tell you this over the phone, let alone leave a message on your machine but," there was another long pause. It sounded as if she was crying, muffled sobs and sniffles. "I'm pregnant. I love you, Sam. Please call me."

The muscles in his cheeks rippled, his jaw clamped tightly shut. He stared at the answering machine in disbelief. When Sidney was two years old, he and Marcie both realized that more children were out of the question. Sam had a vasectomy.

Hold them off for so long, linked to the family by blood. Who are they? What family? He did not want to be a part of their family. Had his mother known? His head was swimming.

The last message was from Annie. Her plane would arrive in Denver at 2:15 p.m. at the United concourse. He looked at his watch. There was much to be done and he needed help.

••••

"Revenue, Lashly speaking."

"Dale, Sam Dawson."

"How goes the quest, Sam?"

"I'm making progress, but I need your help again."

"Will I get fired?"

"Probably."

"Outstanding. Talk to me."

When Sam was finished, Dale chuckled lightly into the phone. "I will most definitely get fired, most definitely. You're going to tie all this together for me someday so I can understand why I gave up health and retirement benefits, right?"

"I promise," Sam said.

"What the hell, I was getting pretty bored anyway. Same old crap every day."

"Have you got the sequence, names, and times down?"

"Yep. Trust me, Sam."

"I do, Dale. Thanks."

"Good luck, my friend."

When Sam hung up, he knew Dale would deliver. Despite his eccentricities, he was a damn good information officer who knew all the right people, both inside and outside of state government. More importantly, he knew the pressure points, the hidden scandals, and how to leverage them into favors.

Sam showered, the warm water spraying in his face and running from his open mouth. He was tired and his head ached from the confusion of thoughts and emotions. Sarah Adam's image appeared behind his closed eyes, the warm water soothing his pounding temples. The beautiful young girl in her wedding photo, blonde hair pulled upward into a bun, her slender neck revealing the family beauty mark. He saw her as a child, one of the dancers twirling and singing on the grassy knoll among dark tombstones. "Goodbye, Mr. Dawson," she said to him with the same voice and finality of the aged Sarah Wiley.

Dressing was an effort. Bending over to tie his shoes sent white bolts of pain to the top of his head. He felt slightly nauseous and his heart beat rapidly in his throat. His bed looked inviting. The small plastic box on the wall above the nightstand appeared strangely out of place. The red zero that was normally illuminated was absent from the blackened screen of the carbon monoxide detector. He sat staring at it curiously, the significance of its malfunction not registering. Rising, he traced the detector's cord to the outlet behind the nightstand. It was unplugged. With unsteady hands, he lined up the prongs and inserted them into the outlet. A shrill alarm sounded and the red digital display came to life, numbers feverishly changing form, a kaleidoscope of blinking red lines. The sound of the alarm made him wince with pain, his forehead throbbing. Suddenly the flashing stopped and the numbers became fixed. He squinted at the display, the 732 ppm not registering immediately. Get out, get out of the house, he finally told himself, but his body was slow to react. He stumbled outside, turning off the thermostat and leaving the door open behind him; he hoped to provide a crosscurrent to suck the gas from the house. Behind the garage he turned the propane off at the tank. He slumped against the woodpile, the sun in his face. He breathed deeply.

••••

The gas dissipated quickly; the cold air rushing in through open doors displaced the deadly, inviting warmth of his home. He did not have time to investigate the cause. Instead he turned up the thermostats on the electric baseboard heaters.

Sam decided to take the motor home and was busy ferrying supplies to it when the phone rang. He let the answering machine pick it up, his arms filled with clothes.

"Sam, Barbara Sinclair. Pick up if you're there." There was a pause. "Okay, you're not there. Call me as soon as you get this message. I have some new information for your quest. By the way, Oliver said you were exceptionally rude to him yesterday. Anyway, you're gonna love what I found. Your slutty little trollop from the university, Blair Tennyson, is in this up to her gills. Call me ASAP. I'll clear my schedule and meet you. Okay? See ya."

The red light began to blink. Sam stared at it in disbelief. The pulsing cough-drop-red button declared betrayal. A weakness spread down his arms. He swallowed hard then inhaled deeply. He dropped the clothes on the floor and walked unsteadily to the coffee table in the living room where he had placed the information Barbara had given him. Stripping the rubber bands from the ends of the rolled-up plans, he spread them across the table and weighted down the ends with bookends made of petrified wood. He studied it for a full minute, tracing his finger between reference points. From under the table he pulled the sheets of drawings that Marta Eisenoch had copied for him at the historical society. He placed Marta's 1894 map next to the 1894 map Barbara had given him. The stable on Barbara's drawing was between thirty and forty degrees northwest of the structure that appeared on Marta's map. The 1921 map he had seen at the society confirmed the location of the stable as shown on Marta's map. He shook his head in disbelief. Barbara's map had been altered.

Sam ran his fingers through his hair then massaged his still-pulsing temples, his eyes closed. He wanted to lie down on the couch, curl into a ball, and cry himself to sleep. It was more than disappointment that made him weak with grief. He was alone. The people he loved and trusted had abandoned him with their betrayals. The same hollow feeling had filled his chest when his mother died, a sense of loss combined with a breach of faith. Earlier in the week at the El Condor restaurant when Barbara had asked if he was seeing anyone, he purposefully had not mentioned Blair's name.

CHAPTER TWENTY FOUR

THEY ARE NOT DEAD, THEY ARE JUST AWAY.
EPITAPH
—ROBERT AND MAUDE CHARTER

THE UNITED CONCOURSE WAS PACKED with a cross section of American society. Overweight people who dressed badly clamored noisily in a swirling mass of denim-covered flesh. Sam was nervous, self-conscious of his appearance, and was unsure why. He had called Annie George in a weak moment and now wished he had been more thoughtful. Like Sarah Adams, she would be exposed, complicitous in his crime of discovery. He barely knew the woman. Why did he think he could trust her? What was he going to tell her? What did he expect of her?

A group of middle-aged veterans in lustrous VFW jackets gathered between Sam and the gate where the passengers from Cedar Rapids were disembarking. He could smell their odor of cigarettes and beer. Rising up on the balls of his feet to better see over their heads, he spotted her. She was looking directly at him, smiling broadly.

She too wore blue jeans, but like no one else in the airport. In Iowa he had noted how tall she was, but little else. Her gently ribbed, red cotton sweater with a high crew neck clung tightly to her slender frame. She smiled at him, but then looked away shyly, uncertain of the relationship. Her long, dark hair shone with the luster of a well-groomed thoroughbred, spilling over her square shoulders, accentuating her height.

"Excuse me, excuse me, please," he said, wedging his way between the shiny-coated veterans. Her eyes sparkled and her smile revealed amazingly straight teeth as he reached her. There was an awkward moment when he did not know whether to shake her hand or gently embrace her.

Sensing his hesitation, she extended her hand and said, "Hi, Sam. I made it."

"Annie, it's good to see you," he said, taking her thin hand in his. "Thank you for coming."

"I can't believe I'm here," she said with a mock frown.

"I can't believe I asked you to come. But I'm really glad you did. Do you have any baggage?" he added quickly to change the subject.

"Just one, it was too big for carry-on."

"Baggage claim is this way," he said, taking her by the elbow.

They walked along the concourse without speaking. Their silence was awkward and they both were aware of it. They would occasionally look at each other, smile, and shake their heads in disbelief. Finally, Sam stopped, looked at her seriously, and said, "How old did you say you were?"

Annie laughed. "Old enough to know better," she said.

The shuttle took them to the outlying lot. Annie stood staring at the motor home. "This is your car?"

"I don't own a car. I have a pickup and this," Sam said proudly, extending his hand, palm up, toward the huge tin machine.

She entered hesitantly, looking to its length in both directions. "I don't know about Colorado, but in Iowa if a guy picks you up in a motor home, it's going to be a very long date."

"Date?" he said, attempting to squeeze by her in the narrow hallway. "Annie, let's get one thing straight from the begin—" He was cut off in mid-sentence by her tender kiss, wet and unexpected.

"There," she said. "Maybe now we can communicate more effectively. The sexual tension between us was as thick as molasses. Is that better?"

"I think so," he said, wiping the corner of his mouth with the back of his hand.

"What were you saying?"

"Nothing."

••••

Sam talked almost nonstop for more than an hour. He apologized repeatedly for skipping around in his story, sometimes forgetting to mention key points that would have helped Annie connect the dots. She listened intently, occasionally frowning or squinting when she failed to understand. She shook her head and stared out the side window when he told of the other six states that were probably involved. Annie pushed her hair back against her head and held it there when Sam told her of Sarah Adams' death.

"So they've upped the ante from dog to person?" she said after a long pause.

"These people are serious, Annie. I had second thoughts this morning about bringing you into this."

"What about you, Sam? Are you at least remotely aware that you're in jeopardy?"

He did not respond. Instead he looked out the window into the side mirror.

"Something has already happened, hasn't it?" she said. He did not look at her.

"You brought me into this, Sam from Colorado. If you've placed me in danger, you at least owe me the courtesy of telling me what I'm up against. Tell me. What have they done?"

"They played the carbon monoxide card at my place this morning. I'm a little dumber than I was yesterday, but otherwise okay."

"Did you call the—"

"No," he interrupted. "There was no time for that hassle. Plus, who's going to believe this wild story?"

Annie looked out the passenger window then said softly, "I believe you."

Neither of them talked for several minutes. Finally, Sam broke the silence. "I had a sister, her name was Julie. She disappeared twenty-five years ago just shy of her seventeenth birthday. I believe she was murdered by these people because she had a genetic mutation that was slowly making her deaf and blind."

"Are you sure?"

"Bronco George all but admitted it."

"Jeez, Sam, this just keeps getting darker all the time."

Sam looked at her and could see the fear on her face. "There's more. I found graves in both Oxford and Cambridge of teenage girls who were similarly handicapped. I think these people have been culling the descendants who have this inherited condition, trying to rid their gene pool of inferior traits."

"Culling is too kind of a word," Annie said without looking at him.

Again there was a lull in the conversation.

"I was married for a short time right out of college," he said.

Annie looked at him for a long moment and said, "What happened?"

"It didn't work out. But what's important here is that I have a daughter, Sidney's her name. She's fifteen. We found out two days ago that she has this mutation, Usher syndrome they call it."

Annie stared at him without speaking. She saw his jaw muscles tighten and the whiteness of his knuckles against the black steering wheel.

"They've threatened me with Sidney's safety if I don't back off," Sam said, his lips pursed tightly together.

"My God, Sam, what are you doing here?" Annie almost yelled. "Shouldn't you be protecting her?"

"I've got her under 'round-the-clock surveillance from the Colorado Bureau of Investigation. They're the best there is. There's not much more I can do short of placing her in protective custody." He paused. "Sidney doesn't know about her condition, yet."

Annie stared straight ahead.

"Look," Sam said. "I think the only way to protect her is to expose these people, bring so much public pressure on them that they would be crazy to act on their threat."

"That's a huge gamble, Sam. These people are already crazy. What if your plan to expose them fails? You're betting with your daughter's life against people who have had three-quarters of a century to perfect the art of secrecy. You've got to be right on this, Sam. The slightest misstep and—"

"Don't you think I've considered that?" he said, cutting her off. There was irritation in his voice.

She turned away and gazed out the window again. "This just keeps getting better and better," she mumbled softly.

••••

As they passed the Air Force Academy, she asked where they were going.

"Pueblo," he said.

She did not ask why.

The sky was purple and orange behind the Sangre de Cristo Mountains as the sun set west of Canon City. Sam was tired. It had been a long day and he had slept little the night before. Time had been so compressed that he found it difficult to distinguish between days. He rubbed the back of his neck as they passed Penrose then headed for Florence.

"The sign says Pueblo is that way," Annie said, pointing to the left.

"I know of a little mom-and-pop RV park on the river at Florence. I thought we would camp there tonight. Get an early start in the morning, unless of course you'd rather get your own room at a motel?"

"An early start for what? and no, this will be fun. I've never stayed in a motor home before."

"Great. I'll explain over dinner."

••••

The air was cold and uncharacteristically humid, especially next to the river. Sam stood close to the charcoal grill, occasionally prying up the corner of a steak to check on its progress.

"So that's the Arkansas River," Annie said, her arms folded across her chest, a glass of wine in her hand.

"Yep," he said, looking out between the cottonwoods. A yard light from the campground reflected from the rippling surface. "It doesn't look like much here, but it's a twisting torrent a few miles upstream. The Royal Gorge is just up that way," he said, pointing the meat fork to the west.

Annie came over and stood so close to him that their hips and shoulders touched. "The fire feels good," she said.

They stared silently at the glowing bricks of charcoal. Sam took a deep breath, cleared his throat, and asked the question he had put off all afternoon. "Is there..., I mean do you have a...relationship back there in Iowa? With anyone?" he added awkwardly.

"Are you asking me if I have a lover?"

"I think so," he said, prying up a steak again, not looking at her.

She considered his question, or perhaps the answer for an uncomfortably long moment. It was long enough for Sam to regret asking it.

"I'm here, aren't I?"

"Sorry, it was a stupid question. Forget I asked it," he said.

"I think it could begin to snow any minute," Annie offered, rubbing her upper arms.

"It's late October. It's Colorado. How do you like your steak?"

"Medium well."

"Open the door, it's dinnertime," he said as he placed the steaks on a plate.

The dinner conversation was light. Annie was hungry and they both were exhausted. Sam was tired of talking about conspiracy and decided to give it a rest while they ate. Pushing his plate forward, Sam folded his arms across the edge of the table. "You're a good listener, Annie George. I did all the talking on the way down here. You hardly asked a question. I'm getting the feeling you are having serious second thoughts about coming to Colorado."

She sipped her wine then licked and gently bit her lips before looking squarely at him. "Having second thoughts is an understatement." She leaned back against the padded dinette seat. "What makes you so sure that I'm not part of this massive conspiracy? Blair fooled you, why not me?"

"You're right; I don't know your involvement, other than your genetic ties. I'm taking a huge risk here, following my gut."

"I think you're following something a little lower on your anatomy."

Sam did not expect that type of response from her. But it was an honest statement. "Perhaps that's part of it. But I assure you it wasn't a conscious decision on my part. I guess I'd like to believe that a man and a woman can have a relationship where sex is not the motivator."

"Horse pucky! That was awful, Sam. Try again."

He smiled and shook his head. "You're right, that was pretty lame. Hold on," he said, pointing a finger upward. "Try this one: The few friends I have think I'm loony tunes. The few people I trusted have betrayed me. I'm lonely. I'm frightened. You were nice to me in Iowa and I think you're very attractive. And yes, I suppose sex could be considered a motivator."

"That's better, but you still haven't answered my original question. Can you trust me?"

He stared intently into her eyes as they darted back and forth in minute increments, searching his face for an answer. "You tell me," he said, not taking his eyes from hers.

"If you do anything to hurt my family, especially Nana, I'll be your worst nightmare." She looked at him without blinking, a look of determination on her face. "If I get arrested, there will be absolutely no chance of sex." The corners of her mouth turned upward. "Forever," she added, her eyes widening. "If, on the other hand, this wild tale turns out to be true and somehow you are able to expose it, thereby exposing me and my family to legal investigation and public scrutiny, I'll be your worst nightmare and there will be absolutely no chance of sex, forever."

Sam looked down at the table then back at Annie. "So, what you're telling me is that if I ever want to sleep safely and have sex with you, I need to do both tonight."

"Sorry, Sam, but you're missing the obvious alternative here."

"No, I didn't miss it. To walk away from this, to pretend it never happened, is not an option, Annie. Uncovering a historical crime is only part of it. Exposing the ongoing cover-up and the racist motivation for it is important. Did you miss the fact that they killed my sister, destroyed my family, and now are coming after my daughter?"

"No," Annie said softly, looking down. "Revenge is a powerful motivator. But is part of this to get even with Blair, to hurt her for hurting you?"

"I was deep into this before I discovered her involvement. No, don't you understand? It's the right thing to do. I've spent my life looking the other way, pretending not to see, or covering up other people's mistakes and indiscretions. I never cried when my mother died. I didn't take the time to visit her when she needed me the most. She was orphaned at birth by Eris. She was orphaned by Eris's followers when they took her daughter and she was orphaned at death by me. I pretended she went away and that someday she'll show

up in her June Cleaver dress and pearls, smiling broadly, glad
to see me. I've never told Marcie what a miserably weak human being she is. That she needs to take responsibility for
her life. I've never stood up to Pat and told him what I believe in, what I want to do with the rest of my life. I never
told the governor what a slimy, egotistical bastard he is. And
now, I'm not going to stand by passively and let them take
my daughter."

Annie looked at him quizzically. "Who's June Cleaver?
Who are Marcie and Pat?"

"Never mind, the point is that it's time I stand up for
myself, believe in myself, do the right thing, not turn the
other cheek and walk away. I'm sick of putting makeup on
other people's scabs. A terrible crime has been committed.
Hundreds of people were killed. Eris was the greatest mass
murderer in this country's history. This guy makes Ted Bun-
dy, Richard Speck, and that DeSalvo guy, the Boston Stran-
gler, look like a bunch of beginners."

"He was my great-grandfather," she said softly, looking down, her long brown hair curled gently over her face.
"How would you like to be related to a mass murderer?"

"I am," he said. "I'm pretty sure he's my grandfather too."

She looked at Sam. "I'm just saying that there are consequences. On top of that it looks like I now have a bazillion
cousins, some of whom are white supremacists. And the guy
I kissed at the airport turns out to be my cousin too. How
weird is that? I can see the national news media turning this
into, first, a circus and then, a witch hunt. I can see my picture on a supermarket tabloid with a headline reading 'Iowa

Eris kin suffers rare genetic disorder: Has both male and female genitalia.'"

Sam raised his eyebrows.

"You know what I mean," she said, frowning at him. "And what about your career, do you want to be forever known as the guy who discovered the biggest mass murderer and most prolific father in our history? I haven't known you very long, but you don't impress me as the kind of guy who would use this to spin book sales."

"This is all bull, Annie. Don't place the burden of exposure on me. You now know as much as I do. If I die in my sleep tonight, what are you going to do?"

"That's not a realistic possibility," she said, shaking her head.

"Yes it is," he said, staring intently at her, his brow furrowed. "Who are you going to tell? What will you do with this information? Will you keep it to yourself, take it to the grave with you? Who you gonna call?"

"Ghostbusters?" she said, squinting at him. "Jeez O' Pete, Sam, I don't know. It's an unfair question."

"Jeez O' Pete?" He cocked his head and grimaced. "Annie, it's the same question you're asking me. Should I look the other way, pretend this never happened? Should I protect you and your bazillion cousins or, should I pull the alarm and expose these crazy bastards and their secret plan to build the master race?"

"You know what you're going to do. I seriously doubt if there is anything I could say that would change your mind. I'm just a little confused. I still don't know why you called

me. Why I'm here. It all seems a little more dangerous now."
She turned and looked out the window. "The darkness does
that."

Sam spoke to her reflection in the window. Their eyes
met on the dark glass. "You're here because I trust you, Annie." He reached across the table and took her hand in his.
"I see the same thing in your eyes that I saw in Iowa. You're
a caring and compassionate person. I knew you wouldn't
turn away from the young lives that were frightened by the
darkness too. Imagine them, Annie. Imagine them on a
night like this, alone, imprisoned in a cold stable, their bel-
lies swollen with an unknown life. Their only crime was that
they were young, attractive, and smart. Imagine them, Annie. Taste their tears as they cry themselves to sleep. Feel the
cold as they shudder under a thin blanket. Hear the muted
cries of other young girls on the other side of the wall. Remember how it used to be before you came there. Dream
how it might be if you were rescued. Can you see it? Can
you hear it, Annie? Do you have any idea of how scared
these girls must have been? Can you hear them calling for
recognition, for justice, for someone to care for them, for
someone to miss them? Can you imagine dying and no one
knowing about it?"

He looked down at the table. "Eris committed his crimes
more than a half century before my sister, Julie, was born,
but he screwed up. He didn't know that he was a carrier of
Usher syndrome. His followers have been culling the herd
of anybody who displays a hearing or seeing handicap. All
my life I've repressed thoughts of Julie's fear, her pain, and

her unfound body. I turned away from the torment, choosing not to experience what Julie had. Like the police, like my parents, I gave up trying to find her. Life goes on, time heals. But time has no meaning when you're dead. There's little difference between eighty years and twenty-five years when someone has cheated you out of life and hidden the one thing that proved you existed. I need to find their remains, the tangible proof of their lives. And maybe, just maybe in the process compensate, in part, for my inability to find my sister."

Annie turned from the window and looked directly at him; tears were in her eyes.

"They were people, Annie, flesh-and-blood human beings. Each of them was some mother's child." He looked down at the hand he was holding. Her long, delicate fingers were warm and sensual. "Sometimes at night when the wind blows through the aspens outside my bedroom, I can hear their voices."

"What do they say?"

"I don't know. I can't make it out, just voices. But I know it's them. They've waited for a long time. I think they're scared I might give up. I can't turn away from them now."

The tears in her eyes finally spilled over and ran down her cheeks. "Every instinct I have tells me to run away from you as fast and far as I can," she said, wiping away the tears with her free hand. "But if all this is true, the least we can do is let the world know they existed. Count me in."

"And Annie, I'll do everything I can to protect you and your family," he said, squeezing her hand. "Because forever is a long time," he added, smiling in an attempt to lighten the mood.

Annie smiled.

"Forget I said that," he said. "Tomorrow's a big day. We'll need to get an early start. You take the back bedroom and I'll convert the dinette. You know where the bath is. Go easy on the hot water. I'll clean up the kitchen."

"It is," she said.

"It is what?" Sam said, a puzzled look on his face.

"Forever, it's a very long time."

CHAPTER TWENTY FIVE

DO NOT STAND AT MY GRAVE AND CRY...
I AM NOT THERE. I DID NOT DIE...
EPITAPH
—ELIZABETH PETERSON

NEITHER OF THEM SPOKE. They stared at the tunnel of illuminated asphalt ahead of them. The sun would not creep above the flat eastern horizon for another hour, if at all. The sky was overcast and heavy with moisture. Sam was nervous. He slowly turned his head to look at Annie. She was sitting uncomfortably straight, ready to bolt and run at the slightest provocation. She wore a Chicago Cubs baseball cap, the bill carefully cupped. Her hair, fixed in a ponytail, was pulled through the back of the cap with a fluffy, red ponytail holder snugged up against the cap's adjustable band. The collar of her fleece-lined denim jacket was turned up. She clutched the padded armrests of the passenger seat. The soft, green glow of the dashboard lights accentuated her delicate features, the sharpness of her nose, the definition of her lips, and the dark curl of lashes above wide eyes.

He too was nervous. Timing was critical. Anything out of sequence and the plan would unravel. "Hungry?" he blurted out a little too loudly.

Annie jumped. "Jeez O'Pete, Sam. You would have thought your hair was on fire or something."

He could not help smiling at her obvious irritation. "Sorry, I didn't mean to startle you. Are you hungry? Do you want something to eat?"

"No," she said, a sharpness in her voice. "No, thank you. Sorry, if I'm a little edgy. I was lost in the thought of showering with lots of other women for the next ten years."

"I used to have that dream when I was younger," he said, smiling.

"You know what I mean. Do you think we'll get arrested? I've never been arrested before. I've never even had a traffic violation. I don't have an attorney. Shoot, I don't even know an attorney."

"Take a breath, Annie, a deep breath. I'm anxious too. I'm scared that some patrolman or county Mountie will pull us over before we get there."

"Why would they do that?" Annie asked.

"It's possible that I'm wanted for assault, maybe breaking and entering." He could feel the burning stare that Annie was giving him. "What?" he said, turning to meet her glaring eyes.

"Better and better," she said. "I wish you would have told me you were a felon before I agreed to be your accomplice in yet another crime."

"The real crime was committed a long time ago," he said. "Eris has had generations of accomplices that make your involvement look pale in comparison."

"I hope we get locked in the same cell," she said without turning.

"Really?"

"Yes, I want you to truly experience what forever without the possibility of sex feels like."

Sam smiled.

••••

Just west of Pueblo the first flakes of snow appeared in the headlights. Sam looked at the green numerals of the dashboard clock—5:46, he was early.

"Do you have a plan?" Annie asked softly.

"A plan?"

"Doesn't the state hospital have guards or security or something? What makes you think you can just drive in there with a motor home and not get challenged by the cops?"

Sam thought for a moment. "Sex," he said without turning.

"Sex?"

"It's all about sex."

"You've got a one-track mind," Annie said, a note of seriousness in her voice.

"Senator Harold McFadden, president of the senate, crusader for moral reform, godfather of Pueblo's good-old-boy club, and friend of the governor just happens to like young boys," Sam said matter-of-factly. "The session before I left the governor's office, the good senator negotiated for a child prostitute with an undercover vice cop. The governor put me on it the next morning, and by the evening news I had so much spin on the story that the senator appeared to be a savior of street waifs who were being abused by over-zealous cops. Harold owes me big-time."

"And...," Annie drawled, not understanding the connection to the plan.

"And the Pueblo County coroner is Senator McFadden's brother-in-law. If everything went according to plan, the coroner paid a visit to District Court Judge Michael Olivetii last night. Judge Olivetii plays poker with Senator McFadden on Thursday nights when the legislature is not in session. Olivetii should have issued an exhumation order that will be served by Sheriff Tony Garcia at," Sam looked at his watch, "seven o'clock this morning. Did I mention that Tony and Harold played basketball together in high school and scratch each other's backs politically?"

Annie placed her hands on her knees and rubbed them lightly over her jeans while slowly shaking her head. "I thought Iowa was a small town."

Sam smiled. "Politics is a small-town game no matter how large the city or state. It all boils down to connections and favors. Believe me, public policy is seldom based on public need. It's like making sausage—not a pretty sight."

"This all sounds a little too smooth," Annie said, looking out the side window at the flurries of snow racing by. "What are Blair and Bronco George doing to stop you?"

"I'm more worried about Barbara Sinclair. She's an excellent attorney with strong connections to the attorney general, not to mention the fact that she's a member of the governor's cabinet. We could be in trouble. I doubt if she would get an injunction without running it by the governor first. That's why I had him sent to Grand Junction today to receive a phony award from the Colorado Press Association."

"You had him sent?"

"It was certainly not on his schedule, but he's a sucker for any kind of award. My bet is that we're a few hours ahead of Barbara. We'll need to find bodies in order to establish a criminal investigation and counter the injunction."

"Do you know where the bodies are buried?" Annie asked.

"I have a general idea. They're somewhere between where the stable used to be and the river."

"Sounds like a lot of random digging to me. It will be like looking for a needle in a haystack."

"You're right. We'd be digging for days. That's why I called the CBI."

Annie turned to look at him.

"Colorado Bureau of Investigation," he corrected himself, realizing Annie was not familiar with the acronym. "The same people who are watching over Sidney. They're sending a crime lab technician to meet us this morning with a portable ground penetrating radar unit."

"Radar?" she said.

"As long as the bodies aren't buried too deep, a good operator should be able to detect them. It sort of works like sonar on a submarine."

They were silent for several minutes. The lights of west Pueblo came into view when they crested a hill. Fuzzy halos surrounded each point of light as the snowfall intensified.

"Hope it works in the snow," Annie said without warning.

"Me too," he said softly, turning toward her. Her long, slender fingers were gripping her thighs.

"Sam, what if we don't find any graves? What happens then?"

"You spend the rest of the day licking egg off my face," he said, smiling.

"No, seriously?"

"I don't know. I haven't given it a great deal of thought. I would definitely lose points with the people I've asked to help me. Including you, I suppose." He turned toward her to register her response.

"You're fishing again. I'm not biting. Do you have a backup plan?"

"Not really. I have the ledger. When I get out on bail, I can start gathering DNA samples from those who would cooperate. I won't be able to leave the state, so you'll have to help me with the Iowa clan."

"If this turns sour, buster, you are on your own," she said, looking at him with a straight face.

On the outskirts of Pueblo the neon sign for the King's Inn Buffet cut through the morning gloom. Sam slowed and put on his turn signal.

Annie looked at him and asked, "Hungry?"

Sam did not answer. He again looked at the dashboard clock. It was 6:02. At the far end of the parking lot he saw a long gooseneck trailer with a yellow John Deere tractor and backhoe. It was attached to a silver one-ton Dodge with duel rear wheels. A plastic, magnetic sign on the driver's door advertised "AAA Excavation." Sam pulled in next to the long rig.

Annie looked at him, her brow furrowed slightly.

"You didn't expect we were going to use shovels, did you?" he said.

"How do you know this guy?"

"He was the first listing in the yellow pages when I called directory assistance."

Sam parked the motor home next to the long rig.

"Sit tight, I'll be right back," he said as he exited the side door.

The backhoe operator met Sam halfway, they shook hands, and both folded their arms across their chests as they negotiated the job. The operator was a slim man in his mid-forties, clean shaven, wearing a cap with a yellow backhoe embroidered on it. They shook hands again and Sam returned to the motor home.

"We're in luck," Sam said, sliding into his seat. "This guy began his career as a groundskeeper for Roselawn Cemetery down by the fairgrounds. He's had experience. Said they had to move thirty-some graves when the city annexed a portion of the cemetery when they widened Central Avenue."

Annie said nothing.

"You okay?" Sam said, reaching across the console, taking her hand in his.

"I'm fine," she said and gently squeezed his hand in return. "It's just the realization that we are really doing this that has me a little spooked."

"No turning back now," he said, starting the motor home and circling out of the parking lot. The pickup and backhoe followed.

The snow swirled in frenzied crosscurrents when they reached the sprawling campus of the state hospital. A brick wall with a spiked wrought iron fence atop it, surrounded the facility and stretched nearly three-quarters of a mile from north to south and more than a quarter mile east to west. The main entrance was a divided street with a guard station in the middle, a small brick castle on an oval island.

"Everybody's right on time," Sam said, nodding toward the curb across from the entrance. The Pueblo county sheriff's Chevy Blazer was conspicuous. Parked behind him was a white Ford van with "Colorado Bureau of Investigation" printed boldly in straight black letters along its side."

"Who's in the car behind the van?" Annie asked.

Sam noted the state license plates on the nondescript car. "That should be Susan Murray, the state archaeologist."

"Why an archaeologist?"

"Besides the historical significance, who better to determine sex, age, when they were buried, even cause of death? She's actually a forensic anthropologist. These people know their bones."

Sam double-parked next to the sheriff's Blazer, the excavator behind him. Sam exited the motor home.

"You Dawson?" the middle-aged man asked, stepping from his vehicle. He was not in uniform. Instead he was wearing black jeans, cowboy boots, western shirt with a turquoise bolo around his neck, and a corduroy sports coat with a western yoke.

"That's me," Sam said, extending his hand.

"Tony Garcia," the man said, accepting Sam's hand.

"The sheriff himself," Sam said. "I expected you to send a deputy or someone."

"Anybody digging for bodies in my county gets my personal attention. Besides, Harold—Senator McFadden—called me yesterday and asked me to personally take charge of serving the order. Seems he's indebted to you," he said, probing.

"Harold's a good man," Sam said, brushing off the sheriff's curiosity.

"He's some sort of queer and you know it. But he's still my friend and one helluva politician," Tony said without flinching.

Sam returned the stare, a slight smile on his lips. "We have the CBI, state archaeologist, and Triple A Excavation. We'll be right behind you."

Sam quickly walked to each vehicle and introduced himself to the CBI technician then to the archaeologist. Someone was sitting in the passenger seat of the state sedan. Sam leaned down to look past Dr. Murray. Marta Eisenoch smiled shyly at him. "Hi, Marta. What a pleasant surprise."

"Good morning, Mr. Dawson. I hope you don't mind my tagging along."

"Not at all, Marta; without your help, we wouldn't be here. I hope this doesn't turn out to be a wild-goose chase."

"That's the nice thing about being a volunteer, Mr. Dawson. Doctor Murray can't fire me."

At the gate, the guard, a heavyset Latino, offered no resistance. Sam rolled down his window and heard the sheriff and the guard speaking Spanish. From the smiles and gestures, it appeared they knew each other. No papers were served. The guard waved everyone through the gate, smiling and nodding. In the large side mirror, Sam saw the guard pick up the telephone after everyone had passed.

"That was easy," Annie said.

"Too easy! I have a feeling the hospital director's breakfast is being interrupted as we speak. Let the games begin."

••••

Rows of three-story brick buildings were set back from the cottonwood- and spruce-lined streets. Red brick, green roofs, and white trim on military-looking buildings all added to the institutional appearance. The light snow melted without accumulating. The air smelled metallic.

At the old power plant, the sheriff pulled over and yelled up to Annie, "I don't know where you're going. You take the lead and I'll follow."

At the south end of the facility, Sam pulled over and stopped. The snow was beginning to stick on the huge, sloping field of brown, native grass that stretched before him; perhaps thirty acres of open land that extended toward a chain-link fence, railroad tracks, a flood wall, and finally the Arkansas River.

"Like a needle in a haystack," Annie said softly without looking at him.

Sam looked at the dashboard clock. It was 7:15 a.m. By eight o'clock the walls would begin closing in on him. He needed to find that cemetery. There were no structural landmarks. Most of the older buildings at that end of the campus had been razed long ago. There was no telling how the landscape had been modified in three-quarters of a century. He imagined huge bulldozers rolling over the field, blades down, reshaping the natural contours of the land, scattering and crushing the bones of those buried beneath, covering them under tons of rock and dirt. "They're here," he said with a soft certainty. "I know they're here." He pulled from the console the folded map and photocopies Marta had made for him. "Sit tight, I need to get my bearings, no need both of us getting wet." With that, he stepped from the motor home, motioning to the others with a raised hand to remain in their vehicles.

Annie watched Sam pull up the hood of his coat as he walked into the field, his dark form fuzzy in the blowing snow. He stopped, looked at the maps, glanced left and right, moved farther into the field, stopped again, and repeated the entire process. It was snowing harder, large wet flakes driven by a northwest wind. At times he seemed to disappear completely and then reappeared in the space between squalls. He faced into the storm, staring in the direction of the power plant. The wind blew back his hood. Snow clung to his eyebrows and lashes, foggy vapors rose from his lips. He studied the maps then turned toward the river, then back toward the power plant. Sam appeared small in the large field. He suddenly pointed at the CBI van and, with broad sweeps of his arm, motioned for the technician to join him.

At 7:45 a.m. an emerald green Lincoln Town Car, followed by a hospital security sedan, came to a fast stop next to the sheriff's car.

"What the hell is going on here, Tony?" Dr. David Herrenstein demanded as he rounded the rear of his car and approached the sheriff.

"Good morning, Dave. Think it will snow?" the sheriff smiled.

"You have no right to be here," Herrenstein barked, his face red with anger.

Sam approached the small gathering and was joined by Annie, her hands stuffed inside her jacket pockets.

"Sam Dawson," the sheriff said, "this is Doctor David Herrenstein, director of the state hospital."

Sam stepped forward to offer his hand, but Herrenstein ignored him and turned toward the sheriff.

"This is an outrage. I demand to know under what authority you have brought this circus to my hospital."

"Under the authority of the State of Colorado, as ordered by District Court Judge Michael Olivetii," the sheriff said, retrieving the exhumation order from inside his sports coat.

Herrenstein snapped the papers open; his eyes darted back and forth as he scanned the order. "This is bull. It's an exhumation order. There's nothing here to exhume, no cemetery. Even if there were, you're trespassing. This piece of crap paper only gives you the right to dig. I've already talked with the director of Institutions this morning and she assures me the attorney general has been notified. You can't come marching in here without probable cause and a warrant. And you'll pay hell getting one. The A.G. and I will see to it. Escort these people from the property," he said to the security officer.

"I thought you might try that, doc," the Sheriff smiled. Reaching into his other breast pocket he pulled out another set of papers. "This is a search and seizure warrant issued concurrently with the exhumation order," he said, handing the papers to Herrenstein.

Sam smiled his surprised approval to the sheriff. Herrenstein's face grew redder. "You are so sued. You won't even be able to get a job as gate attendant when I'm through with you, Garcia." He motioned for the security officer to follow him. The big Lincoln fishtailed, its tires spinning on the wet pavement as he drove away.

"He'll get an injunction, you know," the sheriff said to Sam.

"Yeah, I figured. But it'll take them a few hours," Sam said. "Can you stick with us for a while?"

"I wouldn't miss this for the world. Anytime I can make Herrenstein's butt pucker, count me in," he said, grinning.

"Do you think someone has gotten to him already?" Annie said, nodding toward the speeding Lincoln.

"Probably Barbara Sinclair," Sam said, noting that Annie's eyes were a little wider than usual. "But who knows, he could be your cousin."

"Not funny, Sam," she said weakly.

The CBI technician unloaded the ground-penetrating radar unit, an awkward looking contraption mounted on two large spoked wheels and one small wheel in the rear. It reminded Sam of the ice cream pushcart the Good Humor man used at the zoo.

Sam asked the backhoe operator to unload and stand by. He gave the thumbs-up sign to Marta Eisenoch and Dr. Murray, and followed the technician and pushcart into the open field to show him where to search.

••••

The wind intensified as the temperature continued to drop. The wet, flaky snow turned into stinging missiles of ice that forced Sam to stand with his head tucked toward his chest, the bill of his cap deflecting the snow pellets. The technician pushed the cart slowly in a grid pattern over the snow-covered field. He stopped occasionally to wipe the radar screen with his handkerchief.

Sam could not make sense of the pattern. At first he thought it was one of ever-widening straight lines, a rectangle that got larger with each pass. Then he was certain the technician was converging from larger to smaller. At certain points the technician stuck small orange flags into the ground. None of it made sense to Sam. He was cold and starting to shiver. He looked at his watch. It was almost nine o'clock and he was running out of time. At times, the technician faded into the whiteness of the storm then reappeared mystically between squalls. Sam looked at his watch again. Someone grabbed his arm and he spun around quickly, startled. It was Annie.

"Sorry, I didn't mean to scare you," she yelled above the wind.

"What is it?" he snapped, his irritation obvious.

"Come in for a little while and warm up. I've made hot chocolate for everyone. There's nothing you can do out here to speed this up."

"That injunction will be here any minute," he said.

"I can hardly wait," she said, staring up at him, a devilish smile on her face.

"Why's that?"

"That's when I get to lick the egg off your face," she said, her smile broadening. She took him by the arm. "Come on, let's have some hot chocolate."

A tangible tension, intertwined with the smell of cocoa, permeated the inside of the motor home. Exaggerated comments about the weather, the hot chocolate, and the motor home filled the dead spots. Sam knew that everyone was secretly asking if they had foolishly accepted an invitation from a crazy person to a wild-goose chase.

Leaning over the kitchen counter, Sam stared out the window toward the open field. The technician had disappeared into the storm. He looked at his watch.

"Don't worry, Mr. Dawson," Marta Eisenoch said quietly from beside him. "You'll find it. You always do."

"Thanks, Marta, but I'm starting to have my doubts. This whole thing is based on a hunch and the statement of a very old woman, now deceased. I don't even know if we are in the right area. There's a lot of ground out there."

The unintelligible hiss and garbled voice of someone calling the sheriff on his two-way radio silenced the group. The sheriff walked slowly toward the rear of the motor home with the radio to his ear and responded with numeric codes, all of which began with the number ten.

"Problems?" Sam asked when the sheriff returned.

"No, nothing I can't handle," Tony Garcia said. He placed his hands on his hips and pushed his sports coat back to reveal his shoulder holster and pistol. "You're about out of time, Sam. There's a convoy of state patrol, county, and municipal cars all running hot, headed in this direction. There's been an injunction issued."

"Christ," Sam said as he removed his hat and ran his fingers through his hair. "Sounds like overkill just to deliver a court order."

Garcia smiled. "They're also carrying a warrant for your arrest, Denver County, assault charges. We've been advised you are possibly armed and we should proceed with extreme caution."

Sam looked at him with disbelief. Only the wind buffeting the motor home could be heard. Annie stepped forward and slipped her arm around Sam's.

"Any more hot chocolate, Annie?" Garcia asked, holding up his cup.

The faint cry of multiple sirens could be heard above the wind. Simultaneously, everyone turned toward the source of the emergency, staring out the windshield toward the street that paralleled the railroad tracks. The flashing red lights, softened by the storm, formed a chain that stretched more than a quarter mile.

"I think I'll get loaded up," the backhoe operator said. "I sure as hell don't need this."

"I understand," Sam said softly. "Marta, Doctor Murray, maybe you should beat the rush. And would you take Annie back to Denver with you?" he added suddenly.

"No way, Sam," Annie protested. "I'm here until the bitter end."

"Don't you understand? This is the bitter end," he said. He stared at her, attempted a smile, but the pain of defeat was evident in his eyes. "It was a race and I came in second. Go back to Iowa. I'll send you a postcard and let you know the conditions of my parole."

There was a feeble knock on the door, a light pecking upon aluminum. The sheriff, standing closest to the door, opened it.

The CBI technician, his windbreaker hood pulled tightly around his face, looked up at the sheriff through thick, wet glasses. "Is Mr. Dawson here?" he asked with uncertainty.

"You can pack up your machine," Sam said, stepping around the sheriff, "Looks like we're done here. Be sure to tell your boss thanks. I really appreciate you driving all the way down—"

"I'm finished, I think. I have the corners and each row marked with flags. I couldn't find any others," he said, pushing up his glasses.

"Finished with what? What are you talking about?" Sam said.

"The graves you asked me to find."

"You found something?" Sam almost shouted.

"Oh yes, immediately. They were right where you told me to look. The graves are arranged in six rows of about twenty bodies each. The rows are a little crooked and the graves are not aligned very well. They're not very deep, around four to five feet."

"You found 120 graves?"

"Actually 119, one row was a grave short. But there are no caskets, Mr. Dawson. The radar only picked up the bones, no caskets."

Sam leaned around Annie and pointed at the backhoe operator. "Can you do it?"

"Hell yes," the operator said, pulling his John Deere hat lower on his forehead.

"Then go," Sam ordered. He turned to the technician and said, "Show him where to dig, start at a corner—and be careful!"

The backhoe operator pushed his way out the door and ran toward his machine.

"Doctor Murray," Sam said. "I think that guy is pretty good, but can you supervise? I have shovels and rakes in the rear compartment."

"I brought my own equipment, Mr. Dawson, including sifting screens," she said, sliding out from the dining nook. "Come on, Marta, we have work to do."

There was a shift in the sound of the sirens as they turned at the entrance to the hospital campus. "Sheriff, I need some time," Sam said, looking directly into Garcia's dark eyes.

"Show me dead people and I can stall."

"I'll do my best. Thanks," Sam said. Turning toward Annie, he said, "Run interference for me?"

"You got it," she beamed. "Go, we'll take care of the posse."

Annie and the sheriff watched as Sam disappeared into the storm. The line of law enforcement vehicles stopped a safe distance from the motor home. The convoy was led by Hale Robertson, one of the sheriff's deputies. Robertson's cruiser was followed by three state patrol cars and at least three municipal cars, two marked and one unmarked, that stretched down the street, disappearing into the depths of the storm. Red lights flashed illuminated halos of moving snow that gave the scene a festive, holiday appearance. Sirens stopped and car doors opened. In the distance, additional sirens could be heard as they raced toward the hospital, whipped into a frenzy of dangerous excitement. No one approached the motor home.

"Christ," Garcia said. "I hope they don't shoot my ass." He opened the motor home door slowly, knowing that weapons were pointed at him. "Hale, it's me, Tony," he yelled, stepping from the motor home, his hands held slightly in the air. "Holster your weapons, fellas, we've got the area secured," he said, approaching the deputy's car. He turned toward Annie, who stood in the doorway, and motioned for her to join him. "Jesus Christ, Hale. Who do you think you are, Broderick freaking Crawford?"

"Sheriff," a tall, crisp state patrol officer said, stepping forward. "We have a warrant for a Samuel Theodore Dawson, issued by Denver County."

Garcia squinted at the military-looking officer, his Smokey Bear hat pulled tightly down over close-cropped hair. "Do I know you?"

"Captain Summers, C Springs district office," the patrolman said. "Do you have the suspect in custody?"

"I do," Garcia said, nodding his head.

"Excellent, we'll take over from here," Captain Summers said.

"Not so fast, captain," Garcia said, holding up his hand. "I've placed Dawson under protective custody as a material witness at a crime scene."

"What crime scene?" Summers said, straightening.

"My crime scene, and you're standing on it."

"This warrant originated with the state's attorney general. The director of public safety personally took the call this morning," Summers said.

"I assume that's why the state patrol is involved?" Garcia said.

"That's correct, sheriff. Now if you would hand over Dawson, we can all be on our way."

"Not that simple, captain," Garcia said, scratching the back of his head. The snow was sticking to the shoulders of his sports coat. He turned in the direction of the backhoe's diesel groan, but could not see it through the haze of the storm. "First, this is a potential murder scene. Your own CBI just identified over a hundred possible victims buried out there," he said, gesturing with a sweep of his arm. "Second, you're in my jurisdiction."

"That's horse crap, sheriff, and you know it," Summers said loudly. "Don't make me pull rank on you, Garcia. The state takes precedence here."

"You can pull my dick, captain. I've got an active crime scene here and a material witness."

"I can make this very simple for both of you," Annie said with authority as she stepped up from behind the sheriff. "I'm placing this entire sector under quarantine. The federal government is now in charge."

"Who the hell are you?" Summers said, his eyes narrowed and brow furrowed.

"I'm Doctor George with the Center for Disease Control. The CDC has strong reason to believe that anthrax is associated with this site, perhaps interred with the bodies in that field. Anthrax spores, buried for years, are just as dangerous when released into the atmosphere."

"Do you have some form of identification, Doctor George?" Summers asked skeptically.

"Yes, I do, captain. It's on the table in that motor home," she said, gesturing with her thumb over her shoulder, "right next to the first sample of contaminated soil from this site. You're more than welcome to come in and inspect my credentials. But once you step from that road you'll be mine, at least until the hazmat team arrives from Denver. They'll suit you up and transport you to Fort Carson where you'll remain until we can clear you or you die, whichever comes first. Sheriff," she barked, turning toward Garcia, "secure the perimeter of this site. No one comes in, no one goes out. Do you understand?"

"Yes, Doctor," Garcia said, his eyes wide with amusement as he watched her turn and walk briskly toward the motor home. "Hale, call for backup, I want this site tighter than Captain Summers' ass." He looked squarely at the patrolman to see his response. "And, Hale, you arrest anyone, and by God I mean anyone that challenges you. You copy?"

"Yes, sheriff," the deputy said, his voice cracking.

••••

The red flashing lights from the squadron of police vehicles cast a pulsing glow in a limited radius of the gray morning. Snow continued to fall. The last of the sirens arrived at 9:15 a.m. Annie watched as a dark-haired woman with dark-rimmed glasses stepped from the state patrol car. She approached Captain Summers and they talked. Summers gestured toward the motor home and field. The woman walked toward the open field. Hale Robertson called to her, but she did not respond. He ran toward her, slipping and almost falling in the wet snow. Sheriff Garcia caught the deputy by the arm as Robertson attempted to draw his weapon. They both watched as the woman disappeared into the swirling fog of snow. From Sam's description, Annie knew it was Barbara Sinclair.

Looking up, Sam saw her dark figure materialize from the snowy haze. Her hands were stuffed deeply into the pockets of her long wool coat. Snow frosted the top of her bare head. She stopped in front of him but did not look at him. Instead she gazed in the direction of the backhoe's groan.

"You always were persistent," she said without looking at him.

"You were my friend," he blurted out, surprised by his own words and the force of emotion behind them.

"I'm still your friend, Sam," she said, looking at him, her eyes filled with tears.

"Friends don't deceive each other, Babs. Friends don't try to kill each other. You're not my friend," he said, shaking his head.

"Sam, I never wanted it to end this way. I never wanted it, any of it, to hurt you or Sidney. But you wouldn't give up. You took on something much bigger than you can possibly comprehend."

"Try me," he shot back. "I don't have to be real smart to understand right from wrong, to understand the significance of hatred and bigotry, to understand the value of human life."

"Sam, you're a product of contemporary society, a misguided, politically correct, liberal society that refuses to accept or even discuss the overwhelming truths of human, not just racial, differences; a society that refuses to deal with the consequences of indiscriminate breeding by inferior people. Don't you see, Sam, that our society is doomed unless we build on our strengths and limit our weaknesses?" Her red lipstick was curiously out of place against the white background of snow.

"Who defines strengths and weaknesses in your warped Utopian society?"

"We do, the brightest and the best."

"Who proclaimed you the brightest and the best? Who gave you the right to define inferior people?"

"We did, because you let us. Unlike you, we've taken responsibility for the future and tried to do something to change it. The ills of society can't be cured by political rhetoric and Band-Aid public policies. Welfare, child abuse, unemployment, crime, teen pregnancy, drug abuse, and all the other social maladies that threaten to destroy our way of life are shown conclusively to be correlated with low intelligence."

"All this was about IQ?" he said, waving his hand in an arc over the ground around him. "Eris's brood stock were blue-eyed blonde morphs of each other. Don't tell me he wasn't into physical characteristics, building the master race."

"He knew that northern Europeans were of the highest intelligence. Physical characteristics were secondary, but indicative of race."

"That's bull and you know it. Why didn't he propagate Asians or Jews? I've read that both have higher IQ's than us white folk."

She looked down and shook her head, dismissing Sam's argument. "Galton understood the racial differences of intelligence. Eugenics was an offshoot, the practical application of what Galton discovered in his primary research on intelligence. He spent his life laying the groundwork for intelligence testing. He knew that some people were smarter than others. What troubled him was that the dumb ones were outbreeding the smart ones. It's not just race, Sam. Even today, white women in the bottom five percent of intelligence are six times more likely to have illegitimate children. Fifty-three percent of Hispanic babies and seventy-three percent of black babies are illegitimate. Minorities start younger, finish later, and have more of them. We know that drug use, crime rate, dropout rate, incarceration rate, and all the other social maladies of society rise with the illegitimacy rate. They are the least educated, least paid, least prepared to—"

"You're a racist, a white supremacist," he said, cutting her off. "A Nazi!" he yelled.

"I'm a realist, Sam. I'm not a racist who hates but doesn't understand why. Wake up, Sam. Can't you see what's happening to society? In some minority groups three-quarters of all children born are fatherless. They're raised by single women of low cognitive ability and the cycle of poverty, crime, welfare, drug abuse continues."

"Stop," he said, vapor rising from his mouth. "You're a zealot filled with hate and lots of worthless statistics that I could easily challenge, if the field were level, if I'd spent my life memorizing bogus figures to make my case."

"I've heard all the arguments, Sam. You want to tell me there are environmental or cultural reasons for low IQs in minorities, that there are test biases. They've all been considered in dozens of studies. You and your politically correct society are terrified to admit there are genetic differences between races. And that, Sam, is the greatest danger of all. An entire society that has convinced itself that such differences don't exist will only lead to extremism. Don't you see? That's why we have racists. By failing to admit there are differences, you'll never be able to prevent extremists from forming and doing extreme things to get their point across. The white, liberal society is so smug in their unjustified defense of racial equality that they have helped create the very thing they find so reprehensible: racists."

"I don't want to hear this."

"Of course you don't."

"It's insane. You're insane. These people have done nothing to hurt you."

"IQ in this country is plummeting and all the societal cancers that go with it are increasing. The cognitive elite are footing the bill while being biologically, socially, and politically outcompeted by people with low intelligence and cultural values that threaten to destroy the greatest society in the history of mankind. Threatened? You're damn right I'm threatened. Doctor Eris chose to fight back."

"How can you possibly justify the one hundred nineteen dead girls buried in this field and God knows how many other women buried in seven other states—donors, surrogates, or innocent bystanders that simply got in the way?" he said. Anger reddened his face as jets of vapor were forced from his mouth.

"A small price, a tiny fraction of what we are up against. Open your eyes, Sam. A third of the public schools in major cities can't meet the minimum scores on standardized tests. Less than half of high school students in our largest cities graduate, only twenty-four percent in Detroit, Atlanta the same thing. Government policy subsidizes births among poor women of low intelligence. It's social engineering in the wrong direction. If this country spent as much time and money encouraging intelligent women to have babies, you and your liberal, educated, white friends would scream bloody murder, accusing the government of bioengineering society. Instead, you champion for more financial support in order to reward low-income women for reproducing, while demanding the country throw open its gates to an immigrant population with equally low intelligence who can't find jobs, who tax our health and social welfare system, who fill our schools with kids who can't speak English, who drop out, commit crimes, and go to prison all at your and my expense. You and your environmentally conscious friends blame agriculture, logging, and mining for all the ills of our planet and refuse to accept the fact that it's overpopulation competing for resources that—"

"Shut up, Barbara, just shut your stinking mouth. Nothing you can say will ever justify the sick and selfish approach that Eris took. Your involvement, your protection or cover-up or whatever you're doing is a crime against humanity. Your arguments turn my stomach," he said, clenching his fist, his eyes fixed on hers. "You classify people by groups and refuse to acknowledge the value of individuals. You don't celebrate differences, you mock them," he said, shaking his head. "How'd you get like this, Babs? How can you believe this crap? Your righteous plan was flawed from the start. That dirty SOB, Eris, was a murderer, a sick, demented serial killer who did unspeakable things to innocent, young girls, our grandmothers. You can't defend what he did. You can't defend killing my sister. You can't defend eugenics."

"Yes I can," she smiled. "And the sad truth is that you know I can. But you're unwilling to hear it, brainwashed to believe in equality. I understand."

"Condescension doesn't become you, Barbara. If you want to talk brainwashed, let's talk about the children of Cambridge. Not what I would call a normal childhood."

"Sam, surely you've figured out by now that you're one of us. You're flesh and blood. Your mother—"

"Shut your mouth, Barbara. Don't you dare bring my mother into this, I'm warning you," he said, his fists formed at his sides.

"Enough, Sam, enough arguing. I'm tired." She pulled an envelope from her pocket and looked at it then smiled. "You can't believe the lies I told to get this injunction." She slapped the envelope against the palm of her left hand, looking down, contemplating. "I'm tired, Sam," she repeated, looking up, her eyes glassy with tears. She stared at him for several seconds. Tears finally spilled over her eyelids and streamed through the heavy makeup covering her cheeks. She tore the envelope in half and dropped the pieces to the snow-covered ground, turned, and walked away.

Sam wanted to call after her, to yell "Bravo! Encore!" He wanted her to come back smiling, eyes flashing, and tell him the whole thing was an act, a huge practical joke. The elaborate hoax was on him. That she would be joined by Blair, Bronco George, Sarah Adams, the salamander brothers, Annie Dillon, and Annie George, the entire cast all holding hands, smiling and bowing in unison. Barbara disappeared, swallowed into the chaos of storm and emergency lights.

••••

The backhoe operator lit a cigarette and tossed the match from the cab window. Sam smelled the acrid odor of sulfur and the sweetness of tobacco several yards downwind from the muddy tractor. The smells contrasted with the musty odors of dank earth piled next to the three exposed graves. The CBI technician worked ahead of them, marking the ground with yellow flags. Dr. Murray, in muddy coveralls, called from the bottom of the third grave. Marta, aluminum clipboard in hand, took notes, her back to the wind and snow.

"CHS site 1SH Burial Number 3, Field Specimen 3.1, human remains, again no coffin wood, nails, buttons, or clothing fragments. No artifacts. It appears the bodies were buried unclothed. Pelvis wide and low, definitely female, the pubis and sacrum indicate she had given birth. Facial bones are consistent with northern European ancestry, definitely not Native American. Teeth indicate an age of roughly mid-to-late teens. Again, an intermastoid incision has been made across the top of the skull and across the front quadrant consistent with a frontal craniotomy. Marta, tell the sheriff to call the coroner. This is more than an unmarked cemetery. Someone was harvesting brain tissue or hormones. Oh, Marta, ask him to call the honor farm over at the prison to see if we can get some inmates to help dig while we catalog and tag. Tell the backhoe operator to slow down a little. He's good, but it's like picking your nose with a telephone pole."

The snowflakes, wet and large, swirled restlessly in the currents of wind that seemed to come from two different directions. Sam's arms were heavy, and breathing seemed a conscious effort as the stress dissipated from his body. But there was no relief. A cold despair descended over him, starting at the base of his skull then slipping down his neck and radiating across his shoulders. He shivered. A tangible heaviness pushed him downward, cold hands gripped painfully over his collar bones. He resisted, but his knees began to tremble. He no longer heard the roar and clanking of the backhoe or the new sirens that wailed in the distance. Instead he heard the cries of young girls, their muffled sobs of fear. He smelled the sweet aroma of horses. A baby cried, perhaps his mother, perhaps his aunt, muted by plaster and lathe. They were kin, part of his equation. His grandmother was here. She, like his mother, like his sister, had died alone. Leather heels clicked sharply on wooden floorboards as the Pumpkin Eater came for them. Sam could feel their fear, the terror of being alone, and the hopelessness of their imprisonment. No one knew they were there. Young girls secretly pushed between the cracks of a misguided social system.

No one knew of their suffering. They were orphans in an uncaring, deafened society. No one knew of their naked, mutilated bodies withering under the weight of cold soil. They had called to Sam. They had cried out for recognition, for acknowledgment that they had once lived, that they had been people. They called for him to find them, to end their torment. Above the din he heard the familiar voice of his daughter as a child. She cried out that she could not hear or see him. He wanted it to be a dream.

The intensity of the storm subsided momentarily, a lull between the gray cells of snow. A wet fog had descended from the storm-laden clouds and settled over the area. The field developed slowly as Annie strained to see through the wet windshield of the motor home. Gray and vaporous fog with snow fell lightly and drifted over the ground. It sat and lifted. The whiteness of the snow-covered field melded into the nebulous horizon. At first Annie was unsure of what she had seen, something dark, vertical in a horizontal landscape. Sam's form appeared slowly, a grainy black-and-white image of a man with his head bowed. In and out of focus, animated by falling snow, she saw him drop slowly to his knees, frame by frame between strobes of snow-reflected light. Her eyes burned from the tears that formed there. She tried to swallow the hard lump in her throat. She wanted to go to him but could not move, immobilized, captivated by his pain. The continued rumbling of the backhoe told her that he had won, but there was no victory, only grief. His fists were clenched and pushed against his thighs with elbows bulldogged outward, his head hung low. He wept.

EPILOGUE

WELLBORN ARE MY CHILDREN
EPITAPH
—EUGENE ERIS

HE COULD HAVE FLOWN, BUT THE thought of holiday crowds at the airport and crowded planes convinced him to drive. The whimpering in the background, when he had talked to Annie on the telephone, told him he may have a live passenger on the return trip. At Thanksgiving she had casually mentioned discovering a bloodhound breeder in Maquoketa. She had been cryptic and giggly in the last few telephone conversations. They now talked nearly every day. Their often late-night conversations had turned intimate—premature, he thought, given that he had not seen her since October when the relationship was best described as a friendship reinforced by crisis. Both had stopped short of using the word love, but he knew it lingered hesitantly just behind their lips. The eagerness in her voice, the abandonment of coyness, and the softness of her goodbyes spoke volumes about the bond that had formed. He continually questioned his own feelings, ever cautious of setting himself up for disappointment. A few months ago he had loved Blair Tennyson. No matter how hard he tried to dispel the affair as infatuation, temporary insanity induced by hormones, he could not. Comparing his feelings for Annie with those he had for Blair seemed unfair. He believed comparisons were only valuable when making a choice. There was no longer a choice.

The city of Golden was gaudy with holiday decorations. Lampposts had become candy canes; garlands dripped from the "Welcome to Golden" sign that arched over the street. Red, green, gold, and silver sparkled from every storefront with the radiance of fireworks. Tiny white lights outlined the geometric features of the two-block main street. Even the litter barrels were ringed with lights. Christmas music blared from hidden speakers, the repetitive jingle of bells almost nauseating. His motor home seemed much too large and out of place. Horses pulling sleighs would have completed the Currier-and-Ives scene. Sidney stared in fascination from the passenger seat. She loved the holidays, Hanukkah with her mom and Christmas with her dad. She signed the word pretty to her father. "Let's see," Sam said. "That was either pretty or dirty, I can't remember which." They both laughed.

He liked driving at night; the traffic was lighter and his thoughts were deeper. He hoped to make North Platte or maybe Grand Island, Nebraska, by one or two in the morning. There were several RV parks along the interstate where they could sleep for a few hours. They would arrive in Oxford midafternoon the next day, Christmas Eve.

The cheerfulness of holiday lights faded, becoming smaller in his rearview mirrors, then disappeared completely as he left town. Sidney had crawled into bed in the back. Cold darkness crept from the black on either side of

the road, pressing hard against the motor home and taking the heart out of Christmas. The unanswered questions
again swirled with confusing persistence in his mind. Sentence fragments without order. He had learned to accept the
fact that life was often unfair, that evil sometimes won, and
loose ends remained, becoming dormant and then obscure,
finally fossilized. No one seemed to care and he was learning to accept that. He slipped quietly into the background.
He watched from afar as the governor's office turned the
discovery into a nonevent. The press secretary did her job.
An unmarked cemetery on the grounds of the state hospital
received little attention. The media failed to make the connection with Barbara Sinclair's suicide. Instead they went
after the legislature for cutting her budget, which the media
intimated had led to her despondency and death.

Sam had played only one card, an hour-long talk with
the governor who, for a change, listened, understanding
the political consequences of disclosure. Two cabinet members were quickly summoned: agriculture, who oversaw the
Brand Board, and higher education, who represented the
University of Colorado. The dominoes fell silently.

The brand commissioner was unavailable for comment
concerning his dismissal, and the cattlemen avowed a bitter political fight with the governor's plan to privatize brand
inspection.

Neither the president of the Board of Regents at CU,
a wealthy alumnus who had helped elect the governor, nor
the president of the university was questioned regarding the
dismissal of an assistant professor of biology, a geneticist.

A call to the county attorney that took less than a minute of the governor's time resulted in Sam's assault charges being dropped.

There were too many questions and not enough room inside his head. He slept to escape. He dreamed of Eris who, with a twisted smile, whispered, "Wellborn are my children," his beady eyes glistening like those of his earliest creation, the salamander brothers. How many Eris brothers were there? Nervously, he had scanned the maps of the other six states. Tiny rural communities presented in the smallest print with names like Dover, Manchester, Bristol, Birmingham, Sheffield, and Southampton were scattered innocuously within a landmass that nearly equaled that of half the country. How many salamander brothers, who assisted their Doctors Frankenstein, were there and now watched over their graves? How many identical sisters did his mother have? If he thought about it too long, it made him nauseous. He sought relief in sleep. He dreamed of little girls, blonde and fair in white dresses, dancing and playing among gray tombstones on a green hilltop awash with wildflowers. In a frightening, erotic dream, he made love to Annie who morphed first into Blair then into a hideously decomposing Barbara Sinclair. During the day he dreamed of exhuming the Eris twins, of genetically typing their offspring, of exposing to the world their selfish crimes, committed in the name of eugenics. Annie's words, of her being his worst nightmare if he did anything to hurt her family, echoed in his mind and subdued his desire for justice.

Sam had struggled to develop a draft of the Iowa project. Cemeteries and pictures of them repulsed him now. In desperation, Pat offered Sam an advance on a book of black-and-whites. Sam pitched an idea that had been twitching restlessly in the back of his mind for several years. The book would be called *Snags* and would depict the stark beauty of dead trees in remote places. He loved the contrast of orange bark curled around the ancient wounds from lightning strikes. He saw broken-off trees with woodpecker holes and fire-blackened trunks, velvety moss clinging to the north side, a shelf fungus jutting abruptly outward, and brown-eyed Susans growing between exposed roots, promising renewal. It was all about light and the promise of life. Beneath such a tree he had buried the master ledger in a waterproof, fireproof box. It was his life insurance.

••••

The Conoco station, just off I-70 where Sam stopped for gas, was nearly deserted. A single station wagon with fake, peeling wood on the sides was parked at the island nearest the convenience store. Ivan Manfred stood patiently staring at the pump.

"Hello, Van," Sam said, stepping around the gas island.

Manfred turned quickly, his gray ponytail swinging into view. Half the collar of his Hawaiian shirt poked from the neck of his gray trench coat. "Well, if it isn't Blair's ex-friend."

"Sam Dawson," Sam said, but he did not offer his hand, not knowing whether Manfred would accept it.

"You know, I should be pissed at you," Manfred said, his eyes reduced to slits as he stared upward at Sam. "Blair had the cutest little ass of any faculty member on campus. She got that sweet little bottom canned on account of you, Dawson. For what, I'm not sure. All I know is she's mad as hell at you. It'll take at least a year to fill that position, and more than likely we'll get some neophyte post-doc that nobody can understand."

"Sorry," Sam said. He did not know what else to say. There was so much he wanted to say, but none of it would have made sense to Ivan Manfred. The whole story, the truth, had never reached the public. There were no criminal charges, only suggestions of complicity in a crime where the statute of limitations had expired long ago. "I thought she was tenured," he offered weakly, knowing the answer.

"She was scheduled to go through tenure and promotion this year. The Board of Regents was totally mortified about something. I assumed you were going to publish nude photos of her, eh. Do you have any? How much?" he said, reaching for his wallet.

Sam forced a smile but did not respond.

"The provost, who hasn't done a thing in six years, told her there would be no tenure decision and it would be best if she moved on. I told her to go to the press and scream rape, but she decided to go quietly. There's been quite a buzz on campus about it. The media never even picked up on her getting canned, thank God. They got pretty distracted when they discovered that the governor had been porking the staff. Christ, now there's a story. So many offended women, they filed a class action suit. Have you seen the one with a lisp? Looks like my butt, eh."

"Where's Blair now?" Sam said.

"Packed up and gone. Don't know where she is. Her dad won't talk about it, but I think he's devastated. I think she's back home on the ranch. Too bad, she was one talented lady. And what a cute little—"

"Her dad?" Sam interrupted.

"Bill? What about him?"

"I don't recall Blair ever mentioning her father. It just never came up. I guess I assumed he was dead."

"Gettin' old, but he's far from dead. I've worked with Bill Tennyson for fifteen years, long before I met Blair."

"Worked with him?" Sam said.

"Yeah, Bill—Doctor Tennyson—is the physician who founded the fertility clinic at the med center. He's one of the true pioneers in human embryo transplant procedures. Infertile women come from all over the world for transplants. The waiting list is nearly three-years long. Bill was first in the country to start an egg donor program; got bloody, stinking rich by patenting his flushing system. Good-looking, blue-eyed donors are lined up in the hall every week; long-legged coeds selling eggs for big bucks. You've never seen so much blonde stuff. Hell, old Bill's got some pyramid scheme going on campus where chicks recruit other chicks. Kind of like Tupperware or Mary Kay, eh."

Manfred continued to talk, sarcastic and vulgar one-liners thrown in for affect. But his words had no meaning to Sam. He heard Manfred's voice but the language was foreign. It was just a man, slightly out of focus, standing in front of him making noise, unintelligible utterances of human speech. Beyond the man, in the winter glow of the convenience store neon, Sam could see and hear the little blonde girls as they twirled and danced among the dark tombstones. Their white dresses flowed gracefully around tanned legs; their golden hair reflected the tree-filtered sun. One girl, older, hung back from the group, a blurred image that rose from the fog at the edge of the hill. She looked beyond the dancing girls. She smiled at Sam. Her gold-and-white cheerleading uniform was radiant. The girls held hands in a circle that turned 'round and 'round as they sang "Peter, Peter, Pumpkin Eater."

THE END

CPSIA information can be obtained at www.ICGtesting.com
Printed in the USA
BVOW08s1835180116

433371BV00002B/49/P